~ The Summer Girls ~

"Monroe knows her characters like no one else could, and her portrayals of the summer girls are subtle, realistic, carefully crafted, and pitch-perfect."

—*Publishers Weekly*

"More than just a beautifully written, moving portrayal of three sisters finding themselves and each other after years of separation . . . [*The Summer Girls*] deals head-on with significant issues so skillfully woven into the narrative that I often stopped to consider the import of what I'd just read. If you're a dedicated environmentalist, this book is a must-read. If you're just someone who enjoys a good story, you'll get that, too, and much more."

—*New York Times* bestselling author Cassandra King

"This book contains drama, humor, and romance which any good summer read does. Plus it has the message about the care and treatment of dolphins. Monroe is an expert at making this blend, and *The Summer Girls* is one of her most successful efforts."

—*The Huffington Post*

"A song of praise to the bottle-nosed dolphins that bring so much joy to the men and women who gaze at the creeks and rivers of the lowcountry each evening."

—*New York Times* bestselling author Pat Conroy

Also by Mary Alice Monroe

LOWCOUNTRY SUMMER TRILOGY

The Summer Girls

Beach House Memories

The Butterfly's Daughter

Last Light over Carolina

Time Is a River

The
Summer
Wind

Mary Alice Monroe

G

GALLERY BOOKS

New York   London   Toronto   Sydney   New Delhi

G

Gallery Books
A Division of Simon & Schuster, Inc.
1230 Avenue of the Americas
New York, NY 10020

Copyright © 2014 by Mary Alice Monroe, Ltd.

First Gallery Books trade paperback edition June 2014

GALLERY BOOKS and colophon are registered trademarks of Simon & Schuster, Inc.

For information about special discounts for bulk purchases, please contact Simon & Schuster Special Sales at 1-866-506-1949 or business@simonandschuster.com.

The Simon & Schuster Speakers Bureau can bring authors to your live event. For more information or to book an event, contact the Simon & Schuster Speakers Bureau at 1-866-248-3049 or visit our website at www.simonspeakers.com.

Interior design by Jaime Putorti
Cover design by Laywan Kwan
Cover images: photo of woman © Tim Pannell/Corbis;
    photo of grass © Vera Kailová/Alamy

Manufactured in the United States of America

10 9

Library of Congress Cataloging-in-Publication Data

Monroe, Mary Alice.
    The summer wind / Mary Alice Monroe.
        pages cm.—(The lowcountry summer trilogy)
    1. Grandmothers—Fiction. 2. Granddaughters—Fiction. 3. Sisters—Fiction.
4. Self-realization in women—Fiction. 5. Sullivan's Island (S.C. : Island)—Fiction.
6. Domestic fiction. 7. Psychological fiction. I. Title.
PS3563.O529S88 2014
813'.54—dc23   2014008588

ISBN 978-1-4767-7002-4
ISBN 978-1-4767-0901-7 (pbk)
ISBN 978-1-4767-0904-8 (ebook)

For Kimberly Whalen and Robert Gottlieb

Chapter One

≈ ≈ ≈

J uly was said to be the hottest month of the year in Charleston, and after enduring eighty Southern summers, Marietta Muir, or Mamaw, as her family affectionately called her, readily agreed. She delicately dabbed at her upper lip and forehead with her handkerchief, then waved to shoo off a pesky mosquito. Southern summers meant heat, humidity, and bugs. But being out on Sullivan's Island, sitting in the shade of a live oak tree, sipping iced tea, and waiting for the occasional offshore breeze was, for her, the very definition of summer. She sighed heavily. The ancient oak spread its mighty limbs so far and wide, Marietta felt cradled in its protective embrace. Still, the air was especially languid this morning, so thick and cloyingly scented with jasmine that it was a battle to keep her eyelids from drooping. A gust of wind from the ocean carried the sweet scent of the grass and cooled the moist hairs along her neck.

She set the needlepoint pattern on her lap to remove her

glasses and rub her eyes. Cursed old age. It was getting harder and harder to see her stitches, she thought with a sigh. Glancing at Lucille beside her on the screened porch of the guesthouse that Lucille called home, she saw her friend bent over the base of a sweetgrass basket, her strong hands weaving the fragile strands into the pattern, sewing each row tight with palmetto fronds. A small pile of the grass lay in her lap, while a generous heap sat at her feet in a plastic bag, along with another bag of long-leaf pine needles.

Seeing her longtime companion's hands lovingly weaving together the disparate grasses into an object of beauty made Marietta think again how imperative her challenge was this summer: to entwine her three very different granddaughters with Sea Breeze once again. Her *summer girls*.

Mamaw sighed softly to herself. They were hardly girls any longer. Dora was thirty-six, Carson thirty-three, and Harper twenty-eight—women now. Back when they were young girls and spent summers together they had been close, as sisters should be. Over the years, however, they'd become more strangers than sisters. Half-sisters, Marietta corrected herself, shuddering at the nuance of the term. As if by only sharing a father, the women's bond was somehow less. Sisters were sisters and blood was blood, after all. She had succeeded in corralling all three women to Sea Breeze in June for the summer, but here it was, only early July, and Carson was already off to Florida while Dora was fixing on returning to Summerville. And Harper . . . that New Yorker had her sights set north.

"I wonder if Carson made it to Florida yet," Lucille said without looking up. Her fingers moved steadily, weaving row after row.

Mamaw half smiled, thinking how Lucille's mind and

her own were in sync . . . again. Lucille had been hired as her housekeeper some fifty years back, when Marietta was a young bride in Charleston. They'd shared a lifetime of ups and downs, births, deaths, scandals, and joys. Now that they were old women, Lucille had become more a confidante than an employee. Truth was, Lucille was her closest friend.

"I was just wondering the same thing," Mamaw replied. "I expect she has by now and is just settling in to her hotel. I hope she won't be away long."

"She won't be. Carson knows how important this summer is to you, and she'll be back just as soon as she finds out what's done happened to that dolphin," Lucille said. She lowered her basket to her lap and looked Mamaw straight in the eyes. "Carson won't disappoint you. You have to have faith."

"I do," Mamaw exclaimed defensively. "But I'm old enough to know how life likes to throw a wrench into even the most well thought out plans. I mean, really," Mamaw said, lifting her hands in frustration. "Who could have foreseen a dolphin tossing all my summer plans applecart-upset?"

Lucille chuckled, a deep and throaty sound. "Yes, she surely did. That Delphine . . ." Lucille's smile slipped at the sound of the dolphin's name. "But it weren't her fault, now was it? I do hope that place in Florida can help the poor thing."

"I do, too. For Delphine's sake, and for Carson's." She paused. "And Nate's." She was worried about how hard Dora's son had taken the dolphin's accident. Only a young boy, he had put the blame on himself for luring the dolphin to their dock and getting it entangled in all that fishing line. In truth, they were all to blame. No one more than herself.

"For all our sakes," she amended.

"Amen," Lucille agreed soberly. She paused to sweep bits of scattered grass to the wind. "Don't you fret none, Miz Marietta. All will be well. I feel it in my bones. And in no time you'll have all your summer girls here at Sea Breeze again."

"Hi, Mamaw! Lucille!" A voice called out from the driveway, cutting through the two women's conversation.

"Here comes one now," Lucille murmured, returning to her basket.

Marietta turned her head and smiled to see her youngest granddaughter, Harper, jogging toward them in one of those skimpy, skintight running outfits that looked to Marietta like a second skin. Her red hair was pulled back in a ponytail, and sweat poured down her pink face.

"Harper!" Marietta called out with a quick wave. "My goodness, child, you're running at this time of the day? Only tourists are fool enough to run here under a midsummer sun. You'll have a heat stroke! Why, your face is as red as a beet!"

Harper stopped at the bottom of the porch steps and bent over, hands on her hips, to catch her breath. "Oh, Mamaw, I'm fine," she said breathily, wiping the sweat from her brow with her forearm. "I do this every day."

"Well, you look about ready to keel over."

"It *is* hot out there today," Harper conceded with half a smile. "But my face always turns red. It's my fair skin. I've got a ton of sunscreen on."

Lucille clucked her tongue. "Mind you drink some water, hear?"

"Why don't you jump in the pool and cool yourself down some? You look to be wearing a swimming suit . . ." Mamaw trailed off, fanning her face as she spoke. It made her hot just to see Harper's pink face and the sweat drenching her clothing.

"Good idea," Harper replied, and with a quick wave took off toward the front door. She turned her head and shouted, "Nice basket, Lucille!" before disappearing into the house.

Lucille chuckled and returned to her weaving. "Only the young can run like that."

"I never ran like that when *I* was young!" Mamaw said.

"Me, neither. Who had the time?"

"No time, and *certainly* not dressed like that. What these girls parade around in today. That outfit left little to the imagination."

"Oh, I bet the young men can imagine plenty," Lucille said, chuckling again.

Mamaw huffed. "What young men? I simply cannot understand why she's not getting any calls. I've seen to it that she was invited to a few parties in town where other young people would be present. There was that nice boating party at Sissy's yacht club . . . Several eligible young men were invited." Mamaw shook her head. "Harper is such a pretty girl, with good breeding." She paused. "Even if her mother *is* English." Mamaw picked up her needlepoint and added archly, "Her father is from Charleston, after all."

"Oh, I wouldn't say she hasn't been asked out . . ." Lucille said, feeding more grass into the basket.

Mamaw narrowed her eyes with suspicion. "You wouldn't?"

Lucille's eyes sparkled with knowledge. "I happen to know that since she's been here, several young men have called our Miss Harper."

"Really?" Mamaw fumed silently, wondering why she hadn't been made aware of this. She didn't like being the last to know things, certainly not about her own granddaughters. She reached for the *Island Eye* newspaper and used it to fan the air. "You'd think someone might've told me."

Lucille shrugged.

Mamaw lowered the paper. "Well . . . why hasn't she had any dates? Is she being shy?"

"Our Harper might be a quiet little thing, but she ain't shy. That girl's got a spine of steel. Just look at the way she won't touch meat, or white bread, or anything I cook with bacon grease."

Mamaw's lips curved, recalling the row at the dinner table Harper's first night at Sea Breeze. Dora was nearly driven to distraction by Harper's strict diet.

"She's only just been here a month," Lucille continued. "And she's only staying another two. She don't have her light on, is all. And who can wonder? With all she got on her mind, I reckon dating a young man is low on her list."

Mamaw rocked in silence. All Lucille had said was true enough. It seemed everyone had a lot on their minds this summer at Sea Breeze—she certainly did. The summer was flying by, and if she couldn't find a way to forge bonds between her granddaughters, Mamaw knew that come September, Sea Breeze would be sold, the girls would scatter again, and she'd be sitting on the dock howling at the harvest moon.

The previous May, Mamaw had invited her three granddaughters—Dora, Carson, and Harper—to celebrate her eightieth birthday at Sea Breeze. She'd had, however, an ulterior motive. In the fall, Marietta was putting Sea Breeze on the market and moving into an assisted living facility. With the demands of an island house, she simply couldn't keep up living alone any longer, not even with Lucille's help. Her hope was that, once here, all three women would agree to stay for the entire summer. She wanted them to be her summer girls again—as they had been as children—for this final summer before Sea Breeze was sold.

Countless previous invitations of hers had been rebuffed by all the girls over the years, with just as many excuses—*I'd love to but I'm so busy, I have work, I'll be out of town*—each sent with gushes of regret and replete with exclamation marks.

So this time, Mamaw had trusted that her granddaughters had inherited some of her ancestral pirate blood, and she'd lured the girls south with promises of loot from the house. And the little darlings had come, if only for the weekend party. Desperate to keep them on the island, Mamaw had resorted to a bit of manipulation when she'd threatened to cut them out of the will if they did not stay for the entire summer. She chortled out a laugh just remembering their shocked faces.

Carson had just lost her job and was pleased as punch to spend the summer rent-free on the island. Dora, in the midst of a divorce, was easily persuaded to stay at Sea Breeze with Nate while repairs were done on her house in Summerville. Harper, however, had thrown a hissy fit. She'd called it blackmail.

Mamaw shifted uncomfortably in her seat. Blackmail, really. Harper could be so dramatic, she thought as she rolled her eyes. Surely there was a more refined, gentler term for the actions of a concerned and loving grandmother set on bringing her granddaughters together? A smile of satisfaction played at her lips. And they'd all agreed to stay the summer, hadn't they?

But now, only midsummer, and Carson had already left—though she promised to swiftly return—while Dora had one foot out the door.

Mamaw closed her eyes, welcoming another soothing ocean breeze. She couldn't fail in her mission. Eighty years was a long time of living. She'd survived the loss of a husband and her only child. All she had left that mattered were these three precious jewels, her granddaughters. Mamaw's hands tightened to fists. And come hell or high water—or hissy fits—she was going to give them this one perfect summer. Her most private fear was that when Sea Breeze was sold and she'd moved on to a retirement home, the fragile bond between the sisters would break and they'd scatter to the four winds like these bits of sweetgrass that fell loose from Lucille's basket.

"Here comes another one," Lucille said in a low voice, indicating with her chin the sight of Dora rounding the corner of the house.

Mamaw's gaze swept over her eldest granddaughter with a critical eye. Dora was dressed in a khaki suit and a blouse the same pale yellow color as her hair. As Dora drew closer, Mamaw noted that she was wearing nylon stockings and pumps. In this heat! She could see pearls of perspiration already dripping down Dora's face as she dragged a suitcase behind her through the gravel toward the silver Lexus parked in the driveway.

"Dora! Are you off?" Mamaw called out.

Dora stopped abruptly at hearing her name and turned her head toward the guesthouse.

"Hey, ladies," she called out with a wave, upon seeing the two women sitting side by side on the front porch. "Yes," she replied, pasting on a smile that didn't quite meet her eyes. "I've got to dash if I'm going to get to my lawyer's appointment on time. It's going to be a long morning."

Dora left her suitcase and came over to join them. "Look at

you two, sitting there like two birds on a wire, chirping away the morning." Dora stepped up onto the porch and into the shade.

Mamaw set her needlepoint aside and gave Dora her full attention, studying her eldest granddaughter's face. Of all three women, Dora was the one who could best mask her emotions with false cheer. Had always done so, even as a child. On her wedding day, her father, Mamaw's only child, Parker, had arrived at the church unforgivably drunk. Dora had smiled as she walked down the aisle with her stepfather instead of her biological one. She'd smiled through the whispers behind raised palms, smiled during Parker's rambling toast, smiled while friends escorted Parker to the hotel to sleep it off.

Mamaw studied that same fixed smile now. She knew too well the sacrifices Dora had made to present the facade of a happy family. This divorce was striking at her very core, shaking her foundation. Yet, even now, it seemed Dora was intent on giving off the impression that she had everything under control.

"You look very . . . respectable," Mamaw said, choosing her words carefully. "But isn't it a bit steamy today for that suit and nylons?"

Dora lifted her blond hair from her neck, to allow the offshore breeze to cool the moisture pooling there. "Lord, yes. It's so hot you could spit on the ground and watch it sizzle. But I've got to make the right impression in front of Cal's lawyers."

Bless her heart, Mamaw thought. That suit was so tight. Poor Dora looked like a sausage squeezed into its casings.

Dora dropped her hair and her face shifted to a scowl. "Calhoun's being flat-out unreasonable."

"We all knew when you married him that his elevator didn't go all the way to the top."

"He doesn't have to be smart, Mamaw. Only his lawyer does. And I hear he's got himself a real shark."

"You called the Rosen law firm like I recommended, didn't you?" Dora nodded. "Good," Mamaw said. "Robert will catch that shark on his hook, don't you worry."

"I'll try not to," Dora replied, smoothing out wrinkles in her skirt. "I still want to set a good precedent, though."

Mamaw reached up to the collar of her dress and unpinned her brooch. It was a favorite of hers. Small pieces of bright coral were embedded in gold to form an exquisite starburst. Her granddaughter needed a bit of starburst in her life right now.

"Come here, precious," she said to Dora.

When Dora drew near, Mamaw waved her hand to indicate Dora should bend close, then she reached out to pin the large brooch to Dora's suit collar.

"There," she said, sitting back and gazing at her handiwork. "A little pop of color does wonders for you, my dear. The brooch was my mother's. It's yours now."

Dora's eyes widened as her stoic facade momentarily crumbled. She rushed to hug her grandmother with a desperate squeeze. "Oh, Mamaw, thank you. I didn't expect . . . It means a lot. Especially today. I have to admit, I'm nervous about confronting Cal after all this time. And his lawyers."

"Consider it ceremonial armor," Mamaw replied with a smile.

"I will," Dora replied, standing erect and smoothing out her jacket. "You know, I'm so tickled I can fit back into this suit. Between Carson not letting us have any alcohol in the house and Harper getting us to eat all that health food, I've actually lost a few pounds! Who would have thought?"

A genuine smile lit up Dora's face, and Mamaw suddenly saw a flash of the dazzling young woman who once had enchanted all who met her with the warmth of that smile. Over the past ten years of an unhappy marriage and caring for a child with special needs, Dora had committed the cardinal sin of a Southern wife—she'd let herself go. But worst of all, her sadness had drained the sunlight from inside of her. Mamaw was glad to see a glimmer of it resurface in her eyes this morning.

"Is Nate going with you?" Lucille asked.

Dora shook her head and grimaced. "I'm afraid not. I just came from his room. I begged him to come with me, but you know Nate when he's got his mind made up. He barely said more than one word—*no*. I don't think he likes me very much right now," Dora added in a softer tone. "It was like"—her voice choked with emotion—"like he couldn't wait for me to leave."

"Now, honey, don't pay him no mind," Mamaw said in a conciliatory tone. "You know that child's still hurting from what happened to that dolphin. It was traumatic for him. For all of us," she added.

"Carson should be calling with news about that dolphin soon," Lucille said comfortingly.

"And I just know it will be good news," Mamaw agreed, ever the optimist. "I'm sure Nate will come around then."

"I hope so . . ." Dora replied, and hastily wiped her eyes, seemingly embarrassed for the tears.

Mamaw slid a glance to Lucille. It wasn't like Dora to be so emotional. Dora checked her watch and gasped. "Lord, I've really got to go or I'll be late," she said, all business now. "Are you sure y'all can handle Nate while I'm gone? You know he can get squirrelly when I leave."

"I feel sure that three grown women can handle one little boy. No matter how testy," Mamaw said, arching one brow.

Lucille laughed quietly while her fingers worked the basket.

"Yes, of course," Dora muttered, digging into her purse for car keys. "It's just he is particularly difficult now, because he's all upset about that dolphin, and that I'm going to see his father."

Mamaw waved Dora off. "You go on and don't worry about anything here. We'll all be fine. You have enough to contend with getting your house ready for the market."

Dora's eyes narrowed at mention of the house. "Those workmen had better be there or I'll raise holy hell."

Mamaw and Lucille exchanged a glance. That was the Dora they knew. Pulling out her keys, Dora turned to go.

"Dora?" Mamaw called, stopping Dora as she made to leave. Dora stopped, turned her head, and met Mamaw's gaze. "Mind you remember who you are. You're a Muir. The captain of your own ship." She sniffed and added, "Don't you take any guff from the likes of Calhoun Tupper, hear?"

The brilliant Muir blue color flashed in Dora's eyes. "Yes, ma'am," she replied with heart, and straightened her shoulders.

The two old women watched Dora rush to her car, load the suitcase into the trunk, and roar out of the driveway, the wheels spitting gravel.

"Mmm-mmm-mm," Lucille muttered as she returned to her basket weaving. "That woman's hell-bent on taking her fury out on all the men in town today."

Mamaw released the grin that had been playing at her lips all morning. "I don't know who I feel more sorry for," she said. "The workmen at the house, or Calhoun Tupper."

Chapter Two

Charleston, South Carolina

Dora sat clenching her hands tightly together in her lap in her lawyer's office. The air-conditioning was working valiantly against the day's record-breaking heat, but the two lawyers and Cal had removed their suit jackets and rolled up their sleeves. Dora was the only woman in the room, and she still had her suit jacket on. She was resolved not to remove one shred of her armor. And in her mind's eye she could see the safety pin holding her skirt together because she couldn't quite fasten the button. So she sat with her jacket on, chafing at the collar and sweltering with a simmering fury while Cal's lawyer, Mr. Harbison, went on explaining why the amount they were offering for settlement was exceptionally fair.

It was all she could do not to jump from her seat in frustration and rage. Fair? The amount offered wasn't enough for her to live on, much less take care of Nate and all his therapy sessions. She glanced at her lawyer, Mr. Rosen, hoping to catch his attention. He had been very clear that she mustn't engage but simply respond when directly questioned. His gaze was fixed to the pile of papers beside his open laptop and he was busily making notations as the items were discussed.

Frustrated, Dora glanced across the long conference table at Cal, raising her brows in a signal. Her soon-to-be ex-husband sat resolutely looking at his hands. He'd not bothered to meet her gaze when she'd stepped into the office. Nor did he offer a word, or even a glance of comfort or concern during the entire morning's meeting. He never once established eye contact. Cal had never been a touchy-feely sort of man, but today at the lawyer's office he was positively void of all feeling.

She hadn't seen Cal in the past few months, though they'd talked on a need-to-know basis. When she walked into the office earlier that morning, she'd been surprised to see he'd lost the spare tire around his waist and that he was taking more care with his appearance. He wore the classic Southern seersucker suit and she'd had to take a second look to believe his dapper bow tie.

She kept her rigid posture and blasé expression, but beneath the table her foot was shaking. She glanced at the clock on the wall. It was nearing noon. She had endured a brutal morning listening to the cold recitation of positions from both lawyers. Now they had moved on to itemizing her and Cal's possessions.

She followed the long itemized list as the lawyer droned. But when Cal's lawyer began divvying up the Muir family antiques, Dora sat straight in her chair and blurted, "No!"

The room immediately went silent as the three gentlemen turned their heads toward her.

"There must be some mistake," she said. "We are *not* divvying up the family antiques. Cal and I have already agreed that he would get his family furniture and I would get mine."

Mr. Harbison offered her a benign smile. "I'm afraid, Mrs. Tupper, that wouldn't be equitable."

"I don't . . ." She stopped when Mr. Rosen placed a hand on her arm.

"You see, all your possessions are considered communal property," Mr. Harbison continued.

"No, they most certainly are not," she barked at him, feeling her face color. "I don't care if it's equitable, communal, or whatever you want to call it." Her voice was rising. "My family furniture is mine and he can't have it. We've already discussed this and agreed."

Cal's face mottled. "Dora, we may have discussed it, but it was premature. It's clear that's no longer fair."

Dora's eyes narrowed. "Because now you know how much some of my pieces are worth. You went and had the furniture appraised. I can read the report."

"If it were just a few hundred dollars . . ." he said. Cal tapped the papers in front of him, a slight flush rising in his cheeks. "But the Chippendale chairs and sofa, and the Empire chests . . . Those alone are worth over one hundred thousand dollars! The silver is worth another thirty."

Dora lifted her brows in acknowledgment. Their value had been a pleasant surprise, but she couldn't bear the thought of selling off pieces of her lineage to the highest bidder.

"This is not about the money. I don't want to sell my furniture. It's been in my family for generations. And it'll go to Nate after me. We're only the caretakers for the next generation. We don't sell."

"We do when we have to," Cal said succinctly. "And with the costs of Nate's therapy and the fact that the house you wanted has turned out to be a money hole, we have to now."

"Those expenses are not new," Dora fired back. "And let me remind you that you wanted that house every bit as much as I did. You saw the potential profit. But you never thought we needed to fix the house up before. You wouldn't let me do anything. It was good enough for us to live in. Suddenly we need the money to make all the repairs and update the appliances?"

Mr. Harbison cleared his throat, entering the fray. "Mrs. Tupper, I realize this is an emotional subject. The repairs are minimal, just enough to make the house marketable. In the end, the purpose is to bring in a better price, for both your sakes."

Tears threatened and Dora pinched her lips to stop them from trembling. The men in the room shifted in their seats and exchanged glances in a manner that seemed to say, *What could we expect?* She was a woman, after all. She couldn't handle the proceedings without a display of emotion.

Of course she was emotional! These men were dispensing her personal possessions with the same nonchalance as if they were divvying up potatoes. And she was getting cheated in the bargain. Dora remembered Mamaw's words—*You're a Muir. The captain of your own ship*—and bridling, she turned to Cal's lawyer with resolution. She was not accepting Cal's ultimatum.

Dora delivered a hard look to Mr. Harbison. "Let me make my position clear. I don't care what price the house brings in. Nor do I care what the value of my possessions are," she said, making an effort to speak in an even voice. "I'm not parting with my family antiques. They belong to my family. I'll have my grandmother write a letter to that effect. Y'all know Marietta Muir well enough that she'll make certain nothing leaves the family's hands." She sat back in her chair and folded her hands in her lap. "That's all I have to say."

Mr. Harbison's lips tightened in acknowledgment of the truth in that statement. He shot a glance at Cal, who stared at Dora with barely concealed frustration.

"Very well, Mrs. Tupper," Mr. Rosen said in a conciliatory tone. He adjusted his spectacles and addressed Cal's lawyer. "I suggest that we discuss this matter with our clients individually and meet again. We can consult our calendars and pick a date at a mutually convenient time."

Dora resolutely looked at her hands during the uncomfortable time it took the lawyers to tidy up the few remaining details. She felt battered by the ordeal, refusing to look up for fear that now she'd meet Cal's wrathful gaze. When at last the gentlemen began rising to their feet, Dora joined them. She reached for her purse and, muttering something about powdering her nose, hurried from the room before she had to face Cal again.

Summerville, South Carolina

The afternoon sun was lowering as Dora drove along the shaded streets of Summerville, South Carolina. Sunlight dappled through the thick foliage, and summer flowers burst in brilliant colors wherever she looked. Dora always felt at home in the historic district where beloved Southern traditions were reflected in streetscapes, parks, and gardens. She never tired of glancing dreamily at the charming raised cottages, the classic

Greek Revivals, and sweeping Victorian homes. Cal's family had lived in Summerville for generations, but it was the timeless quality of these historic homes in this district that ultimately prompted her to settle here.

Dora had thought herself so clever to "steal" her large Victorian at an auction ten years earlier. The historic location was very desirable and boasted one restored home after another. A house down the block from hers sold for a staggering sum. It had caused a ripple throughout the neighborhood and a flurry of renewed pride of ownership. She and Cal had been so young when they'd moved into the house, so full of hope, so sure they were on the cusp of change and poised for prosperity.

They had been so naive, Dora thought with a stab of sadness as she passed the town square framed by quaint shops that, in the spring, came alive with the azaleas that gave Summerville the moniker "flower town." She passed St. Paul's church, where she'd volunteered in the Women's Mission; the quaint Timrod Library, which she'd helped to support through fund-raisers and where she'd spent hours with Nate while she homeschooled. This was her community, her home . . . yet driving through the winding roads she knew so well, she felt like a stranger.

She'd spent years developing her network of friends in her church and community. People she'd thought she could count on when the chips were down. Yet once she and Cal received Nate's diagnosis of autism, it altered the nature of her friendships.

One by one, her so-called friends grew uncomfortable with Nate's behavior. The children ignored him and the mothers stopped inviting her to bring Nate over for play dates. For her part, she'd stopped trying as well. Eventually, she simply dropped out—of volunteering, school activities, and entertaining. Instead, Dora dove heart first into therapy and homeschooling for her son. Only the parent of a child with a disorder would understand that kind of commitment.

Dora took a long, steadying breath, focusing on the present. None of that mattered, she told herself. None of *them* mattered. She'd managed well enough on her own, didn't she?

Dora glanced at the coral brooch on her lapel. The sight of it comforted her, like a mental hug, reminding her that there were others who did care and who did matter—Mamaw, Lucille, Carson, and Harper. She felt her shoulders soften as she let go of the hurt and rejection that she still harbored in a place deep within. She had created a world of self-sufficiency. Her mother, Cal, the women she'd surrounded herself with were takers, not givers. When the time came that she needed help, they'd disappeared. But perhaps now, she thought with a glimmer of hope—with them—she could begin a give-and-take.

She turned on a road that led away from the park and arrived at the long driveway to her house. From the street entrance, she saw the house the way strangers might as they drove past. The white Victorian peeked out from the cloak of green foliage like a shy bride, enchanting with its charming red pyramid roof trimmed with elaborate bric-a-brac. Unfortunately, it turned out to be more of an old Miss Havisham.

Behind the veil of distance and foliage, the house revealed its turpitude and age. Decades of peeling paint, the crumbling brick foundation, porch pillars tilting under the weight of overgrown vines could not be clouded over with daydreams. She pulled in front of the old house and turned off the engine. She sat in the stifling heat and stared at the large white Victorian. She didn't feel a shred of the old excitement. Instead, despair spread through her bloodstream. Dora no longer saw what could be. Everywhere she looked, Dora saw the rot that festered from foundation to roof and the realization that no amount of effort on her part could save it.

The comparison to her marriage was too obvious and too painful to ponder.

Heart weary, she reached for the bag of groceries, the chilled bottle of white wine, and the box of fried chicken she'd picked up on the way home from the lawyer's office. Dora felt exhausted and utterly depleted, barely able to make it up the brick stairs to the front door. After a brief struggle with the lock, she pushed open the door and was met with a wall of musty heat. Her heart sank and her shoulders slumped.

"How many more disasters do I have to face today?" she groaned as she mentally added *Call air-conditioning repairman* to her burgeoning to-do list.

The house was as quiet as a tomb. The crews had left for the day but the heavy odor of paint and varnish hung in the air. Dust motes floated in shafts of light as she gazed around the rooms, checking the progress of the workmen. The antique pieces of furniture that she and Cal had inherited were clustered in the middle of the rooms. Wallpaper had been scraped off and repair on drywall had begun. Rotten windowsills had been removed. There was a long way to go but it was a start.

Seeing the improvements was bittersweet. She'd always dreamed of restoring the house—a new coat of paint, some cheery wallpaper, new fabric for the furniture, even flashy new appliances. She had manila folders overflowing with clippings from magazines. But Cal had told her there was no money to update the plumbing or appliances. Now, at last, the work she'd begged Cal for years to get done was finally under way—and she wouldn't get to enjoy any of it.

The lawyers had made it clear the house was to be sold as soon as possible. She had to pack up and move.

Dora suddenly felt as if the hot and humid house were closing in on her. She couldn't catch her breath. She stripped off the constricting suit jacket, then rushed from kitchen to dining room to living room opening windows, since only a few windows in the kitchen had been cracked open. The wood was swollen with the humidity, but an inner rage that had been building in her chest while she'd sat helplessly in the lawyer's office fueled her strength. Dora groaned, sweat, and swore, pounding the window frames with the palm of her hand until, at last, the stubborn windows yielded. She opened every last one of them wide.

She stood for a moment breathing in the fresh air, letting her heart rate slow. Turning, she surveyed the mayhem of her house. The afternoon at the lawyer's had shaken her. She felt rather like this old house, she thought, leaning against the wall. Beneath her ever-present smile, she was crumbling.

Dora had been raised to believe if she followed the rules of behavior for a Southern belle—a well-brought-up Southern woman, especially one with a pedigree—she could expect the fairy tale. Her life would be a smooth continuation of the one her mother had led, and her mother before her. These rules were not written but passed down by example and reprimand from mother to daughter to granddaughter, from generation to generation.

So Dora had lived by the rules. She'd been a good girl. She

went to cotillion, dutifully wrote thank-you notes, debuted in white at the St. Cecilia ball, and married an upstanding man from a fine Southern family. As a bride she supported her husband's career and volunteered in her community and church. And, after years of trying, she'd at last produced a son. Dora had believed the perfect life was spread before her for the taking.

Such a fool, she cursed herself, her hands covering her face. All her expectations were nothing more than illusions. And the supposed rules . . . She dropped her hands with a grimace. What a farce! Was she supposed to write a thank-you note to Cal for the pittance he'd offered?

She gazed at the collection of antiques clustered under plastic in the living room. Yes, this house might be falling down around her ears. And yes, the furniture needed reupholstering. But this furniture, her china and silver—these were all treasured objects that held deep significance. They represented a continuance of *family* from one generation to the next. Why should she give them up now, when she needed them the most?

And besides, *she* wasn't the one ending the marriage in the first place!

Emotional, my ass, she thought as she angrily walked to the kitchen. She grabbed the bag of takeout chicken she'd brought home and tore it open. The steamy, greasy deliciousness wafted into the air and made her mouth water. A wave of guilt swept over her as she pulled out a fried drumstick. Harper and Carson would have a fit if they saw her eating this. Dora shook the vision of their scolding faces from her head. Let them be angry. And damn the diet and her figure. She deserved a treat tonight. Closing her eyes, she bit into the high-calorie food and swallowed hard. Taking another bite, she didn't enjoy the taste.

Dora knew the food might fill her up for now, but it wouldn't touch the real hunger gnawing inside of her.

She was only a few bites into her meal when the doorbell rang. Dora swung her head toward the front door and debated whether to answer it. With a yearning look at the side of mac and cheese, she put the drumstick on her plate with a resigned sigh. Dora never was one to let a doorbell or phone go unanswered. Dabbing at her mouth with a paper napkin, she hurried to the door.

The last person she expected to see was Cal.

Dora's heart immediately commenced pounding and her hand unconsciously went to her hair. Cal had removed the bow tie and seersucker jacket he'd worn at the lawyer's office. He stood in a relaxed pose in a white shirt rolled up at the sleeves, a bottle of wine in his hand and a sheepish half smile on his face.

"Cal! What on earth are you doing here?"

"I just thought I'd stop by. See how you were doing. After today, well . . . I thought we could talk a bit," he said, hoisting the wine bottle as a peace offering.

Dora surveyed him coolly, despite her still-jackhammering heart. "You don't think we talked enough this morning?"

Cal shook his head. "The lawyers did all the talking today. I thought maybe we deserved a chance, too."

Dora could hardly believe her ears. Could she have misread him? She remained hesitant, her hand clenching the door handle.

"I don't know if we should talk without our lawyers present," she hedged.

"That's what they tell us, while they charge us by the hour

to let them do the talking for us. Dora, we both know it was plain ugly today."

Dora only nodded.

"For all the ups and downs," Cal continued, "we've always tried to be fair and sensible. Why stop now? Let's you and me try to cut through the chaff and reach a meeting of the minds." He laughed in a self-deprecating manner. "And save thousands of dollars in fees in the process. Besides," he added, his smile slowly widening, "it's been a long time since we talked." When she still didn't respond he added, "At least we can try. What do you say?"

Dora looked long and hard at her husband. Calhoun Tupper wasn't a handsome man when she'd married him, but his once gawky appearance was aging well. Some men were lucky that way. His undeniable Southern charm was what had first caught her fancy. And he was working that charm now.

"I can't help but wonder where we'd be now if you'd made that offer a year ago," she said in a softer voice. "Even six months ago, instead of walking out this door."

Cal had the grace to appear shamefaced. "Maybe you're right."

Dora studied the man standing before her. He appeared to be offering an olive branch and she wished she could believe him. He was still her husband, the father of her child. He was saying all the right words. But she'd been served a dish of humble pie at the lawyer's office that was hard to swallow. Now her practical nature reared up and she kept up her guard. She swung wide the door and coolly ushered him into her house. *Their* house, she amended—at least until the judge deemed otherwise.

Following his familiar figure down the front hall toward the kitchen, Dora thought of the countless times he'd walked this path back into the kitchen when he returned home from work. He'd loosen his tie, drop his briefcase, give her a peck on the cheek, and turn to the fridge for a beer. Tonight he'd brought wine, she noticed. A drink *she* preferred. While Cal made himself at home opening the kitchen drawer for the bottle opener, Dora went to the fridge for the bag of green seedless grapes she had brought with her. While she rinsed the fruit at the sink, she watched Cal deftly turn the screw into the cork and remove it with a gentle pop.

They carried the wine and grapes to the dining room, where they shoved aside the plastic tarp to sit at the table. Night was falling and shadows played on the walls. Dora turned on a few table lamps. Soft yellow light flowed across the floors, but the mood was hardly one of romance or even reconciliation. It was strangely awkward. She took a seat, thinking how odd it was to be sitting with a man she'd lived with for so many years and feel as if they were strangers.

"The air-conditioning is out," Cal said, stating the obvious.

"Yes. I'll give the repairman a call tomorrow."

"Let's just pray the whole system doesn't have to be replaced. It's got to be over twenty years old now." Cal didn't need to say *add it to the list*, because they both knew the other was thinking the same thing. He leaned back against the chair and let his gaze wander the room. "Well, looks like the painters got started."

"No surprises. Yet."

"Good to see the roofers have gotten started, too." When she nodded, he added, "You have to stay on top of them, hear?

They'll take forever if you let them, and we want the house to go on the market as soon as possible."

"Uh-huh."

"Then there's the garden," he continued. "The real estate agent was clear it needs attention. It's completely overrun. I don't know why you started that butterfly garden. It's all weeds now."

"It was for Nate," she replied, irked that he didn't remember. "For his science lessons, remember?" Nate had been fascinated with the caterpillars. Monarchs, swallowtails, Gulf fritillaries—they'd brought them indoors and raised them, watching them go into chrysalis and later change into butterflies.

Cal snorted derisively. "It was an expensive lesson. It's a jungle out there now. You let the whole thing go."

"I don't have any help here, Cal," Dora said quietly.

"The real estate agent said you'll have to do something to make it look better. Whatever is cheap. Hire someone to just mow it back."

Dora clutched her glass and sipped her wine, saying nothing.

"How's Nate been handling the racket of all the repairmen?"

She was glad he'd finally thought to inquire about their son. "He's not here."

This caught Cal by surprise. "Where is he?"

"Out at Sea Breeze with Mamaw. We're staying there for the rest of the summer."

"The entire summer?" he asked, incredulous. "When did you decide this?"

"Last month. I told you we were going."

"For your grandmother's birthday. Not for the summer."

"Mamaw *invited* us"—she raised her fingers around the word

"invited" to make quotation marks—"to stay for the whole summer. In fact," she added with a short laugh, "Mamaw told us we had to stay the summer or we were out of the will."

Dora held back a smile at seeing his stunned expression, remembering the same looks on her sisters' faces when Mamaw had dropped that bomb.

"The old battle-ax," Cal said. "That's pretty high-handed, if you ask me. Even for her. How did she figure you could all just pack up and go away for the summer like you did as little girls? Your sisters have jobs, and you . . . you have responsibilities here, to this house. What about all that's going on here?" He waved his arm, indicating the work being done at the house. "You can't leave now."

Dora felt her spine stiffen at the audacity of his command. First he insulted her efforts with Nate, and now he was ordering her around? She recalled Mamaw's admonition to channel the Muir spirit and lifted her chin.

"You forget, Cal. I *can* just up and go if I want to. I no longer need to consult you, or ask your permission. You've changed things between us."

She paused, acknowledging his tightening lips and flushed face. His eyes looked as if they were about ready to explode, but he pulled himself together.

Cal cleared his throat. "Dora, be reasonable . . ."

"I am being reasonable," she said with a forced smile, chafing under the implication that she was once again being emotional. She sat straighter in her chair and began to explain her decision, trying to keep her tone level.

"I thought this through carefully. It makes sense for me to stay with Nate at Sea Breeze while the work is being done here.

The men will be working round the clock. Nate wouldn't be able to tolerate the hammering, the strange smells, the heat. He'd also be spooked by having strangers around him all day. We're lucky to have Sea Breeze to go to! Of course, you could stay at the house during the renovations. To keep an eye on things," she added with a sweet smile. *There, not the least bit emotional,* she thought with smug pleasure.

Cal's face tightened but he didn't respond.

"Plus, I want to spend time with Mamaw and my sisters again. Mamaw intends to sell Sea Breeze. It's our last chance to be together again."

Cal's gaze sharpened. "She's selling Sea Breeze?"

Dora wasn't surprised that this tidbit caught his attention. Sea Breeze was worth millions on today's market. "Yes."

"That should bring in a pretty penny."

Dora merely shrugged. She could almost see the numbers rolling in his brain.

"I reckon I can see how *you* could decide to stay," he said, considering. "You don't have a job. Now don't get your back up," he added, raising his palms in an arresting gesture. "I meant a real job, at a place of business. What I don't understand is how your sisters manage it. I mean, who can just up and leave for three months? Even for them . . ."

Cal had never had a high opinion of her half-sisters, though he barely knew them.

"Timing is everything, I guess. Carson's TV series was canceled so she's between jobs. She was all over the prospect of staying at Sea Breeze rent-free for the summer."

"What's she worried about? Don't folks working in Hollywood get paid the world?"

"That was the big shocker. Carson doesn't have any money. In fact, she's flat broke."

He released a short laugh of surprise ringing with satisfaction. Cal had always been sensitive to the fact that he wasn't earning nearly as much as many of his childhood friends. Promotions and increases in salary rarely came his way.

"What about Hadley? Granted, *she* doesn't have to work."

"Her name is *Harper*," Dora corrected him, annoyed by the error. True, they hadn't been close with Harper all these years, but to not get her name right was flat-out ridiculous. "Don't you remember how Daddy named each of us after a favorite Southern author?"

"That's right," he said in a drawl, as though remembering a joke. "Let's see, that's Harper Lee, Carson McCullers, and"—he indicated Dora with a gesture of mock gallantry— "Eudora Welty." Cal picked a single grape from the cluster, then held it a moment between two fingers. "Parker Muir, the great author. Given that your father never published a book, it's almost pathetic, isn't it?" He popped the grape in his mouth.

Dora flushed at the sting of his words. "Not in the least," she said, rising to her father's defense. "I think it reflects his sense of culture—and a certain Southern charm." She reached for her wineglass, needing to bolster her confidence.

Cal merely shrugged.

She could feel a subtle shift of emotion between them. A new tension bubbling under the surface.

"So, how's Nate doing out at Sea Breeze?" he asked at length. "I'm surprised he let you leave him behind. No fireworks?"

She wanted to reply, *If you'd bothered to call in the past few weeks you'd know.* But wanting to continue taking the high road, she answered, "Well enough, under the circumstances."

"Circumstances? I don't understand."

"It's a long story."

Cal sighed with impatience.

Dora decided to give him the short version. She knew his attention span was limited when it came to her family, even his son. "Nate fell head over heels in love with a dolphin at the dock. You know how he gets when he's interested in something. He studied dolphins, talked incessantly about them, and spent a lot of time with Carson swimming in the Cove." A smile blossomed as Dora remembered Nate's face, so vibrant and alive in the water with the dolphin. "Oh, Cal, I wish you could've seen him swimming. He's gotten so strong and tan. So handsome . . . He just loved it."

"That's a change. It's always been a fight to get him into the water."

"I know." She paused, getting into the difficult part. "He also liked to catch fish to feed Delphine. That's what caused the accident, you see. Luring the dolphin to the dock. She got horribly entangled in all that fishing line. Oh, Cal, it was awful . . ." Dora closed her eyes, remembering how the lines cut deep into the dolphin's flesh each time she rose to catch a breath.

"Did it die?" he asked.

"Too soon to tell. Carson followed the dolphin to Florida, to the rehab center." She shook her head. "I'm worried for Nate if she dies. Since the accident he's been back in his room with those damn video games. He won't go outdoors or swim in the Cove. I'm afraid he's in one of his bad periods."

"I never was much of a help during those spells," Cal admitted.

"You could have tried," Dora said pointedly.

To her surprise, Cal nodded. "I admit there are times I could have been a little more patient with him," Cal said.

Dora was taken aback. Cal had never before acknowledged his poor treatment of Nate. "He's only nine. You still have plenty of time to repair bridges."

"That's true."

For a moment, Dora felt almost hopeful. Maybe there was a way they could still work this out, still be a family. They owed it to Nate to try. She was about to utter those words when Cal spoke again, his tone suddenly businesslike and strained, any hint of a remorseful father wiped clean.

"Anyways, Dora," he said, his eyes focused on a point just over her shoulder, "that's not what I've come to talk to you about."

Dora felt her stomach rise to her throat and a burn blaze across her cheeks. Against her better judgment she'd let her guard down for a moment, thinking he might have changed. And she knew he was about to stomp all over that vulnerability.

"I see," she said in a carefully measured voice. "What do you want to talk about?"

Now Cal was studying the wineglass as if it held the secrets of the universe. After a moment he folded his hands together on the table and met her gaze.

"I came to discuss an amicable divorce."

"An amicable divorce?" she repeated, not comprehending the meaning of the phrase.

"Yes." Cal leaned forward slightly and began to speak in a

controlled and deliberate voice, as though he'd memorized each word. It frightened her more than if he'd shouted.

"You see, a divorce doesn't have to be a free-for-all. You saw how much tension and anger was pent up in the lawyer's office this morning. Divorce can be amicable if the divorcing couple communicates frankly about their needs and desires while resolving the issues they face."

"*The divorcing couple*," she repeated, incredulous and enraged by his pretentiousness, his distance. "Lord in heaven, Cal, you sound like you're on some advertisement. The divorcing couple? There's just you and me."

Cal sat back, slightly insulted. "Right," he said.

"Go on. I'm listening."

He continued. "Basically, you and I will work out the details ourselves," he said, dropping the officious tone. "Not the lawyers. If we ask the attorneys to resolve our issues, it can get nasty and our case can go on forever and cost a fortune in legal fees. Look at what happened today. Your lawyer was blindsiding my lawyer. It was getting contentious. The way I see it, we can make a settlement plan ourselves, have our lawyers look at it, and we can remain friends. I'd like that, wouldn't you? It'd be better for Nate, too, don't you think?"

Now that Cal had effectively burst her bubble of denial, Dora could listen to his words and hear the veneer he was spreading on thick. *Her* lawyer blindsiding? It had been just the opposite.

"I don't think so, Cal," she replied in an even tone. "I heard what you offered today. If that's your idea of working things out, then you can take your settlement and stick it where the sun don't shine." She smiled sweetly.

Cal's face colored. "So, you're going there, are you?"

"I'm only continuing down the path you started us on."

"I thought, well . . ." Cal sat back in his chair, slapping his palms on his thighs in a gesture of impatience. "I don't know why I'd expect you to be reasonable."

"You thought I'd just sit back and do whatever you told me to do, like I always did. Didn't you? Good ol' Dora. She'll toe the line." Dora jabbed her finger at him. "*You* left, Cal. You walked out that door, not only on me but on your son. I expected a man who did something like that would feel some guilt. I expected you to be generous. To *be reasonable*." She laughed insultingly. "I saw how reasonable you were. Nate and I can't live on what you offered!"

"If I had more I'd offer more!"

"I know exactly what you make and I know when I'm getting the short end of the stick. You always were cheap, Cal. But I'm not just talking about the money. We always said if anything ever happened to us that the antiques you inherited would go back to your family and mine would go back to mine. But now you want my family antiques, too."

"Everything we own, including the furniture, is considered communal property. The lawyers explained that. We have to divide it equally."

"Have to? If we do this amicable divorce thing, we can do what we want. You just said so."

Cal set down his glass and stood abruptly. His chair scraped the wood floor. "I can see there's no discussing anything when you're in this mood. This is where Nate gets it from."

Dora gasped and felt a sharp pain, as though the words had stabbed her heart. She'd always known that deep down he'd blamed her for Nate's autism. Dora's heart began pumping hard in her chest and her mouth felt so dry that she couldn't respond.

"I'd better go," he said.

"Yes, go. You're good at that!"

His face pinched and he turned to leave.

"You didn't just leave me, you know," she cried after him. "You left Nate."

He turned back to face her. His own face was set in resolve. "Yes."

Her heart ached for her son, her sad, lonely boy. "You haven't called or visited him. You're a lousy father, do you know that?" She could feel the emotion rising and was powerless to stop it, didn't want to stop it. "You never even once took Nate fishing!"

"Fishing? What the . . . Where did that come from?"

"He wanted to learn how to fish. What boy doesn't? Mamaw taught him. Not you. You never taught him anything. He was always a disappointment to you."

"Dora, we're getting off track. Why are we digging up all this anger when the only reason I came over tonight was to try to find a peaceful settlement? You always do that. You get so emotional."

"You want to see emotion? I'll show you emotion!" Her voice rose to a shout. "Why did you leave me? You never told me. Why?"

The louder she yelled, the more withdrawn Cal became. He blew out a plume of air. "I hated my life," he answered simply.

Dora went silent, mouth agape, blindsided.

"Every night when I came home I stood at the door and resented that I had to enter this house." His gaze swept the room. "I hate this goddamn house," he said in a cold monotone. "It's been an albatross around my neck. Then the minute I'd walk in you'd start rattling on and on about Nate's problems or the house's problems, or the yard's problems. There were always problems! I couldn't get five minutes to sit down and relax before you'd start right in wanting to discuss some earth-shattering problem, like the garbage disposal was broken."

"You could have told me! I'd have given you space."

"It's not only that."

"What else?"

"It's us."

"What about us?"

"There is no us!" Cal exploded. "There hasn't been for a long time. There's only you and Nate. I'm the odd man out. Sure, I understand that Nate needs a lot of your time. I get that. But once you got his diagnosis you were obsessed. You couldn't do enough. You've been *over*involved. Our entire lives revolved around him. Dora, you hover. You plan every moment of his life."

"It is my job!" she cried, almost in tears. "I'm his mother!"

"You were also my wife! You forgot that part. I became an afterthought in this house."

"An afterthought? I cooked your meals, cleaned your house, did your laundry."

"I want a wife, not a goddamn maid!"

Dora sucked in her breath. More than all the words spoken in the lawyer's office, more than all the lists on ledgers, this moment told her for certain that her marriage was over. He didn't love her, had not loved her for some time. Would never love her again.

"I . . . I didn't know you felt that way." She choked back tears.

Cal wagged his head with exhaustion. He was the picture of a man throwing in the towel. He softened his voice. "Don't cry, Dora. Please . . ."

His words just made her sob harder. She gulped for air, unable to catch her breath. It felt as though he'd taken her heart in his hands and was squeezing it, tighter and tighter. She felt pain under her rib cage and, clutching her chest, she doubled over.

"Dora, what's wrong?" he asked, taking a step toward her.

Her heart was pounding so hard she could barely hear him for the thundering in her ears. She staggered forward, her knees buckling.

"It's my heart. I can't breathe."

Chapter Three

~~~~

A sultry, salty breeze lifted Carson's long, dark hair like a sheath of silk from her shoulders. It was the only visible movement as she sat still as a statue on a metal chair, leaning forward with her chin cupped in her palm. She had an athlete's body, strong and trained. She could hold this position for a long while, her gaze laser-focused on one particular blue tank in the Mote Marine cetacean hospital.

This rear area of the hospital was more utilitarian than the larger, beautiful Mote aquarium. A large wall was dominated by an attractive sea-green and white mural depicting dolphins. The mural distracted the eye from the industrial gray stucco walls and towering water tanks in the behind-the-scenes outdoor arena. A few blue holding tanks occupied a corner of the space. All the tanks were empty save one, which held a dolphin.

"Oh, Delphine," Carson murmured.

Carson had barely recognized the beautiful, beguiling Delphine she knew from Sullivan's Island. That dolphin was a vigorous, sleek female in her prime. This dolphin's skin was a dull gray, she was listless and weak, and her long body was crisscrossed with scars.

Staring at the listless dolphin, Carson couldn't move or speak. Her heart was crushed under the weight of her guilt. Sitting in the glare of the sun, feeling the burn, Carson had to own that it was her fault this dolphin had been so badly injured. As Blake had told her, this is what her selfishness had brought them to.

Blake Legare worked for the National Oceanic and Atmospheric Administration in Charleston. He'd been her friend, her lover, but the fact that she'd kept from him the truth that she'd befriended a dolphin at the dock at Sea Breeze had forged a wedge between them. She'd gone against all that he worked so hard to educate the public against doing, and in the end she'd proved him correct. She'd fed a wild dolphin and the dolphin was injured. Yet Blake still arranged for her to visit the Mote Marine cetacean hospital, where he'd brought Delphine for treatment. For this, she'd always be grateful.

Carson had driven to Sarasota from Sullivan's Island the day before. Tired and hungry, she arrived in town late and checked into a modest motel as close to the Mote Marine hospital as she could afford. She'd barely slept a wink waiting for dawn, and was standing at the doors of the hospital when they opened.

The staff had received word of her impending arrival and were friendly enough, but until formal permission was granted for access, all Carson was permitted to do was enter the hospital area, wait patiently, and watch. She'd been sitting for over an hour and that was more than enough time to observe how sick Delphine truly was. Even with Blake's warning, she hadn't been prepared for the extent of the dolphin's injuries.

A short while later, Carson heard a voice call her name. She turned to see a tall, attractive woman in a swimsuit and bright blue rash guard with MOTE emblazoned across the chest. She wore her blond hair in a long ponytail and carried a clipboard. Carson sprang to her feet, eager to talk to someone about Delphine.

"You're Carson Muir?" the woman asked.

"I am," Carson replied, reaching out her hand.

"Lynne Byrd," the woman replied in greeting, giving Carson's hand a perfunctory shake.

Lynne looked at her clipboard, her demeanor all business. "It says here that you're requesting to be allowed to volunteer with the dolphin rehabilitation program."

"Yes."

"Okay. Let's see." She checked her notes. "Dr. Blake Legare contacted us." She glanced up. "Do you know Blake?"

Carson looked at the exceptionally pretty woman and felt a flutter of jealousy. "He's a friend."

She smiled. "Yeah, Blake's a good guy. We've worked together," she said in an offhand manner that spoke only of a professional relationship. "He asks that you specifically be allowed to volunteer with the dolphin Delphine." She glanced up, questioning. "Why this dolphin?"

"I know this dolphin."

"You *know* her?"

Carson heard the same censorious tone in Lynne's voice that she'd noticed in Blake's when he'd first learned that Carson had befriended a wild dolphin.

Carson nodded. "It's a long story."

"I'd like to hear it."

Carson shifted her weight, resigned to the retelling of the painful incident. She knew that Lynne would be listening carefully not only to what she said, but also to what was left unsaid. Carson brought to mind the first time she'd seen Delphine in the Atlantic Ocean on that fateful morning.

"I was surfing outside Isle of Palms and a dolphin protected me from a bull shark that was messing with me. I'd read about this kind of thing happening, how dolphins save people's lives, but you never really believe it, you know? But it happened to *me*," she said in a somber tone. "I believe—I know—this dolphin saved my life."

Lynne tilted her head in the way that told Carson her interest was piqued. "I've heard the stories, too. And I believe them," Lynne conceded. "There are too many documented cases not to."

Carson immediately liked the woman. "But Delphine paid a price for her heroism. As she tried to get away, the shark lashed out and bit her fin."

"We figured the missing chunk in her fluke was from some sort of attack," Lynne said.

Carson nodded. "A few days later, I was paddleboarding in the Cove—that's a body of water behind Sullivan's Island in South Carolina—this dolphin began following me, checking me out. When I saw the bitten fluke, I knew it was the same dolphin that had rescued me. I couldn't believe it." She let out a short laugh. "The dolphin recognized me before I recognized her."

Lynne shook her head.

"I'm always amused when people are surprised at how

smart dolphins are. We know they're exceptionally intelligent creatures, but whenever we attribute them with any of what we think of as human qualities and smarts, we find it hard to accept. The truth is, dolphins are that kind of smart." She paused to scribble something down on her clipboard. "So, how did she end up getting ensnared in all that fishing line?"

"This is the part I'm ashamed to tell," Carson said. There was no skirting around her part in this. "I guess I was flattered that the dolphin recognized me. She seemed eager to befriend me, as much as I wanted to form a relationship with her, too. I know now that I should have stopped there. But I didn't. I thought somehow I was special. So, I encouraged her. I named her. We swam together and I called her to the dock." She paused, cringing. "We fed her fish. I know, I know . . ." she said quickly, seeing the flare-up in Lynne's eyes. "I shouldn't have. We did everything wrong."

"Yeah, you did," Lynne said, but there wasn't scorn in the tone.

Carson continued. "One night, my nephew set up fishing lines to catch fish to feed Delphine. He's only nine and his heart was in the right place. The next morning, I discovered Delphine entangled in the fishing lines."

She closed her eyes. Carson would never forget the sound of Delphine's screams piercing the early morning quiet, or the sight of her struggling to catch a breath in the choppy water. Each time the dolphin rose up in the water to take a breath, the razorlike filament cut deeper into her flesh.

"I called Blake and the NOOA team rescued her. My grandmother arranged for the plane to transport her here." She looked at her feet. "You know the rest."

There was a moment's silence as Lynne seemed to be considering the story.

Carson cleared her throat. "How is Delphine now?"

Lynne's face was grave. "Well," she began matter-of-factly, turning again to her notes on the clipboard. "This dolphin is in critical condition. She suffered multiple lesions in her pectoral and dorsal fins, and severe slicing across her body. The fishing line had embedded deeply and required surgical removal." Lynne flipped to the next page, and reading farther, she frowned. "What was really bad were the two fishing hooks that were embedded into her soft palate." Lynne shook her head. "That was one badass hook. I've rarely seen a mammal so close to death that makes it. She was slack-jawed, her eyes glazed. I thought she was gone. But this dolphin has a strong will to live. She's on antibiotics and fluids. We thought we were making progress."

"Thought?"

Lynne looked up from her clipboard. "She stopped eating. Delphine has been showing no interest in food. It's a serious worry."

Carson's stomach clenched. "What can you do?"

Lynne suddenly dropped her professional demeanor, leaning into Carson and lightly touching her wrist in sympathy. "All we can. It's touch and go at this point. Delphine continues to be cared for around the clock by trained volunteers who are keeping a close eye. They're a dedicated group. Some of them are taking the midnight shifts. We're grateful to them."

"I could do that," Carson said automatically.

Lynne paused. "I'll be honest with you. When I first heard that you were coming I was annoyed. I figured the last thing I need is some rookie wanting to play Flipper in my tank. But I know Blake Legare. I trust him. He said that I should give you a chance with this dolphin."

Carson remained silent.

Lynne continued. "Delphine's weak but swimming for short periods on her own and in a more upright position than she had been when she arrived. The staff is working to encourage her to swim herself for longer periods of time." She looked out at Delphine in the tank and sighed with worry. "She's just so listless."

Carson followed Lynne's gaze. "She looks depressed."

"I don't like to use human terms in referring to dolphins, but . . ." Lynne lifted her shoulders slightly. "Yes, I'd say she looks depressed."

"She's all alone in there."

"We don't want to encourage too much human interaction. We don't want her associating humans with food, so the more hands-off we can be, the better it will be for her in the long run." Lynne lowered the clipboard to her side. "But . . . I've been doing this for over twenty years. Every once in a blue moon I meet up with a dolphin who is extremely social. I think Delphine is one of these dolphins." A small smile of memory flitted across her face. "Usually we don't touch them. One time when I was in the tank with her I accidentally rubbed her skin with my palm. She whistled and looked at me. I mean, she really looked at me, like you were talking about. I swear, if she was a cat she'd have purred."

The memory of Delphine in the Cove, her head tilted and her dark eyes shining, flashed in Carson's mind. "I know that look."

Considering this, Lynne studied Carson's face. "If this dolphin has a bond with you, if she recognizes you, it might be what helps her turn the corner."

"I did bond with her. I know she'll recognize me," Carson said resolutely.

Lynne nodded firmly, then looked at her watch. "It's time to give Delphine her meds. You can come into the tank with us. Let's see how Delphine responds to you. We'll let her decide."

"Thank you," Carson said.

"Don't thank me," Lynne replied, back to her brusque manner. "We both want what's best for this dolphin."

Carson was guided to a restroom, where she changed into a swimsuit. A volunteer gave her a blue Mote rash guard, then led her to where Lynne and another Mote staff member stood outside a large blue holding tank. The sun was shining bright overhead and the cement burned her feet as she crossed the square. Carson's heart was beating fast; she was both anxious and fearful of being close to Delphine again. Would she welcome her? she wondered. Or was she so far gone that she wouldn't even recognize Carson?

Lynne and the vet tech climbed up the ladder to enter the tank, and Carson followed. Peering over the edge, she saw Delphine on the opposite side of the large tank, and her breath caught in her chest. Closer, Carson could vividly see the glaring white scars crisscrossing Delphine's gray body, still so fresh. She followed the other two women down the ladder to enter the tank's cool water. The water in the pool was up to her waist. Lynne and the tech were already beside Delphine, holding her steady. Carson held back, her eyes glued to Delphine. She floated more vertically than was normal for a dolphin. Her beautiful eyes were open, but mere slits in the large gray head. She looked almost lifeless.

"We need you to help hold her head so I can deliver the meds," Lynne said, waving Carson over.

Carson approached Delphine with slow steps.

Delphine, aware of each presence in the tank, tilted her head toward the new person approaching. Carson stared into Delphine's eyes. Suddenly the dolphin let loose a loud whistle and wriggled out of the tech's hold with one firm push of her tail.

"Delphine!" Carson cried, and held her arms out as the dolphin made a beeline for her.

Delphine let her body slide against Carson's as she swam past her. She circled the tank, whistling with excitement. Then she returned to Carson, her large eyes wide and eager looking. Carson reached out, but before touching Delphine, she looked to Lynne.

"Can I touch her?"

Lynne smiled wide and nodded. "Go ahead. It's clear she wants you to."

Carson relished the feel of Delphine's rubbery skin under her palms as her hands caressed her large head and more gently slid along her side, careful of the wounds. Skin to skin, it was a glorious moment of reconnection. Carson felt a rush of love for the dolphin and gloried in knowing it was reciprocated. When Delphine came to a rest in front of her, her mouth open wide in a seeming grin, Carson shuddered at seeing how badly the hooks had ravaged her mouth.

"What have we done to you?" she murmured.

In a surprise move, Delphine rolled over to present her belly to be stroked. Carson heard Lynne suck in her breath at this show of obvious affection and trust. Carson reached out to stroke the sleek, smooth belly, the water rustling between her fingers. The dolphin's whitish skin became rosy colored with pleasure.

Delphine turned upright and rested in the water, facing Carson.

Lynne came closer and rubbed Delphine's big head.

"Well, I'd call that a positive response," she said with a light laugh. The vet tech smiled in agreement. "That's more movement than we've seen from her so far. Let's see if she'll take some fish."

Lynne handed Carson a container of live fish. "Toss one to her. Head first. It's easier for her to swallow."

Carson did as she was instructed. She'd tossed many a fish to Delphine from the dock back home, so she knew Delphine could catch it if she wanted to.

"Delphine," she called out. The dolphin's dark eyes were watching her, curious, even expectant. Reaching into the bucket, Carson grabbed a single, slim fish in her hand.

"Delphine, hungry? Want a nice herring?" she called out.

Delphine watched.

"Here you go," Carson called, and tossed a fish. In a flash, Delphine caught it and sent it down the hatch.

The three women cheered with mutual relief while Delphine looked back, eager for more.

Carson fed Delphine the rest of the fish, praising her for each bit she ate until the bucket was empty.

"This is excellent," Lynne told Carson. "Better than I'd hoped. She needs to eat about eight pounds of herring and capelin a day. So," she said, smiling broadly, "how long can you stay as a volunteer?"

"A week, maybe. I don't have a job or a place to live. I can't afford to stay much longer. Is a week long enough for Delphine to turn a corner?"

"I think she's already doing better. Just starting to eat again is huge." She gazed out at Delphine swimming in slow, tight circles around the tank. "Sometimes, all we need is a little love."

Carson thought of her grandmother, of her sisters, of Blake. Of how the love shared this summer had already changed her.

"I'll put you in charge of Delphine's feeding," Lynne said. "Angela will show you what to do in food prep. You can continue hand feeding her for a little longer, just until she's stronger. Then we'll get her eating on her own. I'd like to get Delphine in the large pool soon. There'll be more room for her to swim and we'll just toss the fish in for her to catch rather than hand feeding. This is an important step, should we return Delphine to the wild. The more hands-off we remain, the better it will be for her."

"Return to the wild?" Carson asked, surprised by this possibility. "I thought Delphine was going to a care facility."

"That's not for certain yet. Before today, I wasn't sure she'd survive. Our first goal is always to return the dolphins to the wild once they're healthy. But she's got a ways to go. We'll just have to wait and see."

"If you release her, where would she go?" Carson asked worriedly.

"Back to her community. Dolphins are very connected to their family pods. Communication within community structure is critical for their survival."

"And if she can't be released back to the Cove?"

Lynne paused. "Well, that's our first goal, of course."

"I'm confused. Didn't Blake tell you that there have been questions about whether she's part of the Cove community? He hasn't found Delphine in his database yet. He's still looking."

Lynne shook her head. "He didn't mention it. That's a serious issue. We don't make the final decision. If she can't be released to the wild, we'll find a suitable care facility for her."

"Blake mentioned the Dolphin Research Center."

"An excellent location. Have you ever been there?"

Carson shook her head.

"You should go. Check it out. I'd be curious to hear your feedback."

"I hold hope Delphine will be able to go back to the Cove."

"You know what that means for you, though, don't you?" Lynne asked. "You could observe her, but you could never interact. Delphine might well want to return to your dock, mooch a free meal. It's easier than hunting."

"Blake's raked me over the coals on that, you can be sure of it."

"Yeah, I can imagine. He's seen too much to be laid-back about it. We all have." Lynne signaled to the other Mote staffer. "You can stay in here awhile. I'll lower her toys and you can try to engage her. If she seems tired, just stand nearby and observe. Let us know if you see anything strange. And hey, I'm glad you're here. You did good."

Carson was left alone in the tank with Delphine. She couldn't just yet extinguish the hope that flared in her heart that Delphine might return to the Cove. But before today, she hadn't really seen how severe her injuries were, how compromised she was.

Delphine came to rest again in front of Carson. They gazed eye to eye for several minutes in companionable silence. The sun was hot on Carson's back. The water rocked gently with Delphine's movements. From somewhere in the distance, gulls cried.

Carson closed her eyes and felt the first peace she'd known in what felt like a long while. It would take time to work through the harsh truths revealed in the past month: how her mother had died in the house fire, her parents' alcoholism, and the likelihood that she, too, suffered from the disease.

But looking into Delphine's eyes, and seeing the unconditional forgiveness and love there, Carson felt the hardness of her heart soften and the process of absolving herself of her past mistakes begin.

Sullivan's Island, South Carolina

Harper stood outside the library door and peeked in the dimly lit room. Inside, Nate was sitting cross-legged on the floor in front of the television set. He was a slight, pale boy, his fair hair badly in need of a haircut. He sat motionless except for his nimble fingers rapidly working the remote control of the game he was playing. His concentration was intense; he was utterly unaware that she was watching him.

Seeing Nate in this room, small and alone, absorbed in his own world, reminded Harper of herself at that age. Harper had often squirreled herself away in this very room, only she wasn't into games back then. She escaped to her books. She still treasured the books of her youth, counted them as friends: *A Wrinkle in Time; The Lion, the Witch, and the Wardrobe;* and anything by Judy Blume. So many books, so many hours . . . She remembered being engulfed in stories, completely engaged in the enchanted worlds. During those times she hadn't felt lonely.

Like Nate, she had spent much of her childhood alone. Harper had been raised as generations of James children were raised before her. The upper-class British family subscribed to the *children are best seen and not heard* school of child rearing. James parents did not kiss or coddle their children. Emotional displays were frowned upon. No one could say that Georgiana neglected Harper's physical needs. Quite the contrary. Harper was always well dressed, well fed, well tended by a fleet of nannies. Neglect took many forms, however.

Her mother schlepped her between their homes in Manhattan, the Hamptons, and England, leaving her in the care of a nanny, a woman who usually sat and watched Harper play alone while her mother conducted endless business meetings or engaged in the whirlwind of her social life.

When Harper was six, she was deemed old enough to visit Sea Breeze during the summer break. Her mother never liked the idea of sending her daughter to the Muir family in the South for an extended stay, but the summer sojourn away did prove convenient, so she'd agreed to Mamaw's invitation.

Only here, at Sea Breeze, did Harper's pattern of isolation finally break. When she'd first arrived, everything on Sullivan's Island had felt so strange—so foreign. The enormous oak trees dripping with moss, the pounding surf, the lack of routine. Mamaw did not allow nannies at Sea Breeze and let the girls run wild on the island, requiring them only to show up washed and tidy for meals.

At first, Harper had felt like a boat adrift without a rigid schedule to follow or a nanny to tell her what to do. The freedom was frightening to a lonely six-year-old. She also felt shy and awkward with her two older sisters. Carson and Dora were closer in age to each other—and five and eight years older than Harper. They knew the house, the landscape, the culture. Sea Breeze was *their* place and Harper felt like an interloper. The first few weeks of that first summer, she spent huge amounts of time hiding in her room, reading.

Until Mamaw intervened. "Child, you must play outdoors!" Mamaw would say. Her grandmother shared Harper's love of books, but under her tutelage, Mamaw shared with Harper her other loves—fishing, boating, swimming, and the magic of the lowcountry. Mamaw took it upon herself to be the girls' pied piper. She packed lunches and took them out exploring the island and the waterways while telling tales of their infamous ancestor, the dashing Captain Muir, a fearsome pirate. She inspired the adventurous spirit that lay dormant in their blood and seeded in their young hearts the dream of finding the buried treasure that was, she claimed, rightfully theirs.

Dora was transitioning to her teens that summer and had set her sights on local boys. Carson, in need of a summer friend, turned to Harper. They soon discovered that they were kindred spirits, both creatures forged of imagination and dreams. The five-year difference in age evaporated in light of Harper's intelligence and Carson's love of adventure. Harper's love of reading often was the creative fodder for exciting new ideas to act out in their world of play.

Her summers at Sea Breeze had been a saving grace for her as a young girl. She wasn't alone with her books. With Carson, she had brought her imagination to life. She'd had a friend to play with.

Harper peeked in once again at the little boy sitting alone in front of the console. She quietly backed away from the door, a smile playing at her lips. She knew what she had to do next.

Chapter Four

~~~

*D*ora awoke in a strange room. She blinked slowly as it dawned on her where she was and how she had gotten here. She remembered the pain in her chest, the shortness of breath, Cal helping her to his car and driving her to the hospital. The mattress was thin and the sheets starchy, like the green and white hospital gown bunching at her hips. She felt woozy as she continued to blink in the light.

"Hi," Cal said at her side. "Glad you're awake."

She mustered a weak smile. "Hi." She looked blearily around the room, allowing her eyes to adjust. In the corner, she saw Mamaw sitting upright in a metal chair. She looked smart in her usual tunic—an aqua blue today—and tan linen pants. Mamaw smiled with encouragement when their gazes met.

A voice rang out from across the room. "Lord, you had us so worried! I was fixing to have a heart attack myself!"

Dora saw Mamaw's eyes roll before she turned her head in

the other direction to see her mother hurrying to her bedside. Winifred Smythe wore a sparkly white top that clung to her ample curves over black stretch pants, like snow on a mountaintop.

"Mama?"

Winifred rushed to Dora's side. Her once blond hair was now mostly gray and worn in the utilitarian bob and bangs style that Cal referred to as "the helmet." Under her blue eyes, a string of pearls graced her neck and dangled from her ears in delicate drops.

"Yes, it's me, darling. I'm here!" she said, clutching Dora's hand.

"When did you get here?"

"I dropped everything and drove straight here the moment Cal called. Bless his heart, he was so upset about you, he forgot to tell me what hospital he'd taken you to."

Dora tried to imagine Cal being that worried about her.

"Honey, you gave us such a scare," Winifred continued, squeezing her hand. "When I got to thinking my baby girl had a heart attack. I cried all the way from Charlotte. I am a wreck!"

Mamaw spoke up. "Don't get your knickers in a knot, Winnie. We don't know it was a heart attack."

"Well, of course it was," Winifred replied dismissively. She released Dora's hand with a pat. "A mild one, I'm sure . . ." she added to Dora in a consoling tone.

Cal stepped closer to the other side of her bed. Dora shifted her head on the pillow to focus on his face. Deep circles darkened his eyes and his usually neatly combed hair was disheveled. His expression was worry filled, even penitent.

"Dora," he said in a low, broken voice. "I never meant for

anything like this to happen. When I saw you hit the floor . . ." He shook his head in misery.

Winifred clucked her tongue in sympathy.

"I . . . I was thinking . . ." He hesitated. "Maybe we should talk about this whole divorce thing a little more. Maybe we're moving too quickly."

Dora heard her mother suck in her breath.

Mamaw suddenly appeared at his right. "Cal, you look exhausted. You went through a scare and haven't left Dora's side. The doctor isn't going to be in for a while. Why don't you take a minute to go down to the cafeteria for some coffee. Winnie and I are both here. We'll call you if the doctor comes."

Cal looked at Dora and she nodded in agreement.

"Okay," he said. "I could use a minute. I'll be back soon."

No sooner had the door closed behind him than Winifred clasped Dora's hand again and squeezed it with enthusiasm.

"Did you hear that, honey?" she said with a gush. Her eyes gleamed. "Cal doesn't want a divorce!"

Dora looked back with apathy. She didn't feel the same giddy rush her mother did. She didn't feel much at all. It was as though all the pent-up emotion that had roiled inside of her had expelled itself through whatever had happened to her in the house.

"He didn't say that, Mama," she said impassively. "At least not exactly."

Winifred waved her hand. "He's opened the door and you should rush back in. It's time to mend those fences."

Dora's head was swimming in her mother's overuse of mixed metaphors. Winifred loved pat sayings and used them excessively.

When Dora didn't reply, Winifred said with shock, "You don't want a divorce, do you?"

"And why not?" Mamaw asked her in an imperious tone.

Winifred turned to face Mamaw with a pinched expression. No love was lost between the two women, and the last thing Dora needed now was a showdown. She'd always felt that her mother unfairly blamed Mamaw for Parker's faults. Mamaw had done all she could to support Winifred during her marriage to Parker and throughout the divorce. After all, Mamaw had introduced the couple, and they'd been so young when they'd married. With Parker having just graduated from college and Winifred a sophomore-year dropout, never to receive a degree, Mamaw had purchased a lovely house for the young couple in the fashionable Colonial Lake area of Charleston. Edward got Parker a job in his bank. Dora had always thought no parents could have been more generous. Two years later, after it was discovered that Parker was having an affair with Dora's nanny, Mamaw had rallied in support of Winifred, threatening to cut Parker off if he didn't end the affair with eighteen-year-old Sophie. The whole mess was a big disgrace that took Winifred years to get past. Memories were long in Charleston. But it certainly wasn't Mamaw's doing.

"Divorce is painful to bear," Winifred said pointedly. "I should know. Not to mention the scandal of it all. If Cal is willing to reconsider, Dora should do whatever she can to save her marriage."

Dora felt a twinge at her heart.

"Winnie," Mamaw said, stepping closer. Her tone had shifted to conciliatory. "I realize your divorce from Parker was difficult. It broke my heart. You were both so young and you with a baby."

She shook her head remorsefully. "It was all very sad. But Parker never changed, did he? He would have broken your heart over and over again if you had stayed together. You were set free by the divorce. If you'd stayed in that marriage, you never would have met Henry. And you've been happy with him, haven't you?"

"True," Winifred said, mollified. "But Cal isn't Parker. He's much more stable, reliable. He's not an alcoholic," she finished, her tone slightly smug, as though she knew the sting of those words would cut Mamaw deep.

Mamaw let the dig slide. "But does he love our Dora? That is the only criterion she should consider. Dora deserves more than a life filled with resentment and regrets. Both of us know too many women who are desperately unhappy because they stayed in a loveless marriage."

"Marriage is not just about love," Winifred countered, raising her voice sharply. "Love is merely passion and infatuation. Marriage is duty. Obligation. Commitment. It's hard work."

Mamaw scoffed. "You make it sound like a prison term. And I daresay, if those are the only reasons one chooses to live with a man, it will be."

Dora felt this battle of wills stir her heart. She cringed, her body reacting to what she was hearing, like nails scraping a blackboard. Her mother's position was clear. Dora should not get a divorce. Dora looked at her mother standing as erect as a soldier, glaring at Mamaw, ready to do battle with a formidable foe. Her mother used the word *should* a lot, she realized. She didn't care if the marriage was happy or even content. Winnie had never invested in relationships. It had always been about maintaining the social conventions, about doing what one *should*.

Dora was about to remind them that she was in the room when the door opened and the subject of their conversation entered carrying a cup of coffee. Immediately the two women stopped talking and tight smiles appeared on their faces as they welcomed him back. Dora said nothing, but realized that it hadn't occurred to Cal to ask the older women if they'd wanted coffee, tea, or even a donut. They'd been pulling equally long hours at the hospital. But he'd never been thoughtful in that way. Dora tried to brush off the thought. After all, Cal was here and he was trying. That had to be enough.

Dora's mind froze. *That had to be enough.*

Wasn't that her pat answer whenever Cal disappointed her? When he refused to babysit Nate, or pick up dinner when she was tired. When he'd said they couldn't afford a dishwasher, or forgot their anniversary. Or when he'd recoiled from her touch. But he loved her, she'd kept telling herself. He was a good man. A good provider. He didn't drink and have affairs, as her father had done. He was her husband. *That had to be enough.*

Trouble was, it had never felt like enough. She'd talked to her mother about it, hoping for some bolstering mother-daughter advice. Winifred had blown off Dora's complaints with a light laugh, explaining that all wives were ignored in some ways and that it was perfectly normal as the years went by. *The blush is off the rose*, she'd quipped.

A brisk knock on the door drew Dora's attention away from her musings. She turned her head in time to see a doctor walk in, followed by a tall, pretty blond nurse.

"Hello, Dr. Newell," Mamaw said.

Dora watched Dr. Newell skim through her chart. The cardiologist reminded her of Opie from Mayberry—freckled and freshly scrubbed, like he just got out of school. She wondered how someone so young could have so many degrees.

"How are we feeling?" he asked her with a quick smile.

Dora hated when doctors used the royal *we*. "I don't know how you're doing, Doctor, but I feel like something the cat dragged in."

He chuckled, amused. Dora decided to like him.

"That's to be expected," he replied amiably.

Mamaw spoke up. "Was it a heart attack?"

Dr. Newell glanced up from the papers he was carrying and, directing his attention to his patient, offered Dora a professional smile and a short shake of his head. "No. Dora's symptoms mimicked a heart attack, but we've looked at the tests and the good news is that you actually have a different type of heart problem called stress cardiomyopathy."

"I didn't have a heart attack?" Dora asked, relief flooding her body.

"No. Have you been under an unusual amount of stress lately?"

Dora glanced at Cal and saw his brows furrow in concern. "Yes."

"I see. This condition is usually brought on by severe stress or grief. We call it the 'broken heart syndrome.'"

Dora stared back at the doctor in silence. She couldn't believe it. That was exactly what it felt like—as if her heart had broken.

Mamaw's relief was visible on her face. "That is good news. But I've never heard of this broken heart syndrome. And you called it a heart condition. Is this serious?"

"Not necessarily. You see, a stressful event triggers the sympathetic nervous system, which is also called your fight-or-flight mechanism."

"I've heard of that," Winifred chimed in.

Dr. Newell smiled in the manner a teacher would at a pupil who shouted an answer out of turn. "Yes. It's a normal reaction. Your body unleashes a flood of chemicals, including adrenaline. This sudden flood can stun your heart muscle, leaving it unable to pump properly. We all have stress in our lives. Stress cardiomyopathy is a condition that comes on suddenly and unexpectedly, mostly among postmenopausal women. And"—he paused with another smile—"it resolves itself quickly. Especially in Dora's case, because her heart appears to be in good shape. So even though broken heart syndrome may feel like a heart attack, it's a lesser problem that requires a different type of treatment."

"How exactly do you treat this, Doctor?" Mamaw asked. "Are there medicines she should take? More tests?"

"When can she go home?" asked Winifred.

The doctor listened to the flood of questions, then turned to address Dora. "I want to keep you here for the night. Maybe two. You're a little dehydrated and I'm waiting for the results of a few more tests. You won't need medications. At least not yet." He looked at the others. "Dora was actually very lucky."

"Lucky?" Dora asked.

"Lucky that we can look at your heart health now, before any more serious problems arise. I'm glad you're here," he said, turning to Mamaw. "I'd like to confirm family history. I understand your husband died of heart disease? And your father?"

"Yes. The family is riddled with heart disease," Mamaw exclaimed. "Edward, my husband, died of a heart attack at seventy-two. His father and two brothers, all from heart problems. My son died at only fifty-five. We lost him so young. Muirs die of heart disease—or war," she added darkly.

"And you?" Dr. Newell asked Mamaw.

"Not me, thankfully. Colsons get the cancer. Though I do get those heart palpitations when anxious."

Dora thought about what Mamaw had just said about Parker. "Mamaw, I thought you always said it was the drink that killed Daddy."

"True enough, but the immediate cause of death was a heart attack. Poor man was thin and malnourished. It was only a matter of time till the liver got him. But," she added with emphasis, remembering an important point, "Parker had heart palpitations just like this when he was but a few years older than you are now, Dora. Edward and I took him to the doctor but he couldn't find anything wrong."

In the resulting silence, Dora could hear the scribbling of Dr. Newell's pen as he wrote quickly on the chart. She'd never known that her family had such a strong history of heart disease . . . and it frightened her.

"The good news today is that your heart shows no sign of disease," Dr. Newell told Dora. "But with your history, and this incident, it's time to make changes. Are you a heavy drinker?"

"No," she replied quickly. "I drink wine, mostly red," she added, having read somewhere that red wine was good for the heart. "And the occasional cocktail. But just last month my sisters and I went cold turkey for a week, just to be sure we could. We worried about it, because of our father's alcoholism. I didn't have a problem stopping."

"Good. What about your job? Sedentary?"

"I'm a stay-at-home mom. I homeschool."

"Exercise?"

Dora shook her head, shamefaced.

"How many children?"

"One. My son, Nate. He's nine years old."

"What about your diet?" Dr. Newell looked at his chart. "You're overweight and I'm concerned that you carry so much of your weight around your waist, which is a clear indicator of possible heart disease. Nurse Langelan is a nutritionist and she can give you advice on what you can do to change your diet and lifestyle." He waved his hand toward the nurse beside him. She was tall and slender, an example of good nutrition and exercise. "You know the drill. But no more putting it off, Mrs. Tupper," he said in earnest. "You must do it. *Now.* This has been your wake-up call."

Dora looked at Mamaw and Winifred. Mamaw's eyes had taken on a new gleam, while Winifred appeared haunted, as though she'd just heard herself diagnosed.

"Other than that, you're free to go home as soon as the tests are done."

Dora managed a smile, relieved.

"Thank you, Doctor," Winifred said magnanimously. "We're so grateful for the good news. Dora, you can come home with me to Charlotte. Henry would love to have you for as long as you wish. And Nate, of course," she added. "Doctor, how long should she be on bed rest?"

"Bed rest? That's what Dora does *not* need. I want her up and moving, doing nonstrenuous exercise to start." He turned again to Dora. "Take long walks along an even surface. A half hour minimum and work up in ten-minute increments. Once you're comfortable with that, you can and should ramp it up with a regular exercise routine. Nurse Langelan will give you suggestions. If you have any further questions, don't hesitate to call." He smiled at Dora with encouragement. "Do take this seriously, Dora. You're young and you still have time to make changes. Good luck."

Dora smiled weakly, wondering about all those forthcoming changes.

After Dr. Newell left, Nurse Langelan assured Dora she'd be right back and followed him out. For a moment all in the room were silent.

Mamaw was the first to speak. "It doesn't make sense for Dora to go to Charlotte. She is already comfortably settled at Sea Breeze. There's nothing but fresh air and beaches to walk, and Lucille will prepare a healthy diet. And best of all, Nate is already settled there. He doesn't like change," she reminded them.

"But she needs her mother now," Winifred said.

"Oh, Winnie, do be sensible," Mamaw snapped, her patience running out.

For a moment the two women eyed each other.

"Mamaw—" Cal began.

"Excuse me," Mamaw interrupted him, looking at him with disdain. "I only allow my family to use that term of endearment. You can call me Mrs. Muir."

The color drained from Cal's tight face. "Mrs. Muir," he conceded. "I'd like to speak to Dora alone for a moment."

"Don't you upset her!" Mamaw warned.

"I won't."

"I wish I could believe you."

Cal drew himself up. "I own that I've made mistakes." His eyes flashed. "But I don't have to explain them to you. Only to Dora."

There was a momentary pause. Then Mamaw said to Dora, "It's quite late. Time I left for Sea Breeze. And you need your rest. Call me in the morning, won't you, dear? I do hope you'll return to Sullivan's Island. We all do."

"Good night, Mamaw," Dora said with a smile. She wanted to go home with Mamaw right this minute. To leave this sterile hospital with its uncomfortable bed and more tests on the way. To get away from Cal and her mother. To see Nate. She longed for her son. "Give Nate a kiss from me, will you?"

Mamaw bent to deliver a kiss to Dora's cheek. "I surely will." When she straightened, she turned to Winifred. "Winnie, do you have a place to spend the night? You're welcome to stay at Sea Breeze."

The invitation clearly took Winifred by surprise. Her face softened for the briefest moment but quickly returned a mask of indifference toward Mamaw. "Thank you, but no. I'll stay at my usual hotel. I want to be close to my daughter," she added with self-importance.

"Of course," Mamaw said. "Well then, I'm off."

Winifred also said her good-byes, laced with assurances of her love and promises to take good care of Dora in Charlotte, where she belonged. Before she left she offered Cal a kiss on the cheek, then said, "You children have a good talk. Patch things up."

When the door closed again, Dora closed her eyes as well, drawing her strength to deal with whatever Cal had on his mind. She was bone tired and heart weary. Barely able to open her eyes again, but she managed. Cal was standing beside the bed, his hands in his pockets, looking down at her, waiting.

Dora said, "I think we've said all there is to say for one day."

"Dora," Cal said, his eyes imploring. "I meant what I said earlier. About us reconsidering the divorce."

"Cal . . ."

"All this"—he waved his hand, indicating the hospital—"made me think again about how serious a step this is. About how short our lives are. We shouldn't be so quick to throw away all that we've built together."

He had her attention. Dora listened.

"Perhaps . . ." he began, taking her hand.

She stared at their joined hands.

". . . you should stay with me at my condo."

Dora gave him a quick glance but didn't respond.

"It's a nice building in our neighborhood with an elevator, close to shops. You could walk through the park to the house." He smiled with encouragement. "It will give you exercise and you can keep an eye on the repairs. Kill two birds with one stone."

"I find it hard to believe you."

Cal opened his mouth to reply, then closed it again. He paused, putting his hands back in his pockets. "I know," he said. "I don't blame you. Dora, I'm sorry I hurt you. Believe me now."

Dora looked long and hard at her husband. His face was drawn and pale. It struck her that Cal didn't look happy. She struggled to remember the last time she had seen him happy. She couldn't. She tried to recall when *she'd* last felt happy. The answer came quickly. It was at Sea Breeze on the dock with Nate, Mamaw, and her sisters. That crazy dolphin in the water making them all laugh. She still could see the breathtaking, ear-to-ear grin on Nate's face, his usually taciturn expression filled with joy.

"What about Nate? Your condo is small. Won't it be tight?"

Cal's face clouded and he rubbed his chin with consternation. "Right. Nate . . . That's a tough one."

She gave a tiny shiver at the obvious implication that, for Cal once again, Nate was an afterthought. Dora watched him walk to the window, look out a moment, then return to her side.

"You're right," he said in a normal voice. "It is small. There really isn't room. But here's the thing," he added quickly. "We aren't talking about a long time. Just long enough for you to recuperate. And in the meantime, we can look for a bigger place. Can't Nate stay at Sea Breeze?"

Dora felt outrage bubble in her chest; how could Cal be so willing to leave Nate behind at Sea Breeze?

"No!"

"It makes sense. You said he liked it there. He's settled. Comfortable. Moving him twice will be disruptive for him. You know he doesn't like change. And," he added with import, "it will give us time to talk. Just us. We need that."

"But . . ."

"Just for a little while."

"How long?"

He shrugged. "A few weeks. Maybe a month."

Her mind felt stunned by disbelief that he would think she'd be willing to leave Nate behind for even a few weeks, much less a month. Yet, his offer of reconciliation, so close on the heels of the lawyer's office debacle, muddled her thinking. Her mother's words came back to her: *If Cal is willing to reconsider, Dora should do whatever she can to save her marriage.*

"You're right, Cal. We don't want to just throw away our marriage. But I'm tired now. My head feels fuzzy and I need to sleep."

"Right. Of course. I'd better go."

Dora managed a meager smile.

"I'll be back in the morning."

"Will you go to see Nate tomorrow? I don't want him to worry."

His face was all remorse. "I wish I could. But I've got a full day of appointments. I'm sure he's in good hands at Sea Breeze."

Dora tugged the thin blanket higher around her neck as she felt a sudden chill. She looked at her nails. They were short and unpainted. She couldn't remember the last time she'd had a manicure. On her left finger she was still wearing the slim channel-set diamond wedding band. Cal had not once, in all his arguments, declared that he loved her. He'd not told her that he'd missed her, or missed their son.

Dora took a breath that exhaled all the angst, anger, and worry that she'd harbored in her chest for too long. A change of address was not going to change Cal. He didn't want her back because he loved her. That was what she *wanted* to hear. What Cal wanted was for her to monitor the house renovations. He wanted to soften her up to get the better deal with the divorce.

She deserved better. Nate deserved better. It was not enough.

"You don't have to come by the hospital, then, since you're such a busy man," Dora said flatly. "I'll be fine. Thank you for the offer that I move into your condo. But it's too soon. I need time alone to think—about our marriage, about me . . . about so many things before I'm ready to talk."

Cal cleared his throat to speak but she pushed on, not giving him the chance to interrupt.

"As soon as I'm released, I'm going back to Sullivan's Island. You're right. Nate is happy there. And you know what? I'm happy there, too. I think we all deserve some happiness. We can talk again in a few weeks. Maybe a month." She ventured a small smile on reiterating his words. "As for watching over the house improvements . . ." She shrugged. "Good luck with that."

Chapter Five

~~~~~

Mamaw loved holidays. Christmas was her favorite, of course. Then Valentine's Day, with its hearts and chocolate, and Easter, with the brightly colored eggs and pastel flowers. And now it was time to celebrate the Fourth of July. On the island, crowds of tourists thronged the flag-strewn streets.

She and Lucille were crawling through traffic to pick up Dora at the hospital and bring her home to Sea Breeze. Lucille drove her old Camry across the Ben Sawyer Bridge to Mt. Pleasant. It was a faithful car—ten years old with low mileage and nary a dent or scratch. Since Mamaw had given Carson her vintage Cadillac, she was without a car of her own. Just as well, she thought as she gazed out the window of the passenger seat. Her vision wasn't what it used to be, nor was her reaction time. She sighed. For that matter, neither was Lucille's.

Mamaw looked out the window as they rolled past the vast lowcountry wetlands. The tide was high, covering the oyster beds. Only the tips of the grasses were visible now, bright green from the recent heavy rain. This was the busiest week of the year on the island and even at midday the traffic was heavy and slow on the narrow road that crossed the marshes from island to mainland. Mamaw noticed, however, that there was a great deal of space between their car and the one in front.

"You drive as slow as a turtle," she said to Lucille.

"I'm not slow," Lucille replied with a scoff. "I'm careful."

Mamaw looked in the rearview mirror. A long line of cars trailed behind them. This was a no-passing zone on a two-lane stretch. She could imagine the drivers of the cars behind them cursing the two old women who were leisurely leading the pack. She chuckled. Every time she used to drive she'd get at least one honk. Likely from a tourist, she thought. No one from Charleston would be so rude as to honk at an old lady. Once they were on the mainland the road opened to four lanes and cars zoomed past them, some of the young ones scowling as they roared by.

"Let 'em go," Lucille muttered, her chin thrust forward and her hands tightly gripping the steering wheel. "I ain't rushing on their account. I never got a ticket and I'm not going to start now, not after all these years. Them folks keep driving like that, they won't reach my age. That's for true."

"The young are immortal, Lucille. Didn't you know that?"

"Humph," she said with a frown.

"Speaking of the young, I wonder what time Carson will arrive home today. I'm so proud that as soon as she heard about Dora's broken heart syndrome she headed right home."

"Told you she would."

"With Dora coming home, there are changes to be made at Sea Breeze. We must follow the doctor's orders to the letter."

"*More* changes, you mean," Lucille added. "I already never get to cook pork or grits no more."

"If I have to forgo my little rum drink at night . . ."

Lucille guffawed. "Not exactly every night, are you?"

Mamaw swung her head to stare at Lucille. So . . . she knew about the hidden flask!

"I can't see the harm of a small libation when I read my book at night. I'm alone in my room, after all."

"If I have to give up my chitlins for Dora, then you've got to give up the rum for Carson. And Harper . . ." Lucille made a face. "Not eatin' anything white. Who ever heard of such a thing? I'd of starved coming up!"

"It's a different world. We have to support them." She lowered her voice. "But that doesn't mean we can't cheat once in a while and have our little treats, does it?"

"No ma'am," Lucille agreed with gusto. "Maybe I'll start cookin' more in my cottage."

Mamaw's eyes gleamed. "Yes! I'll stop by there for our tête-à-tête. Often."

Lucille chuckled, eyes on the road. "Uh-huh."

"But back at the main house, we must remain vigilant," Mamaw said. "Heart-healthy diet only!"

"Doctor said it weren't no heart attack. What they call it?"

"Stress cardiomyopathy."

"Mm-mmm." Lucille ruefully shook her head. "Imagine that. Now them doctors have this fancy name for something we all knew happened all along. Broken heart syndrome," she said with a firm nod of her head. "That's the right name for it.

My grandparents were sweet on each other from the moment they met. Married more than sixty years when my grandmother Etta passed. My grandfather died only a few months after. No matter what the doctors said, we all knew Daddy Earl died of a broken heart."

"I had an aunt who had the same thing happen. She just up and died after her husband did." Mamaw sighed. "We should never underestimate how important our loved ones are to us. Or how powerful one's grief can be."

She turned to look at the woman beside her. Lucille's lips were a thin, clenched line of concentration; she was barely able to see over the wheel. Today she wore a plain, light blue cotton shirt-dress; this had been her favorite dress style for as long as she'd worked for the Muir family. Mamaw had seen the waistband expand over the past fifty years, same as hers. Now Lucille's hair was more salt than pepper and she wore wire-rim glasses when she drove. But her skin was still as smooth as a baby's butt. It irked Mamaw no end that Lucille steadfastly refused to give her the recipe of the face lotion she'd concocted. It was a long-standing feud between them.

"I don't know what I'd do without you in my life," Mamaw said suddenly, overcome with a wave of affection.

Lucille swung her head, surprised. "Oh, you're just being silly. You'd get along fine without me."

"Why, Lucille," Mamaw said, a bit hurt at having her sentiment brushed off. "You know how much you mean to me. You're my dearest friend. Of course I wouldn't be just fine if you left."

Lucille frowned but kept her gaze on the road ahead. "Yes'm, we are good friends, that's for true. But you wouldn't pine away if I should die, now, would you?"

"The things you say. No, I probably wouldn't. After all, I didn't pine away after my husband died. Though, I think I might depend on you more than I ever did Edward."

"That's just nonsense talking."

"It isn't. We're like salt and pepper, the two of us."

Lucille kept her eyes on the road.

"Do you realize this will be the last holiday we'll celebrate at Sea Breeze?" Mamaw said in a wistful tone, as they continued along Coleman Boulevard.

"I reckon that's true." Then she added with a grunt, "If the house sells."

"It'll sell," Mamaw said conclusively. "There's already a list of people who'd like to get their hands on my property." She sighed again. "I truly wish I could leave it to the girls, so that they could continue to come here in the summers, to see one another, their children. But, it just might not be meant to be."

"You might get more than you think for it," Lucille said.

"I hope I do, of course. But the house is so heavily mortgaged, and the cost of the retirement home so high, after they do all the subtractions, there'll be much less than you think left over. There hasn't been an income in this family for a very long time." She sighed. "I've been advised to prepare for ever-increasing medical costs, living expenses . . ."

Mamaw paused to glance at Lucille. "You know, of course, that you will be taken care of. Mr. Edward had the arrangements made before he passed. You'll have the money from the sale of the cottage, free and clear."

"Yes'm. I know."

Mamaw sighed. "I'm resigned to it. The house must be sold, and the sooner the better."

Lucille didn't respond, but a heavy pall slipped over them.

"Let's not be gloomy," Mamaw said in a cheerful tone. "Let's make this Fourth of July a real firecracker! The best party ever. All the girls will be at Sea Breeze again and we'll gather a few rosebuds while we may."

Lucille glanced quickly her way. "What's that about rosebuds?"

Mamaw laughed at her frivolity. "It's from an old poem I once memorized as a schoolgirl." She brought to mind the stanza she could recall. "'Gather ye rosebuds while ye may, / Old Time is still a-flying: / And this same flower that smiles to-day / To-morrow will be dying.' There's more, but I don't remember it. I'm pretty pleased I remembered that much."

"Don't seem too cheerful," Lucille said. "All that talk of dying."

"It's about enjoying the present. And that's exactly what I intend to do. We've had a few bumps in our summer plans, what with the Delphine debacle and Dora's health. But we still have the rest of the summer, right? Let's gather our sweet rosebuds—Dora, Harper, and Carson—at Sea Breeze and be happy. No more bad news!"

"No more bad news," Lucille agreed, and laughed under her breath. "Just rosebuds."

⌇⌇⌇

Later that afternoon, as she sat in the rear of Lucille's car on the drive home from the hospital, Dora thought Sullivan's Island had never looked more beautiful. American flags hung from every street lamp, houses—and even the golf carts—were festooned with red, white, and blue. Everywhere she looked people were on foot, most with a beach bag and folding chair underarm, heading to and from the beach.

She'd been so ready to leave the hospital. The two days felt like two years, what with nurses waking her up at all hours of the night to draw blood or conduct a test of some sort. And the food . . . Dora couldn't wait to bite into some of Lucille's home cooking. But these complaints were trivial compared to the constant barrage of cajoling and urging from both her mother and Cal to change her mind about returning to Sea Breeze. It was silly, really. Aside from the fact that Dora wanted to be at Sea Breeze with her sisters, Nate was the best he'd ever been after just a month on the island. Imagine how much he'd improve after an entire summer in the sunshine.

Dora was exhausted from her mother's not-so-subtle arguments for her to take Cal up on his offer to stay with him at the condo in Summerville. But she and Nate were a package deal and she'd made up her mind. At the end of her hospital stay she felt physically and emotionally drained, and her final good-byes with both of them had been cool.

The car turned off Middle Street onto the curved back island road and all went quiet. Lucille slowed as she guided the wheels off the pavement to bump along the dirt road. Large oaks and palms created a tunnel of shade and shadows, shielding the houses from view. Dora leaned forward, feeling excitement bubble as they approached the familiar tall green hedge. "Sea Breeze," Dora murmured.

She opened the car door and stepped out into the sultry air. The shade of the ancient oak was a welcome shield from the harsh midday sun. She'd half expected the front door to swing open at the sound of slamming car doors. But no one appeared.

"Let's get you inside," Lucille said, rounding the car. "I'll get Harper to collect your suitcase later. You shouldn't be lugging anything heavy up the stairs, leastwise not yet. Come on, Miss Dora," she said, nudging her forward.

Dora followed Mamaw's slow pace up the stairs. She felt tired but not ill. Under normal circumstances Dora would have hurried up the stairs without a second thought. But the attack had made her nervous about her heart, despite all the doctor's reassurances.

Inside the house, all was quiet.

Mamaw set her pocketbook on the front hall table and called out in a cheery voice, "Harper!"

There was no answer.

Dora immediately felt her heart quicken with worry. "Nate?" she called out, walking into the living room.

No answer.

Dora felt a surge of energy and rushed through the living room and down the hall of the west wing of the house. The door to the library, where Nate slept, was closed. Without knocking, Dora pushed open the door, eyes searching for him.

Harper and Nate were sitting side by side, cross-legged on the floor in front of the video game screen. Harper wasn't much bigger than the boy; she looked like a kid as they both leaned slightly forward, their gazes focused on the screen and fingers flying over the remotes. From time to time, one would grunt or the other would shout out "Oh, no!" It took a moment for Dora to digest that Harper was actually playing video games with Nate—and that she was having a good time.

Mamaw and Lucille had followed Dora and joined her at the library door. The noise they made alerted Harper and she swung her head around. On seeing Dora, her large blue eyes sparked to life and her face opened up in delighted surprise. She lowered the remote and exclaimed, "Dora, you're back!"

"Yes, just," Dora replied, still a little bewildered at the sight of the two of them playing games together.

"Look at you!" Harper said. "You don't look bad at all. And here I thought you'd be hobbling around like an old crone."

"No, I'm fine, really. More a scare than anything else." Dora's gaze sought out her son, desperate to lay eyes on him. Nate had not come to visit her in the hospital. She knew he didn't like hospitals, but she had missed him like crazy and was hoping he would give some signal that he was glad she had returned. But Nate's gaze remained resolutely on the screen.

Harper turned to Nate and said pointedly, "Nate, your mom's back!"

Nate continued to play his game.

"Hi, Nate," Dora said.

He looked briefly in Dora's general direction, then just as quickly returned to his video game and continued playing.

Harper frowned and leaned close to him. "Nate, go say hello to your mother. She's just come back from the hospital."

He ignored Harper's admonishment.

Dora could see that Harper was upset that Nate wouldn't leave his video games for his mom, but Dora was familiar with her son's ways. He often ignored people and didn't pick up on normal social cues, especially when he was engrossed in one of his games.

"He's not being rude," she told Harper. "I wish you wouldn't encourage him to play video games," she said tersely. "You know I'm trying to get him to ease up on them, to go outside.

Why would you do that?" Then, trying to modulate her voice, Dora looked again at Nate.

"But Nate, your *behavior* is rude. When your mother returns home from the hospital—or from anywhere—it's polite to stop what you're doing and greet her. So come now, and say hello to your mother."

Nate stopped playing the game and set his remote on the floor. Harper moved aside, allowing him to slowly rise and approach his mother. When he stood before her, Nate looked up and impassively studied her face.

"You look sick. Are you going to die?"

Dora could hear Mamaw suck in her breath behind her, but she smiled and replied, "I'm not sick, Nate, and I am not going to die. Not for a very long time, I hope. I'm just pale because I am tired. Did you think I was going to die?"

"Yes. You went to the hospital, like Delphine. And she might die."

Dora wanted to hold him tight to her breast, to comfort him and smother his cheeks with kisses, but she knew he would recoil; instead, she merely reached out to cup his face in her hands and smile into his eyes.

"I've missed you," she said, her heart pumping with love.

Nate didn't respond other than to pull his head back from her hands.

"Did you miss me?"

He nodded, looking at his hands.

Dora bent closer to his ear. "Were you worried?"

Nate nodded again.

Dora felt her heart bloom. "You don't have to worry anymore. I'm home."

"You are?" he asked, glancing up at her. "Is this our home now?" he asked, seemingly confused.

Mamaw, overhearing, said, "Of course it is, Nate! All summer."

Dora knew that Mamaw was trying to be loving, but Nate was taking her comment literally. Plus, his frown reminded Dora that he didn't like being the center of attention. It could be frustrating for him.

"Yes, it is our home," she answered straightforwardly. "For the summer. Like we talked about, remember? Is that okay with you?"

He looked away. "Can I go back to my game now?" he asked.

Dora didn't want him stuck playing games in the dark room with Harper any longer.

"I think we are done with the game for a while."

"Harper is winning and I don't want to lose." His voice was getting whiny.

"But I haven't seen you in days," she said. "Let's go outdoors. It's a beautiful day. I'll make you something to eat. Are you hungry?"

"I want to go back to my game."

"You've been playing for hours," Dora replied more firmly. "It's time to turn off the game."

His expression immediately turned mutinous and he began shaking his hands erratically high in the air. "No!" he shouted at the top of his lungs.

"That's enough," Dora said sharply.

Nate began jumping up and down on the balls of his feet. "I hate you!" he said over and over. Then in a rush of defiance he ran to grab his remote from the floor. "I won't turn it off."

Dora felt her anger zoom and stomped over to Nate's side to grab the remote from him. "It's time to turn off the game."

Despite his small size, his anger was quick and powerful. Nate's face colored and he balled his fist. In a flash he swung back and struck Dora, right over her heart. The punch packed a wallop, but more than cause pain, because it was her heart, because she was afraid, the hit shook her. Dora stumbled back, hand over her breast and sucking in her breath.

Nate threw himself onto the ground in a full-blown tantrum.

Dora watched him howling and kicking with a feeling of helplessness. She couldn't move, couldn't find the energy to go to him, to soothe him. She felt swallowed up by panic and despair.

"I can't do this anymore!" The cry ripped from her throat. She backed away from her son and covered her face in her hands. "I need help!"

In a breath, she felt Mamaw's arms around her, heard her voice at her ear. "We'll help you, Dora. You're not alone."

Chapter Six

~~~~~~~~

Days passed and Dora did not leave her bedroom. She couldn't muster the desire, much less the energy. She lay listlessly on the twin bed, wearing a thin white cotton nightgown, staring at the patterns of light playing on the ceiling. It was another in what seemed a steady stream of hot midsummer days. The air-conditioning hummed, but Mamaw never kept the temperature very cool. The ceiling fan did a good job stirring the air, though the blades were slightly off balance, shaking the fan and making monotonous clicking noises as it whirred.

Dora had shared this small bedroom with Harper since they'd arrived at Sea Breeze in May. When she'd returned from the hospital, however, she found Harper had temporarily moved into Carson's empty bedroom. Dora had expected Harper to move back in with her when Carson returned the night before, but she heard the two of them giggling and talking in the other room like little girls till the wee hours of the morning.

Dora hadn't minded sharing a room with Harper. She couldn't have wished for a better roommate. She was tidy, excessively so. Her younger sister lived like a nun, albeit a well-dressed one. All her clothing, shoes, and jewelry were stored in attractive storage boxes or velvet bags. Her laptop and books were stacked in orderly fashion on the small table in the corner. Her bed was made every morning, complete with crisp hospital corners. Even in the bathroom, not only did she clean up after herself but she compulsively cleaned up after Dora, as well, picking up towels from the floor, wiping the sink and tub, putting away toiletries into the baskets she'd purchased.

Still, sleeping in the same room, in twin beds no less, was a bit more togetherness than either of them wanted. Harper was on her computer or reading a book until late at night. Dora usually could fall asleep, but on nights she couldn't she pretended to be asleep while the clickety-clack of the computer keys occasionally set her teeth on edge.

Everyone was gathered out on the porch. Dora could hear the chatter and the clink of dishes from her room. She strained to listen but couldn't make out the words, only the soft murmur of conversation punctuated by the occasional laugh. She could get out of bed, of course, but no one had thought to come check on her, or invite her to join them.

She turned on her side, feeling a tidal wave of sadness as cold and blue as the deep Atlantic Ocean. Why would they ask her to join them? she thought morosely. Why would anyone? Cal had told her she could be boring, and she believed it was true. People didn't warm to her like they did to Carson, who never met a stranger she couldn't charm and make feel like family. Carson was like Mamaw, spontaneous, fun to be around. People flocked to her side. Harper, too, despite her seeming reserve, seemed to have a million friends. Someone was always texting her, or e-mailing her. Her phone was always making noises.

Dora had no friends, no lovers, no life. Even her son didn't want to be with her. What was wrong with her? She clenched the pillow tight with her fists, remembering her breakdown.

"Lord help me, I'm so ashamed."

Her own meltdown had rivaled Nate's. Only now, with hindsight, could she see how she'd missed all the signs. It was easy to see now that Nate was not merely annoyed at being told to turn off the game. A meltdown was never just about rage. While she was at the hospital he'd been worried, frightened, lonely, frustrated, and perhaps even sad. Dora's ultimatum had just delivered the last straw. If she was honest with herself, she didn't recognize them because all she could see was that Harper had found a way to play with Nate, just as Carson had before her.

Dora knew her sisters were only trying to help. To get to know their nephew better. Part of her was thrilled that they were making the effort. Grateful. Yet, another part of her was jealous to see them playing together. *Why didn't her son want to play with her?*

She knew that answer. She was the enforcer in her son's eyes. The rule maker. In contrast, her aunts were fun. Carson swam with dolphins. Harper knew the good games. Her breath hitched in her throat as the truth became obvious. *I don't know how to play with him.*

She heard a faint footfall in the hall and she turned her head toward the door, on the alert. *Go away, go away,* she thought, clenching her eyes tight and holding her body still. She just wanted to be left alone in her misery. A moment later, she heard a faint knock on the door. Her first thought was not to answer; to pretend she was asleep. Then she heard Mamaw's voice.

"Dora? Dora, dear, are you awake?"

Before Dora could decide what to do, the door opened and Mamaw's silvery head peeked through.

"Am I waking you up?"

"No," she said begrudgingly.

"Good," Mamaw said, and walked in. She went directly to the bed.

Dora expected her to rest her hand on her shoulder, offer a gentle pat of encouragement. Instead she took hold of the sheet and whipped it off her body.

Dora swung around and stared at her agog.

"Dora, it's high time you stopped this pity party and got out of bed!"

"I don't want to." Dora grabbed for the sheet and pulled it back over her shoulders.

"I don't care. I'm telling you I want you up and out of this bed this instant. Do you hear me?"

Dora hadn't been spoken to like that since she'd been a little girl. She was too stunned to speak. Instead, she turned her back to Mamaw and curled up in a ball and began to cry.

"Oh, Dora," Mamaw said with exasperation, sitting on the bed beside her.

"I'm so unhappy," Dora wailed.

"Darling, you passed unhappy miles ago. You're right at the corner of depressed and downright miserable."

"I know," Dora sobbed. "I hate my life, I hate myself. I hate everything."

Mamaw, unforgivably, laughed.

"It's not funny," Dora ground out.

"No, it's not. But you're having what my mother would call 'a case of the vapors.' Lying in this bed wallowing isn't helping."

"I like it here."

Mamaw stood up and put her hands on her hips. "Dear girl, when I invited you to return to Sea Breeze from the hospital, I intended for you to begin your healing here. If you wanted to stay in bed and wallow, you should have gone home with your mother."

Dora grunted and curled her legs tighter against her chest.

Mamaw went to the windows and opened the curtains wide, flooding the room with sunshine.

"Look outside, child! There's the ocean, the beach, the sunlight, the sweet-smelling air—and it's all just waiting for you. You mustn't turn your back on it any longer." She tapped Dora's shoulder. "Or on me, for that matter. You're acting like a spoiled child and I won't have it."

This was classic Mamaw, coming to the point, not the least afraid of speaking her mind. Honesty was always easier to deal with, and suddenly Dora felt glad Mamaw had come into her room like a ray of sunshine. A bit ashamed of her behavior, Dora rolled over to face Mamaw.

"I feel like such a fool," she said. "I've failed as a wife. As a mother."

"Of course you haven't."

"Haven't I? My mother certainly thinks I have. I feel like I've broken some rule of womanhood. I've fallen down and just can't get myself up. Every time I try, I just fall back again."

Mamaw's face softened. "Let me help you."

Mamaw took Dora's arm and gently tugged her into a sitting position.

"There. That's better." Mamaw stood back and surveyed Dora, her eyes narrowed in scrutiny. "Child, you are one hot mess. When was the last time you washed your hair? And you look so pale. Fair skinned and pale are not the same thing. I know just what you need. Stand up, girl. You heard me. Stand up!"

Dora obliged. She wasn't one to ignore Mamaw's order. She slowly stood, a bit off balance from all the time spent lying horizontally, sighing dramatically in a small show of rebellion.

"Good. Now, look at me, Dora."

Dora slowly, hesitatingly, raised her gaze to meet Mamaw's. She met Mamaw's eyes and felt the timeless connection of her grandmother's gaze.

"Come with me, child."

Dora didn't speak but offered her hand to Mamaw while her heart whispered, *Yes!*

Mamaw took hold of Dora's hand and led her down the hall to her bedroom. Dora felt like a child, her gaze darting from left to right, not wanting her sisters to see her in this state, as she allowed herself to be herded along. She was aware of Mamaw's hand in hers, dragging her from the abyss. She didn't want to let go.

Once in Mamaw's suite, with the door firmly shut, Dora felt safe. This was Mamaw's feminine sanctuary—plump chintz chairs, lots of pretty pillows, paintings of the ocean and wetlands, fringe on the curtains.

Mamaw released a slow smile. "There, that's better. Whenever I feel chewed up and spit out, I take a nice, hot, perfumed bath. It does wonders for my spirit. How does that sound?"

Dora's face perked up a bit at the suggestion.

"Wonderful."

"You sit here, dear, while I fill your tub," Mamaw instructed. "No, no, don't do a thing, just relax!" she added cheerily, brushing away Dora's halfhearted effort to help.

Dora sat on the big queen bed, feeling very much a child again as Mamaw disappeared into her bathroom. Dora heard the thunk of the pipes and the gush of water. Shortly after, a sweet scent wafted into the room. She closed her eyes and breathed deep. Roses . . . it was intoxicating. Mamaw came back into the room with a big aqua-colored towel and handed it to Dora.

"Undress," she ordered. "The bath will take a few minutes to fill. While you wait, drink this." She handed her a small glass of amber liquid.

"What is it?"

"Rum. Neat. It's aged and as smooth as a baby's butt, so enjoy it. But don't whisper a word of this to Lucille. She'll have *my* butt if she finds out I've still got a bottle hidden." She giggled and her eyes shone with triumph. "Behind the toiletries. The small bottle blends right in!"

"But Mamaw, I shouldn't drink this." She moved to hand the glass back. "We all agreed. No alcohol."

Mamaw gently pushed Dora's hand back. "Precious, this is one thing I'm *not* worried about with you. None of us are perfect. We don't need perfection. Balance will do."

Dora sipped from the glass. The rum was smooth and burned only slightly on the way down, warming her chest. It felt utterly lovely, and, this early in the day, decadent.

She removed the nightgown with lace trim that always made her feel like an old lady. Kicking it across the room, she swore she'd never wear it again. She slipped into Mamaw's thick terry robe.

Mamaw stepped from the bathroom and called her name. "Dora! Come, child."

Dora stepped into a room filled with steam and scent. Mamaw helped remove Dora's robe and guided her into the steaming tub. It was so hot Dora lowered herself into the water by fractions of an inch, giving her body time to acclimate. Gradually she stretched out and let her body ease fully into the perfumed, bubbly water. She leaned back and let her head rest against a pillow at the edge of the tub. Closing her eyes, she inhaled the steam and felt the tension flow from her body to vanish into the water. She sighed, feeling as though somehow she'd been rescued. The drops on her face were not tears but perspiration.

Mamaw served sweet tea on the back porch while Lucille passed blueberry scones from the Village Bakery. She'd called together this impromptu family meeting while Dora was soaking in the tub. It was a lovely afternoon in the shade of the black-and-white-striped awning. Large, white cumulus clouds drifted over the sweeping view of the Cove. Pots of colorful flowers set about the porch added punches of color and the air was heady with their scent.

Mamaw tapped her spoon against her glass to silence the chatter. Carson and Harper stopped talking and Harper closed the lid on her laptop.

"Where's Dora?" asked Carson.

"Still sleeping in her room?" asked Harper.

"No," Mamaw said with a reprimanding glance at Harper's thinly veiled criticism. "But that's precisely the reason I called us together. Dora is not herself."

"I'll say," Carson said. "I've never seen her so low."

"The way she flew off the handle . . ." Harper added with a shake of her head.

Mamaw corrected Harper. "She wasn't upset as much as she had a breakdown. There's a difference. The important point is that Dora asked for help."

"I can't ever recall her asking for help before," Lucille mused.

"Exactly. We need to put our heads together and come up with ways that we can help Dora through this difficult time. Thank the Lord, she did not have a heart attack. But this definitely was a warning. A shot over the bow. The doctor was clear that Dora must make serious changes in her eating habits, exercise patterns . . ." She sighed. "Or lack thereof." She paused to glance toward the porch door to make certain it was closed. She didn't want Dora to overhear and have her feelings be hurt.

"Unfortunately, instead of trying to make changes, she's holing up in her room. She says she's still too tired, but . . ."

Mamaw sighed dramatically to indicate there was much more involved than fatigue. "I thought we might find ways to be her cheerleaders. Rally around her. Show we care."

"Get her out of bed," Lucille added drily.

The sisters were silent for a moment. Then Harper spoke up. "That's all good . . ." she began, her tone hesitant.

Mamaw tilted her head, waiting. Harper, for all that she didn't gab much, was a deep, careful thinker. When she offered an opinion, it was her own and reflected an intellect mature beyond her years.

" . . . but the will to change has to come from her. She's not a little girl. We can't *make* her do anything."

"True, but we can encourage her," Carson said. "I was grateful when y'all stood by me when I wanted to stop drinking. You took every bottle out of the house. I know because I looked for them," she added in a lightly self-deprecating manner. She joined in the laughter, then continued in a more serious tone. "If there had been wine in the fridge at night, I could not have resisted."

"And there's still none in there, in case you go looking," Lucille told her pointedly.

Carson made a face while the others chuckled.

Harper leaned toward Carson. "How are you holding up on that front?"

Carson swirled her iced tea a moment. "I had a lot of time to think while driving to and from Florida. I don't want to think I'm an alcoholic, but with both my parents being alcoholics, and with my track record . . ." She shrugged. "There's definitely a problem. Truth is, the craving for a drink just won't let go. I used to think that I just drank socially. Most single girls our age go to bars or restaurants and just hang out. But it always involves alcohol. Right?" she asked Harper.

Harper nodded. "And the hope to meet some guys."

"When I totaled it up, I figured I used to drink at least five drinks in one night."

"But those five drinks would be consumed from, say, eight p.m. until one a.m.," Harper said. "That's about one drink an hour. In that context, it hardly seems excessive."

"And yet, I went out drinking with friends several times a week. Plus had a glass or two at home." Carson frowned. "Any way you do the math, that's a lot of drinking." She took a breath. "I'm thinking of joining AA, just as a precaution. It might help to hear other people's stories and get a sense of where I stand with this whole thing."

Mamaw's brows rose. "Do you think that's necessary?"

"It is if she thinks it is," Lucille rejoined emphatically.

"I haven't decided yet," Carson hedged. "Still just thinking about it."

"You go on thinking," Lucille said. "Don't you be lazy and let it slide."

Mamaw leaned forward to pat Carson's hand. "That's a brave decision. One your father should have made. I regret I didn't encourage him to do the same. If you suspect you need AA, then go. I'm proud of you."

Mamaw shared a gaze with Carson that pulsed with affection.

"See, that's my point," Harper said, returning to Mamaw. "Carson's decision to do something about her drinking came from *her*. She'll succeed because she wants to. If Dora is going to succeed in changing her diet and her lifestyle, the desire has to come from her. Without that, all the cheerleading and good suggestions in the world won't make a difference."

"I agree the decision has to come from her," Mamaw said. "But we can help her reach that point. And encourage her, to ensure her success. Girls, our Dora's been through the wringer at the hospital, and I'm not just talking about her medical problems."

"What happened?" asked Carson.

"She was bullied, plain and simple. Her mother"—Mamaw rolled her eyes—"horrible woman, pressured Dora to come back with her to Charlotte, delivered with that tone of disapproval Dora usually caves under. And Cal . . ." She made no attempt to keep the scorn from her voice. "He suddenly *suggested* that they rethink the divorce. He asked her to move to his condo in Summerville."

"Really?" Harper said, surprised. "Isn't that a good thing?"

"It is not," Mamaw answered emphatically. "He is being shamelessly selfish. It was all I could do not to put him in his place. Winnie, of course, was all agog with the possibility of a reconciliation. No divorce—no scandal. She didn't give a thought to what was best for Dora."

"Mamaw," Carson said cautiously, "I'm sure she does care about Dora. She's her mother, after all, and entitled to her opinion."

"I agree with Carson. How can saving their marriage be wrong?" Harper asked, still not convinced.

"But of course it's not wrong, if the reasons are sincere," Mamaw replied. "Cal Tupper doesn't give a hoot about Dora. Or his son." She straightened in her chair. "He might fool Winnie but he can't fool me. She really knows nothing about the man. He wants to keep Dora in Summerville, close to that behemoth of a house, so she can supervise the repairs. Chop-chop. That was his motive."

"Excuse me, but again, what's wrong with that?" asked Harper. "It's what she'd be doing if they weren't having problems in their marriage, isn't it? She is his wife, after all. And being a homemaker is her job."

"That's not the point."

"What is the point?" Harper asked.

Carson narrowed her eyes and wagged her finger. "What aren't you telling us?"

Mamaw glanced toward the door and lowered her voice. "The point is Nate."

"What about Nate?" Harper asked.

"He's not included in the invitation to live at the condo."

Carson was incensed. "Not included? But he's their son!"

"*That's* the point," Mamaw said, nodding with satisfaction that her side had been vindicated.

"You mean, he wants *us* to take Nate off his hands?" Carson asked, incredulous.

"Exactly."

Carson leaned back in her chair. "You're right. He is a shit. Poor Nate. Poor Dora."

"I don't know him from Adam so I'm not defending him," Harper said. "But do we know both sides of the story?"

"How can you say that?" Carson blustered, turning to face Harper. "He's a jerk. We all knew that before the divorce."

"But he's Dora's jerk!" Harper argued back heatedly.

She paused, hearing her words, and they all burst out laughing.

Mamaw brought the conversation back on track. "Dora's made her decision to return here with us, so let's not waste our time debating the merits and flaws of Calhoun Tupper." Her tone of voice made it perfectly clear that she'd already wasted enough breath on the man.

"Dora has spent most of her life doing what she was told. And putting others in front of herself—especially Nate. This is the first time she spoke up for herself about what she wanted, by insisting she and Nate would be best off at Sea Breeze. It's a good start," she added.

Looking at Harper, Mamaw continued, "You're quite right that Dora has to make this decision on her own. But we can guide her toward new habits that help her feel good about herself. Inside and out. Little things that you two take for granted—getting manicures and pedicures, taking time to exercise, going out with the girls—these are all foreign to her. She dotes on Nate and his needs, and then Cal's, and then the house. She puts herself last, over and over. It's no wonder she let her figure go. She just gave up. Plus, I doubt there's been much money for such extras."

"Mamaw," Carson said, leaning back in the wide chair and tucking her arms around her legs, "Dora wasn't like that as a girl. During our summers, she made sure she had things her own way. I never thought of Dora as shy and retiring. In fact, she still isn't. She's downright bossy."

"Yes, she is," Mamaw agreed. "Now think about it for a moment. Dora is a stickler for *what?*"

"Nate's schedule," answered Carson promptly. "Nate's food, Nate's clothing . . ."

"Following the rules," Harper said quickly. "The Southern belle rules, I mean. Like not showing too much bosom or wearing skirts too short."

"Never wearing white before Easter or after Labor Day," added Carson.

"Manners, swearing, yelling, churchgoing," continued Harper.

Carson smirked. "Being a lady."

In a flash, the girls swung their heads around, pointed at each other, and blurted out, "Death to the ladies!"

Mamaw had to laugh. When Carson and Harper were little girls, they prowled the island pretending they were pirates searching for buried treasure. Mamaw knew full well the two tomboys chafed under her rules and squirmed when she told them to take their sandy feet off the beds and elbows off the table, to spit out the chewing gum and use tissues rather than shirtsleeves for wiping noses. She'd made them clean up for dinner, brush their hair, lower their voices, and always told them to "act like a lady." So the girls had created a secret mantra that they'd shout as they escaped out the door—*Death to the ladies!*

"Exactly," Mamaw replied. "Dora is like some herd dog who barks and nips to keep the sheep in line. She takes pains to follow the rules. To be the good, well-brought-up girl." She offered a sly grin. "I say she needs to channel a bit more of the pirate in her blood, don't you?"

Carson and Harper both responded with grins.

"Death to the lady—of course!" Carson exclaimed, catching on.

"Dora needs to break a few rules," Harper said, obviously enjoying where this was heading. She leaned forward. "What can we do to help?"

Dora didn't have any idea how long she'd been lying there, immersed and fully relaxed, but the water was cool when Mamaw returned. She held out the thirsty terry-cloth robe like a lady's maid for Dora to step into, then escorted her into the bedroom.

Mamaw's vanity was a piece of art. It was a French antique, triple mirrored with a glorious slab of white marble in the brass frame.

Dora remembered when she was a young girl watching Mamaw dress for one of her nights out with Granddaddy Edward.

Dora sat cross-legged on Mamaw's big bed, transfixed at the sight of her beautiful grandmother sitting at her shiny mirrored vanity. She thought her grandmother looked like a queen in her ruby-colored robe. The silk fell glamorously from her slender shoulders to puddle on the floor. Dora looked at her My Little Kitty pajamas and wished she could be as beautiful as her grandmother, with her long golden hair gathered on her head by jeweled pins. Mamaw lifted a brush and delicately dipped it into one of her pots of color. She leaned closer to the mirror and applied the makeup with deft strokes. Dora sighed when Mamaw brought various pairs of earrings to her ears, turning her head from left to right as she caught a glimpse of her reflection in the three mirrors to better decide which to wear. For the coup de grâce, when she carefully applied the ruby red to her lips, Dora almost swooned.

Mamaw turned on her bench and smiled at her. "Would you like to try a little?"

"Who? Me?" Dora asked, sitting bolt upright. Her mother had never offered to put makeup on her face. The one time she'd asked to try her lipstick, Winnie's eyes widened with shock and she exclaimed, "You're much too young for makeup!"

"Yes, of course you," Mamaw replied, rising from the bench. She reached out to take Dora's hand and led her to the bench. Dora stared in awe at her reflection in the magnificent three mirrors.

Mamaw picked up a boar bristle brush and began brushing Dora's hair in long, smooth strokes. It felt dreamy.

"Your hair is the same color as mine," Mamaw said in a tone that indicated she was pleased with that fact. "You must brush it one hundred times each evening so it will shine."

Mamaw set the hairbrush on the vanity and reached for her makeup brush. She dabbed it in some pink powder, then gently applied a few strokes to Dora's cheeks. Dora held her breath when Mamaw applied a hint of blue to her eyelids.

"Just a light touch when you apply makeup," Mamaw instructed. "You want to enhance your beauty, tastefully. Too much, and you look like a common floozy."

Dora wasn't sure what a floozy was, but she caught the gist of Mamaw's meaning. When she saw her reflection in the mirror, Dora had felt so grown-up—even beautiful! In that moment, Dora loved no one in the world more than her grandmother.

Now, all these years later, Mamaw was once again setting her in front of these same triple mirrors. Dora slumped her shoulders and averted her gaze, still feeling like the gawky girl. Without looking at her reflection, Dora felt more the jester than the queen.

"Now, dear girl, drink this," Mamaw told her, handing her a glass.

Dora looked at it with suspicion.

"It's only water," Mamaw said with a light laugh. "After a hot bath you must replenish your moisture. Your skin must never be dehydrated."

Dora obediently took the glass and sipped.

Mamaw pulled open a mirrored drawer and took out a jar of cream. Dipping in, she applied moisturizer to Dora's skin with gentle strokes, taking time to make small circles at her temples. Dora kept her eyes closed as once again Mamaw brushed her hair, one smooth stroke after another.

"You are a beautiful woman," Mamaw told Dora when she had finished. "Open your eyes and see how your skin glows!"

Reluctantly, Dora opened her eyes. In the reflection she saw a pair of luminous blue eyes staring back at her. Around them, her skin was pink from the steam bath. She stared back at her reflection, surprised that the woman there was actually rather pretty.

"You've always had the best complexion," Mamaw went on speaking as she brushed. "So soft. Look, not a wrinkle. You get that from me, of course. When you take your walks, be sure to wear sunscreen and a hat. The sun is not your friend."

"My walks?" Dora asked.

"Of course. You must take long walks every day, like the doctor said. Early in the morning or late afternoon, when the sun isn't too harsh. It's the best exercise for your heart—and your figure will thank you, too," she added. "You can begin this afternoon."

"I don't know . . ."

"Of course you do. We've already been through this at the hospital, dear. You know full well it's time to begin anew."

"I don't know if I can. I want to hide. I feel so hurt. So disappointed—in life, in Cal. In people."

Mamaw stopped brushing and met Dora's gaze in the mirror. "'People give pain, are callous and insensitive, empty and cruel . . . but *place* heals the hurt, soothes the outrage, fills the terrible vacuum that these human beings make.'" She put her hands on Dora's shoulders. "Do you know who said that?"

"No."

"Your namesake. Eudora Welty."

"Her," Dora said with a frown. "Not very lucky in love either, was she?"

"How do we really know? Besides, whether or not she was married or lucky in love is immaterial. She *knew* herself and lived her life fully."

"She spent her whole life alone, in the small town she was born in," Dora argued.

"You keep missing the point," Mamaw said, tapping Dora's shoulder. "The life Eudora created for herself was of her own making. No matter where she may have spent her life, she was at home within herself. Yes, she spent most of her life in a small town in Mississippi, but what Eudora understood, and wrote about so beautifully, was how love of place can fill the soul.

"I sympathize with that sentiment. I take that to mean a deep-rooted attachment to the place where we find ourselves at peace. Content. Where we have roots."

Mamaw shook the brush for emphasis. "Dora, I've seen many sunsets all over the world, but to me, nothing matches a lowcountry sunset when the entire sky is alive with hues of sienna, purple, and gold. Or the thousand and one different ways one stretch of beach can appear on any given day. I resonate to *this* place because this is my *home*. This is where I'm *from*. It's where I can be *me*."

Dora's eyes moistened, making the blue shine like a torch. "I don't know where my home is anymore."

Mamaw lowered to slip her arms around Dora and place a kiss on her head, moist and sweet-smelling from the bath.

"Feel our love around you. We are holding you up. You're safe. So go out, Dora. Walk the beach. Feel the sand in your toes. Prowl the streets, haunt the vistas. Walk, walk, walk. And I believe, in all your wandering, you will discover a place of stillness and peace. Find yourself, and you will find your way home."

Chapter Seven

*I*mmediately after the family meeting, Carson hopped into the golf cart and made a beeline to Blake's apartment. It had been less than a week since she'd seen him, and she was surprised how much she missed him. She had the pedal to the metal, but the cart couldn't go beyond fifteen miles per hour.

"Come on, come on," she murmured, leaning forward with a sense of urgency.

At last she arrived at the long stretch of white wood apartments that once had been quarters for the military when they had a presence on Sullivan's Island. She parked the cart and hurried up the stairs to knock sharply on the door. She heard a warning bark—Hobbs—then a moment later the door swung open and Blake was standing there in tan shorts, a brown T-shirt, sandals, and an expression of delight on his attractive features.

"At last!" he exclaimed, and reached out to grab her around

her waist and hoist her against his chest before he planted a solid, impatient kiss on her mouth.

As usual, the natural spark between them exploded. Carson wrapped her arms around him, starved for his kisses. She hung on, still kissing, as Blake walked her into the room, tottering as he reached out to close the front door. Hobbs barked excitedly beside them, pawing to get their attention.

Blake tore his mouth away to growl at his dog, "Hobbs, get down!"

Hobbs grunted and went to his bed and settled with a disappointed thump.

"This one's all mine," Blake said against her lips, his eyes gleaming, and claimed her mouth again.

Giddy, laughing, kissing, they stumbled into Blake's bedroom, kicking off shoes en route to the bed.

Later, lying naked in Blake's arms, Carson wondered at the red-hot quality of their passion. Undressing and getting into the bed was a blur, all part of one seamless, hungry, relentless kiss that demanded more. It was often like this with him, she thought as she let her finger slide lazily up and down his arm.

She played with the soft, dark hair of his chest, thinking how she'd driven twelve hours home from Florida, slept in her own bed, reconnected with Mamaw and her sisters. Yet only now, in Blake's arms, did she feel truly home again. It was a new sensation for her, as confusing as it was pleasant.

She leaned back to look into his face. "I missed you."

He laughed in that satisfied, ego-laden manner men sometimes did. "I could tell."

She smirked and gently, teasingly tugged at his hair.

"You done good with Delphine," he told her.

She smiled against his chest. The subject of Delphine's accident was still a tender subject between them. She knew, despite his spoken forgiveness, some part of him was still angry at her for drawing a wild dolphin to the dock with food and attention, so this praise fell sweet on her ears.

"Lynne told you?"

"She called after you left. Actually, it was kind of a thank-you call. She told me how Delphine turned the corner after you visited. She was very pleased. And impressed."

Carson felt warmth bloom in her chest. "I felt badly leaving so quickly and on such short notice."

"She understood. It was a family emergency. Besides, she thought it might've been for the best."

"Really? Why?"

"Your bond with Delphine is so strong. If she's got any hope to be released to the wild, she can't continue to seek out humans. Especially not you."

Carson turned on her back and looked at the ceiling. The fan's blades slowly stirred the air above them. She still couldn't imagine a world without Delphine in it. A small pang of sadness pierced her insides whenever she thought about it. Yet she knew if she truly loved the dolphin, she had to let her go.

"I want that, too." She moved to sit up on the bed, comfortable with her nakedness. "I need your advice on something," she began.

Blake moved to put his hands under his head. His dark eyes gazed at her with full attention.

"It's about Nate. We're worried about him. He's having a hard time getting past Delphine's accident. Harper did research about dolphin programs for children with special needs and wondered if a program like that wouldn't help Nate get past his guilt over what happened with Delphine."

"Could be." Blake's brows gathered, a signal she recognized that he was considering the question. "I don't know anything about the benefits of dolphin programs with special-needs kids. It's not my area."

"But you know the Dolphin Research Center."

He raised his brows.

"That's the program we're interested in," she explained.

"And it's no coincidence that the DRC is also the place they're thinking of moving Delphine."

Carson smiled conspiratorially. "I figured, why not check out the facility while I help Nate out."

He raised himself on one elbow. "*You're* going to take Nate to the DRC?"

She shrugged. "Me or Harper, or both of us. It's still up in the air."

He gave a little groan. "I can't see Dora letting you or Harper take Nate."

"It's complicated."

"I think I can follow."

Carson reflected on the long family meeting earlier that day. They still hadn't presented the idea to Dora. That would come next.

"In a nutshell, Dora's pretty fragile right now. She had, well, kind of a meltdown the other day. With that on top of her health, Mamaw wants Dora to take some time to heal without worries or responsibility. So Harper and I thought if we took Nate to this program, it would provide both Dora and Nate time to heal. I think it's a win-win deal. So I'm asking if you can help me make arrangements for Nate at the Dolphin Research Center?"

"You're asking me to help you to leave again."

She licked her lips, knowing it was a tender point. "Yes, I suppose I am. But not for long."

"That's what you said last time."

"And I was gone less than a week."

"And now you want to leave again."

"It's not about leaving," Carson said with a hint of frustration. "I'm taking Nate to Florida for a weeklong program. Hey," she said brightly as a new idea emerged, "why don't you come with us?"

"I can't. I took time off to go to Florida the last time. With Delphine. Plus I'll be out in the field for a week gathering samples. I have to be here for that."

She looked up at the ceiling again.

Blake said quietly, "Like I said, I don't know much about the special-needs program but I've met Joan, the woman who heads it up. I like her and I hear she's a great therapist. She tailors the program to meet the students' needs."

Carson felt a glimmer of hope. "So, you think it's a good idea?"

"It can't hurt." He begrudgingly smiled. "Yeah, I think Nate will do well there."

"You'll help us get an appointment?"

"I'll give Joan a call and explain the situation. That's all I can do."

Carson leaned over to kiss him, filled with gratitude. "Thank you, Blake."

He returned the grin of a man who'd just been played. "Come here," he said, holding out his arms.

Carson sighed and climbed into his arms.

Blake lowered his lips to her head and slid his arms around her and held her, his cheek resting on her head.

She closed her eyes and nestled against Blake's chest. Listening to the strong and steady beat of his heart, she felt safe and secure. She didn't want to go anywhere. She thought, *I could love this man.*

Lucille returned from her appointment and joined Mamaw on the porch. She brandished a deck of cards.

"At last," Mamaw exclaimed, eager for a hand of gin rummy.

Mamaw cut the deck and Lucille dealt the cards and turned over the discard. Mamaw wasn't happy with her hand but refrained from making a face. She knew Lucille would be watching for any clues. She rejected the discard and picked up the jack of clubs, then, frowning, immediately discarded it.

"I was thinking . . ."

"Oh Lord, here comes trouble." Lucille drew a card, kept it, then discarded a queen of hearts.

Mamaw drew a card. "The tension between Harper and Dora is so thick at times I could cut it with a knife. I thought if they had something they could do together, something that would bear fruit, it might bring them closer." She discarded.

Lucille picked up her discard and placed it in her hand. "I thought them two were a mite too close together already." She discarded.

Mamaw looked up from her cards. "What do you mean?"

Lucille looked at Mamaw as if she'd lost her marbles. "I mean, them two are sharing a room! They sleep in twin beds! That's a lot of togetherness for two young girls, but for two grown women? It's no wonder them two are testy with each other. Your turn."

Mamaw was stunned by this observation. Of course Lucille was right. She usually was. Why hadn't Mamaw seen this for herself? She'd blithely assumed the tension between them was merely the difference in their ages or their backgrounds. Leave it to Lucille to figure out something as basic as proximity.

Mamaw picked up a card and was delighted it was the card she was hoping for. "You are absolutely right," she said. "It's as plain as the nose on my face. But how? I'm plumb out of rooms and I certainly can't afford to add on to the house again."

"Don't need to. Discard."

Mamaw looked at her hand and quickly discarded. "Dora doesn't want to sleep in the library with Nate and we learned we can't move him. Where do you suggest we put another room?"

Lucille considered Mamaw's discard, then drew from the pile instead. She made a face and discarded. "You came up with the idea yourself a while ago."

Mamaw leaned back in her chair and racked her memory banks. Then her face lit up like a morning's dawn. "My sitting room!"

"It's low-hanging fruit." Lucille picked up the card.

"Right. It wouldn't be much to do and the cost would be

reasonable." She sat straighter, excited at the prospect. "Each girl would have her own room." Mamaw was beaming as she studied her cards. "We settled the problem of rooms, but we haven't come up with an idea to get Harper and Dora to do something together."

"Well, what do they have in common?" asked Lucille.

"Not much, as far as I can tell. Dora's kind of a Southern snob about Northerners, and I fear it's reciprocated in Harper. Harper likes to run, and Dora is starting her walking program. There's a start."

"But not something they do together."

"True. Cooking, maybe?"

"Dora's on a diet and Harper don't eat nothing but rabbit food."

Mamaw knew Lucille could never accept Harper's vegetarian diet. "The only other thing I see Harper do is be on that computer. She's always typing . . ."

Lucille set her cards on the table. "What's she writing? That's what I want to know. Her fingers are flying."

Mamaw nodded, and she lowered her voice. "Carson says she's not just surfing the net. She's writing something."

"Surf the net? What's that mean?"

Mamaw made a face. "I had to ask, too. It means she's not searching around, or watching videos. Harper is actually writing something, like a diary or journal. Or maybe some travel article on the islands."

"What's so secret about that?" Lucille wanted to know.

Mamaw nodded in agreement. "Exactly."

"Well," Lucille said, picking up her cards. "I 'spect she'll tell us when she's ready."

Mamaw raised her hand, picked up a card, looked at it, then immediately discarded it.

"None of that aids and abets our cause. Maybe if we think of things Dora likes to do."

There was a silence as both women stared at their cards. Truth was, Mamaw was hard put to think of anything that Dora loved to do.

Lucille picked up a card, then quickly discarded it. "I know!"

Mamaw's attention was piqued as she picked up a card.

"Dora likes to garden. She used to have that big garden in Summerville."

"But do you think Harper likes to garden?"

"Don't know," Lucille replied. "You asked me what Dora likes to do."

Mamaw laughed and moved a few cards in her hand. "We'll have to keep thinking on it. The way I see it, it's a two-pronged plan to bring Harper and Dora closer together. First we get them separated by giving each girl a room of her own. Then we bring them together by finding a project they can work on. It will come to me," she said, drawing out a card and brandishing it in the air. "And when it does, I'll pounce." She set the card on the table and sang out, "Gin!"

⁓⁓⁓

Dora couldn't procrastinate any longer. Wearing old gym shorts and one of Cal's old Gamecock T-shirts, Dora laced up her old tennis shoes and headed out for a walk. Mamaw and Lucille were out on the porch, and not wanting to draw their attention, she hurried out the front door. She didn't have any plan—unlike Harper, who shot like a bullet out of the house early each morning. It was already midafternoon, but Dora wasn't measuring her distance or heart rate, or wearing high-tech wicking clothes or running shoes, like her sister. Her intention was simply to start moving. Mamaw had told her to just go out and explore, not to have an agenda, but instead to look around and soak in the sights. To allow herself the freedom to simply roam without someone or something calling her back.

Dora took the advice to heart. She drew in a breath, then began walking at a moderate pace—not so fast that she started to sweat, but quicker than a stroll. Large, drooping oaks provided welcome shade along the side streets. As she passed the few visible houses, she admired the landscape designs, checked out what plants were in bloom. It was a lovely day, with blue skies; she had to ask herself why she'd been so hard-pressed to get out of the house before now. The answer was, she knew, because the black cloud hovering overhead made the world appear dismal.

But she was walking now, pumping her fists with determination. Dora reached the end of the pavement, and then she started down a sand- and rock-strewn beach path bordered on either side by an impenetrable maritime shrub thicket. She paused to study the groundsel, the wax myrtle, the yaupon bushes that survived—even thrived—under the harsh effects of wind-blown salt and sand. Survivors, every one of them. A lesson to be learned, she told herself as she moved on.

Dora followed the narrow path to where it opened up, revealing with a gust of wind the panorama of the Atlantic Ocean. The brilliant sea mirrored the azure skies, sunlight reflecting on its surface like diamonds. Heartened, Dora took off on a quicker pace, keeping to the hard-packed sand. She reflected on the many years she'd walked this same stretch of beach. When they were girls, she and Carson would pretend they were Chincoteague ponies, kicking their knees high and neighing as they galloped along the surf.

Her mama would drop her off at Sea Breeze in early June when school let out and come collect her in early August in time to get her outfitted for school. Carson would cry when Dora had to return with her mother to Charlotte. Dora had always felt for the little girl without a mother. But she was a bit jealous of her, too. Carson got to live full-time with Mamaw in her great house on East Bay, the loveliest street in the world, she thought. And on weekends and holidays, she'd go with them to Sea Breeze. Mamaw tried not to show favoritism when the girls were together, but everyone knew Carson was special to her. As a grown woman, Dora could understand that it was only natural for Mamaw to feel more for the girl she mothered. But as a child, Dora envied Carson for the silliest things, like how Carson got the best bedroom, which, as eldest, Dora thought should have gone to her.

Years later, she gave up girlish games to sit in the sun, coated with baby oil, roasting like a plucked chicken. Carson used to beg her to play, but Dora was three years older and her interests had shifted to the more sedentary scene of sitting on a towel, talking to her girlfriends, flirting with the boys, or reading a book. She had been awash in a sea of hormones, vacillating between laughter and tears, wanting to play the old games with Carson one day and trying to ditch the younger girl the next. It was a confusing summer of budding breasts, boys, and best friends.

That first summer when Dora was on the precipice of womanhood was also Harper's first summer at Sea Breeze. Carson was eleven and Dora was already fourteen. Then this tiny, doll-like girl of six years of age arrived from Manhattan with expressive blue eyes and ginger hair. She was introduced as their half-sister, Harper. Everyone catered to her, oohing about how pretty she was, how well behaved, how smart. Dora had heard of this younger sibling, of course, but she'd never met her. The age difference was too great for them to really play together, as she had with Carson. At best, they'd find a few activities they could share over the summer; at worst, she'd get stuck babysitting.

When Dora remembered those summer days, however, she always returned to one day during that first summer when all three sisters were at Sea Breeze together. Mamaw had taken them to the beach, as she did many days. Mamaw sat in a folding canvas chair under a large, colorful umbrella. Beside her, three towels were spread out on the sand. While Mamaw read, the girls played—making sand castles, collecting seashells, playing tag in the waves. Mamaw's strictest rule was that no one was allowed to go into the water unless she was watching.

On this particular sunny day Carson had been pestering Dora to ride the skim board along the shoreline. Dora was getting annoyed. Carson was such a tomboy it could be embarrassing. After all, only boys skim-boarded and Dora wasn't about to look like a fool in front of people she knew. Harper was building a sand castle in the moist sand at the low-tide mark. Dora lay on her belly on her towel, pulled out *Seventeen*, and soon got lost in the magazine.

Then she heard Harper scream.

Instantly Dora dropped her magazine and leaped to her feet, scanning the beach for the little redheaded girl in the pink swimsuit. She spotted Harper standing frozen by her sand castle, arms out as though poised to run, staring at the massive cargo ship passing the island. Dora ran to her side and grabbed her hand. Carson had also heard the scream and abandoned her skim board to reach Harper's side just after Dora. The little girl was trembling with fear as the monstrous ship passed. The enormous, black, rusting hulk coming so close to the shoreline was very frightening for a child, even for Dora. Fully as tall as a high-rise building, it moved at a leviathan's pace, skimming past the island.

What Dora remembered most was standing on the beach, side by side with Carson and Harper, holding hands, bolstering one another as the behemoth cast its shadow over them. Both she and Carson had come running when Harper cried out. Dora felt a keen sense of solidarity with her sisters at that moment.

When the ship had gone and the sun shone warm on the beach again, the girls dropped hands and each went back to their individual play. But that moment had sealed an unspoken pact between them. They were sisters. They'd be there for one another.

Mamaw, Dora realized now, had never forgotten the sisters' unspoken promise to one another, though the sisters had in the many years they'd been apart. Mamaw had been standing behind them on the beach, watching. Years later she'd brought them back here, to this same island, to this same beach, to feel that bond again.

Was it possible? Dora wondered. Could anyone recapture the innocence and trust of youth once she had transitioned into the cynicism of adulthood?

She continued walking, lost in her thoughts, before she turned a curve and saw a dozen or more kite surfers gliding across the water, their colorful kites like brightly plumed birds in the sky. She grinned, mesmerized by the sight. Carson had told her about this new sport and, curious, Dora took a spot with others along the shoreline, watching the amusing aerobatics out on the water. Of course, Carson had already learned to kite surf from Blake. Dora smiled and thought, *Maybe next year.*

Reaching the tip of the island, she looped around and began her long trek back along Middle Street. She hadn't realized how far she'd walked. She'd reached the northern end of Sullivan's Island. Her throat was parched and her body ached; she was exhausted, sweaty, and had a long way to go before reaching Sea Breeze, clear on the other side of the island. Dora scolded herself for having left without water, but she'd not planned to go so far! But as there was no place to get any or buy any, she had no choice except to put one foot in front of the other and keep walking.

Sweat dripped from her face and was pooling along her neck and between her breasts, blotching her T-shirt. Her thirst became palpable, and she began to worry. *You're such an idiot for going so far on your first day. What if you have a real heart attack this time?*

A car honked beside her and she nearly jumped from her skin. Blinking in the bright sunlight, Dora put her hand up over her eyes like a visor to see who it was waving her over. A shiny red pickup truck with big wheels and a shiny front grille was idling at the curb.

"Hello?" she called out in a questioning tone.

"Dora! Dora Muir, is that you?"

Dora didn't recognize the man at the wheel, nor did she want anyone she might know to see her dressed like this and all sweaty. She waved and kept walking.

The truck followed.

"Dora!" the voice called again.

She didn't stop.

"Hold on a minute. It's me. Devlin."

Devlin? Dora stopped again, then squinted toward the man in the truck. He was a barrel-chested man with shaggy, sun-bleached hair and deeply tanned skin; he was wearing a pale blue polo shirt. He had the look of an islander. She couldn't put a finger on exactly what it was that gave someone that look, but it was as deeply embedded as DNA.

"Devlin Cassell?" she called out. Earlier in the summer, Carson had told Dora she had run into Devlin.

The man in the truck grinned wide. "The one and only."

That was a name that brought up memories that had been packed away in a pretty box labeled "old boyfriends" and tucked into the deep recesses of her brain. If Dora's face hadn't already been so flushed from overheating, Devlin would have seen her cheeks pinking. She'd heard he'd become a successful real estate agent, and that he was divorced. Dora wiped her brow. It was just her luck that she'd run into Devlin Cassell again after fifteen years when she was exhausted and soaking in her own sweat.

"Hey, Devlin," she called out halfheartedly. "Nice to see you again."

"Well, come on over here, girl," Devlin called back, waving his arm in a come-hither gesture. "We don't want to keep shouting."

"I'm all sweaty," she begged off.

"So what?"

"So, I don't feel like stopping right now." Nervousness made her dry mouth feel like a desert. She started to cough, and it was one of those hacking coughs that could go on forever.

"You okay?" Devlin called out.

She waved her hand dismissively, wishing either that he'd go away or the earth would just swallow her up.

Dev put the truck in park and rushed to her side with a bottle of water. He handed her the bottle and gently patted her back. She drank thirstily, and as the coughing fit subsided she took great heaving breaths, embarrassed to the core.

"Thanks," she said between breaths. She was so hot, if she were alone she'd take the rest of the water and pour it over her head.

"Come on, sit a spell in my truck. It's air-conditioned."

She wanted to. Desperately. Dora looked from left to right, to see if anyone she knew might see her step into the car of a man who wasn't her husband. Silly, of course, given that she didn't really have a husband any longer. But old habits died hard.

"Sure, thanks," she said. Dora followed Devlin to the truck, plucking at her T-shirt as she walked so it wouldn't cling so tight.

Inside the truck it was blessedly cool. She almost wept with gratitude when he moved the fan to blow directly onto her.

Devlin leaned back against the door and grinned like a Cheshire cat as they studied each other. His eyes were shockingly pale blue against his dark tan and she remembered how, when they were teens, the girls all said he looked like Paul Newman. Well, she thought, swallowing another gulp of water from the bottle, she wasn't the only one who had put on some weight since the good ol' days. But Devlin wasn't heavy as much as solid. He had filled out his girth and had the sheen of a man who loved the outdoors and his drink in equal measures.

"Dora Muir," he said in a tone that implied he couldn't believe he was seeing her again. "As I live and breathe."

"Well, *I'm* barely breathing," she said with a self-deprecating laugh.

"What are you doing running in the heat like that? It's gotta be close to a hundred out there."

He thought she was running? Dora let that one slide. "I didn't know it was that hot. I, uh, might have gone a little too far."

"Your face is as red as a beet. Let me drive you back to Sea Breeze."

She could've kissed him. "That'd be nice," she replied, wiping sweat from her brow in as demure a manner as she could manage. "Thank you."

Devlin fired up the big engine. It purred to action.

"Nice truck," she said. Then, remembering the dented, vintage gray Ford pickup he used to drive, she added, "Nicer than the one you used to drive."

His grin spread across his face and he laughed. "You remember that old clunker?"

"Remember it? Some of my fondest memories were in that smelly ol' truck."

His eyes sparkled with mirth and memory, and she knew they were both remembering the heavy-petting sessions they'd had in the torn-up front seat of that truck when Dora was sixteen and Devlin seventeen. Over the course of one long, hot summer, Dora had rounded first, second, and third base with Devlin Cassell and, on one particularly steamy night, almost scored a home run.

"Yeah," he said in a slow drawl as he shifted into gear. They took off down the road. "It near broke my heart when I had to let that truck go. Hung on to it long as I could." He glanced her way. "It sure is good to see you again. You're as pretty as ever."

"Oh, get out of here," she said with a wave of her hand. "I look terrible. I'm sweating like Pattie's pig."

"You're out running. You're supposed to."

Dora wasn't going to argue with that.

They reached the corner where Dunleavy's Pub sat.

"Hey," Dev said. "Can I buy you a drink? There's a parking spot right in front. That don't happen every day."

"Good God, no. I'm not going in there dressed like this."

He continued on past Dunleavy's and the strip of restaurants on Middle Street, most of them not crowded yet. In another hour, all of them would be overflowing with guests.

"Well, how about I drop you off, then you can spruce yourself up. Then I'll swing by and pick you up in, say, an hour? How does that suit you?"

"I don't know . . ." she hedged. This was going too fast.

"Come on, Dora," he cajoled in that easy drawl she never could say no to. "We've got a lot of catching up to do. Let me buy you a drink. Or dinner."

Right now, all she wanted was to shower and collapse back

into bed. Maybe she'd watch a little television. Going out for a drink was not part of her usual repertoire.

"Not tonight."

"Tomorrow night?" he persisted.

"I don't know."

"I'm just gonna keep on asking, so you might as well say yes."

She laughed, falling under the charm of his smile. "Okay," she said, surprised that she was sincere. "What time?"

Devlin pulled into the gravel driveway of Sea Breeze, put the car into park, and turned toward her, letting his arm slide over the top of the seat. He had that same irascible grin on his face now that she remembered all too well.

"Honey," he said, playing out each vowel, "I'll sit there till judgment day if you tell me you'll be there."

She tilted her head, believing he might just do that. "We can't have that. Let's say the day after tomorrow? Five o'clock."

~~~

Dora waited till Devlin's car drove off before letting loose the belly laugh that she'd been holding down. What a hoot! After all these years, Devlin Cassell had invited her for a drink.

She felt flustered. Giddy. She hurried to the house to shower and change, then stopped short as a new thought took root. She recalled how Harper and Carson always went to the outdoor shower after a run or a trip to the ocean to hose down before entering the house. There hadn't been an outdoor shower when she was a girl coming to Sea Breeze. Back in the day, they'd just used the hose to wash off.

Dora retraced her steps and followed the stepping stones

around the enormous gardenia bush to the outdoor shower. It was just four wood walls with no ceiling. Dora stepped inside, avoiding the spiderwebs in the corners. There was only one spigot; in the summer on the island all the water came out warm. Mamaw had lavender soap, shampoo, and conditioner in wooden bins, and smelling them, she recalled catching that scent on her sisters.

Dora stripped down and stood under the miserly spray of water. Even still, it felt luxurious on her hot skin. Being buck-naked outdoors under the sun was exhilarating—freeing—and she laughed for the pleasure of it. And the idea that she was like her beautiful, trim, sexy, and single sisters. Sure, she had a way to go before she got back in shape, but for the first time, she felt like she could do it. Her goal wasn't to be thin. After the scare with her heart, Dora just wanted to be healthy and glowing with the confidence of a woman at ease in her own skin.

Harper and Carson sat at the kitchen table eating fresh strawberries and rehearsing what they would say to Dora.

"I don't think she'll go for it," Carson said.

"I think she will," Harper countered. "We've done all the research." She lifted up the pile of papers she'd printed about various dolphin therapy programs and pertinent medical reports as proof.

"*You've* done the research," Carson amended.

"*You* asked Blake to help. I still can't believe he got us a slot at the Dolphin Research Center so quickly." She looked at her sister, eyes narrowed in speculation. They'd both been excited about the plan, but now Carson appeared hesitant. "Are you getting cold feet because you don't want to take Nate? If so, I can take him alone."

"No, it's not that at all. I was just remembering how Dora responded when Cal suggested she leave Nate at Sea Breeze."

"For the *summer*," Harper reminded her. "This is only for a week. And it's completely different. She won't be dumping Nate. We're offering to take him. This is for Nate's benefit. And hers. Once she understands that, I think she'll go for it."

Carson puffed out a plume of air, then slapped her hand on the table. "All right, then. Let's do this."

They gathered the reports and Harper's laptop and headed to the bedroom Dora shared with Harper. After a quick knock, they pushed open the door, rushed inside, and jumped onto her bed like they used to as girls.

Dora grabbed hold of her magazine, laughing.

Carson and Harper moved to sit cross-legged facing her, their eyes wide with excitement. Harper could smell the clean, lavender scent of her soap and shampoo.

"What's going on?" Dora asked them.

"You look good," Carson told her. "Your cheeks have some color."

"Thanks. I was walking."

"Good for you!" Harper exclaimed, settling onto the bed. "Did you do warm-ups?"

"No."

"I'll teach you some. You don't want to get stiff."

"Okay," Dora drawled.

There was a beat of silence while Harper and Carson shared a glance.

"We have a proposition for you," Carson announced with import.

"Just hear us out before you say anything," interjected Harper at seeing the quick flare in Dora's eyes.

"Okay," Dora replied, this time more hesitant.

"So," Carson began while Harper opened her laptop and flicked it on. "While you were out walking, we've been talking. Here's the thing," she said, putting her hands out to emphasize the point. "We think you deserve some time for yourself, totally selfish time, without anything to worry about."

"Kind of like going to some spa for a week, only the spa is here," added Harper.

Dora smirked. "I like the sound of that."

"We were also talking about Nate," said Carson. "What he needs."

Dora's focus immediately sharpened.

"And how he's having a hard time letting go of what happened to Delphine," she continued.

"We know you're worried about how he's holing up in his room too much," Harper said. "So we asked ourselves, what would bring him out of his shell? And the answer came quickly—dolphins. But he feels guilty about what happened to Delphine, even though he shouldn't. You know that, we know that. But Nate doesn't. So I did some research and discovered that there are several places that offer special dolphin programs for kids. A place where he could interact with them in a safe and secure way to give him a new perspective. We checked with Blake and he agreed that the program at the Dolphin Research Center in Florida would be a good one."

"Is it a therapy program?" Dora asked, more than a hint of skepticism in her voice.

Harper answered, "It's not a therapy program per se, but a program for children with special needs. The goal of the week's program is set by the staff and you, to personalize it, which I think is important, especially for Nate."

"Nate will be with dolphins again," Carson said. "Only this time, it's the proper setting. Not in the wild. He can feel safe and know he can't hurt them, or they him."

"Take a look," Harper said, moving the laptop so Dora could see the screen. "Here's the website."

Dora took the laptop from Harper. "It looks interesting. Nate had always responded better to animals than to humans, especially dolphins. So you think I should take him there?"

Harper looked at Carson before turning back to Dora. She knew this part was going to be the hard sell.

"Actually, we think we should take him and you should stay here."

Dora drew back. "What?"

"We know this is outside your comfort zone, so try to indulge in a little sideways thinking," Harper said. "You need a break, Dora."

"Absolutely not. I can't let you take Nate without me."

"Why not?" asked Carson.

"First of all, he won't go with you. Secondly, well . . ." she sputtered. "I won't let you take him."

"It's your decision, of course," Harper said in a persuasive voice. "But consider this. Mothers of special-needs kids need a break. Right? Does Nate have special needs?"

"Of course he does," Dora said with short temper.

"Are you his mother?"

Dora shook her head, her brow furrowed. "I know where you're going with this," she said irritably, "and I can't let him go."

"Listen to what you just said," Carson said gently. "You can't let him go. Dora, sweet sister, you're holding on to him so tight. Ease up a little. There's no way we can persuade you that what you fear might happen won't happen, but trust Nate. Trust us. We'll be fine."

"He's still angry at you!" Dora countered. "What makes you think he'll go with you?"

Carson smiled and in that moment Dora thought she looked uncannily like Mamaw.

"Delphine," Carson said cagily.

Dora narrowed her eyes.

"I'll take him to see Delphine after the program," Carson added.

"How many extra days will that be?"

"Just one. And you're missing the point."

"And that is?"

"If he needs to see Delphine, he'll say yes and that will be our answer. If he says no . . ." She flipped her hands up. "We'll agree with you and we'll nix the whole idea."

"Regardless of what he answers, why don't *I* just take him to this program?" Dora said.

"You could," Harper answered. "Or, you could take a break instead." She took hold of Dora's hands and inspected them. "Look at your nails. You desperately need a manicure."

Dora tried to tug back her hands but Harper held tight.

"You need time to notice such things," she said gently. "To take some time for yourself."

"One week," Carson said. "That's not long. If you went away to a spa, it would be at least five days."

Dora turned to Carson, the struggle visible on her face. "Carson, do you think you could handle Nate? He is a sweet boy, but he can be difficult."

"Did you forget I took care of him for almost as long last month and look how well he did."

"But that was here . . . with dolphins."

"We're going to see dolphins!" Carson persisted. "Dora, I love Nate, and even though he's mad at me, I know he loves me, too."

"And me," Harper added. "We've become fast friends."

Dora took the papers Harper had printed and began leafing through them. Harper exchanged a hopeful look with Carson. After several minutes, Dora set the papers aside and looked long and hard at Carson, trying to make up her mind.

"This is scary for me."

"We know," Carson said.

"It seems like a good idea . . ." she hedged.

Harper and Carson remained silent, giving Dora time. The silence stretched on while Dora rocked slightly in thought. When she stopped, she reached out to rest her hand on Carson's arm.

"I couldn't trust Nate to anyone but you."

Carson's face softened as she put her hand over Dora's. "Don't worry, I won't let you down. I'll take good care of him. And I'll call you if I need you. But, hey, he's my nephew. I've babysat for him before, remember? We'll be fine."

"You're so kind to do this."

"You'd do the same for me," Carson replied.

Harper shifted back, feeling her enthusiasm wither. She knew in her heart that it made sense for Carson to take Nate to Florida. Carson and Nate had shared experiences with dolphins, Carson could take him to visit Delphine. It was their thing. Yet it had been her idea in the first place to go to the program, and Carson had run away with it. That and the fact that Dora didn't even consider her qualified to take Nate made her feel as she did when she was very young and her two older sisters walked off together engaged in intense dialogue that didn't include her, not even realizing they'd left her behind.

"Here's the good news," Carson said, leaning forward with excitement now that the decision had been made. "Blake called the director and got Nate a slot in the Pathways program." She paused for dramatic effect. "They got him into a slot later this week!"

Dora was stunned. "So soon?"

"Someone canceled. Otherwise we would have had to wait for who knows how long. The sooner the better. Everything just dovetails. It's like it's meant to be, right?"

Dora laughed lightly and lifted her hands. "I guess so."

"You can talk to the director of the program tomorrow," Carson continued. "Together you'll set goals for the program."

"I don't know what to say," Dora said, looking at both her sisters. "Thank you."

Harper saw the relief and gratitude in Dora's eyes, then dug deep and let the perceived slight go. It was better this way than if they both went to Florida, she thought. Divide and conquer. Carson could take care of Nate, and she'd take care of Dora.

"The other day you asked for help. We're just trying to give it to you," Harper told her. "While Carson takes Nate to Florida,

I'll help you get started on a workout program. We'll have fun. We'll get manis and pedis. We'll have massages. We'll do whatever you want to do without thinking about schedules or routines or who needs something. Best of all, while *you* are healing, you can relax knowing that *Nate* is healing, too."

"I don't care if I get my nails done," Dora told her, and sniffed as tears flooded her eyes. "I just want to roam the beaches and sleep."

God help me, Harper thought. She wasn't sure handling Nate wouldn't be easier than her opinionated and currently emotional sister.

Chapter Eight

~~~

T he two-block strip of restaurants on Sullivan's Island was buzzing with chatter and laughter from the summer crowds. Dora grumbled to herself upon seeing the throng of tourists from all over the area crowding the streets looking for an island restaurant to enjoy dinner. The days of Sullivan's Island being a slow, quiet Mayberry by the sea were long gone. Word got out and now it was tough to find a parking spot for dinner, much less a table. A golf cart, however, was small, and she found a spot on a side street between a tree and a cluster of rocks that she could squeeze into.

She pushed the parking brake and sat for a minute in the island quiet, feeling uneasy. What was she doing here? she asked herself. She was still a married woman, and here she was, going to a bar to meet a man she hadn't seen in some fifteen years. She should have stayed home with Nate. After all, he was leaving for Florida in a few days. Though, when she'd left, he was playing video games with Harper and had barely said good-bye. Lucille would feed him dinner and she'd be home by the time he went to bed.

Dora knew the anxiety lay in herself. She was reluctant to let Nate go, afraid that something might happen to him if she wasn't with him. She was also nervous about tonight—saying the wrong thing or doing something tactless with Devlin. What would they talk about?

She checked her watch. If she was going to meet Devlin, she had to go now. She hated being late. She brought to mind Devlin's face. At the memory of the spark she'd felt when he'd asked her for a drink, she felt again a flutter of anticipation. It had been a very long time since she'd gone out with a man for a drink.

Dora gathered her purse and strolled behind a young couple walking arm in arm, talking in that polite way that told her it was probably a first date. It was a night for romance. The air was balmy, not humid, and the fairy lights along the outdoor eating areas were twinkling in the dusky light. Dora felt pretty in her Lilly Pulitzer summer shift. Her blond hair fell softly to her shoulders, tucked behind her ears, which bore pearls. She knew her hairstyle and clothing were much the same as they were in high school, but her mama told her classic never went out of style. When she reached the corner, diners spilled out onto the outdoor umbrella tables.

Dora checked her watch; it was two minutes after five. She sucked in her tummy and stepped inside the door. The booths were crowded with patrons laughing, eating, having a good time. Overhead, the fans were whirring and all the windows were open. She nervously searched the tables for Devlin.

He wasn't there.

All the giddiness she'd felt coming here fizzled in her stomach. She stood awkwardly at the door, feeling heat color her cheeks. Devlin had not waited for her after all.

Her disappointment was greater than she should have felt. After all, it wasn't a real date. Devlin merely suggested they have a drink. It was a last-minute gesture, a kindness to an old friend. He may have waited a few minutes, but why would he choose to spend the night here on the off chance she'd show up?

Another couple was trying to enter the restaurant. Dora stepped aside to let them pass. All the tables looked full but she didn't want to tuck tail and go home. Searching, she spied an open seat at the bar.

She could hear her mother's voice in her head: *Nice girls don't sit alone at a bar.* Dora never had. She'd always followed the rules of a good girl. *And look where that got you*, she reminded herself. Tonight she'd showered and put on a pretty dress, took care with her makeup, and even spritzed a bit of scent. To go home now felt defeatist. Dora decided she'd had enough of retreating.

Quieting her mother's voice in her head, Dora walked straight to the bar stool, feeling like a brazen hussy as she took a seat. She folded her hands on the bar and looked from left to right. Truth was, she felt awkward sitting alone on the stool, as if she were wearing two left shoes.

"What can I get for you, miss?" asked the bartender, stepping up. She recognized the gray-haired man from the times she'd eaten lunch in this pub. He was the manager, and Carson's former boss. She couldn't remember his name, and he didn't recognize her, either.

"A glass of white wine, please," Dora answered.

"Chardonnay's the house."

"That'll be good."

He delivered it quickly, then served another customer. Dora took a sip, needing the bolstering.

Time passed agonizingly slowly. She looked idly around at the photographs, designer beer cans, and sports memorabilia that decorated the pub, pretending to take an interest, but it was no use. She wasn't enjoying herself. Outdoors, the light was fading. She didn't relish driving home in the dark in the golf cart. Wasn't even sure the front lights worked. She looked at her watch, then glanced behind the bar, hoping to catch the bartender's eye for her bill.

"Dora! You came!"

She felt an arm slide around her waist.

"Devlin! You're here," Dora said, trying to keep her voice pleasantly disinterested instead of immensely relieved.

"Sure I'm here. Told you I would be."

"But I didn't see you."

"Had to make a quick call. Can't hear my phone in here. You didn't think I stood you up, did you? I knew if I did that, Dora Muir would never give me a second chance. Hell, I'm dumb, but I'm not that stupid. I told Bill to keep an eye open for you." Devlin turned and signaled the bartender, who promptly came with a cold beer and set it in front of him.

"Thanks, Bill. Hey, I told you to keep a lookout for Dora here."

Bill looked at her, eyes narrowing. "You're Dora? Sorry. He told me you were Carson's sister but I didn't see the resemblance."

"No one usually does," Dora replied, then added, "We're half sisters."

Devlin said, "Dora's the pretty one."

It was cheesy, Dora knew, but his eyes gleamed with sincerity and the compliment warmed her.

"They have the same eyes. That blue," Devlin said, shaking his head with appreciation.

"Nice to know you," Bill said with a curt nod. "How's Mrs. Muir? Haven't seen her about lately."

"Good. Real good."

"Put hers on my tab," Devlin told him, indicating the wine.

"Got it," Bill said, then moved on to another customer.

The couple beside Dora stood to leave and Devlin smoothly slid onto the vacant stool.

"You hungry?" he asked, playing the perfectly solicitous gentleman.

Dora shook her head. She hadn't eaten dinner and the French fries smelled heavenly. Ordinarily she'd have ordered some, just to nibble, but they no longer were on her diet.

Devlin took a long swallow of his beer.

"Bill knows your order without you telling him?" she observed.

"Oh, sure. We go way back. This is kind of my office."

Dora raised a brow. "Really? I can't imagine you get much work done here."

"Enough," he said with a sly grin. "Real estate is a lot about who you know. And everyone on the island stops by Dunleavy's."

"And there's plenty of beer on tap."

"That, too," he agreed with conviviality. "I haven't seen you in here this summer. Or anywhere, for that matter. Where you been hiding yourself?"

"Hiding? I live in Summerville. I come here for a few weeks in the summer with my son, Nate. I don't go out much."

"What about your husband?"

She paused, noting his increased interest. "He stays in Summerville during the week and comes for the weekends. Or did," she amended, looking at her wineglass.

"I'd heard you might be getting a divorce."

Dora looked sharply up. She didn't like hearing that her private life was being talked about on the island. "From Carson, I suppose?"

He shrugged.

"Uh-huh." She looked at her wineglass. "We're separated," she replied, deliberately vague.

"I'm divorced."

"Yes, I heard. Sorry."

"It happens. I'm not gonna lie, it's tough when you go through it. But I have my little girl to show for it. Cute as a button. The same age as your son."

Dora turned her head, interested. "How did she fare in the divorce? I've heard it can be hard on children."

His face clouded and she caught a glimpse of hurt behind his happy facade.

"I tried to make it easy for her. Gave my ex-wife all she asked for. But she still made me jump through hoops to see Leigh Anne. That was the hardest part." He paused for a swig of beer.

"Leigh Anne—isn't that your mother's name?"

His eyes sparked with pleasure. "You remembered," he said with a hint of surprise that she did.

"Of course. Your mother was always very kind to me."

"She liked you."

Dora smiled, remembering the heavyset woman with the beautiful, sad eyes.

"She passed a year after Leigh Anne was born. Too young. I felt robbed." He drew a long swallow of his beer. "Well, she lived to see her first grandchild. I got that much right, at least."

"I'm sorry, Devlin. I didn't know your mama passed." Devlin was an only child, and his mother, divorced, had raised him on her own. They'd been very close.

"It was hard," he admitted. "I had a couple of dark years after. Looking back, I can see how it wasn't easy for Ashley. I drank a lot, went out a lot. It cost me my marriage."

Dora leaned closer as his voice lowered.

"But after a while you work things out, and the hurt and pain passes."

"I am sorry you went through all that."

"Life goes on," he said in a more upbeat tone, clearly wanting to let that line of conversation drop. "You and I, we had something special, you know?" Devlin said, changing the direction. He waved his hand when she made a face. "I'm not just saying this 'cause you're sitting here. I often think back on those days we were together. How long did we go steady? Four years?"

Dora smiled into her glass. "At least. Till you went off to college."

"Columbia is only two hours away," he chided.

"You forget my home was in Charlotte, and without a car, you may as well have been clear across the country," Dora said archly.

"I called you, you know, when you went off to Converse College."

She smiled, remembering the tingle she'd felt just hearing his voice again on the phone. "I was already dating Cal."

"Yeah," he said slowly. "Bad timing." His glance leisurely swept her face. "You know, if we'd gotten together again a mite sooner, I might not have married Ashley and you might not've married what's-his-name, and we'd be married right this minute."

She laughed into her drink. "Maybe," she agreed. "But then I wouldn't have Nate and you wouldn't have your sweet Leigh Anne."

"We can't change the past." Devlin grinned and leaned forward. "But we can change the future," he added flirtatiously. He turned and signaled to Bill for another round.

Dora slid her elbows onto the bar and swirled the wine in her glass as she listened to Devlin tell a colorful story of how he and his buddies had bagged a marlin. She noticed the pleasant cadence of his speech, the way his Southern accent, heavier than Cal's, drawled out vowels, and the mirth in his blue eyes as he chuckled.

Devlin was the same amiable person she'd remembered, and yet so very different from the boy she'd dated so many years ago. He'd gained a confidence that replaced his cockiness, an assuredness that came from success. As she watched his animated face, it occurred to her that she wasn't enjoying the story as much as the music of his voice.

In a moment of sudden clarity, she understood that was how it was for Nate, too. At bedtime he liked her to tell him stories until he fell asleep. When he had a meltdown, she knew *what* she said didn't matter as much as *how* she said the words to calm him.

She listened to Devlin and sipped her wine, enjoying the simple pleasure of being out and having the attention of a man again. She no longer felt awkward or nervous sitting at the bar. She wasn't a woman alone. She was with Devlin—an old friend, a former lover. She was merely having a drink at a bar. Yet it wasn't a date, either. She could stay or she could leave. There were no expectations. No pressure.

And that, she realized with amusement, was enough.

Three days later, Carson was on her way to the Florida Keys. Her hands clenched the wheel of the Blue Bomber as she stared at the highway, counting the miles. She was overtired, over-caffeinated, and at her wit's end. Florida was one long state—it went on forever!

The sun was beginning to set by the time she got off the mainland to the first of the islands of the Keys. She'd hoped to get to the motel before dark. The planned twelve-hour trip was taking fourteen because of all the stops Nate had to make. She glanced in the rearview mirror, relieved to see the boy sitting quietly absorbed with his handheld video game. "Thank God," she muttered.

The trip had been grueling. The front seat was littered with various brands of wipes she'd bought before Nate finally accepted one. Lord knew, the boy needed to keep his hands clean. Eating had been a nightmare. Dora and Lucille had specially prepared food that they packed in a cooler. Unfortunately, something was "wrong" with the sandwiches they'd made. Carson still wasn't sure what. It was something about the way they were made or looked or how they smeared . . . Nate flatly rejected them. She'd resorted to trolling fast-food chains along the road, hoping he'd find something acceptable. The car smelled like a fast-food restaurant because she'd bought Nate hamburgers, fish burgers, submarine sandwiches, pancakes, until he finally agreed to eat chicken nuggets and French fries—as long as there was not a drop of catsup or sauce on them. She'd found that out the hard way.

If eating was tough for Nate, elimination was worse. As far as she could tell, Nate had the bladder of a pregnant woman. He had to stop to pee every two hours like clockwork. He was terrified of having an accident, and the minute he felt the urge he screamed for her to take the next exit.

"We're on the Keys now," she called in a cheery voice to Nate in the backseat after another shout for a bathroom stop. "Hold on. Shouldn't be long now!"

"It's six forty-seven," Nate said. "We've been on this trip for twelve hours and thirty-two minutes. We should be there."

Carson glanced in the rearview mirror to see Nate looking at his watch. She blew out a plume of air and wiped a strand of hair from her forehead. He was a good kid, she reminded herself. Dora had prepared her for his idiosyncrasies—how he didn't show emotion in his voice or face. How he could develop an obsessive interest in something. How he could overreact to something seemingly inconsequential. But driving to Florida with Nate was like being in the car with a dictator. Meet his demands, or meet his wrath!

"Yes, we did plan to be there by now," Carson said evenly,

marshaling her frustration. "But we made so many stops it slowed us down. We've got at least another hour."

"Oh." A moment passed. "I can't wait an hour. I have to go to the bathroom *now*."

The motel was a 1950s-era stucco two-story painted lime green and billed as a "resort." Carson had booked the room online, and as often was the case, the professional photos looked better than the actual location. Calling the small, scruffy, off-the-highway motel a resort was a long stretch, but it was close to the Dolphin Research Center and cheap and they had a room available. An undeniably attractive trifecta, in her budget-conscious mind.

It was dark by the time she parked in the gravel lot. After she checked in, she gathered their suitcases and led a wary Nate along the narrow, poorly lit pavement pathway to the rear of the motel, praying a snake or iguana or some rodent wouldn't jump out from the shadows. The light over the cottage door was dim but she got the door open without trouble. Her hand felt along the wall for the light switch. In an instant, the room was revealed.

It was a small cottage, spartanly furnished with cheap, beachy white wicker furniture. And it was pink. Pink walls, pink fabric, pink bathroom tile, and splashes of pink in all the nautical prints on the wall. The space was divided into two sections by a half wall open to the front windows. The front area was narrow and long. To the left, a cluster of mini white appliances made up the in-room kitchenette. To the right was a lumpy-looking futon and an ancient TV atop a white wicker stand.

The rear was a bedroom with a queen bed, a wicker bureau, a small wicker desk, and the bathroom.

Carson dropped her bags to the floor and walked around, surveying. She opened the fridge and checked for ice. There wasn't any.

"Make yourself at home," she told Nate. "This is where we'll be living for the next five days."

Nate stood by the door, ramrod straight and clutching his bag. "I don't like it here."

"It's not a palace, but it's clean."

"It smells bad."

"Yeah, it does," she said. The scent of mildew was prevalent. "We'll open the windows, okay? Get some of that nice ocean breeze in here."

"It's dirty."

She followed his gaze to the corner where the linoleum was chipped and curling. "It's not dirty, Nate. It's just old."

"I want to go home." Nate's face crumpled.

Carson's heart went out to the little guy who'd tried so hard all day to keep it together. She brought to mind Dora's warnings of a meltdown and immediately walked close to Nate and gently took his bag.

"Hey, little man, let's check out the bedroom. We're tired and it's dark. We'll feel better in the morning. Tomorrow we'll eat breakfast, then go right off to see the dolphins," she told him, hoping he'd feel more comfortable if she laid out the plan of the day. "You can have the bed in front of the TV. Does that sound good? This is your space," she said, walking over to pat the futon mattress. "Tell you what. While I jump into the shower, you can watch TV and unpack. Take your time. Okay?"

He stared at the futon but didn't respond.

Carson felt the miles clinging to her skin and couldn't wait to wash them away. She turned on the television, found a local station of cartoons, then pulled down the futon into a bed. The sheets were crisp and smelled clean. She poured him a glass of water, set it on the table by the futon, and waited. Soon, Nate's interest was captured by the cartoons. She wanted him to acclimate at his own pace. She went to the back room, stripped off her clothing that reeked of fast food, and went into the pink bathroom. It was barely large enough for one person to stand in but the water in the shower was hot. After a blissful scrubbing, she felt revived.

Wrapping herself in a towel, she went back out into the room. She found Nate standing in the back bedroom, putting his many dolphin books and clothes into the bureau drawers. On top of the bureau, he'd laid out in a neat row his toothbrush, toothpaste, hairbrush, comb, shampoo, liquid soap, and a book.

"Nice job," she told him, feeling relieved that he was settling in. She followed suit, unzipping her bag. She casually set her toiletry bag on the dresser.

"No!" he exclaimed with alarm. "This is where my things go."

"Can't we both put our things here? There's plenty of room."

"No."

Biting her tongue, Carson withdrew her toiletry bag and went to put it in the bottom drawer.

"That's where my books go," he told her in a voice bordering on panicked.

"Nate, there are three drawers. We have to share."

"No!" he exploded. "My books go in there."

"Where do my clothes go, then?"

"I don't know." He thrust out his chin and turned his back to her.

Carson heard obstinacy in his tone and knew he was teetering on the brink tonight. Hearing the triggers, she held her tongue and went to the small closet and set her suitcase in there. She'd lived out of a suitcase before, she told herself.

"When you're done, it's your turn for the shower," she said in a cheery voice.

"I take baths." His voice, though monotone, trembled.

Carson skipped a beat and cursed her luck. No tub . . . She knew he was struggling with everything being different; he was out of his routine. Sensing he was a time bomb about to go off, she tried for humor.

"You're in luck. You don't have to take a bath tonight! You can take your choice. You can brush your teeth first or get in your pajamas first."

"I'll get in my pajamas."

"Good."

Carson, exhausted after fourteen hours of driving stop-and-go and dealing with the child's demands, knew her work wasn't over yet. Leaving Nate to change clothes, she went to the door and stepped out on the front porch. She dialed Dora's number and said a prayer of thanks when Dora answered on the second ring.

"Are you there?" Dora asked, sounding slightly breathless.

"Yes, we got here. The motel's okay, not great. It'll do. But it doesn't have a tub."

"Oh, Lord, batten down the hatches," Dora said in mock horror.

She laughed. "And Nate says it smells bad."

"Oh, Lord," Dora said again.

It was exactly what Carson needed to hear. She'd been worried that Dora would freak out and then she'd have two hysterias to deal with. But here she was, making a joke and defusing the tension. She was pleasantly surprised by how her older sister was reacting.

"What's he doing now?" Dora asked.

"He's changing into his pajamas. I told him he didn't have to take a bath tonight. Bought me some time."

"Good thinking. The thing to keep in mind is that right now Nate's dealing with a lot of new stimuli and he doesn't have any place safe to sort things out. You and I have the apparatus to deal with these things, but he doesn't. He's rearranging his mental map of the world. It's a scenario for a meltdown. Remember, though, if he has one, he's not angry, he's reacting."

"Tell me what to do."

"You're doing real good all on your own. You took away the conflict when you told him he didn't need to take a bath. I'm impressed."

"I'm scared." Carson made it sound like a joke, but she wasn't kidding. She wished she could tell Dora how inept she felt dealing with this child. What was she thinking? She didn't know the first thing about children. But she'd made sweeping assurances so that Dora would go along with their plan. She couldn't make her sister nervous now.

"Aw, sis, I feel for you. You know I do. But don't be. He's the one who's scared." Dora's voice hitched a bit. "Just a scared little boy. Remember that, and you'll do fine," she said, her voice returning to normal. "If he has a meltdown, just hold him tight until he gets through it. It won't be easy. You'll be just as exhausted as he is when it's over. But you will get through it. I think right now the main thing is to get him on a routine as soon as possible. Maybe make him a schedule."

"You mean with gold stars and all that?" She looked toward the interior of the room, wondering where she'd put it.

"Kids with Asperger's do better with pictures than charts. How good are you at drawing?"

Carson slipped on her flip-flops and hurried in the dark to the car to fetch the box of art supplies that Dora had packed for the trip. Little did Dora realize that it would be Carson who would use them. She fumbled with her key but managed to get back into the room before Nate realized she'd left. She carried the box to the small glass-topped table and pried open the box. There was the usual assortment of computer paper, colored pencils and markers, watercolors, coloring books, glue, and Scotch tape. Carson smiled when she saw dolphin stickers. Her sister really was a great mom.

Fifteen minutes later she had a small stack of drawings. She carried them and a roll of tape to the bathroom, where Nate was idly letting water pour over his toothbrush. He seemed to be self-soothing so she didn't interrupt him. She reached up to tape a picture to the left side of the mirror. It was a rudimentary, stick-man drawing of a boy brushing his teeth under the sun. Next she taped up a similar drawing of a boy brushing his teeth under the moon and stars. Nate studied the drawings.

"This is to remind you to brush your teeth in the morning. And this one is for the evening," she told him.

She went directly into the bedroom, pleased that he followed her. She taped a drawing of a woman sleeping in a bed under where she'd written her name. The nondescript woman had long, black hair, which was the best she could do to indicate it represented her.

"This is where I sleep."

In similar fashion, Carson went to the bureau that Nate had claimed and put his name on it. She put her name on the closet, a drawing of a boy in bed with Nate's name over the futon, and on the fridge she taped up a large meal chart. The drawing of a spoon and sun rose over the drawing of a clock at seven a.m. for breakfast. A plate, fork, and a moon were over six p.m. for dinner.

"This is our schedule," she said, pointing to the drawings. "We have new rules. Starting tomorrow, every morning we will get up at seven, get dressed, and eat breakfast. At eight thirty we will go to the Dolphin Research Center. And every night we will eat dinner at six. You will go to bed at the same time you do at home, eight o'clock, and you can watch your television or play games for an hour." She could see the tension in his body relax as he studied the chart on the fridge. "It's already after nine, so hop into your bed, but because it's our first night and special, if you like you can watch a little TV until nine thirty. Or you can go right to sleep. Which would you like to do?"

Nate's wide eyes studied her and she could almost see the wheels turning in his head as he considered the choice put before him. Dora was right; the pictures had provided him with a map to his world.

"I'll watch TV. Please," he added.

"You got it."

She placed his pillow from home on the bed and he climbed onto the futon. He looked at her drawing of the boy on the bed and giggled. "You're a bad drawer, Aunt Carson!" he exclaimed.

Carson burst out laughing. "You're right! I'm a terrible drawer. Look at the feet. They're huge!"

Nate looked at her, eyes wide with both astonishment and pleasure that she'd laughed. "It's a very bad drawing!" he exclaimed, catching the gist. He pointed. "You gave the boy six toes."

This made Carson laugh all the harder. It was infectious. The more one laughed the harder the other laughed. Not that any of it was all that funny, but they were both laughing together at the same thing and it felt good. As she laughed she could feel the stress flowing from her body. Seeing Nate holding his belly and howling with laughter, she knew he felt the same. She hadn't seen him laugh like this since they were in the Cove together, before Delphine's accident. This was the first sharing since then of something that was good and fun. A wave of peace swept over her, knowing she'd done the right thing to bring Nate here.

She could do this, she realized as she wiped her eyes and leaned back against the lumpy futon beside Nate, enjoying his company.

Chapter Nine

*T*he following morning Dora awoke to pounding in her temples. Blinking in the morning light, she realized the pounding was coming from outdoors. She dragged herself from her bed, padded to the kitchen to pour herself a cup of coffee, and followed the sound of voices to the back porch.

Stepping outdoors, she paused, catching a waft of the sultry air. The pungent scent of pluff mud was strong this morning, tingling in her nose. She breathed deep. This brown, sucking, rich mud redolent with the scent of spartina grass and tidal flats was the perfume of the lowcountry. It was the scent of home.

As she sipped her coffee, her thoughts quickly shifted to Nate. She wondered how he would enjoy his first day at the Dolphin Research Center. Last night she'd talked on the phone with Carson until late. Dora had already been second-guessing her decision to let Carson take Nate to Florida without her; she still had a hard time believing she'd agreed. So when Carson had called to ask for her help with Nate, Dora was a breath away from hopping in her car and driving south to rescue them. But she forced herself to make light of the situation, for her own benefit as much as to keep Carson calm. And it had seemed to work. For the first time, she'd let go and let Carson have a chance at resolving the problem. She was as proud of herself as she was of Carson. Dora had learned to trust someone else—to trust Nate.

She'd also learned that she was not indispensable. This realization was as humbling as it was freeing.

The morning sky over the ocean was brilliant with puffs of white clouds dotting the blue. Dora took a deep breath and blew out slowly. The thought that she was free to do whatever she pleased that day came unbidden, surprising her with possibilities.

Under the shade of the large black-and-white-striped awning, Mamaw was sitting in her favorite oversized black wicker chair with her feet propped on the ottoman, a glass of iced tea on the table beside her, reading a book. She looked like a queen in a white linen tunic and scarlet pants. The morning's peace was abruptly rent by a sudden pounding and the high-pitched hum of power tools.

"What in the name of all that's holy is all that noise?" Dora asked, setting her coffee mug on the glass-topped wicker table.

Harper emerged from the garden, holding clippers and a clump of sorry-looking roses in her hand. "Top secret," she said, climbing up the steps to join them on the porch. She smiled under her broad-brimmed straw hat. "Mamaw's having some remodeling done in her bedroom, but she won't divulge the details."

Dora greeted her sister and strolled over to place a kiss on Mamaw's cheek. "Do tell, Mamaw. What you got cooking over there?"

"Can't a woman have a few surprises, even in her own boudoir?" Mamaw said archly.

"No," both girls answered at the same time.

Dora lowered into a wicker chair beside Mamaw and stretched out her long legs with a soft moan. "What time did they get here? I thought the pounding was in my head when I woke up."

"Did you go to Dunleavy's again?" Harper asked. "I noticed you got in rather late last night."

Dora gave Harper a warning glare but it was too late. Mamaw caught that comment and she pounced.

"Were you out with Devlin again?" she asked.

"Mamaw, retract your antennas. Dev and I are just two old friends who are catching up on old time. 'Nuff said."

"Old friends, huh?" Mamaw said in a slow drawl. "Well." She put on her sunglasses. "I have to say, hearing the name Devlin Cassell again is déjà vu." She looked pointedly at Dora's short nightgown. "Though if you were sixteen, I wouldn't allow you to still be lounging in your nightgown at ten o'clock in the morning. Aren't you supposed to be doing your walk now?"

Dora stifled a yawn. "I know, I know. I'll walk later."

"I'm just trying to be supportive."

Harper placed the stems of a clutch of the small yellow roses into her water bottle and carried them to Mamaw. "All I could find, I'm afraid."

"Why, thank you," Mamaw said, setting down her book to accept the flowers. She delicately plucked the browned, curling leaves from the stems. "Poor things, look how stunted they've become. Pitiful, really. My roses used to be so large and fragrant they took my breath away."

"I remember. What happened to the garden?" Harper asked, pouring herself a glass of iced tea from the pitcher and lowering herself into a chair beside them. "There always used to be lots of flowers and butterflies out there. There's not much left out there now but the weeds."

Dora sat up in the chair to peer out at the garden that was located along the border of the porch. It was a small, narrow plot of land between the house and the wild cordgrass that bordered the Cove. She had studied horticulture in college and, though she'd never received her degree, instead choosing to leave college to marry Cal, she'd continued taking master gardener courses. One of the aspects she'd loved most about her home in Summerville was the acreage that surrounded the house itself.

She'd planted an extensive garden the first year that they'd moved in, investing an enormous amount of time and energy into the project. She could still remember how fulfilled she'd felt at the end of an afternoon in the garden, covered with dirt and sweat, grinning like a fool. After Nate came along, however, her focus had shifted to him, and as he grew and his needs became more demanding, the garden slipped into an afterthought.

"It looks like my garden in Summerville," she said with a hint of cynicism. "This climate turns the land into a jungle in no time. Especially out here on the islands. The heat is a furnace blast and the humidity is crushing." She sat back and turned to Harper. "You must feel it when you're running?"

Harper lifted her hair from her neck. "That's why I run early in the morning." She let her hair drop and said pointedly, "So should you."

"Nag, nag, nag," Dora teased. "I swear, just walking leaves me hot, winded, and drenched." She looked again at the remnants of the garden. "Mamaw, I have to say, roses were always an ambitious choice. It doesn't pay to plant anything but indigenous plants on a barrier island."

"I don't care. I love roses. There isn't much soil out here, I grant you. But I try. When I think of the beautiful walled garden at my Charleston house . . ." Mamaw said wistfully. "The camellias and roses . . . Do you remember it, girls? The loveliest dappled light . . . The wall protected the plants from the wind and salt from the sea. I tried to create something similar here, but . . ." She sighed. "The combination of weather and old age got the best of me, I'm afraid. I couldn't keep up and eventually I just lost the heart for it. I do miss my roses, though. Actually, Dora, they did surprisingly well here, despite the odds. Those poor plants are just old and tired, like I am."

Harper patted Mamaw's leg. "Not so old."

"When I'm working in that heat," Mamaw said, "I feel as old as Methuselah."

"You're going to live forever," Dora said. "But I sympathize. I couldn't keep up with my garden, either. It's a labor of love."

"True, true," Mamaw said, and returned to her book.

"I wouldn't know," Harper said wistfully. "In the city we don't even have a patio, much less flower boxes." She looked out over the property. "I always wanted a garden of my own."

"What about your house in the Hamptons?" asked Dora.

"Oh, there are gorgeous gardens there, to be sure. But I only visit there on weekends or for a week's vacation, hardly time to tend a garden. Besides, my mother pays a fortune to a fleet of gardeners and they'd have a conniption if I brought a shovel or spade to *their* flower beds.

"You should see my granny's garden in England. It's a true English garden with masses of flowers and flowering shrubs. Granny cuts them fresh every morning and does arrangements for the house. Quite lovely. She's rather like you in that way, Dora. Passionate about all things gardening. The gardens were designed ages ago but she makes changes here and there and has the final word on all plantings. Still, all the digging and weeding is done for her."

"That makes things easier," Dora said with an edge.

"Exactly," Harper agreed. "Poor Granny broke her leg recently, though; I don't imagine she'll be able to do even that much gardening this summer." She paused and said with a twinge of guilt, "I really should visit."

"Do you go to England often?" Dora asked.

Harper began removing her garden gloves. "Not as often as I should." Then she said in a lower voice, "It's a very big house with very big expectations to fill."

"What does that mean?" Dora asked.

Mamaw set down her book and listened.

"My mother is an only child, and I am her only child. The house in the country is the James family seat and I am the heir. There is," she added diffidently, "no spare. Whenever I visit I feel like I'm living in a glass tower." Harper tugged off the fingers of the glove with short, angry tugs. "Everyone is watching, waiting for me to find the right husband and carry on the James name." She pulled off the glove and stared at it in her lap. "They're quite disappointed that I'm twenty-eight without a prospect in sight."

"Do they expect you to marry and live in England?" Dora pressed on, realizing how little she knew about the pressures her younger sister faced. She had always assumed Harper was living quite the charmed, carefree life of a wealthy urbanite.

"Granny would love it, of course. Whenever I visit she throws elaborate parties to introduce me to all the eligible young bachelors. Not unlike you, Mamaw," Harper gamely added in Mamaw's direction.

Mamaw feigned shock. "I have no ulterior motive. I only want you to feel at home here!"

Harper laughed lightly. "You are the dearest. But you're fooling no one. I'd rather find my husband on my own terms, thank you very much." Her tone grew wistful again. "He's out there somewhere."

"That all sounds very romantic," Dora said. "But tick-tock, sister. You're not going to find him sitting here by your lonesome. You haven't gone out on a date since you've arrived."

"Well, look who's suddenly Miss Lady Out on the Town!" Harper remarked playfully.

"True, true," Dora said with a laugh. "But seriously, you're so young and so pretty."

Harper sat straighter in her chair, lifting her chin. "I'll know him when I meet him," she said. "I've always dreamed when I do, it will be a thunderbolt. I've heard of such things happening, haven't you? You look into a stranger's eyes and boom, you just know."

Dora thought of how she shivered whenever she looked into Devlin's eyes. She spoke as much to herself as to her sister.

"I never thought of you as a romantic," she said with a short laugh. "That's the stuff of fairy tales. What you're referring to is plain lust. Marriage is another thing altogether. Thunderbolts are fun, but a husband has to be a good provider. And in your case, your man has to have a long and illustrious pedigree."

Mamaw turned in her chair to look askance at Dora. "When you talk like that you sound like your mother," she said drily.

Dora paled and brought her hand to her mouth. "I do, don't I?" She turned to Harper. "Oh, hell, don't listen to me. What do I know? Look at the mess I've made of my life."

"You're doing just fine," Harper said. "Let's forget about me," she said, deflecting the attention from herself back to Dora. "I'm glad to see *you* going out for a change."

"As should you," Dora replied, tossing the spotlight back to Harper. "You're becoming an introvert," Dora argued, "only talking to people on the Internet. That's not good."

"But it *is* good," Harper said insistently. "For me. My whole life, even as a girl, I was on a treadmill, always pushing toward some goal." She paused, then said evenly, "Mother was very good at setting goals."

Dora snorted in an unladylike manner. "I get that."

Mamaw set her book down again and looked at Dora.

"Dora, *you* might need people now," said Harper. "But I need solitude."

"Solitude is different from isolation. I isolated myself in Summerville even though there were lots of people around me, and let me tell you, I was lonely. I can understand seeking moments of peace, but be careful that you are not hiding out."

"I know the difference," Harper said defensively. "It's hard to explain. I didn't realize it when I first arrived here in May. I thought I'd come in for Mamaw's weekend party, then be on my way. Of course"—she looked sheepishly at Mamaw, catching her eyes and smiling—"it didn't turn out that way. Since I've been here, though, it's like my whole body has slowed down. I'm paying attention to the minutiae that suddenly loom so large. And I like it. I'm off the treadmill. I don't have set goals, I don't feel I have to live up to someone else's expectations. I can just *be*."

"That's the magic of being at Sea Breeze," Dora said. "But it's not real."

"Isn't it?" Harper asked rhetorically.

"No. You're on vacation," Dora persisted.

Harper let her gaze sweep the vast wetlands that stretched across the vista. "Mamaw, you never made me feel like I had to measure up to some standard here. Quite the opposite. As far as you were concerned, I was family and all that was required of me was my occasional presence." She glanced at Mamaw with a wry grin. "That and good manners."

Mamaw made a face.

Harper stared down at her sweet tea and stirred the ice with her finger. "It sounds escapist, I realize that," she said. "But when I come here to Sea Breeze . . . I don't know how to explain it." She looked back out at the Cove. "I feel so far away from that other world. It's truly different here. Time is inconsequential. My internal clock is set by the sun and the moon and the tides. I feel unfettered. And, if I stay long enough, in the stillness I sense something's opening up inside. Something important."

A short silence fell as Harper continued staring out at the vista.

Harper looked back at the two women and shook her head, seemingly embarrassed for the confession. "I'm sure that all sounds very New Age or whatever. I'm okay, really I am," she said evasively.

There followed another momentary silence. Dora looked at Mamaw to see her studying Harper.

"Girls," Mamaw said, her eyes gleaming. "I've just had the best idea."

Eager for a change of subject, Harper brightened. "I'm all ears."

Mamaw set her book aside and leaned forward, closer to the girls. "Dora, you love gardening and know a lot about it. Harper, you want to learn how to garden. Why don't the two of you take this poor pitiful garden on as a project? It's something to work on together. I'll supply the plants. I'll even pull out my garden gloves and help you. What do you say?"

"Mamaw," Harper said with enthusiasm. "That's a splendid idea!"

"I don't know," Dora said, dragging her heels on the idea. She already had so much on her plate. "Do you have any idea how much work is involved? And how hot it is out there?"

"But, Dora," Mamaw said, a bit put out. "You love gardening. It doesn't have to be a massive project, like your garden in Summerville. It won't take that much time if you keep it small. Besides, isn't gardening supposed to be good for the soul?"

Dora cast a dubious glance at her grandmother. She stood and looked out over the garden, her finger tapping against her lips as she considered the possibilities. It might be good for her to get her hands back in the soil again, she thought. To create something. She needed creativity in her life—what woman didn't? It occurred to her that she'd let that important part of her life go.

"We'd have to come up with a plan, first," Dora said.

Harper opened her laptop with alacrity. "Right."

"It's already midsummer, so we'll only want plants that can withstand the lowcountry summer heat. I don't know what the garden centers have left in stock. Offhand, sweetgrass would be nice, and they don't flower till October, a profusion of pink fluffy heaven. It will look showy when you put the house on the market, Mamaw. Then there are hardy plants like gaillardia, lantana, verbena . . ."

"Slow down," Harper said. "I'm typing them up."

"And roses," Mamaw added, getting swept up in the idea. "We must have a few roses."

"Roses too," Dora said with a dramatic sigh. "If that's what you want. There are knockout roses now that can handle the heat. We'll plant them just for you. Harper, when you research plants, remember to keep in mind zones. This is Sullivan's Island, not the Hamptons."

Harper snorted. "That much I figured out."

Mamaw clapped her hands. "Oh, girls, this is a wonderful idea!"

The pounding ceased and a sudden peace descended.

"I'm heading inside in search of breakfast," Dora said. "Or is it lunchtime? Whatever, my diet is all pretty much the same these days—vegetables and fruit. By the way, where is Lucille? I haven't seen her pattering about in the kitchen."

"She has a doctor's appointment. She'll be back soon," Mamaw answered, picking up her book again.

Dora's brow furrowed with concern. "Nothing serious, I hope."

"Darlin'," Mamaw said, "at our age, we go in for regular maintenance."

Dora walked off to the kitchen. Before she left the porch, she looked back to see Harper bent over her laptop, her fingers tapping away. Harper was always typing. What was going on in that clever mind of hers? She'd discovered this morning how little she really knew about her. Digging around a bit might indeed be a good idea.

Florida

It was a hot and steamy July morning that made even a low-country girl sweat. The air-conditioning in the cottage rumbled noisily but did a poor job cooling the space. Carson's alarm went off at seven. She'd blearily opened her eyes as the sunlight pierced through the drawn curtains, but Nate was already awake, playing his video game. She figured it gave him a measure of comfort in the strange place and she let him play until it was time to dress.

They spoke little as they fumbled through the morning routine. The dreaded shower was not mentioned and Nate dressed himself in his usual soft-fabric, elastic-waist clothing. Breakfast was touch and go in the hotel's dining room. Nate scrutinized every option, laboriously deciding a blended fruit yogurt and a piece of white toast was acceptable. He was amused by the packaging of the tiny boxes of cereal and took one, though he ate little of the cereal. For Carson, coffee was enough and she drank it like a camel, storing caffeine in her body for whatever surprises the day held.

It was a short drive to the Dolphin Research Center, barely long enough for the air-conditioning to cool the car. Yet Nate was already anxious when they pulled into the parking lot beside the giant sculpture of a dolphin and a calf. Nate danced on the balls of his feet, tugging at her skirt to hurry her as she locked the car. They walked at a clip through the front entrance and the gift shop, past souvenirs and T-shirts that held no interest for Nate. He tapped his fingers by his mouth as she registered at the desk and received their passes. As soon as she opened the door to the park, Nate shot out and began running.

"Nate! Wait!" she called out, and took off after him on the winding walkway past cages of exotic birds calling hello, a water park, and a few quaint cottages. She turned the corner to see Nate standing frozen, arms out stiffly in an arrested posture. Before him a large lagoon spread out along the glistening Gulf of Mexico.

"Why did you run off?" she asked, catching up to his side.

Nate didn't respond. He remained motionless, staring in disbelief and wonder at the lagoon. Only his fingers moved, and they trembled.

"Are you okay?" she asked, suddenly concerned that he was on the verge of a meltdown.

Then she heard the high-pitched whistle. To her ears it was a concerto of welcome that she translated in her heart. In the front of the lagoon she saw five dolphins clustered along the walkway, watching the passersby and waiting. Returning her gaze to Nate, she understood immediately why he'd balked.

"Do you see all the dolphins, Nate? Isn't it wonderful?"

"I can't go near them."

"Yes, of course you can. That's why we're here."

"No. Blake said we are not supposed to go near the dolphins."

"Blake was talking about the wild dolphins. The dolphins in the Cove. These dolphins live in this lagoon. It's their home. It's okay to visit them, Nate."

"I . . . I don't want to hurt them," he said in a trembling voice.

Her heart nearly broke at hearing this. She'd known that he was deeply disturbed by Delphine's accident at the dock. But she'd never understood how much blame he'd assumed for his part in it. She could hear in his voice that he'd taken on *all* the blame, and that was far too big a burden for these young shoulders to bear.

She knelt next to him and spoke gently. "Nate, what happened to Delphine was an accident. It was my fault for bringing her to the dock in the first place. But she's doing better. She's going to be okay. You'll see for yourself when I take you to see her. These dolphins are healthy. They're used to people visiting them. Here, it's okay for us to swim with them. We can get close to them. That's why I brought you here. So you can understand the difference between dolphins that live in a facility like this one and dolphins in the wild. Okay?"

He brought his fingers to his mouth.

"Listen! They're whistling for you. They want you to come over. Let's get closer, okay?"

She led the way to the covered walkway that lined the front lagoon. It was a beautiful, natural setting with seawater and fish flowing in and out. Nate inched closer to the rope fence that bordered the lagoon. He peered over the edge, poised for flight. Just a month earlier, Nate had run down the dock at Sea Breeze and leaped into the Cove. He'd been fearless with Delphine. Now Carson watched his cautious, even timid posture and felt the weight of her responsibility in helping this boy through his sense of loss.

A long, sleek dolphin swam right beneath Nate, tilted to look up at him, then began making clicking sounds. Carson was relieved when she saw Nate smile.

"Mrs. Tupper?"

Carson turned toward the voice. A slender woman with flowing brown hair in nylon fishing pants and a pale blue dolphin T-shirt approached, carrying a clipboard. She smiled as she drew near, and her beautiful, warm eyes captured Carson's attention, making her feel welcome.

"I'm Carson Muir. Nate Tupper's aunt. I'm here with him for the program."

"Nice to meet you. I'm Joan, the director of the program. I'll be working with Nate this week."

"Thank you for squeezing us in on short notice."

"Happy to do it. I understand we have a little boy who's had a bad experience with a dolphin." Her gaze searched out Nate. When she found him leaning over the rope fence making clicking noises back to the dolphin, a grin spread across her face. "I'm pretty sure the dolphins are going to take good care of him."

~~~

"Small steps," Carson told herself, repeating the advice that Dora had given her on the telephone the night before.

The first session with Joan at the Dolphin Research Center was going better than Carson had hoped. They began in the small classroom, where creative activities with a dolphin-based theme introduced the goals set by Dora and Joan. Dora had spoken with Joan by telephone prior to Carson and Nate's arrival, and had communicated that she wanted Nate to work on overcoming his guilt over the accident, but also to help him with his interpersonal skills. Joan had formed "Team Nate," telling Carson that they'd work together to make sure Nate met his goals.

When she handed Nate his schedule, he clasped it firmly and immediately bent over the table to study it thoroughly. Carson could almost hear his sigh of relief at the sight of the schedule, a simple piece of paper that promised him order throughout his day and removed the threat of the unknown.

For most of the classroom session Carson sat along the wall as an observer. From this vantage point, a fly on the wall, she was fascinated to watch Joan slowly, firmly, steadily build on skills that allowed Nate to grow comfortable. She spoke with a warm lilt in her voice that eventually broke through Nate's reserve. Carson was proud when Nate revealed how bright he was, and how knowledgeable about dolphins. From time to time Joan would turn her head to meet Carson's gaze, brows raised in surprise that Nate knew the answer to a question.

When the classroom session ended, it was time to begin working with the dolphins. Carson could feel the excitement as Team Nate walked to the front lagoon. He was nervous, but Joan and Rebecca, the dolphin trainer, kept their voices upbeat and cheery, distracting him with questions as they outfitted him in a life preserver.

When they took Nate to the lower dock, Carson went in search of a place in the shade to sit and observe.

She spied a long, wooden bench set against the wall of the

trainer's building. It sat in the deep shade of a long thatched roof. One man sat there, staring out over the lagoon. He might have been a bodybuilder, his muscles bulging from his black T-shirt. But the rigid posture, the chiseled cut of his chin, the shorn hair, the black sunglasses, and the way he crossed his arms across his chest made her wonder whether he was in the military. He gave off a strong vibe that said *Stay away*. There was no place else to sit, however, and Carson didn't scare easily, so she walked to the bench and took a seat on the opposite side.

He glanced her way when she sat down and nodded politely in acknowledgment.

"Hi, there," Carson responded. Then, because she was curious, she asked, "Are you here to swim with the dolphins?"

His lips turned upward in mild amusement. He had a beautiful mouth, she thought, and a strong, straight nose that made her think of Michelangelo's *David*. As a professional photographer of movie stars and models, she had a habit of noticing and filing away physical details. He was, in fact, stunning in a masculine way. If she were working, she might have handed him her card for an audition.

"You could say so," he said.

Carson wasn't sure what that was supposed to mean. Yes or no, she thought, mildly annoyed. Nor did he offer a rejoinder to keep the conversation going. Curious, and stubborn, Carson refused to let his coolness deter her.

"I'm here with my nephew. That's him with the dolphin," she added, pointing to the dock in the lagoon right in front of them. Another group was at the dock at the far right of the lagoon. They appeared to be a family, parents with two young children around eight years of age. "Is that your family?"

He glanced at the family, then shook his head with a chuckle. "No."

Talking to this man was like talking to Nate, she thought. Except this man wasn't family or nine years old, and she certainly didn't have to deal with *his* rudeness. She gave up and pulled out her camera and lens and instead focused on Nate, who was sitting on the dock with his legs in the water. A sleek gray dolphin waited only a few feet in front of him. Carson moved closer, watching through her lens as Nate tentatively put out his hand and gave a signal to the dolphin. In a flash, the dolphin rose high up in the water and toggled back on his tail in an impressive show of strength and agility. Rebecca blew her whistle and Team Nate released a hearty cheer for the dolphin and Nate. In the close-up view of the lens, Carson saw the boy's eyes light up and a huge grin ease across his face. Carson snapped a quick shot to capture the moment, then put her hands to her mouth and fired off a whistle.

She was still smiling when she returned to the bench.

"Nice whistle," the man said, his lips twitching in a grin.

She glanced at him and, feeling happy about Nate, said with a cocky air, "Thanks."

After a pause, he spoke again. "Is this his first time with a dolphin?"

Surprised the man was initiating a conversation, Carson half turned to face him. His gaze was on the water, but she sensed that behind those sunglasses he was watching her every move.

"No. He's spent a lot of time with a wild dolphin by our house in South Carolina."

He turned his head, suddenly interested. "You're from South Carolina?"

"I was born there. But I spent most of my life in California."

"Whereabouts?"

"LA."

"No, I mean where are you from in South Carolina?"

"I was born on Sullivan's Island. But I lived in Charleston as a girl. On East Bay," she said, dropping the name of the tony street in town. "We spent summers at my grandmother's house on Sullivan's. That's where I'm living now."

"Sullivan's Island is a pretty spot," he replied, unfolding his arms to stretch one over the top of the bench. It seemed their mutual South Carolina connection had somewhat loosened the tense guard he kept around himself. "We used to go there sometimes, to the beach. My family lives not far from there. In McClellanville."

"Oh, sure, I know McClellanville. A real pretty spot right on the water. Where the shrimp boats are, right?"

"What's left of them." He leaned back and crossed his leg over his knee. "My dad was a shrimper. He had to get out of the business, though. Like most of the boats."

"Is that where you're living now?"

"No, I live hereabouts. But I'm thinking of heading back home. When I'm ready."

Carson wondered about that comment but didn't want to pry. She didn't get the sense this was a man who gave out personal information readily. "So, we're neighbors," Carson said, glad for the icebreaker.

"Almost," he added drily.

"We're just down here for the week," she said. "Nate, that's my nephew, came down for the Pathways program."

"He's working with Joan?"

Carson tilted her head, curious that he knew Joan. "That's right."

Again, he only nodded, not divulging any more information. There followed another long silence during which they watched Nate giving more commands to the dolphins, to the loud cheers of the team. Carson whistled and clapped in support of Team Nate. After a final rousing cheer, the team climbed to their feet and began gathering supplies. The session had ended.

Carson rose to her feet as well and stooped to gather her camera equipment and pull out a towel from the huge canvas bag. She turned again to the man on the bench.

"It was nice talking with you. I'm Carson." She reached out her hand.

He took it readily and returned a firm shake. "I'm Taylor. Nice to meet you, too. He seems like a good kid," he added, motioning toward Nate.

The compliment filled her with pride. "He is."

Chapter Ten

≈ ≈

The following morning's wake-up call was sharp raps on the door and the rallying call "Rise and shine!"

Dora threw her pillow at the door. "Go away, Harper!"

"Delivery!"

Despite herself, Dora smiled. Harper had moved into Carson's room while Carson was away, but despite the fact they weren't roommates, she was making a concerted effort to get closer this week. Dora was moved, even flattered, by her little sister's persistence. Feeling a boost of energy, she kicked off her cotton blanket and walked across the room to open the door.

"What are you . . ."

Harper wasn't there. On the floor in front of the door lay a shoe box and a shopping bag. Dora picked up the parcels and carried them back to the bed. She sat on the bed beside the loot, feeling a bit like it was Christmas in July. Inside the shoe box she found a new pair of walking shoes, the fancy brand that Harper wore. Dora ran her fingers across the white shoe with the pink trim to check the size—perfect. Excited now, she dug into the bag and gasped as she pulled out a pair of white stretchy running shorts, a running bra, and a pink-patterned tech running shirt. She checked the tags and her mouth slipped open at the prices. These were from the upscale company from which Harper purchased her athletic clothing. And . . . Harper had selected them in Dora's favorite pink color.

Dora held up the shirt, then set it back on the bed. Looking at the clothes, she felt a little embarrassed. Did she look that bad in her old T-shirt and shorts? Lord, Devlin saw her in them. Maybe she didn't want to look all fashionable when she exercised, she thought mulishly.

Looking at the clothes, Dora knew that wasn't true. She'd just never been involved in an exercise program before and didn't know what to pick out. She'd always been a tad jealous when she saw women jogging by in their athletic gear.

Stapled to the bag was a handwritten note: *Meet me out front at 7 sharp!*

Dora glanced at her alarm clock. It was ten before seven. Feeling a surge of adrenaline, Dora peeled away her pajamas and slipped into the new running clothes. She sighed with relief when everything fit. Before she left she quickly checked her reflection in the mirror. The woman in the reflection didn't look the least bit dowdy in old gym shorts and her husband's baggy T-shirt. Dora felt buoyed by the sporty look and hurried out of the room with a spring in her step.

Harper was waiting for her with a bottle of water.

"Look at you!" she exclaimed as Dora trotted near.

Dora ran straight to Harper and delivered a big hug. "Thank you, thank you! I love them. But it's too much. My Lord, I could buy an evening gown for what these cost."

"You're exaggerating. It's nothing," Harper said, waving away the comment. "I have a back debt of birthday presents, so consider this an installment. I enjoyed picking them out."

"I don't know what to say."

"Don't say anything. Save your energy. We're losing daylight. I'm going to teach you a few stretching exercises that you need to do every morning before you head out. You don't want to get any injuries. Okay, ready?"

As much as she enjoyed the stretching, Dora enjoyed doing them with Harper more. Harper took Dora through the routine. Then, with a wave and a wish of luck, Harper took off. Dora watched her trot away, her ponytail bouncing perkily from left to right, and sighed, guessing Harper would probably run some five miles.

Undaunted, Dora took off on her own path.

Florida

Carson was surprised to see Taylor standing by the front lagoon again this morning. He turned his head and half smiled as she strolled up.

"You stalking me or something?" he said with a grin.

"Oh, yeah, that's what I'm doing." Carson settled the gear she carried for Nate on the bench under the thatched roof and took a seat. She looked out over the lagoon. A young woman in a bright blue rash guard and swimsuit sat on the dock in front of two young dolphins. Beside her was a blue cooler filled with fish that the dolphins kept their eyes on. Taylor and Carson watched the trainer put a pair of dolphins through their paces. The morning was punctuated with short blasts from her whistle and her high voice of praise for the dolphins. An older couple and two young children, probably grandchildren, lined up along the lagoon to watch. The little girl was enthralled, clapping her hands whenever the dolphin performed its task.

"Where's Nate?" Taylor asked.

Carson was impressed that he'd remembered her nephew's name. "He's with Joan in the classroom. I'm supposed to butt out for a while so they can work in private. I worried that Nate would have a meltdown when she asked me to leave, but nope. Not a whimper. I've been relegated to pack mule."

"Joan's like that. Everyone falls under her spell. You mentioned he's in the Pathways program—Nate has special needs?"

Carson widened her eyes a bit. Clearly someone was feeling chattier today. "Nate has Asperger's, which is a high-functioning autism. He's very smart," she hurried to add, "but he's become withdrawn lately and we're hoping this program will help him open up more."

"It will," Taylor replied.

She shot him a quick glance, wondering about his certainty. "I hope so. But my biggest worry now is just getting Nate into a routine. He's not very flexible. We narrowly avoided a serious meltdown when we arrived, but I slaved over making a new routine for him." She laughed lightly. "I feel like Suzy Homemaker. I've got pictures posted all over our room and I put a schedule on the fridge—complete with shiny stickers for effort. It's written in stone what time we get up, when we eat, our toiletry habits, and what time we go to bed."

"Sounds good to a Marine."

She skipped a beat. "You're a Marine?"

"Yes, ma'am."

She'd been right that he had the fitness and short haircut of a military man. "I thought you might be a soldier."

"Not a soldier," he corrected. "A Marine. A soldier is army."

"Oh. Sorry." Carson hadn't known the distinction.

"Just different," he explained. "But most military men live on a strict schedule."

"I've never been much of one for schedules. I'm not lazy," she quickly added, seeing his expression grow dubious. "I'm very disciplined. I surf and I'm out on the ocean at dawn most mornings. But living by a clock? Not so much. I have more of the free-spirit mentality. Making a schedule was a new experience, let me tell you."

"You don't have kids?"

"God, no. Far from it. I'm not even married. What about you?"

"Nope. Not married. No kids. Just a dog."

"Girlfriend?"

He tried to hide his grin. "Nope."

She noticed he didn't ask whether she had a boyfriend. His diffidence was intriguing.

"What brings you back here today?" she asked, getting to the question in the forefront of her mind. "Yesterday I figured you were a tourist. But today you're back and you know Joan."

He looked out at the lagoon. "I'm back most days."

Curious, she thought. Getting the man to talk was like pulling teeth, but she could be stubborn, too, so she waited him out. She didn't want to press him. His reticence led her to believe he wouldn't appreciate it.

"I'm doing a program with Joan myself," Taylor volunteered at length.

Surprised that he'd answered her question, Carson turned her head to look at him. He was still watching the group in the water.

As if sensing her curiosity, Taylor stretched and started gathering his things.

"Got to go. My session starts soon."

"Where is your session?"

"The other side of the park, where the boys hang out. They call it the bachelor pods."

"Cute." Carson smirked.

Taylor rose and slung his USMC backpack across his shoulder. "See you."

They said a brief good-bye and she watched him walk off along the path to a different section of the park. She wondered if she'd see him again. She hoped she would. In his long cargo shorts, gray T-shirt, and sandals, he looked like any other tourist clustering the lagoon. There wasn't any limp or physical signal of an injury. And there was no mistaking the power in his muscles as he made his way along the path. Now more aware of his background, she readily picked up how he turned his head from right to left, scoping out the crowd.

Sullivan's Island

Dora got into her running clothes and tiptoed through the quiet, dimly lit house, careful not to wake anyone. She was delighted that she'd awakened before Harper for her morning walk. She moved swiftly down the streets, while above in the trees birds chirped out their dawn song. Soon her feet hit the soft sand of the beach path and then, at last, the great expanse of the beach and sea. She stood on the precipice of the dune, smelled the sea air, felt its breath on her face and her chest expand at the sight of a new day's sun rising. The sky was a glory of pastels that shimmered in reflection on the calm sea.

This early in the morning, the sand was untrammeled. Bits of mica glistened in the lavender light. Dora stopped to take off her new walking shoes, preferring to go barefoot during this stretch. The hard-packed sand was moist under her feet as she walked briskly near the shoreline. It was breakfast time for the shorebirds. Peeps ran on straight legs, playing tag with the waves, gulls cruised low, and higher in the sky, pelicans flew in formation.

Early mornings were an introspective time on the beach. A young couple jogged past her. In the distance, a man played with his chocolate Lab, throwing a ball into the water and watching the big dog jubilantly leap after it into the sea. Dora wasn't jogging yet, but in only a few days, her pace had quickened and there was a snap and precision to her walk. She wasn't as winded, either. As she walked, she kept pace by thinking of new words to describe herself: *alive, empowered, strong.* Just thinking the words made her feel better.

And reminded her that, like Harper, she felt a stirring of rebirth. Maybe even a resurgence of the bold young girl she once was, who she believed was still hiding within her.

She saw in her mind's eye the photographs of Nate that Carson had e-mailed the day before. To see her little boy laughing and playing again was more than she'd hoped for. She wished

Cal could see this more outgoing, playful side of his son. Maybe he'd appreciate Nate's uniqueness more. Mamaw and Lucille had huddled over the photos, arguing over whose idea it had been to suggest the trip.

Dora knew it had been a group effort—Harper and Carson's brainstorm, and Mamaw's generous funding—but in Dora's mind, it was Carson who deserved the credit, for going solo with Nate like the fearless trouper she was, despite her complete lack of experience with children. She and Carson had talked several times in the past few days. At first they discussed Nate's progress, but later their conversation shifted to whatever came into their minds. Not since they were young girls had they spent nights just chatting like this.

She was passing the black-and-white Sullivan's Island lighthouse when she spied a small group of women clustered together atop a dune by the bright orange sea turtle nest sign. Curious, she veered on an angle across the softer sand to the dune. Three of the five women wore matching blue Turtle Team T-shirts. The other two stood by, eagerly watching one of the women kneel beside the sea turtle nest.

Dora walked up to the woman carrying a clipboard, a good sign she was in charge. This woman was tall, like Dora, slender, with glossy, dark brown hair under her cap.

"What's going on?" Dora asked, drawing closer.

"We're doing an inventory of the nest," she replied, bending to her backpack. She pulled out plastic gloves and, straightening, handed the gloves to one of the team volunteers. Then she turned to Dora. "Three days after a nest hatches, we open it up to count the hatched and unhatched eggs. The Department of Natural Resources monitors the success rate of the nests along our coast. Sometimes we find a few hatchlings stuck in there and we release them." She smiled. "That's the fun part."

Something about her was familiar and Dora tried to place it. The woman wore sunglasses, so it was hard to be sure.

"Do I know you?" Dora asked. She hated to ask that question, since most of the time the answer was no.

The woman took off her sunglasses, revealing a striking face with dark brown eyes under arched brows. She was friendly but had the manner of someone accustomed to being in charge. She squinted and slowly shook her head. "Maybe. You look familiar to me, too."

"I'm Dora Tupper. I used to be Dora Muir," she added, using her local family name. "Marietta Muir's granddaughter?"

The dark eyes widened with the woman's smile. "*Little Dorrit?* Oh my word, of course I know you! I see it now. It's me, Cara! I used to babysit you, a long, long time ago."

Dora's mind shot back in time to the early summers she'd spent with Mamaw, back when she was seven and Carson was four. She hadn't been called Little Dorrit since she was a little girl.

"Cara Rutledge! Is it really you? I can't believe it." She stuck out her arm toward the nest. "But of course it's you. You're a Rutledge. You're taking care of turtles."

Cara rolled her eyes. "Yes, my mother roped me in, kicking and screaming all the way. Only it's Cara Beauchamps now."

"How is your mother? I'm surprised she's not here with the turtles, holding court. Even after all these years I never see one of those orange nest signs without thinking of Miss Lovie."

"Mama passed."

"Oh, Cara, I'm so sorry. I hadn't heard. Your mother was an

amazing woman. The pied piper of these islands. We all loved her; do you remember how we used to follow her around the island as she tended turtles?" Dora laughed gently at the memory. "I remember a couple of times you took us to your beach house on Isle of Palms. Miss Lovie used to give us sugar cookies and sweet tea."

Cara added, "I was trying to get my mother to help babysit."

"Do you still have your beach house on Isle of Palms?"

"Of course. I'll never sell it. My mother adored that house. A part of her spirit lives on there. How's your sister? She was such a cutie." Cara shook her head. "I can't remember her name. It's been so long."

"Carson."

"That's right. You two were such a pair. You with your white-blond hair and she with her dark hair. Wasn't there a third sister as well?"

"That's Harper, but I don't think you babysat her much. By the time she started staying for the summers I was old enough to babysit. Mamaw's not above going after free labor."

Cara laughed at that. "I haven't seen your grandmother in ages. Is she well?"

"Alive and kicking. She's going to live forever, I pray."

A squeal of excitement interrupted the two women's reminiscing. Cara swung around and Dora, following her gaze, saw the volunteer who had been digging holding a small loggerhead hatchling in her hand. More people had gathered while she was talking to Cara and now they were crowding closer to the nest for a better look.

"I'll catch up with you later," Cara told her. "I have to get to work."

Cara grabbed a red plastic bucket and brought it to her teammate, who placed the hatchling inside. Dora moved closer to watch in fascination as the two women who were opening the nest brought out dozens of broken eggshells, a few whole, discolored eggs, and, to the thrill of the onlookers, three more hatchlings from the nest.

Cara moved with the same efficiency and grace that Dora remembered in Miss Lovie, and she felt a pleasure in knowing there was a continuity between mother and daughter. She'd always wanted a daughter, someone with whom she could share traditions, go shopping, cook and bake, just be a girl. Then she thought again how this prayer had been answered. She might not have a daughter, but this late in her life she'd rediscovered her sisters.

Dora followed Cara, who was carrying the red bucket closer to the sea. Cara asked the group clustered at the shoreline to form two lines at either side of a wide opening that would allow the hatchlings ample room to find their way into the ocean. Dora took a place close to the water's edge, excitement thrumming in her veins that at last she would witness this. She had come to these islands in the summer for most of her life and yet had never seen a sea turtle hatchling.

Cara put the edge of the red bucket to the sand and gently tilted it. The four dark hatchlings scrambled out, flippers madly pushing as they began their trek across the sand. One of the hatchlings had a slight dent in its shell and was having a hard time of it. She doubted that poor fellow was going to make it far with all the hungry fish in the ocean. The other three were vigorous, racing to the surf.

Cara returned to stand beside her, watching the hatchlings.

Dora said, "I can't believe I've never seen this before."

"I can't either. It happens every year," she said with a smirk.

"How long have you been on the team?"

"Oh, I guess around five years now. I started out helping Mama when she got sick, and then I got hooked. I didn't know my interest in sea turtles would become a lifelong passion."

Passion. There was that word again, Dora thought. The thing that Harper was hoping to find. The thing Winifred told her wasn't worth losing Cal over.

She followed the hatchlings close to the water's edge.

"Keep your eyes on the hatchlings," Cara told her. "When they reach the water, instinct kicks in and they dive. I never get tired of watching that immediate transition from scrambling hatchling to beautiful swimmer. Instinct is powerful."

Dora silently urged the hatchlings on as they swam with all their might through the water; then an oncoming wave swept them up and sent them tumbling back to the beach like pebbles.

"Don't move!" Cara called out to the onlookers. "There are turtles by your feet. Just stand still and let them crawl back."

"That's so sad," Dora said mournfully. "They work so hard to get to the ocean, then they get tossed back. Can't you help them? Pick them up and carry them to the water?"

Cara shook her head vigorously. "No, they need to make it on their own. Nature is an amazing teacher. We've learned that though it looks like the waves are hard on them, in fact the waves help orient the turtles in the right direction. They'll swim for twenty-four to thirty-six hours to reach the Gulf Stream, where there are vast floats of sargassum weed. They act as nurseries for the hatchlings for the next ten years or so."

She paused. "Still, it's estimated that only one in a thousand hatchlings survives to maturity. That's why we're here. Every hatchling counts. And though the number of nests along our coasts is still way down from back in the days my mama was tending turtles"—she paused to grin—"we're trending upward again."

"You sound like your mama."

Cara smiled. "I'll take that as the highest compliment."

Dora looked out as another wave tossed two of the three hatchlings back to the shore. And once again, the hatchlings righted themselves and took off in their comical scramble for the sea. She followed one hatchling to the shoreline, feeling an attachment to this small turtle that she'd never seen before and would never see again. Was it her maternal instinct? This desire to nurture a young life? Like Cara said, instinct was powerful.

This time when the dive instinct kicked in, the hatchling dove deep and made it past the breakers. Dora felt her spirits soar as she stood ankle deep in the warm water, cheering on the hatchling until it dove again, disappearing. She continued watching the smooth surface of the water past the breakers.

There they were! Her breath hitched when she spotted two tiny heads emerge as the hatchlings took a breath.

She stood for a while longer just watching the waves roll in, picturing in her mind the turtles' epic scramble home to the sea. Perhaps for her, too, getting tumbled and tossed around a bit had been a good thing, she thought to herself. With luck, eventually she'd right herself and start heading in the proper direction. She had to trust her instincts.

After all, she thought with a laugh, her odds had to be better than one in one thousand.

On her way back to Sea Breeze, Devlin's truck pulled up along-side her and he fired off a wolf's whistle.

Dora loved it, but she feigned annoyance. "Devlin Cassell, you're embarrassing me."

"Nice outfit," he called out.

Dora blushed, thinking again how Devlin had seen her in her ratty gym shorts and T-shirt. She sauntered toward the truck and leaned against the open window. "Feels a lot cooler in here."

"Hop in."

"Can't. Want to finish my walk."

"Aw, come on. There's something I want to show you. It'll only take a minute. Hop in."

Dora narrowed her eyes with speculation, but curiosity won her over and she trotted around the front of the truck to the passenger side and jumped in. Devlin floored it and the tires spit gravel as he took off toward Breach Inlet.

"You sure look cute walking out there," he told her.

She deflected the compliment. "What do you want me to see?"

"Hold your horses. We're almost there." He pulled into the parking lot at Breach Inlet and swung open his door. "Come on. Hurry."

Together they jogged along the path to the bridge that spanned the turbulent water between Sullivan's Island and Isle of Palms. On the western side of the bridge lay Hamlin Creek, the wetlands, and the Intracoastal Waterway. On the eastern side, the water emptied out into the Atlantic Ocean. It was stunning to see how calm the water was on the western side, and how choppy and turbulent on the east. Devlin led her to the middle of the bridge, then they crossed the road to where they could overlook the creek. She stood beside him as cars passed from one island to the other. Suddenly he pointed.

"There! Look straight out, smack dab in the middle. See the dolphins?"

Dora raised her hand over her eyes and squinted. Then she saw them. One larger dolphin arcing in the water, then—she squealed with delight—she spotted the smaller dorsal fin of its baby.

"I see them. A mother and baby! They're beautiful."

Devlin was watching her, smiling at her reaction. "The mothers like to bring their young here to feed. See how turbulent that water is? There's lots of fish in there and it's easy hunting. I've heard tell mothers give birth to their young here, too, but I've never seen it."

He peered out at the water. The sunlight glistened against the murky brown depths of the rough water. "Right beneath us! See?" he called out, pointing excitedly. "There's another pair."

Immediately beneath them on the bridge Dora spotted another mother dolphin arcing in the water, and immediately after, her young calf. She clutched Devlin's arm and in response, he slipped an arm around her waist.

Dora watched the smooth symmetry of mother and child skimming in tandem across the water. The young calf was riding safe and secure in its mother's slipstream. Her thoughts naturally turned to her own child and she felt a sudden loneliness for him. He'd love to see this and she wished he were here with her. She wanted to share special moments of happiness with her son, like this, rather than always be the disciplinarian.

They stood side by side watching the dolphins, feeling the

warmth of the sun on their backs until the dolphins swam off into the creek. She looked down to see his hand at her waist, then up to his face as he stared out at the water with an expression of a deep appreciation and even peace. She thought to herself, *I like spending time with Devlin.* He was easy to be with and deceptively intelligent. He played the role of a good ol' boy, but he was very smart. Few people knew the lowcountry as intimately as he did. He loved the sea, the land, the culture, the history—all of it. These islands were his home. She found that very attractive.

Devlin turned his head and caught her looking at him. His eyes kindled. "Thought you'd like to see that."

She was touched that he'd thought of what she'd like to see. Dora couldn't remember Cal thinking of her in that way. She smiled and hoped it conveyed all she'd been feeling. "I surely did."

"Best get you back. I've got to get to work sometime today."

Dora reluctantly turned away from the view and followed Devlin back to the truck. "It's been quite a morning," she told him. "First turtles, now dolphins."

"That's just a normal morning in the lowcountry," he said in a magnanimous tone as he opened her door. "You just have to get out and look."

"You're right," she admitted. How many people were like her? she wondered. Living in this paradise and not exploring its wonders. She slid in the front seat and waited for him to hop in beside her. "I've stayed indoors for too long."

Devlin put the key in the ignition, then paused to turn and face her. "Girl, you know what you need?"

Her lips twitched. "Nope."

"I think you need someone to reintroduce you to your own backyard."

She tilted her head, amused by his suggestion. "You think?"

"I do." He fired the engine.

"You wouldn't happen to have someone in mind for the job?"

He shifted into first, then cast her a sly grin that kicked her heart into gear.

"I just might."

"Uh-huh," she said in a teasing tone, then laughed as the truck pulled out of the parking space.

He drove a few blocks through the dappled shade of Middle Street. "How about I start by taking you boating?" he asked at length. "We used to love to cruise these waters, remember?"

Dora looked out the window and recalled countless summer days going out on Devlin's boat when they were young, roaring up the creeks, putting down anchor near some hammock, making out while the boat rocked gently in the waves.

"Yes," she replied dreamily. "I remember."

The truck stopped at the sign. "We'll do it again," he said, swinging his head around. The sparkle in his blue eyes was contagious. "We'll putter along the coastline, have a few drinks, then I'll take you to dinner."

Dora moved her sunglasses down her nose so she could look at him eye to eye. "That sounds rather like a date."

"Well, I hope so!" he blurted. "It was meant to. Took me damn near three days to work up the nerve. So what's your answer? Yea or nay?"

Dora slipped her sunglasses up her nose. "Yea."

Chapter Eleven

～～～

*H*arper couldn't wait to get back into the garden. She'd already ordered four books on the subject of gardening in the South, plants for hot-weather climates, and butterfly gardens. She and Dora had designed a modest garden plan, and Harper had ordered the plants. Dora was keeping firm control— approving or disapproving any of Harper's suggestions. Her lack of trust chafed, especially in light of how Dora didn't trust Harper to take her son to Florida. No matter what they did, or how hard she tried, Dora seemed to keep her at arm's length.

Harper was deep into comparisons of varieties of lantana when the morning's peace was rent by a squeal of delight, followed by the thundering of feet approaching. As she looked up from her computer, the porch door flung open and Dora rushed out, her face beaming with news.

"I lost ten pounds!" Dora exclaimed breathlessly. "Ten pounds!"

Harper turned in her chair, surprised to see Dora practically jumping up and down. "Hey, congrats! That's a lot of weight. Since when?"

"Since the last time I weighed myself in the hospital."

"I told you that you were slimming down."

"You've always been trim and fit. You don't understand how huge this is," Dora said, her eyes still blazing with triumph. "I've been trying to lose ten pounds for ten years."

Harper wondered why her being fit would render her any less excited for her sister. "It's the exercise, more than any diet," Harper said, trying to be supportive. She closed her laptop and rose to her feet. "We have to celebrate."

"What's the point? I can't eat anything good."

"Why do we have to eat at all? Let's go shopping!"

Dora looked surprised at the suggestion, as though she'd never thought of having a celebration without food. "Well, I could use something pretty to wear on my dinner date with Devlin."

"Something that shows off your figure."

"Well, I'm hardly showing off," Dora said, suddenly shy. "I have another ten to lose, at least."

"Glass half empty," Harper told her, wagging her finger. "You can buy another dress when you lose the next ten, too. Come on, sis, life's too short not to celebrate each milestone." Harper scooped up her laptop, water bottle, and pens and paper from the table. "Besides, we haven't had a shopping trip yet. Or a mani-pedi. I seem to recall it was on our list of things to do this week. It'll be fun. Just us sisters."

Though Harper meant the shopping trip to be a bonding experience, so far it was anything *but*. Harper stood outside the dressing room of the fifth store they'd plowed through with all the joy of Sherman's march to the sea. Every dress or top she'd brought in for Dora to try on was figuratively burned and utterly rejected.

Harper stood outside the dressing room door, counting to ten and telling herself that this would be the last bunch she'd select from this cute shop. Harper was at her wit's end. She couldn't get Dora free from her locked-in look of cover-ups in flowing fabric without any discernible waistline, and she wouldn't show any skin. Dora wanted to go to the clothing stores in the mall that catered to overweight women or women of a particular age who didn't want to show too much curve. Stubbornly, Harper steered Dora to King Street in Charleston to some of her favorite stores, hoping to inject a little trend and youth into her older sister's style.

Harper loved clothes. In New York City one of her favorite things was to gaze at all the store windows, swooning over the new styles so fancifully displayed. The bonus of shopping on King Street in Charleston was that there were so many wonderful, chic boutiques, and they wouldn't have to fight the crowds. It should have been fun.

Instead it was war. Dora shot down all the stylish outfits Harper brought in; they were "too tight," or "too small," or "too young." She wasn't even nice about it. Dora was snapping and snarling like a cornered dog in the dressing room, sulking while Harper went back out to find new outfits for her to try on.

Harper resented feeling like she was torturing Dora, rather than trying to help. This batch was her last effort before she bailed. Mustering her resolve, she knocked on the dressing room door.

"Ready?" she called out in a pleasant voice.

"More?" Dora called back with a groan.

Harper closed her eyes, then said with forced cheer, "Last bunch! I'm sure we have a winner here."

Dora opened the door a crack, just enough to reveal her mulish expression. She looked about ready to burst into tears. "I don't want to try any more on. I'm done here."

"Dora, just a few more. I thought you looked beautiful in some of the dresses."

"No, I didn't. I looked fat. Everything makes me look fat!" Dora blurted out.

A salesgirl approached them, young and perky and eager to help. "Anything working for you?"

"We're not sure yet," Harper said in a polite tone.

"Yes, we are. None of these work. You can take them all," Dora snapped.

"Uh, okay," the salesgirl replied, sensing the tension. "I'll just step in and clear these away so you have a little more room," she said, slipping past Harper to the door.

Dora frowned at the intrusion but stepped aside, hastily covering herself with one of the dresses draped across the small chair. When the dressing room door opened, Harper got a glimpse of Dora in her large white bra and granny underpants. Harper stared at the dressing room and was shocked. It looked like Armageddon, with dresses and blouses and skirts flung everywhere. Harper stepped into the capacious dressing room and helped the young lady pick up some of the scattered clothing, embarrassed at the condition of the room, the lack of respect for the clothing. When the clerk left, Harper stayed in the dressing room with Dora, clutching with white knuckles the last three dresses she'd selected.

Dora rounded on her, eyes narrowed with anger. "I want you to stay out. I saw the look on your face when you saw my body. You were shocked."

Harper closed her eyes and groaned. "I wasn't shocked at your body," she said with strained patience. "I was shocked at the state the dressing room was in!"

"Yeah, right."

"Well," Harper admitted with a half grin, "I might've been shocked at your underwear. Next stop, we're buying you a decent bra! Something from this century."

Dora knew she was trying to make light of it, but Harper didn't realize how insulting her quips could be. Didn't she know she already felt like an outdated matron compared to her and Carson? Dora glared at Harper in the mirror.

"Please get out, Harper," she said with forced civility. "I want to get dressed and go home."

"Why are you making this so hard?" Harper cried with frustration. "This outing was supposed to be fun, and all you're doing is sulking and throwing clothes around like a spoiled child."

"Then stop acting like my mother!" Dora shot back.

"What? How am I acting like your mother?"

"You're not listening to what I want. You're telling me what to wear. Ordering me around. This isn't a shopping trip. It's a damn makeover!"

Harper was so angered by Dora's accusation that she tossed the remaining dresses onto the chair. They promptly slid off to the floor.

"I'm trying to be helpful! I know fashion and I'm showing you some outfits that I think you'll look good in. But you won't even try them. God, you're impossible. You're so stuck in your ways."

"I didn't ask for a makeover. Stop trying to change me."

Harper exploded. "You dress like a grandma!"

Dora's mouth dropped open and tears flooded her eyes.

In the shocked silence, Harper felt terrible for losing her temper. In the mirror she saw Dora cowering behind the slip of fabric. Everything about Dora—her posture, her crumpled face, her defiance—spoke of defeat.

"I'm sorry," Harper said, softening her tone. "The last thing I wanted to do today was to make you feel bad. I don't know, maybe I *was* trying to give you a makeover. It's only because I wanted you to see how beautiful you are." Her tone changed to reveal her frustration. "But you won't have it. You're so stubborn, Dora, and for no good reason. I'm beginning to wonder if you don't like the rut you're in because it's comfortable."

Dora didn't answer.

There followed a heated silence, during which Harper bent to pick up the dresses from the floor and hang them on the wall hook. Dora remained rigid against the wall, her face turned away, holding the dress tight against her body like a shield.

Harper turned and faced Dora. "I'm sorry if you don't like the way you look. But you shouldn't take it out on me. And you know what? It's not just today. From the moment I got here you've been pushing me away. You do that a lot, Dora."

"I'm not pushing you away," Dora said defensively. Then she shrugged one shoulder insolently. "I just figured we didn't get along."

Harper appeared slapped. "But *why*? I've tried, God knows I've tried."

"Maybe it's just the way we were brought up. You're from New York and I'm from Charleston."

Harper's voice went cold. "Don't play that north–south card with me. It's such a cliché, and you and I have moved way beyond those differences. This goes deeper. To trust."

"What do you mean?"

Harper looked up at the ceiling. "Where do I begin?" She lowered her gaze and met Dora's. "Okay, here's a recent one. I really had fun playing video games with Nate. But you chewed me out pretty good over that without even giving me the chance to explain why I did it. FYI, games are what he likes, Dora, and what he's good at, and there's solid evidence it's okay for him to play them with someone else. The operative word there, Dora, is *play*. He wasn't alone. We were interacting."

She speared Dora with another hard look. "Another example. *I* was the one who came up with the idea of taking Nate to the dolphin therapy program. I don't want a thank-you and I get why it was Carson who took him to Florida." Harper recited by rote, "She's the one with the experience with dolphins. She knows Florida. She and Nate have this Delphine bond going on." Her voice softened. "But it still hurt that you didn't even consider letting me take him." She asked Dora directly: "Would you have let me take him?"

"I . . . I . . ." Dora stammered.

"No, you wouldn't have," Harper answered for her. "Because you don't trust me with Nate. You don't even trust me with the bloody garden!"

"I don't trust *anybody* with Nate!" Dora fired back. "Not even his father. Do you even know how huge it was for me to let Nate go with Carson? Letting him go was the most trust I've ever shown anyone. And that trust includes you. I trusted what you told me about the program. I listened to you because, well, damn it, I know you're smart and you think things through and I respect you."

Harper went very still.

"I was freaked out letting Nate go," Dora said, shaking with emotion. "I still am. I miss him." She rubbed her arms, suddenly very cold. "Please, just leave now." She shuddered. "I'm so done with this."

"All right. I'm done, too. I'm leaving." Harper turned to leave. Then she swung around again.

Dora turned away.

Harper looked at her sister's back, and her own shoulders slumped. "You're my sister," she said in a flat tone. "I love you. But right now, I don't like you. Do whatever you want. I don't care. I'm going to the coffee shop at the corner. When you're done, meet me there and we'll drive home."

Harper turned and left, closing the door behind her.

───

Dora stood motionless in the dressing room, her body shaking with hurt and shock and anger at Harper's outburst. How dare she say those things to her? Harper didn't like her? Well, she didn't like Harper much, either, she thought, grabbing her shorts and ramming her legs into them. As she fastened the button, she saw again how loose they were at the waist and hips. In a rush, she remembered the elation she'd felt at discovering she'd lost ten pounds, and how immediate and sincere Harper was with her congratulations.

And who was that girl? Dora wondered, stunned at Harper's outburst. The mouse had roared! And Dora had to admit, she admired this side of Harper she'd never seen before. She had gumption, and that was something Dora could respect.

Dora's anger was quickly replaced by remorse. She slumped onto the chair and stared at her reflection in the mirror. Her cheeks were pink from the sun but her hair was mousy and her Bermuda shorts and bra looked like something her mother would wear. How could she be upset with Harper when Harper was right? Dora hated the way she dressed.

Was Harper also right about those other things? Did Dora push people away? She thought of Cal. How many nights had she pushed him away, claiming fatigue and headaches? She knew plenty of women used any number of those excuses on the nights they weren't in the mood, but it got old with Cal, and he got angry. "You're never in the mood," he'd complained. She couldn't explain to him that not feeling pretty, sexy, desirable, or even feminine was often the real source of the problem. Pushing people away was easier than letting them get close.

Harper was right. Again. She had pushed her away. She'd been jealous. She'd always thought both Harper and Carson lived exciting lives. They'd traveled the world while Dora had never left the South. They were younger, slimmer, richer—or at least Harper was. Dora's claim to fame was her marriage, her child, her stability. She'd held up the facade of her being the perfect Southern woman. Until the facade crumbled, leaving her with nothing to feel good about.

Facades were easier to maintain over distance.

But it was about time that *all* their facades were cracking and crumbling. Since they'd all returned to Sea Breeze, the truths were slowly being unearthed. Carson had been brutally honest, sharing the sordid details of her childhood. Harper revealed the loneliness behind the wealth of the James family. Why had Dora been ashamed to tell her sisters about the divorce?

The voice in her head that told her divorce was an embarrassing scandal, something to avoid at all costs, was the same harsh critic that whispered she was fat, not pretty. Were her insecurities what made her act so inflexible and stuck in her ways? Was she too judgmental, always finding fault and pushing people—and any hope for happiness—away?

She brought her hands to her face. In the past week she'd caught a glimpse of how her life could change. She liked the way she was beginning to feel about herself. In her reflection she was catching a glimpse of the young girl she once was. The girl who had confidence and dreams. The girl who believed anything was possible.

How could she break the old patterns that had grown like kudzu vines around her heart? How could she quiet the negative voices and listen to the positive ones?

Dora dropped her hands and slowly raised her eyes to the dresses hanging on the wall hooks. Harper had told her she had looked pretty in the dresses. Devlin had told her she was beautiful. When was she going to start believing?

"Oh, give me that damn dress," Dora said to herself as she rose to her feet and grabbed the first one within reach.

~~~~~~

Harper sat at a small table in City Lights café, a pile of napkins covered in her handwriting on the table before her. Whenever she was hurt or angry, Harper found it therapeutic to write out in dialogue all the things she wished she'd had the courage to say. She'd scribbled in a heated fury a vitriolic scene of Dora and herself in the changing room, hurling insults, throwing clothes, a real catfight. Finished, she sat back in her chair, released the pen, and grabbed her latte.

She finished her drink, set down the empty mug, and looked around the coffee shop. Big stainless-steel espresso machines lined the wall, pastries were arranged on the counter. Women and men of all ages sat at the small tables, talking, reading, typing on laptops. She found the heady scents of freshly brewed coffee and sweet pastries comforting, and she needed that now.

In New York, she often went to coffee shops with her laptop and people-watched. She enjoyed describing what she saw—the people, the setting, what they ordered. She jotted down comments she found amusing or poignant. Sometimes she'd be so inspired by a conversation she'd overheard that she finished the snippet with a short story, letting her imagination run wild. She never showed anyone her writing. She'd learned long ago that she didn't have any talent. But she still enjoyed writing. She either threw the pieces out or hid them away in boxes in her closet. She didn't know why she wrote. It was just something she'd always done.

When Harper was little, she used to show people her stories. They were just silly ones about whatever caught her fancy.

But she'd been proud of them. Then one day, when she was eight, her mother had called her into her office.

⚍

"Harper James-Muir!" Her mother's voice rang out in their New York City condominium. "Come into my office, please."

Harper had been sitting at the kitchen table, idly kicking her legs and eating cinnamon toast while staring at the ice-crystal design on the window. Hearing her mother's voice, she froze and darted a fearful gaze at her nanny. Her mother used her full name only when she was in trouble, and to be called into her office meant this was serious.

Luisa, her nanny, shook her head to indicate she didn't know what this was about.

Harper set down her toast while Luisa rushed to her side to wipe crumbs from her mouth and school uniform. She smoothed Harper's hair, then, taking hold of her shoulders, guided her to her mother's office.

Georgiana was sitting in her book-lined office behind a sleek ebony desk. She was dressed in her work clothes, a stylish black houndstooth wool suit. Harper crinkled her nose at the stench of the cigarette smoke that always made her stomach upset.

"Come in," Georgiana said. "And shut the door behind you. That will be all, Luisa."

Harper heard the officious tone and, nervous, did as she was requested. She stood with her hands held before her.

"Sit down."

Harper walked across the plush carpeting to sit in one of the hot-pink velvet chairs with her shoulders back and ankles crossed, as she'd learned to do. Her gaze swept her mother's desk for clues as to why her mother had called her in. She spotted her handmade book, *Willy the Wishful Whale*. Harper had been especially proud of this story of the adventures of a young whale searching for his family. She'd painted the illustrations herself, bound the book using a three-hole puncher and ribbon. She'd even written a song to go with it. She released a sigh of relief, thinking that her mother, an editor of books, would be proud of her effort. After all, she'd created her first book!

Georgiana lifted the paper book. "Did you write this?"

"Yes."

"Do you write many stories?"

Harper smiled, encouraged. "Yes. Well, sometimes. I mean, I just do it when I get an idea."

"Where did you get the idea for this one?"

Harper shrugged. "I don't know. It just popped into my head."

"It just popped into your head," Georgiana repeated slowly. "I see."

Harper knew that when her mother became frosty, she was on the verge of losing her temper. Harper waited, holding her breath.

"Are you lying to me?"

Harper paled and her stomach suddenly felt sick. "No!"

"You got this idea from one of the books you read, didn't you?"

"I . . . I . . ." Harper didn't know what to say. Her mother was frightening her. "I don't know."

"I thought so," she said, taking a drag on her cigarette, then setting it down on the ashtray. She folded her hands on the desk. Harper stared at her perfect pink nails. "Harper, listen to me very carefully. You must never, ever copy the work of others. In the publishing world, that is called plagiarism. And it's a crime. Not to mention a scandal. I won't have it, not even for play. Do you understand me?"

Harper nodded, rendered speechless at the cruel accusation that she was lying and cheating when she wrote her book. The idea came to her as they all did—while she was dreaming, while reading, while listening to people talk. Sometimes they came to her while she was at the park or zoo with Nanny, just watching the animals. Was that copying? Was she being bad?

"Why are you writing books, anyway?" her mother asked, clearly upset. Then she skewered her with a pointed gaze. "Are you trying to be like your father?"

Harper shook her head no. She knew they'd suddenly moved onto treacherous ground.

Her mother's eyes glittered with anger, as they did each time she brought up the topic of Parker Muir. "Well, don't. You didn't know him. I did, and trust me, you don't want to be like him. He was a lush and ladies' man. A ne'er-do-well." She pointed one of her perfectly polished fingers at her. "You're a James and you're better than him. Better than the lot of them." Her face hardened with the tone of her voice. "Your father wasn't a writer," she said with derision. "His work was derivative. He didn't have the talent. And," she said, lifting Harper's handmade book and dropping it onto the desk as if it were trash, "neither do you."

Harper felt her enthusiasm and pride for her book wither in her heart to be replaced by shame.

Georgiana took a final puff from her cigarette and blew out a stream of smoke as she eyed her daughter sitting slump-shouldered on the chair before the desk. Then she reached over to the ashtray and snuffed it out.

"I'm glad we had this little talk," her mother told her. "You're my daughter. I love you and have great expectations for you. I know you won't disappoint me." She smiled then, the same smile she gave to guests when they left the house, the mega-watt one that made them feel like they'd been given a gift. "You can go now. I'll see you at dinner, all right?"

Harper shivered at the memory and reached for her mug of coffee, frowning when she saw that it was empty and cold. She was bored with waiting and ready to leave. Where was Dora? she wondered irritably. She cupped her chin and let her gaze wander the café, then out the front window. She spied Dora through the window, approaching the store. She sat up, expectantly. The bell over the door chimed and Dora walked in.

Harper felt all the frustration and anger pent up in her chest release in her short laugh of delight. Dora was beaming, wearing one of the dresses that Harper had selected for her. It was a navy print with vertical lines that complemented her figure. Harper didn't know what had brought about this change of heart in Dora, but it meant the world to her. Smiling, she shot her hand in the air and waved it in an enthusiastic arc. Dora spotted her and her eyes lit up at seeing her.

"You look gorgeous!" Harper exclaimed, standing to greet her. "I love you in that dress."

Dora swept her in a bear hug and whispered by her ear, "And I just plain love you."

They held tight for a moment, then a moment longer, not needing words this time to express their apologies and the enduring, unbreakable bond between them.

Dora released her and stepped back, a bit flustered. Harper could see the redness in Dora's eyes that revealed she'd been crying.

"Want some coffee?" Harper asked.

"I'll get it. My treat. I kept you waiting long enough."

Harper watched Dora get in line to place the order with the barista. As she waited, a rush of ideas flooded her head, fun things they could do together—just two women, two friends, two sisters, with a free afternoon on King Street. Smiling, she hurriedly gathered the napkins filled with her angry scribbling and, crumpling them in her hands, walked across the room and tossed them into the trash.

The afternoon sun was lowering by the time the girls returned to Sea Breeze. Mamaw had been waiting by the front windows, watching for them.

"Lucille!" she called out, her heart beating a mile a minute. "They're here!"

Lucille came rushing out from the kitchen in her stiff-legged gait, drying her hands on her starched white apron.

"At last," she huffed. "I hope they didn't eat nothin'. I've been cooking this rabbit food for an hour, trying to give it some taste."

"I hope they'll like what I've done," Mamaw said nervously. She turned to Lucille. "Do you think they will?"

"'Course they'll like it. Who wouldn't?"

"I don't want them to think I'm being, well . . ."

"Scheming?"

Mamaw frowned. "Such a harsh word. I like to think *generous* does the job."

Lucille guffawed. "Well, look at them, laughing together. I 'spect your *generosity* been workin' with those two."

Mamaw felt her worry ease. "Yes. I swanny, they've been like oil and water."

"Baking soda and vinegar, more like it. Hush now, here they come. Lord help us, looks like they done cleaned out the stores."

The front door opened and Mamaw heard the laughter before she saw Harper and Dora saunter in, laden with brightly colored shopping bags in their arms.

"We're back!" Dora called out gaily. "We had the best time! Harper is the sweetest girl in the whole world. Come see what we've bought! Or Harper bought. That woman is wild with that credit card!"

Mamaw turned her head to share a surprised glance with Lucille. This was certainly a change of heart between the girls, and Mamaw's elation bubbled over in her greeting.

"Dora, you look stunning! Why, you're positively transformed!" she exclaimed, walking toward her with her arms open.

Dora's blond hair had been highlighted to punch up her color and trimmed in a sleek new style. The chic summer dress made her look as if she'd lost an additional ten pounds, and Mamaw wasn't sure whether it was her happiness or the new makeup, but her face was positively glowing.

Dora was beaming as she stepped into Mamaw's arms. "It's all Harper. She did a complete makeover."

Mamaw turned to find Harper already busily spreading out the shopping bags on the Chippendale sofa and opening boxes. It didn't appear that Harper had bought anything for herself, which spoke volumes to Mamaw.

"You're quite good at this," she told Harper. "You should open a business!"

"I can't afford it," Harper said with a light laugh.

Dora gushed, "You think *I'm* bossy? I'm a piker compared to this girl. She made me get my hair done, and my makeup, and look! A mani-pedi. Lucille, what do you think of the color?" She held out her hands to reveal a bold hot-pink color. "Doesn't it just scream *summer*?"

Lucille bent over her hands. "It screams somethin', that's for true."

Dora giggled and hurried to the sofa to dig in one of the large bags. She fished out two small ones. "We picked out these for you together. Oh, Harper, you should give them. I'm forgetting my manners."

Harper just laughed and waved her hand, enjoying Dora's excitement. "Go ahead."

Mamaw accepted the bag with surprise. "For me? Gracious, girls, I don't deserve anything. It's not my birthday."

"It's nothing, really," Harper replied, watching. "A *petit cadeau*."

Mamaw pulled a scented candle out of the bag. "Thank you, precious. It's lovely," she said.

Lucille had received a candle as well.

"They're different scents," Harper said. "Hope you like them."

"You should," Dora added. "They cost the world."

Harper laughed and shook her head, embarrassed.

Lucille had pulled on her reading glasses and was studying her candle. "Says here it's called Summer Nights. I don't know what that means, but this smells like jasmine to me. I love me my night-blooming jasmine." She looked up, grinning.

Dora returned to the bags on the sofa. "Wait till you see what else I got."

"Girls," Mamaw said, clasping her hands close to her breast. She glanced at Lucille, who nodded in agreement. "There's something I'd like to show you first. It's my own little makeover."

Dora released the shopping bag and glanced at Harper. "Is this connected to all that knocking and pounding of the past few days?"

"You'll just have to look and see," Mamaw replied cagily.

"I love surprises," Harper said.

"Good. I hope you like this one. Come with me."

Mamaw led them from the living room down the hall toward her bedroom. She opened the doors that led into the anteroom of the suite, where a framed photograph of Mamaw and Granddaddy Edward greeted them over a small foyer table. Immediately to the left was a small computer room that had been built into a large closet. They proceeded into the large bedroom, adorned with a collection of paintings of the low-country landscape that Mamaw adored, all done by local artists. Every spare inch of her walls was covered in paintings. She'd often told the girls that lying in bed, especially now that Edward was gone, she felt surrounded by friends.

Mamaw went to stand before a pair of sliding wood doors separating her bedroom from her sitting room that were not there several days before.

Harper looked to Dora and they shared a look of confusion.

Mamaw's gaze swept over their expectant faces. "I've done a bit of work, as you've heard," she began. She let her gaze rest on Harper.

"Harper, dear, you've been a true gem putting up with being evicted from your bedroom this summer without a peep of complaint. We've all appreciated it."

"Of course, Mamaw," Harper said. "It's nothing. And I've enjoyed bunking with Dora." She glanced at Dora with a smile.

"Precisely the spirit I'm referring to. Nonetheless," Mamaw continued, "Carson and Nate are due back in a few days and I've done a bit of rearranging that I hope will suit you. This is your room now."

Mamaw turned to grasp the large brass door handles and with a push slid open the doors. Sunlight poured into the bedroom from the bay windows, revealing a sitting room transformed into a bedroom. Instead of the settee and armchair, a feminine antique bed with scrolls and curves was set at an angle from the windows, a soft blue patterned Persian rug at its feet.

Harper sucked in her breath and walked slowly into the sunny room, her head turning from left to right to take in the changes. The small desk from Dora's room had been painted a cream color and moved under the bay windows, and atop it, fresh flowers were arranged in the Chinese Rose Medallion vase she'd once told Mamaw she liked. Only Mamaw could be so attentive to the smallest details.

"You created a room . . . for me?" Harper asked in a small voice.

"It wasn't much. I had that bed and armoire in storage. You don't have a closet, I'm afraid. But you can have Edward's computer room for yourself. It just sits there unused. Other than that, Lucille and I just moved things around a bit. Oh"—

she indicated the pale blue coverlet on the bed—"we thought you'd like to pick out a new coverlet yourself."

"Oh, Mamaw, I would have been content with an air mattress on the floor."

Mamaw laughed in the manner that implied what Harper said was absurd. "That is precisely why it brought me so much pleasure to do this." She kissed Harper's forehead. "I had the doors added so you could simply shut me out. They lock, see?" she said, pointing out the brass bolt. "I also had a door added so you can have a private entrance from the porch. I know how you like your privacy."

"Thank you, Mamaw. I'm . . . I'm overwhelmed." Harper had been raised to hold her emotions in check and blinked rapidly, trying to stop the tears.

Dora stood in the background, her eyes taking in the new room with wonder. "I have to admit, I'm going to miss sharing a room with you."

Mamaw looked to Dora to seek out any signs of jealousy that Harper had received such a boon. It was with relief that she saw nothing but genuine pleasure in Dora's face. It made her feel all the more eager about her next surprise.

Mamaw said to Dora, "You don't think I've left you out, do you? We've begun work on your room, too. Come take a look."

They followed Mamaw, giggling, through the living room again to the west side of the house. As they passed the library, the smell of fresh paint permeated the air. Looking over her shoulder to make certain that Dora was behind her, she smiled at seeing all three women with expressions on their faces like children on Christmas morning. Without delay, she pushed open the door.

The small bedroom was in the chaos of transition. Most of the furniture had been moved out, a painter's tarp covered the floor, and all the trim was freshly painted glossy white. One wall was covered with a pale pink-and-white-striped paper, feminine and chic.

"There's a lot left to be done," Mamaw said. "I had to call in every chit and I've been on the phone nagging seamstresses all over town." She proudly walked them around the room, pointing out changes. "The wallpaper will be hung tomorrow and we can get the curtains in as soon as all is dry. I only have a small window of time, and I'm determined to have everything in place before Carson returns from Florida. You'll have to sleep in her room until then. If that's all right with you. Lucille's changed the bedding. All is in the ready."

"Of course," Dora sputtered. "I don't know what to say. I didn't expect anything like this. I would've been happy with a bigger bed. But . . ." Worry had now entered her voice. "Mamaw, all this effort and expense. I . . . we'll only be here for a short while . . ."

"I know, but I'm having so much fun and the Realtor told me I needed to freshen things up a bit. So it had to be done anyway." She shrugged with a roll of the eyes and said, "*Que sera sera*. Now, Dora, there's one object in particular I want you to see. It's what sparked all this effort in the first place," she said, guiding Dora out of the room. "I put it in Carson's room for now. Come see."

"A new bed, I hope?" Dora said. She hated sleeping in that twin.

"That, too," Mamaw assured her. "I'm having a full bed brought over from storage."

"Thanks be to . . ." Dora muttered before her voice stuck in her throat.

Mamaw opened the door to Carson's room and in the corner, dominating the space, she saw Mamaw's imposing French vanity. Dora stood staring at the beloved priceless antique, speechless.

"The vanity is yours, Dora."

Dora walked slowly to the vanity, her hand reaching out to delicately trace the elaborate curves of the brass mirror.

"Oh, Mamaw," Dora said breathlessly. "How did you know how much I loved this?"

Mamaw smiled indulgently. "I'm your grandmother. I *should* know such things."

Dora turned to face her. "But what will you use?"

"Oh, child, at my age, the less I look in the mirror, the better." She glanced at Lucille, who stood by the door beaming with pleasure. "Especially not if that old bird won't give me her skin cream recipe."

Lucille's grin widened. "Too late now, anyway!"

Mamaw sniffed and shook her head with resignation. Turning to Dora, she took her hands. "My dear girl, you've worked so hard to rediscover how very beautiful you are, inside as well as out. I hope you'll look in this mirror every day and see that beauty reflected." She squeezed Dora's hands. "You hear?"

Tears spilled over Dora's eyes as she nodded, her laugh broken with a choked cry.

"You're ruining her makeup!" Harper cried, laughing.

Mamaw held Dora in her arms, relishing the softness of her, the sweet scent of tuberose in her perfume, and the depth of feeling Dora was allowing herself to unleash, at last.

Chapter Twelve

≈≈≈

*T*he glimmering candlelight on thick white cotton table-
cloths, the original lowcountry art on the walls, the orchids in
bud vases, the hum of conversation punctuated with occasional
laughs, the clinking of silverware—all combined to create the
ambience of a perfect dinner date.

Dora shifted nervously in her seat and swirled the cabernet
in the large crystal bowl of her wineglass. She took note of her
perfectly polished pink nails. Tonight she wore her new shim-
mering blue silk dress that Harper had found for her during
their shopping spree. Mamaw's large, creamy pearls graced her
neck, and she knew she looked her best in the elegant Charleston restaurant.

Across the table, Devlin studied the oversized menu. He,
too, was transformed tonight, handsome in his beautifully cut
tan suit, a blush-pink shirt, and a Ferragamo tie. She studied his
hands on the menu—they were not long-fingered, like Cal's.

Rather, they were wide and ruddy from being out on the water. A man's hand. On his ring finger he wore a thick gold signet ring. She sipped her wine, her imagination taking a turn in this romantic restaurant. What, she wondered, would those hands feel like on her body?

Devlin looked up from the menu and, catching her perusal, smiled.

"You look beautiful tonight. That reminds me . . ." He set the menu down and, with a gleam in his eyes, reached into his breast pocket to pull out a small jeweler's box. He set it on the table before Dora.

"What's this?" she asked, feeling a sudden panic.

"Nothing big, just something I saw that I thought you might like. Go ahead, open it."

Dora cast him a glance of mock suspicion and reached for the gray velvet box. Opening it, she found a pair of large blue-stoned earrings within a border of tiny diamonds.

"They're beautiful!" she exclaimed, shocked at their size. They had to have been costly.

"I always said your eyes are the color of aquamarines. Topaz are too clear. Yours are a deeper blue, like the deep ocean."

"I can't accept these. They're too expensive."

"Please, don't play that game. We're way past that. I saw them, I want you to have them, and they match your dress. Aren't those enough reasons to put them on right this minute and let me enjoy seeing you in them?"

Dora grinned and plucked the earrings from the box. It took a moment to slip the pearls from her ears and replace them with the aquamarines. When she was finished, she searched her purse for a mirror and pulled it out to study her reflection. The large aquamarines were dazzling and they were, indeed, the same color as her eyes, making them pop against her soft tan.

"I was right," Devlin said, leaning back in his chair with a smug grin.

"Thank you," Dora said, lowering the mirror to give Devlin her full attention. "Thank you times ten. I've never had such beautiful earrings. I'll treasure them."

"Don't be putting them in a box, afraid to wear them. You should wear them every day. If you lose them, I'll get you another pair."

Dora listened to the words with wonder. Cal had always been so frugal. He never splurged on a gift of jewelry for her. He was the type to buy her an appliance or a scarf. Tonight Devlin was offering her dinner at a five-star restaurant, fine wine, and now a gift—this was a full-court press.

The waiter stepped up to the table. He was dressed in black pants, a white shirt, and a black bow tie. After a few words of chitchat he launched into a description of the evening's specials with a flourish. Dora's mouth was watering after weeks of low-fat, lean meals.

Devlin picked up the menu and began ordering.

"Let's start with some lobster cakes. Then we'd like the she-crab soup." He glanced at Dora. "It's the specialty of the house. You've got to have some." Looking again at the waiter, he said, "That honey-roasted duck sounds good, too. And I can tell you right now we're both going to want some of your famous coconut cake."

"Devlin, wait . . ." Dora interrupted.

Devlin turned his head, expectant.

Dora turned to the waiter. "We're going to need a few more minutes."

The waiter nodded and discreetly stepped away.

"Dev, I can't eat all that. I'm on a . . ." She didn't want to use the word *diet*. "The doctor said I can't eat all that fatty food. Lord, the she-crab soup alone could kill me."

Devlin's smile dropped as his eyes widened. "I'm sorry. I forgot. What an idiot I am."

"No," she said in a hurry, not wanting him to feel bad. "You were being a gentleman. But I think it's best for me to order my own dinner."

"Of course," Devlin said, but she could tell he was flustered at his mistake. He raised his hand briefly and the waiter quickly reappeared.

"The lady will order her own dinner," Devlin said.

"Certainly." The waiter turned his attention to Dora.

She cleared her throat and studied the enormous menu. "I'll have the chef's summer salad, no dressing . . . the grilled shrimp, and hold the hushpuppies. And could I substitute the creamed corn for collard greens?" She closed the menu and, handing it to the waiter, added, "No dessert."

"Well played," Devlin said. He closed his menu and returned it to the waiter. "I'll have the same. Except, I still want some of that coconut cake." He glanced at Dora again. "I might convince the lady to try it."

"Dev . . ."

"One bite!" he exclaimed, then laughed.

Their laughter was interrupted by the ringing of her cell phone. Dora immediately drew her evening bag closer and pulled it out. She kept her phone turned on in case the call was about Nate.

"Hello?" she said.

"Hi, Dora. It's me, Cal. I thought I'd better give you a call and check in."

"Uh, Cal, I can't talk now. Can I call you back?"

"Where are you?"

"I'm out to dinner."

"Oh. Okay." There was a pause. "With who?"

"I have to go. I'll call you back. Bye."

She slipped the phone back into her bag and, a little sheepishly, looked up at Devlin. He was watching her with a skeptical expression.

"Sorry about that. I thought it was about Nate."

"That was your husband?"

The word *husband* coming from his lips while they were on a date sliced the air of intimacy they'd been enjoying.

Dora cringed, thinking, What were the odds that Cal, who rarely called, would pick tonight? "Cal, yes."

"Does he call you often?"

"Actually, no."

"You *are* separated . . . getting a divorce?"

"Yes, of course," Dora replied, bristling. "You don't think I'd be having dinner with you, accepting gifts, if I weren't?"

He spread out his palms. "Just asking."

Dora couldn't respond. An awkward moment passed while she sipped her wine. It was with great relief that the first course arrived.

The remainder of the evening continued in an uncomfortable vein. It was as though Cal had pulled up a chair and joined them at the table. Their conversation was stilted; a bad first date. All the natural ebb and flow that they usually enjoyed had run dry. By the time the famous coconut cake was presented, neither Dora nor Devlin wanted any and were eager to go.

The short drive home to Sea Breeze seemed long, even in his luxury BMW sedan. It was a dark night. Heavy cloud cover obscured the moon and stars. Dora was tired and, closing her eyes, listened to moody ballads sung by Michael Bublé. When they pulled into the driveway, Devlin put the car into park but kept the engine running.

"You don't have to walk me up," Dora said in the darkness. Then, turning toward him, she added in a soft voice, "Thank you for a lovely evening. I had a wonderful time."

There was a pause, then Devlin switched off the engine. He turned and slid his arm around her waist. She stiffened, but he didn't release her.

"You don't have to be polite. You didn't have a wonderful time," he said in a low voice.

"I . . . It was a delicious meal."

He nodded in agreement. "It was. But I'm sorry I got all messed up by Cal's phone call. Plus, that whole scene is not my style. I just wanted to impress you."

"Impress me? Why? I've known you since we were kids."

"That's exactly why. You knew me when I was flat broke. I couldn't ever have afforded to take you out to a restaurant like that or buy you pretty earrings. I wanted to, but I never had the money."

"Dev, you and I . . . we never needed any props between us. It's always been just you and me, having a good time because we were together."

He reached out to take her hands. Looking at them, he

played with her fingers, then tapped the wedding ring she still wore on her hand. "But you married him."

"Yes."

"Tell you what," Devlin said, looking at her face. "Give me another chance to take you out again. We'll go out on the boat, like we used to. Take a spin through the creeks. Do it proper." He drew her closer. "What do you say?"

Dora let her arms slide under his suit jacket and around his waist, and she leaned against him. She felt his warmth and smelled the faint remnants of his aftershave. It was a spicy scent and, smiling, she thought she wouldn't be at all surprised if he was still wearing Old Spice. She turned her head up toward his.

"I'd love to."

His smile came slow and easy as he wrapped his arms around her and lowered his mouth to hers. His arms tightened as his kiss deepened, and all thoughts of Cal evaporated into the night like an exorcised ghost.

The following morning, Dora stood at the wooden kitchen table overflowing with produce that had been delivered from a local farm. She was packing a bag of snacks for her boat trip with Devlin. She'd washed and cut up carrots and celery, added a bag of cherries and almonds, and put them into a large canvas bag beside bottles of water. A month ago she would have packed cookies, a candy bar, and soda. Though she still craved sugar, with every day that passed the desire loosened its hold on her as her refined taste buds began to appreciate the natural sweetness of fruit. After talking with Carson about Nate and his colorful schedule, Dora had affixed her own routine and diet calendar to the fridge. Every X on the calendar gave her strength to stay on her diet another day.

Across the room Lucille was at the stove, stirring a pot of vegetable soup. Lucille and Mamaw stuck by their word unwaveringly, clearing all the processed foods and sweets from the cabinets. There were nights when she'd prowled the kitchen for something *good* to eat—meaning cookies, candy, anything sweet—cursing them for not leaving a single morsel of chocolate. Dora had gained a whole new understanding of Carson's addiction to alcohol.

"That soup smells wonderful!" Dora exclaimed.

Lucille grunted. "It'd be a whole lot better if I could put a ham bone in it. Nothin' a good soup needs more than a ham bone. That's what gives it the flavor."

"So put one in."

She grunted. "Can't. Miss Harper can sniff out a bit of pork like a coon dog does a possum. Nothing gets past her. It'll be good," she said, stirring. "Just not *as* good, that's all I'm sayin'."

"We're sure putting you through your paces this summer with all our demands, aren't we? No alcohol, no fat, no salt, no butter."

"No taste," Lucille grumbled.

"It's healthy," Dora offered.

"I do what I gots to do," Lucille said with the sigh of the long suffering. "But I won't give up my corn bread. I don't care how much Miss Harper complains about my bacon grease, I will not give up my mama's corn bread!"

"God forbid!" Dora agreed. "Bless her heart, she's from New York and doesn't appreciate the virtues of pork. But she's making an effort. And you're a genius in the kitchen. Everything still tastes wonderful. I, for one, know I wouldn't be able to stick to this diet without your support. I swear, Lucille, your cooking is holding this family together."

Lucille appeared mollified and half smiled. "Ain't nothin' I wouldn't do for this family."

Dora paused and stared at the woman bent over the stove. Lucille had the heart of a lion but she was normally shy of expressing her affection in words. She showed her love through action—breakfast in bed on birthdays, an ironed dress for a special occasion, fresh flowers on the bureau. To hear these words now took Dora by surprise. She went to Lucille's side and kissed her cheek.

Startled, Lucille drew back, her dark eyes wide. "What's that for?"

"Does it have to be for something? *You're* family, you know."

Lucille, clearly flustered by Dora's show of emotion, awkwardly tried to smile as she turned back to the stove. "Just caught me by surprise, is all. You're not one to give kisses."

Dora wondered about that comment as she returned to the table. For so long she'd held herself back from excessive shows of affection. Cal was not physically affectionate. No pats on the behind or arms around her shoulder during a movie. She was especially restrained with Nate, knowing that he'd get upset if she spontaneously hugged or kissed him. Did that restraint come naturally to her? Was she, as Cal had insinuated, frigid?

Dora stuffed a few paper napkins into the canvas bag. "I'm sure Cal would agree with you. Maybe I should change that, eh?"

"This surely is a summer for changes."

Dora laughed, hearing the truth in that.

"Where are you off to this time?"

"We're going boating."

"We?"

"Me and Devlin."

Lucille paused her stirring, her lips twisted in thought. "I know that name. How do I know that name?"

"Devlin Cassell," Dora replied. "You remember him. I went steady with him back in high school. Blond hair, blue eyes, tan. Surfer. He was here all the time. Practically lived in the kitchen. Used to steal your cookies."

Lucille swung around, eyes wide. "*That* Devlin? Lord help us. Was that the man you got all trussed up for the other night?"

Dora laughed. "Sure was."

Lucille clucked her tongue. "Back when, your mamaw was on her knees praying most nights that boy wouldn't get into your skivvies, worried 'bout what else he'd steal beside cookies. And now it's startin' up all over again." She turned back to the stove and said in a lusty wail, "My, my, my . . ."

"Mamaw doesn't have to worry about my cookies any longer," Dora said drily. "Let's just say things aren't as hot and heavy now as they were back when we were teenagers."

"You talk like you're an old woman."

"I'm thirty-six. Almost thirty-seven. With a child."

"You got the same parts, don't you?"

"Last time I looked."

"And they still work?"

Dora smirked. "I wouldn't know. It's been so long."

"Seems to me it's high time you find out."

Now it was Dora's turn to be flustered. "Well, it wouldn't be right," she stammered. "I'm not divorced yet."

"You ain't been living as man and wife for a long time."

"It would be wrong for me to, you know, be with another man."

"Who says?"

"My lawyer, probably. My mother, most certainly."

Lucille grunted in a manner that gave no doubt she didn't care for Winnie. "Who's gonna tell them? That's one woman who'd be a lot happier if someone took the long pole out of her backside."

"Lucille!" Dora burst out with a laugh.

"You know it's true. And don't you tell me you're not thinkin' the same thing."

Dora giggled at Lucille's unexpected burst of temper. Her mother had never given Dora that little talk mothers were supposed to give their daughters at puberty. Dora didn't think Winnie could bring herself to say the words. When Dora was thirteen, she had found a pamphlet on her bed written by some priest or bishop. It was all about the mystical body of Christ, and Dora couldn't figure out what they were talking about.

"She was always pretty rigid about rules, I'll give you that. And sex. I don't think she finds sex very ladylike."

"It was a miracle you were born, child," Lucille said. "When Winnie talks about Adam and Eve, I'll wager all she can think about is how they committed some sin. What's that special name they call it?"

"Original sin."

"That'll be it. Ain't we learned nothin' since then? Still calling sex a sin. Sex is as natural as the birds and the bees." Lucille grew agitated, putting one hand on her hip as she spoke. "God put a man and a woman together, buck naked in paradise.

'Course He knew what was gonna happen. Way I see it, that was the plan all along. Else how would Cain and Abel be born? Or any of us?"

She covered the pot of soup and turned off the stove. "Don't listen to your mother. You ain't sixteen no more. You're a woman, fully growed. Make up your own mind. Just remember, we're all Eve's daughters." She caught Dora's gaze and held it. "This is your one and only life, girl. Your time in the garden."

Lucille pointed the wooden spoon at Dora. "What you waitin' for?"

Dora stood on the dock, staring into the current of the Cove. Even with Nate on holiday, Dora still acutely felt the weight of her responsibilities. She felt more and more sure of her decision to proceed with the divorce. This opened a Pandora's box of decisions. Where would she move? She'd have to find a school for Nate, a job for herself. This was a watershed moment in her life.

A large fish jumped and landed in the water with a noisy splash, creating ripples that fanned out farther and larger across the water as Dora watched. She sighed—the ripples of her decisions would have long-lasting consequences as well.

The growl of outboard motors broke her dark thoughts. Lifting her head, she saw the tip of a blue-and-white boat heading toward the dock. Squinting, she spotted Devlin waving at the wheel and immediately broke into a grin and waved back.

As the big boat drew near, Dora couldn't help but notice it was a very nice one. A Boston Whaler, at least twenty feet in length with a pretty, bright blue canopy. Devlin always liked his toys, she thought as she stood on the edge of the dock with her arms outstretched, ready to catch the rope.

Dora loved boating—she was good at it. When the girls came to Sea Breeze for the summers, it was Dora who drove the boat while Carson and Harper rode the inner tubes or water-skied. Dora wasn't much for getting wet. She preferred the feel of the wheel in her grasp and the throttle of engines at her control.

The boat's engine bubbled in the water as Devlin slowly brought the boat alongside the dock. Dora deftly caught the rope and secured it. Her legs stretched precariously between the dock and boat as she tied the line. She almost lost her balance for a moment, not having the control she did when she was younger. She blushed and looked up at Devlin.

He was busy tying up the line in fast, sure movements. He was stocky but moved across the boat like a dancer. Knowing boats, she appreciated his speed and confidence. That, she knew, came only with years of experience.

Devlin looked up from the boat, grinning behind his dark sunglasses at seeing her. A worn Ducks Unlimited cap tamped down his blond, windblown hair and his skin was tanned. Devlin was an outdoorsman, as comfortable on the water as on land, and Dora found that very attractive. She smiled back and tossed him the canvas bag, then reached out to accept Devlin's hand. At his touch she felt an electric-like charge, calling to mind the conversation about natural urges she'd had earlier with Lucille. He must have felt it, too, because he squeezed her hand again before releasing it.

Devlin went to the cooler and retrieved two beers. He put them in koozies and handed one to Dora.

"Make yourself comfortable, pretty lady," he told her as he rushed back and forth across the boat untethering the ropes. When he was done, he went to the wheel.

Dora opened her can, then moved to stand close to him under the awning. He reached out to slip an arm around her and tugged her closer.

"Glad you're here," he said, giving her bottom a modest pat.

Dora laughed for the pure joy of going out on the boat with Devlin on such a perfect day. "Me, too."

It was still early. The sun was rising overhead in a cloudless sky. Devlin slipped his arm away to lean back, half standing, half sitting against the captain's chair. He reached for the throttle with one hand, while the other was on the wheel as he slowly revved the motors. They growled and gurgled as he guided the Whaler through the narrow marsh creeks.

Dora held on to the rocking boat as she moved to sit in the second seat beside him. She held her beer, but her fingers itched to drive the boat. She knew a captain didn't like to give up his wheel and she didn't want to press—at least not on their first outing.

As the boat took off, she thought back to when they were young and she and Devlin had been out on his boat. He used to let her drive. When her hands were on the wheel, he'd come up behind her and put his hands on her waist. He'd told her he was steadying her, but as they bounced along the waterway he'd leaned closer, wrapped his arms tighter around her, and buried his lips in her neck. Her toes curled as she remembered the rush of feelings.

She remembered how great a kisser Devlin was. Day after summer day they went out on the boat alone to explore the winding creeks and deserted hammocks, stopping at frequent intervals to explore each other's bodies with equal excitement and adventuresome spirit.

Dora opened her eyes and studied the man at the wheel from behind her sunglasses. Was it really twenty years ago? Where did the time go? He'd aged some, as she had. She could see the weather-beaten texture of his skin, the first gray hairs at the temple. Their bodies were fuller, softer. Her gaze traveled to his mouth and she smiled furtively. He still had those beautiful lips.

They had traveled years apart, too, she realized. Yet today, back on a Boston Whaler in these familiar creeks, with Devlin, she thought, *I feel sixteen again.*

Devlin guided the Whaler out of creeks into the wide and heady Intracoastal Waterway. Once there he slowed the boat to a stop, stepped aside from the wheel, and waved his hand, indicating Dora should come closer.

"Come on, honey, let's give you a chance at the wheel. I seem to recall you were pretty good at handling one of these things."

Dora burst into a grin. He'd remembered! Clearly she wasn't the only one taking a trip down memory lane. She set her beer into a holder and began walking across the boat when another boat roared past them, sending huge wakes their way. Dora lost her balance in the rocking boat and tottered with her arms stretched out wide.

Devlin grabbed her waist. "Hold steady, girl."

Dora clung to his arm a moment, like it was her anchor. When she got her balance, he released her and she clumsily walked the few feet to the wheel and grabbed hold.

Looking up, she spotted the speeding boat weave past another boat in the queue ahead. It was filled with four teenagers, all insolent, bronzed, and beautiful.

"Damn hooligans. Someone ought to arrest those boys, speeding like that," she blustered.

Devlin laughed beside her. "Aw, hell, Dora. We were just like that. What goes around, comes around. Come on, sugar. Let's show 'em how it's done."

She glanced over at him. She couldn't see his eyes behind his shades but knew there was a boyish sparkle of mischief in them.

"You're a bad influence on me," she said.

"Always have been"—his lips spread to a grin—"Mrs. Dora Tupper."

He'd used her married name for the first time. She hadn't been aware that he knew it.

"What you waitin' for, girl? Let's get this ol' tub going!"

Dora reached down to grab the throttle and pushed it forward. The Whaler's engine growled again and they took off along the waterway. Dora lifted her chin, feeling the vibrating, powerful engines under her control, the push of wind against her cheeks.

"Put a little muscle on it, Dora. You drive like a girl."

Dora burst out in a laugh and accepted the dare. She gripped the throttle with her hand and pushed forward hard. The engines screamed as they churned water and the boat tore off down the Intracoastal Waterway. The boat bounced on the small waves like a bronco, cool droplets splashing her face, and the wind coursing through her hair, streaming it back like a flag. She let out a whoop while beside her, Devlin let loose a rebel yell. She hadn't felt this alive in years.

Devlin stepped behind her and placed his hands on her waist.

"Just like old times," he said, lowering his lips to her ear.

Dora leaned back against him, enjoying the feel of his hard body against hers. She slowed the boat, wanting to enjoy the moments as they cruised the waterway. She rolled her palms along the wheel, one eye on the shallows, the other on signals, passing slower boats with finesse.

"Stay left at the split," Devlin called, pointing out the direction.

"Aye aye, Captain." She veered left, maneuvering the boat to a narrow creek bordered on both sides with cordgrass growing so high that she could barely see over it. It felt more like they were traveling through a long tunnel.

"Where are we going?" she asked. "It's getting narrow in here. If the tide goes out, we can get stuck."

"We're good here," he told her with confidence. "This is deep water." He leaned forward, his lips close to her cheek. "Don't you remember where we are?" he asked, his voice suddenly husky.

She caught the scent of beer on his breath and enjoyed the feel of his chin grazing her skin. She studied the long stretch of cordgrass and for the life of her couldn't remember. She shook her head. "No."

"Keep going," he told her encouragingly.

She drove the boat at a slower pace through the narrow creek before it opened up again to a wide area of water spotted with several small hammocks. The breeze picked up in the open area and brushed away the cobwebs in her memory.

"I know where we are!" she exclaimed, turning around to face Devlin, laughing. "This is our old hangout."

He slipped his arms tighter around her waist and said teasingly, "More than a hangout, if memory serves."

She blushed and faced forward again, her eyes lingering on the rounded hammock in the distance, a jungle of tall palm trees, live oaks, Chinese tallow trees, and shrubs. This had been their spot. The isolated place they'd anchor and make out and talk for hours. This secluded haven was where she'd lost her virginity. She smiled, realizing Devlin remembered.

"You ol' horn dog," she said with a playful push.

"Can't teach an old dog new tricks."

He nuzzled her neck and she felt again she was racing along the Intracoastal.

"We can pull anchor right up yonder," he said, pointing to a shallow spot near what had been their favorite hammock. "Seems as good a place as any to have some lunch."

"Lunch? I didn't pack lunch, just some things for us to munch on."

"You weren't supposed to. You don't think I invited a lady out for a trip without seeing to the details, do you?"

"I don't remember you ever bringing food to this hammock before."

"Yeah, well . . ." Devlin rubbed his jaw in embarrassment. "I've grown up a bit since then. Learned some manners at my daddy's knee."

"Your daddy? I'll wager you learned through trial and error with all the pretty girls you've brought to this hammock since me."

"None of them were as pretty as you."

Dora felt embarrassed by the compliment. Of course she wasn't the prettiest.

"Stop it, Devlin. You don't have to say that."

"Say what? It's the truth. You're beautiful."

"I said stop it," Dora snapped. "We both know I'm not." She turned her gaze away. "At least, not anymore."

Devlin took the wheel as the mood shifted. Dora went to stand at the opposite side of the boat. Devlin brought the mighty engines to a stop and set anchor. The boat rocked lightly in the current, immersed in a sudden great silence.

Dora stared at a pair of white ibis standing in the shallow water along the shore, their elegant orange down-curved bills digging in the mud. They appeared so beautiful, so serene.

Devlin walked to her side and, taking her waist, turned her to face him. He took off his sunglasses. Then he reached out and took off Dora's. This close, Dora could see the network of fine lines around his stunningly pale blue eyes. She couldn't look away.

"Dora Muir Tupper," Devlin said. "You're still the prettiest girl I ever saw."

When Dora looked into his eyes, she saw a pulsing kindness and sincerity that couldn't be faked. She felt her own eyes fill with tears and thought to herself, *Lord help me, I still have a crush on this man.*

Their gazes locked. Everything that needed to be said was said in that long look, words that the intervening years had made too complicated for translation into syllables. Dora raised her arms around his neck, not worrying this time if her body wasn't slim and perfect, if he felt more skin than was there before. He'd called her beautiful and she'd seen the truth in his eyes. She would, she decided, believe him.

When Devlin lowered his head, Dora knew that this time, she wasn't a fumbling sixteen-year-old. No, not at all. She felt every inch a luxurious woman. As she pressed her curves against him, she thought, *We are all Eve's daughters.*

～～～

It was late by the time Devlin drove Dora back to Sea Breeze. He kissed her good-bye once, then again, then once more. They giggled softly, each acknowledging that they didn't want to stop. When, at last, she extricated herself from his arms, she adjusted her shirt and smoothed her hair, glad for the darkness.

"See you tomorrow?" he asked.

"Call me."

"Soon as I wake up."

She looked at him askance. "Lord, what time is that?"

"Whenever I open my eyes."

Dora chuckled. This was one dog that would not be tied to the post.

She opened the car door and closed it as softly as she could, not wanting to wake up the household. Mamaw had kept the light burning for her. She was likely asleep, and Harper was likely still tapping away at her keyboard, lost in whatever it was she was madly working on. Feeling safe from discovery, she waved and watched Devlin drive off into the night.

No sooner did she start walking toward the front door than Lucille's porch lights went on.

"Shit," Dora muttered under her breath.

The cottage's front door opened and Lucille came out in her long white nightgown and blue floral-patterned robe. Dora didn't know if she'd ever seen Lucille in her nightclothes before and she couldn't quite grasp it in her mind.

"Sorry if I woke you up," Dora said in a loud whisper, walking closer to the cottage porch.

"You didn't. I couldn't sleep."

Dora reached the foot of the porch. "Are you okay?"

Lucille waved her hand in dismissal. "Oh, just an old woman's aches and pains. I ain't had a good night's sleep since I turned sixty. Gettin' old is not for sissies. I reckon I'll just sit out on the porch awhile, let this fine night cast its spell."

"Want some company?"

"Why, sure. Love it. Want something to drink?"

"Not a thing," Dora answered, stepping up the stairs onto the porch. She took the rocking chair beside Lucille, dropping the canvas bag on the floor.

Lucille's dark eyes studied her. "You look like you got some sun."

"Lots of it. Hope I don't peel."

"Put aloe on your skin tonight and drink lots of water."

"I will."

They rocked awhile before Lucille said, "That sure was a long boat ride."

Dora closed her eyes as images of Devlin flashed across her thoughts. That first kiss on the Boston Whaler had lit a fire in her that she hadn't felt in a very long time. It felt both as though she and Devlin had picked up right where they left off when they were sixteen, and like they were exploring something fresh and new. They were older, more world-wise, certainly more experienced. Being with Devlin was like scratching an eighteen-year-old itch. She felt again the ripple of pleasure she'd experienced when he'd found the itch and scratched it, but good. Again and again.

Dora stopped rocking and looked at Lucille. "I discovered something today."

"Oh, yeah?"

"I'm sure as hell Eve's daughter."

A knowing smile spread across Lucille's face. "Well, good for you! I'm glad to hear it." She chuckled and commenced rocking. "That boy's been waiting long enough. I reckon it was worth it?"

"Oh, yes," Dora said with a slight laugh. "Definitely."

"You gonna see him again?"

"Definitely," she repeated. After rocking awhile Dora said, "He wants to see me again tomorrow. And the day after that. I think I should cool it a little, don't you? I mean, I feel this nervousness, like I'm in high school all over again. That's not normal, is it? Is it always like this when you have a crush on someone? At my age?"

"Don't ask me. I ain't never felt that."

Dora looked at Lucille and it suddenly dawned on her how little she knew about Lucille's personal life. Lucille was always the much loved woman who lived at Sea Breeze and took care of all of them. That was a child's vision of the person, she realized with a burn of shame.

"Lucille, why didn't you ever get married?"

"I didn't want to."

"You never fell in love?"

"Didn't say that. Said I didn't never want to get married."

"Why not?"

"Why you want to know?"

Dora rocked awhile. "No reason. I just realized I don't know much about you. About your family. And I've known you all my life."

Lucille stopped rocking. "What you want to know?"

"Do you have a family?" Dora asked.

"No, not no more. My family used to live here on Sullivan's Island. You know that."

Dora nodded.

"A lot of black families used to live on Sullivan's. But times got hard, and we left to move to the city when I was not much older than Nate. My mama found work, but my daddy . . . One night he went off and we never saw him again. Never found out what happened to him. My mama died a few years later. I was just thirteen."

"Lucille, I'm sorry. That's so sad. Did you go to live with relatives?"

"My two younger sisters went to live with my aunt upstate. It was hard on them taking on two more mouths to feed. They had their own chilluns to worry about. I was the eldest and they couldn't take on the extra burden, so I went out on my own."

"At thirteen?" Dora asked, aghast. "What about an orphanage?"

"There weren't no orphanages back then, not for colored folk." She shook her head and commenced rocking.

Dora studied the woman's tight lips and didn't press with more questions.

"I made my own way," Lucille continued at length. "My mama, she took in ironing and taught me. When she passed, I had her iron, so I had some work. There were some nice women who looked out for me." She turned away, frowning. "Some not so nice."

Dora couldn't begin to imagine what life must have been like for a young, orphaned black girl in the 1950s, making a living for herself. It would have been Dickensian.

"The Lord looked out for me, though. I went into service with your mamaw when I was eighteen and I been with this family ever since." She turned her head. "You're my family, hear?"

Dora nodded, comprehending the depth of the comment.

"So you think you're in love with Devlin? That what you saying?" Lucille asked in an upbeat tone.

Dora understood Lucille wanted to change the subject. "It's way too early to say that. I like him. A lot. But with all that's going on, I don't think I should encourage him."

"A little late for that."

"A fling is one thing. A relationship is another. I mean, do I really want to take on another relationship so soon? All I want is to have a little fun. I've got enough to deal with without sparking gossip."

"Honey, no one's looking that close. If any tongues wag, they're just jealous. Look at your sister. Carson goes through men like nobody's business. You think she cares what people think?"

"I'm not like Carson."

"No, you ain't. You ain't like Harper, neither. Each of you girls have changed some since you were little and you're gonna change more in the years to come. But you're the same at the core. Carson, now she's what you might call fearless. She takes the world head-on. But she gets knocked down on her bottom plenty, too. Harper, she likes to watch. She might seem to be on the sidelines, but she's taking everything in. That girl don't miss a trick. Something's bubbling in that brain of hers, and I don't know what it is. She might not either. Yet." Lucille half turned to look at Dora and let her gaze sweep slowly over her.

"And me?"

"And you, Dora, you're the rock. You always have both feet planted firmly on the ground. The one we can depend on."

"I don't feel like a rock."

"You're going through an earthquake now. Your world is shifting. That's okay. Happens to all of us. Some folks crumble, but not you. You'll settle again, and when you do, you'll feel solid and strong again. Maybe even more than you did before. I know it."

Dora reached out to take Lucille's hand. "Oh, Lucille, thank you. I needed to hear that tonight."

"It's all gonna be all right," Lucille said in a soothing voice, patting Dora's hand over hers.

"Can I come back again, to chat like this? Just you and me?"

Lucille smiled and her eyes grew misty. "Why, I'd like that. For true."

Chapter Thirteen

~~~

*T*he day was starting out to be a scorcher on Sullivan's Island. No cloud broke the sun's relentless heat, no breeze blew from the ocean. Sweat poured down the overheated faces of both Dora and Harper as they fought backbreaking struggles with deep-rooted monster weeds in the garden. They'd been at it for over an hour and had managed to clear nearly half of the garden. They'd been ambitious with their original design, but once they comprehended the great battle, they edited the garden to a more manageable size.

Today, even that felt like too much.

"Why are we even doing this?" Dora whined, pausing her digging to swipe the sweat from her brow. "My back aches and my mouth feels like it's stuffed with cotton balls."

"Because it's fun?" Harper replied in jest, whacking at the parched earth with her hoe.

"Yeah, it's a riot," Dora said with heavy sarcasm.

Harper leaned on her hoe and caught her breath.

"Really, what's the point?" Dora asked. "Mamaw's just going to sell the place. We won't see it come to glory."

"Maybe not," Harper said. Wiping her brow, she left a mud streak in the sweat. "But we'll know it's here, won't we? Like it used to be."

Dora wasn't convinced. "So what . . ."

"*So what*, indeed," Harper muttered as she let her gaze sweep Sea Breeze.

The view from the Cove was its best side, she decided. Her Muir ancestors knew what they were doing when they'd chosen this spot on the quiet end of Sullivan's Island. The old house was well situated on higher ground, with a broad rear porch facing the Cove. The porch provided a magnificent vantage point from which to view the Intracoastal Waterway. Mamaw had added the long black-and-white awning that provided shade for the oversized black wicker chairs, with their plump black-and-white cushions. A few steps down from the porch was another level of decking that surrounded the swimming pool and stretched the entire length of the porch. From this level, more steps led to the small patch of grass that continued on a downward slope to where the wild grasses bordered the marsh.

This was where the long wooden dock extended over the marsh to the winding water of the Cove. The old, elegant Southern house, the broad veranda with chairs, the dock with a boat tied up were, for Harper, the very definition of a low-country setting. She was surprised by the love she felt for this place and how heartsick she was to see it leave family hands. *So what*, she wondered, feeling a bubbling resistance to the idea that she'd never be able to come back here, to Sea Breeze, to the only place she'd ever truly felt safe. *So what* . . . She didn't want that to happen, that was so what.

She heard Dora laughing and turned her head to see her sister looking at her with amusement.

"What's so funny?"

"You. Even digging in the garden, you make a fashion statement."

Harper looked down at her long-sleeved white cotton shirt and designer jeans. "It's all I had," she said, a tad defensively.

"I don't want to think how much those jeans cost," Dora said.

"After today, they'll be worthless. And this shirt will officially be my gardening shirt because it won't be fit to wear in public. Sort of like yours," she teased, indicating Cal's old Gamecock T-shirt, now relegated to garden duty. Dora's jeans might've been Cal's, too. They were too big and unhemmed. Under her large floppy straw hat, Dora's face was as bright as a cherry.

"Maybe we should both take a break," Harper said. "You shouldn't push too hard, with your heart and all. I don't want you digging your grave here."

"Don't worry about me," Dora said with a dismissive wave. "The doctor wants me to have a good cardio workout every day and I'm thinkin' this applies."

"I have to admit, this is a lot harder than I thought." Harper wiped at her brow. "How big did you say your garden was in Summerville?"

"A quarter acre."

Harper shook her head, incredulous. "Amazing. And ambitious."

"It was already framed out when I moved in. And I was younger." Dora laughed. "It was in the same sorry shape as this when I took it over. Lord, I slaved over that plot of earth. But it was worth every minute. I grew all our vegetables for Nate. Everything was natural, no pesticides. And the butterflies!" She smiled wistfully.

Harper brushed clumps of dirt from her shirt. "After all that work, why'd you let it go to seed?"

Dora had asked herself that question many times over the years. There wasn't an easy answer. "With Nate, it just came down to choices. I could go out to the garden or spend time with Nate. Nate won out every time. And later I homeschooled, which took a lot of time. Then there were his enrichment therapies, speech therapy . . . so many different therapies over the years." She added pointedly, "I don't regret how I spent my time."

"Of course not," Harper readily agreed. "I don't know if I'll ever have kids, but if I do, I hope I'm half as dedicated a mother as you are."

The compliment caught Dora by surprise. Harper couldn't know what it meant to her.

"That was so nice to say. Thank you."

Mamaw called from the porch, "Come take a break, girls. I've brought iced sweet tea!"

"You go get me one, would you?" Harper said. "There's something stuck in here and I've almost got it out." She gritted her teeth with determination. "Hand me that shovel."

Dora relinquished the shovel with relief. She plucked off her garden gloves as she strolled across the scrubby patch of grass, slapping them against her thighs to shake out the dirt. Looking over her shoulder, she laughed at the sight of Harper digging in the hole like a terrier with a bone. That tenaciousness was a side of her sister that she was coming to recognize and appreciate.

"Bless you, Mamaw," Dora said, accepting the glass. The tea was icy sweet, and as she gulped it down, her throat felt like parched ground welcoming a rushing river.

"You're making progress," Mamaw said, lifting her sunglasses as she looked out at the garden. "It does my heart good to see the garden return to its former beauty."

"It won't be as fancy as your last one."

"It'll be glorious, because you girls created it. Now drink up. You know what I always say."

"*You have to stay hydrated,*" Dora replied, then dutifully took a sip.

"And wear sunscreen. I've given you good genes, but you have to do your part." She lowered her voice and took a step closer. "And get Lucille's recipe for face cream. I swanny, she'll go to the grave with it."

Dora chuckled at Mamaw's lifelong quest to get Lucille's face cream recipe. "Where is Lucille?" she asked. "I haven't seen her around this morning."

"No, she's feeling poorly, bless her heart."

"That doesn't sound like her. I can't remember the last time she got sick."

"I know. She's usually fit as a fiddle, but we have to accept that she is getting older. Even if she won't admit it."

The porch door opened and Lucille stepped out, blinking in the light. She was dressed in her usual summer uniform of a pale blue cotton shirtwaist dress. Mamaw had told her many times over the years that she no longer was required to wear a uniform, but Lucille preferred to and stubbornly continued to do so. When Lucille had her mind made up, she couldn't be swayed.

"I won't admit what?" Lucille asked, walking toward them.

Dora didn't like the stiffness to Lucille's gait or the grayish cast to her skin. She looked frail, too, like she'd suddenly aged.

"Are you sure you should be out of bed? You don't look so good."

"That's because I don't feel so good. But I just go stir-crazy lying in my bed all day. I can sit just as well out here on the porch." She turned to Mamaw. "I won't admit what?"

"That you're getting older," Mamaw replied archly, walking over to the large black wicker chairs in the shade.

"I'm still younger than you!" Lucille snapped back, then mumbled something unintelligible.

Dora trotted over to help Mamaw drag a chair deeper into the shade, then carried the ottoman over as well.

"Come sit down, Lucille," Mamaw said. "You should rest."

Lucille obliged, sinking with a soft grunt into the thick black-and-white-striped cushions. She put her feet up on the ottoman and rested her head back, already fatigued from the mild exertion. Dora caught Mamaw's eye and saw her own worry reflected there.

"You don't have a fever, do you?" Mamaw asked, hovering over Lucille. "Is it the flu?"

"No, I ain't got no flu. I'm just tired. Like you said, I'm old."

"Not that old," Mamaw said.

Lucille looked at Mamaw and shared a laugh.

"How about a nice glass of sweet tea?" Dora asked.

"That'd be real nice." Lucille glanced at Mamaw. "Want to play a little gin rummy?"

Mamaw's eyes lit up. "I'll get the cards."

A call from Harper in the garden interrupted her departure. "Hey! I found something!"

Mamaw's hand flew to her heart. "Heavens, she found buried treasure!" she exclaimed dramatically. "We've been looking for the Gentleman Pirate's treasure for generations. Legend has it that pirates buried their treasures for safekeeping in the deserted dunes and woods of these islands," she told Dora. "And, with our history, well, it should be here somewhere. Although," she said with a sigh, "no one has found anything so far."

"I'd better get out there before she claims finders keepers," Dora exclaimed. "Just what a James needs, more treasure," she added with sarcasm. "It'd be just my luck, too." She took a final swig of iced tea. "I'm coming!" she yelled, and trotted to the garden carrying a frosty glass for Harper.

Harper was on her knees before a deep hole at the fringe of the garden, bent over a mud-encrusted object in her lap.

"It looks like some kind of chain," she said as she busily knocked off clumps of dirt. Then she paused to gratefully accept the drink from Dora.

"Maybe it's a gold chain," Dora said, excitement building.

"Or just a chain. It's metal. And it's heavy." Harper gulped down half the glass of tea, set the glass down, and returned to knocking dirt from the object. Gradually the object became a recognizable shape. Harper took off her sunglasses and lifted the item higher in her hands. She cocked her head, studying it.

"I'm not sure," Harper said a bit breathlessly, "but I think it might be handcuffs of some kind."

Dora scooted lower, then looked over to Harper with amazement and awe. "*Slave shackles?*" Though she would have preferred to have unearthed a thick gold chain from pirates, there was a historical significance to the shackles that rendered her speechless.

Harper rose to her feet with the chain. "Let's go rinse it off with the hose and show it to Mamaw and Lucille. They'll know."

Mamaw and Lucille were sitting up in their chairs on the porch, necks craned as they followed Dora's and Harper's progress from the garden to the hose.

"What you got there?" Mamaw called out.

"Not sure," Dora called back. "Be right there."

Dora held out the chain as Harper hosed the gushing water over the unknown hunk of metal. Water sluiced off the final layer of mud and muck, revealing what looked like thick, rusting, heavy metal handcuffs joined together with a chain. Neither woman spoke but stood in almost a reverential silence. Harper turned off the hose, then followed Dora across the porch to the two waiting elderly women. Their eyes were wide with curiosity.

"What is it?" Mamaw asked.

Lucille sat up and lowered her legs from the ottoman.

Dora lay the dripping object on the ottoman. It settled with a clanking sound.

Lucille sucked in her breath and stared at the object. Then with seeming trepidation, she reached out to place her dark, wrinkled hand on one of the handcuffs.

"Lord above, girl, you done found slave manacles," she said in a soft voice that shook with emotion.

"I thought that might be what they were," Dora said.

Mamaw drew closer to study the heavy metal cuffs. "They say if you dig anywhere on this island you'll uncover history. When we renovated the house, we found Revolutionary War bullets, Civil War coins, buttons, broken pottery, all manner of memorabilia. But never any pirate's treasure. Or anything as profound as this," she said, indicating the shackles. "This is a part of our history I'm not proud of."

Lucille's hands shook under the weight as she lifted the manacles and put them in her lap. "They so heavy I can hardly lift them."

"Can you imagine how they managed to walk with those?" Dora said.

Harper asked, "What are slave shackles doing on Sullivan's Island? I thought the slaves all went to the market in Charleston."

Mamaw's face grew reflective. "The slaves weren't sold at the market. They were usually sold at the Charleston ports, right off the boat. After quarantine. The local residents were terrified of infectious diseases like cholera, measles, and smallpox coming in on the ships. This was a major port for the country, don't forget. So they built pest houses here on Sullivan's Island for quarantine. It was a convenient location, a barrier island right along the port entry. Throughout the eighteenth century, slaves flowed through our port in large numbers. And all of them were sent for quarantine before they were sold."

"If they survived the journey," Lucille added somberly.

Mamaw rested her hand over her friend's. "Sadly true."

"How many slaves came through Charleston Harbor, do you know?" asked Harper.

"No one knows for sure," Mamaw answered. "So many died here in the pest houses—men, women, and children."

Lucille said sadly, "I heard somewheres between two hundred and four hundred thousand slaves came through."

Harper gasped. "That many?"

Lucille glanced at her. "You think that's a lot? It ain't so many when you know ten to twelve million were shipped out of Africa." Lucille sighed as she stared down at the shackles. "Africa done bled her children."

"Charleston was the major port of entry for slaves in America," explained Mamaw. "Near half of African Americans in this country can trace their roots through Charleston. And most of them were quarantined right here on this island." She looked at the shackles and added, "I've always felt that we needed to do more here on Sullivan's Island to honor all those slaves who died here. A monument of some kind. After all, this was an Ellis Island for the hundreds of thousands of slaves who passed through."

"Hardly Ellis Island," Harper corrected Mamaw. "Immigrants who passed through that island came willingly and sought a better life, political or religious freedom. Ironic contrast, wouldn't you say?"

Dora felt a flurry of irritation. Harper always had to argue a point. And it rankled because she was usually correct.

"My ancestors came here on a slave ship," Lucille said in a low voice.

She was bent over the shackles, her hand resting on the metal protectively. It appeared to Dora that the old woman was folding into herself.

"Only the strong in spirit survived the journey," Lucille

continued. "Black families lived on Sullivan's for as long as I know. Used to be small farms here." She stretched out her hand toward the garden. "Big gardens. There were chickens, too. Maybe a pig. But they's all gone now. Poor folk moved to Daniel Island when this one got built up. Now they gone from Daniel Island, too." She paused as her mind seemed to drift back to the past.

"Do you miss your family?" Harper asked gently.

Lucille blinked and seemed to return to the present. "No, there's only me." She looked at the other women. "And y'all. And that's all right. We all have our time, there's no use fightin' it. I like to think we'll meet up again someday on the other side."

"You have your ancestors' strength," Dora said emphatically.

Lucille appeared moved by the comment. "I hope so. I'll need it when times get hard." She looked at Harper. "What you plan to do with these?"

"I don't have any plans," Harper replied. "Donate them to a museum maybe?"

"If you don't mind, I'd like to hold on to them, just for a while."

"Of course," Harper said. "Take them. They're yours."

Lucille looked down at the shackles in her lap. "Thank you. I'd just like to study them awhile. Maybe I will go back to my cottage now," Lucille said. "I'm tired." She attempted to rise, but with the heavy chain weighing her down it took more strength than she had. Alarmed, Dora and Harper each took a side while Mamaw grabbed hold of the chain. They helped Lucille to her feet.

"You better go back to bed," Mamaw told her.

"I might do that," Lucille said in a pant. "I am weary." She reached out for the shackles.

"I'll carry those for you," Harper said.

Lucille turned her shoulder and took the shackles from Mamaw. "No, no, child. I got them. I want to carry them. I want to know what it feels like to be worn-out and still have to walk, carrying this burden."

Chapter Fourteen

～～～

Dora received a text message from Devlin asking her to come by a house he was working on. He wanted her to see it and then join him for dinner.

It was easy to text back an enthusiastic yes. Dora loved houses, especially on Sullivan's Island, where so many—large and small, historic and new—had unique settings, or views, or history. She hopped into the golf cart with a bottle of water and bumped along the road to the southern side of the island, checking the address. She turned down a side street that led toward the marsh. Many old live oaks created heavy shade cover, welcome on a steamy summer day. She checked the address again and came to a stop before a small cottage barely visible behind a jungle of overgrown shrubs and palm trees. The driveway had long since been converted to dirt. Revving the engine, she drove the golf cart up beside Devlin's big truck. When she reached for her purse, she heard her phone ringing.

"Hello?" she said, expecting it to be Devlin. She was shocked when she recognized Cal's voice.

"Dora? It's me."

"Yeah. What's up?"

"Well, you never called me back."

Dora cringed. She'd completely forgotten about him. "Oh, I'm sorry. I, uh, I've been really busy."

"Oh yeah? Doing what?"

"Oh, uh . . ." She swallowed, thinking of an excuse. "Harper and I have started a garden. It's been a lot of work."

"A garden? In July? Are you sure you should be doing that kind of intensive labor? With your heart?"

"My heart is fine," she replied, irritated that he still thought she was sick. "And we're being careful. Anyway, I'm sorry I never called back. Is there something in particular you wanted to discuss?"

There was a pause. "Yes," he said in that tone that implied she should have known there was a topic. "We were going to discuss whether you were going to move into the condo. With me."

"I thought I was clear about that. I'm going to stay at Sea Breeze for the summer."

"I thought you might change your mind. You see, there are problems at the house."

Dora's stomach dropped. Of course, that was why he was calling. "What kind of problems?"

"The painters say that there was water damage on some of the upstairs bedrooms. That they can't paint, so they're stalled. They're guessing it's from the roof. So now we have to have someone come in to assess water damage in the attic. It's never-ending," he said with a hiss of frustration.

"What do you want me to do about it? I'm out here on Sullivan's. You're in Summerville."

"Dora," he said, reining in frustration. "That's why it makes sense for you to be here. The house is a bigger project than we'd anticipated. It needs someone's full-time attention to keep the crews in line."

"It's not bigger than we anticipated," she argued. "We always knew it was a big job, and that's why we didn't start, or at least that's what you always told me. I'm going to say again what I told you at the lawyer's office. Sell the house as is if you don't want to take charge of the renovations."

"We can't do that. We'd lose our shirt."

"We've already lost our shirt."

"Dora, please. I'm up to my ears in work right now. Can't you help me?"

Dora groaned inwardly. "Oh, all right. I'll come to Summerville and take a look at the house. Make a few phone calls. But that's it. I'm not moving into your condo, Cal. I'm not ready to go that far."

"Okay, that's fine. But you'll call someone about the leak, right?"

She rolled her eyes and laughed shortly at his transparency. "I'll call. Bye." She ended the call and tossed the phone into her purse.

Dora stretched her arms over her head, trying to release the frustration from Cal's phone call before she saw Devlin. She didn't want Cal in the room between them, again. She heard the high hum of a power tool from inside the house and, curious, followed the noise to the front door. It had been left ajar.

"Hello?" she called out, poking her head in. It was hard to be heard over the roar of the power tool. She stepped inside and saw Devlin in goggles, standing behind a woodcutter and slicing what looked like a piece of wood paneling. She had to pause to take in the sight of Devlin doing construction. It was another side of him she didn't know about.

"Hello!" she called again when he'd stopped.

Devlin jerked his head up and broke into a wide grin. He lifted his goggles from his head, shaking sawdust into the air, and stepped forward to offer a quick kiss.

"You're here!"

"Just got here," she said, brushing away sawdust from his hair. "What's going on?" she asked, looking around the house with curiosity. The cottage had been gutted and was now in the process of a major renovation. A lot of work had already been done—new walls, cabinets, counters, appliances. Dora had dreamed of renovating her house in Summerville for so long that she always got a thrill at the sight of a renovation.

"This is a house I bought last year when the market dropped. Got it on a foreclosure. I'm renovating it in my spare time. When I'm done, I'll put it back on the market."

"*You're* renovating it? I didn't know you were a handyman."

"A carpenter, thank you very much," he said in the manner of someone who'd been doing it for a very long time. "That's what got me in the real-estate business in the first place. I used to work construction—thought you knew that. I bought a fixer-upper back when I could afford anything on Sullivan's, did all the work myself, then sold it for a big profit. I just kept on going, flipping houses, making profits. Found out I had a good eye for real estate." He shrugged. "I was lucky and got in for the boom. The rest is history."

She looked at Devlin, seeing him in a new light.

"Why are you looking at me like that?"

"Like what?"

"Like you're about to have me for dinner."

She laughed, coloring. "I guess because I find the fact that you can do your own renovations very sexy."

He laughed, raised his brows, and set the piece of paneling down. "Well, hell, lady," he said, reaching out and grabbing her around the waist, tugging her closer. "If I'd a known that, I'd a shown you my power tools right off."

He kissed her then, long and slow and deliberate, and she felt the humming in her veins. When the kiss ended, she leaned back in his arms and smiled coyly. "I wish I'd known you had this talent a few months ago. I could have used your help."

"Yeah? Why?"

She disentangled from his arms and began walking around the room, not wanting to bring Cal and the house in Summerville into the conversation. Devlin was installing cypress wood paneling into the back room, creating a lovely lowcountry feel. The back wall had been replaced with a long wall of windows overlooking the marsh. Dora crossed her arms and stood looking out over the wide swath of waving grass and the Intracoastal glistening in the sunlight.

"This view never gets old."

Devlin followed her to the windows and stood beside her. "That's because it's always changing. Folks from off who come to buy always want the ocean views. I can find that, too. But it's the wetlands that shows the change of scenery. The migrating birds, the changing grass—bright green in the summer, gold in the fall, brown in the winter, then the soft greening again in the spring."

He turned his head and looked at her, his gaze serious. "Why could you have used my help a few months back?"

Dora sighed, resigned, and looked up at him. "I have to put my house in Summerville on the market. We bought it as a fixer-upper, only we never did the fixing-up. There was never the money. Now that we're getting a divorce, we're putting the house on the market. Suddenly everything that I've been waiting years to get done has to get done in a hurry."

"So, you're trying to flip the house."

"Not even. We're just trying to get it in decent enough shape to sell it. Cal wants to spend money we don't have, and I want to sell it as is. He won, of course."

"Why of course?"

"Because whenever it's an issue of money, Cal makes the decision."

"Even when the outcome affects your financial situation?"

Dora moved to the other side of the room, where a new fireplace mantel was being installed.

"Cal is not as concerned about my financial situation."

Devlin gave a little laugh. "He's an ass."

"Yes, well . . ." Dora looked closely at the wood trim of the mantel. She heard Devlin draw closer.

"How can I help?"

Dora turned and found he was standing very close. "Cal just called. There's a problem of a leak. It's probably the roof. He wants me to find someone who can take a look and tell us what needs to be done."

"He wants you to find the person?"

She nodded.

Devlin pinched his mouth, keeping what she was sure was a string of unsavory comments from flowing out.

"I'll take a look. And I should send him a whopping bill, just to teach him a lesson. Only you'd get stuck paying the bill. We can drive up together and I'll take a good look around and give you my opinion, for what it's worth."

"That would be so great. Apparently the workers are slacking off, too."

"I've got good crews who can do the work for a good price. If your guys are jerks, we'll send them packing."

"What can I do to thank you?"

Devlin gave her a wicked look that promised mischief, then pointed to the box of paneling. "Grab some gloves, woman, and lend me a hand. I've got work to finish before I cook you dinner!"

They spent the rest of the afternoon paneling the back room together while Devlin's old CD boom box played rock and roll. With the hum of the power tool and hammering, they couldn't talk much. Instead they sang out the lyrics to songs they remembered from their youth, and during the occasional slow song, Devlin strolled over to her side, swinging his hips to wrap her in his arms and dance with her. He held her close, hummed in her ear, and smelled of sweat and wood, and it was pure heaven.

When at last the room was paneled, Dora and Devlin stood back to admire their work. She'd actually helped panel a room, she thought with stunned surprise. And it had been fun! This is what she'd always imagined it would be like for her and Cal in the house they'd bought. Working together, side by side, taking pride in their accomplishments, sharing in the glory. It was never going to happen, not if they'd lived in that house for another ten years. She knew that now. It wasn't the time or the money. Cal didn't have Devlin's skill or the desire to do the transformation himself. He wasn't interested in anything but seeing it done. Cal was, simply, not Devlin.

"Nice job," Devlin told her, obviously pleased with the turnout.

"I can see how you got hooked," she said.

"You had a good time, did you?" he asked, curious.

"I did," she replied honestly. "I never knew how physically exhausting it was, but I had a great time. Can I help with something else?"

Devlin laughed then and wrapped her in his arms. "I knew you were a good 'un." He kissed her nose, then patted her bottom in a signal they were done. "Let's take a swim before dinner."

"I didn't bring a suit."

"Yeah? So?"

Dora made a face. "I'm not going skinny-dipping."

Devlin wagged his brows, then grabbed her hand. "Come on, I won't look. Much."

Dora laughed but pulled away. "No way."

"Chicken. All right. Come on, then, and help me pull up dinner."

"Where are we going?"

"Down the dock, of course."

He took her hand again and she followed him outdoors. They walked single-file in the path he'd made through the tall grass that led to the wood dock. It was very long and very narrow, double the length of Mamaw's dock at Sea Breeze, because it had to stretch much farther out over the grass to reach water.

"It's kinda rocky in spots, so be careful," Devlin warned.

Dora followed Devlin down the rickety walkway over pluff mud and grass. A few slats had rotted through, and Devlin was careful to point each one out along the way. At last they reached the end, where a rickety dock met the waterway.

"I'll have to replace the dock, too," Devlin said. "Whew, it sure is hot today." He took off his T-shirt and wiped his brow with it. "That water sure looks refreshing." He glanced at Dora.

Dora stuck out her hands. "Don't. Just don't!"

"Kick off your sandals, darlin'."

"Devlin!" She kicked off her flip-flops.

In a flash he grabbed her hand, pulled her close to the edge of the dock, and they both let loose a howl as they jumped together into the water.

She hit the water, and it was cool and refreshing. She burst out laughing as she came up for air, her hair flowing back and the sun shining on her face. Devlin swam to her side and kissed her again, holding her close, beginning again the slow dance in the water.

Later, they climbed back to the dock, refreshed. Devlin went to the edge and pulled up on a thick rope attached to the piling. His wet shirt clung to his body, revealing taut muscles straining as he pulled on the rope, hand over hand, until a large, black iron cage emerged, dripping water. Dora drew closer, curious, then stepped back when she saw at least a dozen crabs skittering noisily inside the trap.

Devlin lifted the trap high and laughed. "You're as skittish as one of these crabs. Haven't you ever gone crabbing before?"

"Never!" she exclaimed, warily watching the claws snapping in the air.

"Stand back," he said, easing the trap onto the dock. "We've got dinner!"

Dora helped Devlin again, this time cooking the crabs in a big stainless-steel pot on a gas burner out on the back porch. Dora wore a towel like a sarong and slicked back her hair from her face. There was an old picnic table on the patio that was still standing . . . barely. Devlin spread newspaper over it, set candles in empty beer bottles, and laid out two wooden mallets and a roll of paper towels, while she shucked corn and melted butter. The boom box played golden oldies by Otis Redding.

The sun was setting and Dora was on her third beer by the time the feast was ready. In the distance the glassy waters shimmered in hues of lavender and rose, setting a romantic mood. Devlin lit the candles and guided her to a seat on the bench.

"I know this isn't quite the setting of the restaurant the other night," he said by way of apology.

"No, it's not," Dora replied, swinging her leg around the bend and sitting. "It's better."

Devlin lowered his face to kiss her neck, and she shivered in anticipation of what was to come. Once again, Devlin helped Dora wield a hammer, this time on the crabs to crack the shells and dig out the sweet meat. Putting the crab to her lips, she tasted the pungent Old Bay seasoning and the salt from the sea on her fingers, thinking she'd never in her life tasted anything so delicious.

Tonight, no specter of Cal came between them. They talked seamlessly about whatever came to mind—Nate's progress, Devlin's plans for the house. Later they journeyed back to shared memories of the years they'd dated, laughing at crazy antics, calling out the names of old friends, favorite songs, rumors they'd heard, truths revealed.

When they were done feasting, Devlin took her in his arms and once again they began to dance. He held her close as they moved left to right to the beat of the music, no longer remembering old times they'd shared, but dreaming of new ones to come.

Chapter Fifteen

~~~

Florida

*T*oday was special. Nate was becoming increasingly relaxed in his interactions with the dolphins from the floating dock. He'd learned hand signals and played games with the dolphins using balls and rings. He'd even had a T-shirt painted by a dolphin. Today, however, Nate was going to swim with the dolphins.

"How do you feel about getting in the water with the dolphins today?" Carson asked Nate over breakfast. She put a spoonful of cold cereal in her mouth and began chewing, giving him time to answer. Earlier in the summer, Nate had swum daily with Delphine in the Cove behind Sea Breeze. Carson worried that he'd be nervous about going back in the water with a dolphin after Delphine's accident.

Nate scooped his cereal into his mouth and continued reading the back of the cereal box. When he finished, he set down his spoon and nodded seriously.

"Good," he said.

"What's good? The cereal or swimming with the dolphins?"

Nate scowled, as though frustrated with his ninny of an aunt.

"Good to swim with the dolphins."

That was all Carson needed to know. That, and the excited look in his eyes gleaming against his tanned skin, spoke volumes.

Once there, Nate ran ahead to the lagoon as usual. Carson moved slowly, feeling lethargic in the relentless Florida heat. Watching the boy trot along the path, she reflected on the transformation from a shy, timid boy into this happier, more relaxed version. He wasn't outgoing; that was not his nature. Yet she could see he felt comfortable here after days of routine. Welcomed. The staff called out his name as he ran along the path, and though he didn't verbally respond, he raised his hand in a wave of acknowledgment. Most telling of all was the joy she captured on film when he swam with the dolphins.

Joan and Rebecca were waiting and guided them to a different section of the park. This was on the opposite side from where the female dolphins lived. It was a break in his routine from the front lagoon and Carson held her breath as she watched Nate tap his fingers against his mouth, a sign she recognized now as nervousness. But Joan led the way with confidence, marching Team Nate past the wood railings that bordered the lagoon and the houses where the sea lions lived. Two sleek females were basking like mermaids on rocks. Turning a corner, Carson paused to take in the wide expanse of gorgeous Florida Bay.

"So these are the bachelor pods," she said.

A long coral causeway was covered with the same thatched island-style roof found at the front lagoon. It created a shaded space for guests while they watched the dolphins. Each side was lined with spacious enclosures, partitioned to house different pairs or small groups of dolphins.

When they reached the partitioned dock that Nate would use today, Carson grabbed a spot on the bench in the shade.

"Are you sure you don't want to join us in the swim today?" Joan called to her. "You're welcome to, and it'll be fun."

"No, thanks. I want to take pictures," she called back. She lifted the camera hanging around her neck to prove the point.

"We have a photographer," Joan reasoned. "He'll make sure to get plenty of great shots of Nate."

Carson paused.

A part of her wanted to go into the water with Nate, to feel the rubbery skin of the dorsal fin under her hand again and glide across the lagoon. That feeling was unlike any other. But she couldn't face swimming with another dolphin. Not yet. She'd had such a rare and unique bond with Delphine. She missed seeing Delphine's bright, inquisitive eyes, hearing her high-pitched whistle or her nasal staccato laughs. Swimming with another dolphin would be too painful.

She shook her head. "My stomach's feeling a bit off," she called back. "Better not. But thanks."

Carson bent over her huge canvas bag where she kept all their supplies and pulled out the lenses she wanted to use today. A dog's bark from the far end of the lagoon caught her attention, and turning her head, she was surprised to see a large black dog on the lower dock at the end of the pavilion. A dog near the dolphins wasn't the norm. Curious, she rose and joined the cluster of tourists craning to watch the interaction between the big black dog and a dolphin. They were laughing and pointing.

Carson lifted her camera. Through her lens she saw the big dog lower its pointy nose as it inched with agonizing slowness toward the edge of the dock. The dolphin appeared equally curious about the dog and was rising higher in the water, angling closer.

Carson held her breath, her finger on the button.

The big dog reached the edge, then stopped. The dolphin moved forward to touch its rostrum against the dog's nose.

Carson clicked the camera. "Got it!" she said, grinning. She felt as if she were the big black dog as its tail began wagging a mile a minute. Carson kept clicking away as the dolphin returned for more kisses. It was clear the two animals were having a good time.

When a man came to take hold of the dog's collar and, with a gentle pat, lead it away from the dock's edge, she lowered her camera and joined the chorus of groans from the audience who were enjoying the tender scene. He tied the dog to the dock post in the shade and gave the dog's big head several more pats. When he returned to the lower dock and looked out, Carson realized that the man was Taylor.

She knew she should go right back to Nate's dock, but she couldn't resist watching Taylor give signals to the two dolphins at his dock with the ease and authority of any of the other trainers. He was working with two male dolphins, one huge and the other small. She poised her camera and photographed Taylor giving a command that sent the dolphins swimming off underwater. Clicking rapidly, she caught shots of them leaping skyward in a beautifully synchronized leap. The big dolphin reached a remarkable height, while beside him the smaller one climbed not nearly as high.

Carson's heart lurched when she saw a chunk was missing from the smaller dolphin's tail fluke, like Delphine's. She followed the small dolphin with her camera, focusing in on the details. When the small dolphin emerged again at the dock to receive a fish, she saw that part of its dorsal fin was missing as well. The crowd applauded and Carson caught a great shot of Taylor's face breaking out into a reluctant grin.

"I could watch him all day," a young woman to her left remarked to her friend. "And I'm not talking about the dolphin."

"Mm-hmm," her friend agreed, before they bent their heads together, giggling.

Perusing the group, Carson couldn't help but notice how many of the women had their gazes not on the dolphins but on the handsome trainer. With her camera she captured his muscles exposed beneath his sleeveless T-shirt, the long swim trunks falling from his hips. Besides his good looks, his movements were graceful like a dancer's. What made him all the more attractive was his being oblivious to the attention he was receiving. His focus was solely on the dolphins.

Carson lowered her camera, feeling an undeniable racing in her blood, a spine-tingling attraction to the ex-Marine. She was only human, after all. But then Blake's smiling face popped into her head, and she felt guilty that the first time she'd left Blake, her gaze was wandering.

Carson covered her lens and hurried back to the other side of the pavilion to Nate's dock. She quickly took several photos of Nate chest-deep in the water, grinning ear to ear while confidently giving signals to a big dolphin. Then she went back to the bench and, pulling out her phone, placed a call to Blake. She wanted to hear his voice. Blake had been out doing field-work for the past several days, out of phone range. Once again, her call was sent to voice mail.

Sighing and putting her phone in her bag, she looked up to see Nate engaged in a splash battle with the dolphin. Clearly the dolphin was winning and Nate was loving it. As she watched, her mind drifted back to Blake. She'd never been in love before, but she thought what she felt for Blake might be love. So her attraction to Taylor was a red flag.

"Still stalking me, I see."

Carson whipped her head up to see Taylor standing by the bench, a crooked grin on his face. He held on to a thick, black "Service Dog" harness attached to the black dog she'd seen on the dock. The dog was so big that, sitting on the bench, she was eye to eye with it.

"Taylor!" she exclaimed a little too loudly, rattled that he'd snuck up on her just as she was thinking about him. "I didn't know if I'd see you again. And certainly not training dolphins."

Taylor's grin widened as he took a seat on the bench beside her. He seemed more relaxed today, and she wondered if it was because of his session with the dolphins or because he was with his dog.

"Didn't I tell you I was having sessions here?"

"You did, but I thought you were doing what Nate's doing, not training. You looked good out there, by the way," she said, then blushed slightly at the double entendre. "I took some pic-tures. Here, take a look."

He leaned closer to look into her camera's LCD panel, their shoulders touching. Once again she felt a jolt of attraction. She flicked through the photos, enjoying the sound of his deep laughter and his occasional "That's a good one."

"I've got to get copies of Thor with the dolphin," he told her.

"Sure. I'll send them to you. What's your e-mail?"

"I don't have a pen or paper," he said.

"No problem." Carson turned to dig again into her bag, pulling out her card. "Here's my card. Just e-mail me and I'll send them to you."

"Great. Thanks." He tucked the card into his shorts.

"You were great out there," Carson said.

"I've been training here for almost a year now." He smiled a bit sheepishly. "They've offered me a job."

I'll bet, she thought to herself. There'd be a line of women at the gate clamoring for tickets. "Congratulations." She grinned and, turning her head, stared into a pair of dark brown eyes. "And your dog, too?"

He laughed and reached out to pat the dog's head. "Where are my manners? Carson, this is Thor. Thor," he said to the dog, "say hello to the pretty lady."

Thor shifted his adoring gaze from his master to Carson and lifted his giant paw.

"Whoa," she said as the paw hit her lap. "That's a pretty big paw you got there, pal." Carson loved dogs, especially big, gentle ones. Thor reminded her of Blake's dog, Hobbs, with his large block head, wide chest, and floppy ears. He also had large, soulful eyes she could lose herself in. They reminded her of Blake's eyes.

"He's a great dog," she told Taylor, who was watching Thor with affection.

"Yep, he is," Taylor agreed, patting his head again. "He was rescued from the pound and trained as a service dog. He's a mutt, but I'm guessing he's part Great Dane and part Lab and part something else that gave him that patch of white on his chest that looks like a lightning bolt. Reckon that's how he got his name."

Carson began to absentmindedly scratch Thor behind his ears, and his tail started thumping in response. Taylor was a Marine with a service dog, she thought to herself. Interesting.

"You said you were in a program with Joan?"

Taylor looked across the walkway to where Joan sat on the dock watching Nate.

"I was here for the Wounded Warrior Project."

Carson wasn't surprised to hear that. She'd read that the Dolphin Research Center had a program for wounded warriors. Yet, when she thought of a wounded warrior, she thought of someone with physical injuries.

After an awkward silence Taylor said in a softer tone, "I know what you're thinking. Where's the wound, right? You don't see the injury."

Carson couldn't reply. Blunt though it was, he was right.

"You can't see all wounds," Taylor said. "Especially not in this war. Sure, some of us in the Wounded Warrior program have missing limbs, or are in a wheelchair. Some have serious burns. But *all* of us have PTSD."

Carson knew quite a bit about post–traumatic stress disorder because she'd studied the symptoms after Delphine's accident on the dock. It was a debilitating condition that followed a terrifying event. She'd had bad nightmares after the fire that killed her mother, and she'd tucked away that traumatic memory in her mind for years, only to begin to deal with it now. After Delphine's accident she had been stricken with guilt and regret, but she'd been able to move on. She'd read how PTSD left one feeling emotionally numb, especially toward people they were once close to. Learning that had helped her to understand Nate's angry behavior toward her.

"I think my nephew, Nate, had PTSD from the accident."

"What kind of accident?"

"Actually, it involved a dolphin. Delphine. She used to come by our dock on Sullivan's Island. One morning she got caught in the fishing line and was badly hurt. Luckily we got her to a rehab facility in Florida, but Nate was pretty traumatized by it. You see, he was the one who'd put out the fishing lines."

Taylor turned a sympathetic glance toward Nate. "Poor little guy. He must have taken it all pretty hard."

"So did I," Carson added, her voice catching unexpectedly. She cleared her throat. "Joan's doing a wonderful job bringing him out of it."

"She's good at that."

"What made you want to start training dolphins?" she asked Taylor.

"A lot of it has to do with that little dolphin out there." He jutted his chin to indicate the lagoon.

"Which one?"

Taylor scanned the water, then reached out to point to a smaller dolphin. "That dolphin swimming near the dock closest to us. That's Jax."

"The little guy. I noticed that he's missing part of his tail fluke."

"Yeah, Jax is a real survivor. He was just a calf when he was found near dead in the water near Jacksonville. That's how he got the name. They captured him and brought him to Gulf World in Panama City. The tip of his dorsal fin, half his left fluke, and part of his pectoral fin were bitten off before he got away. You can still see the scars left by the shark's teeth on his flank. From the measurement, they figured he was attacked by a bull shark."

Carson shuddered, remembering her own near miss with a bull shark earlier that summer.

"It's a good guess Jax's mother was killed trying to defend her calf. They saved his life at Gulf World, then he was placed here for a permanent home."

"He wasn't released?"

"He never would've made it out in the wild. Not only because of his injuries, but because without a mother to teach him the ropes, he'd starve or be shark bait. He was only about a year or so when he came here. Now Jax is part of the gang. He has his injuries, of course. And he's younger than the others and still has some growing to do, so he doesn't jump as high as the other males." He grinned. "But Jax doesn't care. There's nothing he can't do. He jumps, leaps, does all the routines right with the pack. Here's the thing. The other dolphins don't see Jax as injured. And Jax doesn't see himself as injured." He swallowed hard. "That says it all."

Carson heard the emotion in his voice and understood why Taylor felt such a strong connection to the brave young dolphin.

"The program directors gave us this," Taylor said, reaching up to pull out a silver chain from under his shirt. He turned so she could see a small silver dolphin tail fin attached to the chain; the left tail fluke was missing. "That's Jax's fluke."

Carson reached out and took the small silver fin between her two fingers, tracing the intricate lines. She looked up at Taylor.

"Aunt Carson!"

Carson had been so caught up in Taylor's story, she hadn't noticed that Nate had finished his session. She was surprised at how fast the time had flown and embarrassed that she hadn't given Nate her full attention. Nate ran up to her, eyes aglow from his session, but stopped short at seeing Taylor and Thor at her side. Instantly he grew wary.

"Nate, you did great! I'm so proud of you," Carson exclaimed. "Come closer, I want you to meet my new friend Taylor. He was a Marine. And guess what? He trains the dolphins."

Nate looked at his feet without a word.

Taylor didn't seem the least bothered by Nate's silence. "Hey, Nate. Do you want to meet Thor?"

Nate looked at the dog. "Is Thor the dog's name?" Nate asked.

"Yes."

Nate studied the dog a moment, then asked, "Can I pet him?"

"Sure."

Nate approached the dog slowly. Thor looked patiently at the boy and remained calm while enduring the petting.

"How much does he weigh?"

"One hundred and twelve pounds of pure muscle," Taylor answered with a hint of pride. "He loves to swim in the ocean."

"With the dolphins?"

"No, they don't come close enough in the wild. But he would if he could."

Nate petted the dog again, then, his curiosity sated, turned to Carson. "I'm hungry."

"I'll bet you are after all that swimming. Let's head back home and think about going someplace special for dinner. It's our last night."

"Why not let me take you to dinner?" Taylor offered. "Since it's your last night and all."

Carson was taken aback by the invitation. It was completely unexpected. Taylor waited for his answer.

"What do you think, Nate?"

Nate looked away and shrugged.

Inside her gut, warning bells were going off, telling her to beg off with some excuse. Ignoring them, she said, "All right, that's real nice of you. I should warn you, though, we'll need to go someplace that serves food Nate will eat. He's pretty picky."

"I'm hungry *now*," Nate said.

"I am, too, pal," Taylor told Nate. "Why don't we get cleaned up and I'll come by your place, and we'll go right out to eat. The Shipwreck is close by and they have a pretty standard menu. It'll be an early dinner or a late lunch. Whatever you want to call it."

You can call it anything but a date, Carson thought to herself as she smiled back at Taylor.

⌇⌇⌇

"Okay, Nate, it's time to turn off the game," Carson called out. "Bedtime."

"No, not yet. Just a little longer," Nate whined.

"We're almost done with this level," Taylor added, not taking his eyes from the screen.

"You're not helping," Carson told Taylor, raising an eyebrow in hopes of transmitting some sort of silent adult signal.

Taylor turned his head briefly from the screen and shot her a teasing glance, then went back to the video game.

Carson stood sipping coffee in the small galley kitchen, watching the big man and the slight boy sitting together on the futon in front of the game screen. Life was full of surprises, Carson thought, but Taylor took the cake. It was surprising enough to discover that he trained dolphins. Then he asked her and Nate to dinner, and they'd had a lovely time. But the last thing she'd expected was for Taylor and Nate to become such pals. Who knew they'd bond over video games? Nate was enthralled by his new hero—Taylor knew all the cheat codes.

She was also surprised by her attraction for him. Taylor had shown up in pressed pants and a long-sleeved shirt. She always was a pushover for a man in crisp attire. His shirt was unbuttoned at the collar and the bright white contrasted with his deep tan. Dinner had been pleasant, if a bit awkward with Nate. It wasn't a date—Carson kept reminding herself—but it felt like it could have been if they'd been alone. The possibility made her nervous. They were just friends, she told herself again. Nothing to feel guilty about. But why, then, did she feel just that?

She reached for her phone and checked her messages. Still no word from Blake. Damn, how long was he going to be out in the field? She needed to talk to him, to hear his voice. To feel a connection with him. She also felt the need to send Taylor packing.

"Sorry, guys, time to break it up. We've got an early start tomorrow. No complaints," she said in automatic response to Nate's immediate outcry. "We're going to see Delphine, remember?"

The mention of Delphine was enough to assuage Nate's outburst. He sighed, more for show, then promptly saved the game and relinquished his remote.

"I think you've got it down pat, buddy," Taylor assured him.

"You get in your pajamas and brush your teeth while I get your futon ready, okay?" Carson said.

Nate rose slump-shouldered and began walking away.

"What do you say to Taylor?" Carson asked, stopping him.

"Thank you," he said dutifully.

Taylor smiled. "It was nice meeting you."

Nate didn't respond. He hurried into the bedroom, closing the door behind him.

Carson looked after Nate's retreating figure with affection. "He really did appreciate it, Taylor. It's rare for him to get along so well with a stranger. He thinks you walk on water. How did you learn to play so well?"

"I'm not that good," Taylor said modestly. "I played a lot of virtual reality games for PTSD therapy."

"You played video games for therapy?" The idea seemed out there.

"Well, the idea is that by reenacting a traumatic experience or confronting an irrational fear in a safe place, we'll become used to that experience. Or fear. The trauma doesn't disappear, but it becomes manageable. It worked for me."

"And the cheat codes?" she asked.

"Ah, well." He rubbed his jaw. "Those I figured out on my own."

She offered a smile. "I've got to get Nate to bed. Do you need to go?"

"I can stick around."

"Oh," she said, surprised. "Uh, okay. I'll just be a few minutes. Do you mind waiting outside on the patio? There are chairs out there." She pointed to the futon and said in way of explanation, "This is Nate's bed."

"Sure," Taylor said good-naturedly. "I'll grab a smoke."

Lord, she thought to herself as she followed Nate into the bedroom. What was going on here? She really didn't need to help Nate much. He was nine and had his routine down. She'd thought it was an obvious hint for Taylor to leave. Going out to the restaurant with him had gone well—and innocently—enough. Sitting on the bench chatting with him in public was okay, too. But being alone with him tonight in the cottage was another thing altogether. Especially with the undercurrent zinging between them.

Once Nate was ready for bed, he and Carson returned to the main room. Nate hopped onto the futon, and she tucked him in. Looking at his tanned face and watching him yawn, Carson thought how much he'd returned to the boy who'd leaped into the Cove and swam like a fish earlier in the summer. The boy who saved his smiles for her. Coming here had been the right thing to do. *Thank you, Harper,* she thought to herself, *for coming up with the idea of bringing Nate here. And thank you, Dora, for allowing it.* She hoped they could keep up the good vibes when they got back to Sea Breeze. A lot, she knew in her heart, depended on what happened with Delphine tomorrow.

"Good night, Nate. I'll just be outside."

"Aunt Carson?"

"Yes?"

"Do you think Delphine will remember me?"

She paused. She'd wondered where his thoughts lay concerning the dolphin. Now she knew he was worried. Perhaps even guilt-ridden. She sat down on the futon beside him.

"I can't say for sure, but I think she will. She's very smart. She remembered me."

"But she loves you."

Carson felt her heart twinge. "Yes, Delphine loves me. But she loves you, too."

Nate yawned the words: "I love her too. I always will. Even if I never see her again after tomorrow."

Out of the mouths of babes. Carson felt love bloom in her heart for the boy. He must have discussed this with Joan. This boy understood the difference between a wild dolphin and a dolphin in a facility better than most adults.

"I couldn't have expressed my own feelings any better," she told him. "Good night, sleep tight. Don't let the bedbugs bite."

"There aren't any bedbugs," he told her matter-of-factly. "I checked."

Carson laughed lightly at the literal workings of his brilliant mind. "Good night," she said again, and then she went to the door, turning off the light as she exited.

Outdoors she could hear the gentle lapping of the waves against the shore. She saw his broad-shouldered silhouette standing on their patio, staring out at the Gulf. A trail of smoke rose from his cigarette.

"Here you are," she said in way of announcement.

Taylor tossed the cigarette to the ground and stomped on it. "I should be going."

MARY ALICE MONROE

"Okay," she said, not sure if it was relief or disappointment she felt. He walked closer to her, and in the shadows she could make out the contours of his face—his strong, Roman nose, his full lips. God, he had a beautiful face, she thought.

"I had a nice time," he said.

"Me, too. And so did Nate," she hastened to add. "It was nice of you to take us out on our last night."

An awkward silence. The night's sultry summer breeze felt like a caress against her skin. It was heavy with the scents of the sea and a sweetness that had musky notes. She felt his closeness, the slim margin of space between them narrowing as they imperceptibly drew closer and desire welled up, unbidden.

Like the dolphin and the dog earlier on the dock, they inched toward each other, each tentative, almost shy. She closed her eyes, surrendering to the tug. In a single move their lips touched. The fullness of his lips cushioned hers. His arms encircled her, so strong, as they pressed harder together.

This kiss felt so good.

Yet it felt so wrong.

Carson opened her eyes, stiffening her back. She put her hands against Taylor's chest and drew away, the light dimming in her eyes. She looked out at the moonlight to allow her breath to slow and gather her wits. What was going on in her head, she wondered. Her body enjoyed the kiss. It wasn't like her to not simply let go with her feelings. The old Carson would have kissed this man good and hard. She wanted him. Yet tonight, even a small kiss had felt like a betrayal.

"Carson?" Taylor's voice was tentative but he held on to her forearms.

"I'm sorry," she said, unsure of how to explain her feelings. "I . . . I can't do this. I'm dating someone."

"Oh," he said, and, letting go of her arms, took a step back.

Carson blew out a plume of air and lifted her long shank of hair from her back. "This is so weird. I don't know what to say."

"Are you engaged?"

"No," she replied, shaking her head. "No," she said again.

"I'm glad."

Carson didn't want to encourage him. "But we have this understanding. It's kind of exclusive."

"I respect that," Taylor said.

A bird called out in the night, a melancholy sound.

"I better go."

"Look, Taylor," she said, stopping him. "I'm really glad I got to know you. You're a great guy." She leaned forward and kissed his cheek. "And I meant it when I said if you're near Sullivan's Island, look me up. We can be friends, can't we?"

He offered her his crooked grin. "Good luck tomorrow with Delphine."

Carson watched him walk away with a pang of regret. Taylor had never answered her question.

Chapter Sixteen

~~~

Sullivan's Island

The moon was a slim crescent in the velvety sky. Venus shone bright to the north. Harper sat at the edge of the dock, her feet dangling in the cool water, and looked up at the night sky, thinking how much she loved being here, sitting under a sky that mirrored the South Carolina flag. When did this love affair with the lowcountry begin? she wondered.

She kicked her legs back and forth, feeling the power of the current. She'd always enjoyed her visits here, but when she was a child she thought of Sea Breeze as a kind of camp. A place to run wild and have fun with the other girls. Someplace that one returned home from. Like Dora had said, being at Sea Breeze wasn't real life.

Or was it? This summer Harper had returned as a woman—despite Mamaw's insistence on continuing to call them her "summer girls." In the past months Harper had come to appreciate that the slower-paced life here in the lowcountry was indeed real. It was just very different from what she knew in New York, or in the Hamptons, or England. Or, she thought, was this summer only a respite from the pressing demands and expectations that she would have to face at summer's end?

She heard a footfall on the dock, felt its vibration, and turning her head, she saw a dark silhouette coming toward her.

"Dora?" she called out.

"Found you!" Dora exclaimed, stepping down to the lower floating dock. "What are you doing out here all alone?"

"Nothing."

"Want some company?"

"Love some." Harper patted the dock beside her.

Harper caught the scent of Dora's floral perfume as she settled beside her and slipped her legs into the black water.

"Seems strange to be out here without Carson," Dora said.

"Yeah. I half expect to see Delphine pop her head out of the water. Poor Delphine . . ." In her mind's eye she saw the sweet smile of the dolphin and felt a prick of conscience for what the consequences of their actions had cost it.

"When is Carson due back?" she asked Dora.

"Not sure. Tomorrow or the day after."

"I saw on the weather report there's a tropical storm brewing off the coast of Africa and the computer models say it will head our way."

"Please . . ." Dora said with a wave of her hand. "Whenever there's any disturbance from that direction, the weathermen go wild, stirring us up into a frenzy. I swear they're disappointed if the storm veers off. I don't pay any of the warnings any mind until it's hugging our coast."

Harper was the type to study the computer models, and at the moment, the majority of them had this storm hitting Charleston.

"You've lived here longer than I have," Harper conceded. "If Carson comes back tomorrow, she'll just beat the storm. I'm hoping she and Nate don't get stuck driving in a downpour."

Dora's face clouded at the slightest possibility of Nate being in a storm. "Maybe I will check those storm warnings."

Harper saw the worry on Dora's face and regretted bringing up the topic of the storm. "They'll be fine," she said in consolation.

"Oh, sure . . ." Dora's voice was troubled.

"You must miss Nate a lot."

"Terribly. It's been wonderful to have some time to myself, but it's been long enough. I want my baby home."

"I miss him, too."

Dora turned to face Harper. "It's also been really nice spending time with you this past week."

Harper smiled into the water.

"I've gotten to know you better," Dora continued. "I feel closer to you. I'm trying to break old patterns, and you've really helped me." She paused. "Thank you."

Harper looked up and in the moonlight saw the sincerity in Dora's eyes. "We're sisters," Harper said. "You don't have to thank me." She broke into a broad grin.

Dora released a wide smile and nodded, looking out at the moonlight dancing on the Cove. "I like that."

"You know, I don't know who was the tougher sell on getting Nate to go—you or Nate."

Dora laughed. "I think it's a miracle he agreed to get in the car with Carson in the first place! But I have to hand it to her. She's done a real good job. She's been sending me pictures every day of Nate's progress. He looks so good, so tan. For a boy who rarely smiles, Nate was smiling all the time! It was a side to my little boy I rarely see. I've sent the pictures to Cal. He needs to see that side of his son." She paused. "Carson doesn't seem to have a problem having a good time with Nate, does she?"

"Carson? She doesn't have a hard time having a good time with anyone. It's her gift."

"And yours. You play with Nate, too. On the video games."

"Well, yeah . . ." she replied hesitatingly, remembering the terse words when Dora discovered Harper playing video games with Nate.

"I shouldn't have snapped at you like that. I'm so sorry. It . . . it wasn't the video games I was upset about. I was jealous," she admitted.

"Jealous?" Harper asked, shocked at the confession. "Of what?"

"Jealous that you found a way to have fun with Nate. Like Carson did. This isn't easy to say, but I don't know how to do that." She mulishly kicked the water.

"He's your son," Harper said, not understanding how a mother wouldn't know how to play with her own child.

"Moms are the rule makers. It's not always a fun job. There has to be balance, and I see now that I've been so obsessed with helping Nate because of his Asperger's, I forgot to have fun with him. I don't want to just be his keeper, the one who tells him what to do, tidies up after him, feeds him." Dora glanced at her sister. "In the dressing room you said something to me that made me think."

"Oh-oh . . ." Harper recalled she'd said some harsh things in that tight space.

"No, really, it was good. I know Nate loves me." Dora took a breath. "But I'm not sure he really likes me."

"Aw, Dora, of course he likes you."

Dora shrugged and said in a small voice, "He doesn't like to play with me."

"It's easy. Find something *he* likes to do."

"I'm trying . . . but it's not easy with Nate. He doesn't like imaginary games and he prefers to play by himself most of the time. I can't count the number of games I've initiated with him or the outings we've gone on that are instructive or will help him learn some skill. He shuts me out."

"That's the problem. Stop being his teacher and just have fun."

"But I *am* his teacher. I love Nate, more than life itself. I'm trying to make life easier for him, to somehow make him *better*. He needs help if he's going to learn to deal in the normal world."

"But not all the time. Nate's a pretty remarkable boy just the way he is. Instead of trying to change him, once in a while try hanging out with him without an agenda. See what he's interested in. He'll let you know."

Dora put her face in her palms. "God help me, I know you're right."

"I'm speaking from personal experience here," Harper said. "There's a difference between compelling your children to do what *you* want them to do, and just letting them discover for themselves what *they* want to do."

"Is that what your mother did?"

"In spades," Harper answered. "That's why I've always enjoyed coming here, to Sea Breeze. Mamaw let us run wild and play our own games." She released a short laugh of pleasure. "You know, whenever I think of the best times in my childhood, they're always here at Sea Breeze."

"Me, too."

"We sure had great summers, didn't we?"

When Dora didn't answer immediately, Harper turned her head. She watched Dora stare out at the Cove as though she were going through personal memories. The moonlight made her hair appear an almost unworldly shade of gold.

"We surely did," she said in a faraway voice.

"So, there's your answer. Be like Mamaw and do the same thing with Nate. Let him go wild. Go exploring. Have fun just for the sake of doing it together." She wagged her finger. "No lesson plans. Okay?"

Dora laughed. "Okay."

Harper took a breath and asked Dora the question that had been niggling at her brain the past few days. "Dora, are you going to introduce Nate to Devlin?"

Dora leaned back on her arms. "I don't know. I don't think so. Not right away."

"Why not?"

"There's no hurry. Besides, Nate doesn't do well with change. He's already upset that his father isn't around. He might feel threatened if Devlin came into the picture right away. And, selfishly, when he gets back, I want some time alone with him."

"Are you sure you're not pushing Devlin away?"

Dora shook her head. "I thought about that, but no. Not at all."

"I think he's good for you."

"You do?" Dora asked, delighted to hear this opinion from Harper, whose opinion she was learning to respect. "Why?"

"He's the yin to your yang. More relaxed, a little wilder, earthy. Not afraid to mess things up. I think this fellow might give you that balance you're looking for."

Dora felt as though Harper's words lit a light inside of her. She felt herself glowing with pleasure.

"We dated all through high school and into college." She glanced at her sister and said, "He was my first, you know."

Harper looked up, surprised. She didn't know. She smiled encouragingly for Dora to go on, reveling in the rare moment of true sisterly bonding.

"Not that there were a lot of others," Dora continued after a huff of embarrassed laughter. "Dev was the only other man I've slept with besides Cal."

"Really?" she asked, her tone incredulous.

"Why? How many men have you slept with?" she asked, sounding a little defensive.

Harper burst out in a laugh. "I don't know," she said, evading the truth. She didn't want to shock her sister with what she'd think a scandal, not when they were finally getting along. "A few more than two, I guess. Let's just say they weren't that memorable."

Dora smirked, indicating she knew Harper was being evasive. "Uh-huh, sure."

"I'm serious."

"Has a man told you he loved you?"

"Sure. Plenty of times," Harper said flippantly. "The problem is, I never believed them."

Dora glanced at her with uncertainty.

"I'm what you might call"—Harper lifted her fingers to make quotation marks—"'a good catch.' I'm decent enough looking, well educated, have—or rather, had—a good job. But that's not the real lure. No, sirree," she said in a self-mocking manner. "I'm an heiress. Rich. With a pedigree. I'm the whole package. Mothers are throwing their sons at me." She laughed bitterly. "Whenever a man tells me he loves me, I'm never quite certain if it's me he desires, or my fortune."

"But even so, didn't you ever fall in love? With any of them?"

Harper considered the question seriously, letting her mind roam over a litany of faces she'd known throughout her teens and into her twenties.

"There were some I liked quite a bit. One or two I dated for several months. There was one chap in England my grandmother almost called the banns for." Harper lifted one shoulder insolently. "Unfortunately, she liked him better than I did. Honestly? I can't say I ever did fall in love. It's rather sad, isn't it?"

"You're only twenty-eight!" Dora said with a light laugh. "You've got lots of time left. Lord, you make it sound like you're over the hill."

Harper didn't laugh. She didn't want to make light of this. "Think of our father and his track record. He never fell in love. He was incapable of making a commitment. And I'm always told Jameses don't marry for love." She changed her voice, taking on a British upper-class accent. "Jameses marry for alliances." She smirked. "My ancestors have married for money for generations."

"How royal of you," Dora said as a tease.

Harper laughed at the truth in that statement. "God knows my mother never loved anyone but herself. I honestly don't think she's capable of that emotion. Not even for her own daughter. She despised our father."

Dora burst out in a laugh. "You mean Mamaw was right after all? Your mama just wanted him for his sperm?"

"I'm afraid so," Harper replied, coloring faintly. "But don't ever tell her I said so. I'll never live down the fact that I am the product of such an ill-advised union."

"My lips are sealed. But I'm glad she did. I have you as my sister."

Maybe it was the oddly intimate spell the night seemed to be casting over them as their feet dangled in the cool water, but Harper finally felt like she could share her deeper feelings. "Do you think there's something inherently wrong with me?"

"What?" Dora blurted. "Lord, no."

"I've been thinking about this," Harper persisted. "Maybe it's in my genetic line to be incapable of love. I worry about that. There might be something missing in my DNA."

Dora reached over to lay her hand on Harper's. "You're crazy if you think that. Love is out there. You just have to find it."

Harper smiled weakly. "I want to believe in love," she confessed. "But I'm not willing to settle. I refuse to be shackled by my fortune. I will *not* be like my mother," she said with heat. "I'm holding out for true love."

Dora studied her sister. "You are wise beyond your years, Harper," she said slowly.

Slightly embarrassed at the compliment, Harper elbowed Dora in the ribs. "That romanticism must come from the Muir side, eh? What with the great love affair of the Gentleman Pirate and Claire, right?"

Dora laughed, then looked out over the water, lost in thought.

"What about you?" Harper asked. "You said you kinda-maybe-might love Devlin. Does that mean you've decided to leave Cal for good?"

A bemused expression slipped over Dora's face. "I've been wondering about that myself," she replied. She shook her head and said in a low voice, "It's so hard to know what to do. I just don't know."

"What don't you know? You know Devlin loves you. Does Cal?"

Dora looked trapped. "I know he needs me."

"Oh, great," Harper exclaimed, throwing up her hands. "That's so romantic." She turned to face Dora. "You just told me how you want to have some fun with Nate. Why should it be any different with your *husband*? Dora, you're a caretaker. It's what you do. Granted, taking care of Cal is one part of a marriage, and an important part, at that. But do you have fun with him?"

Dora gave a tiny shiver. "No."

"I didn't think so. I've been watching you these past weeks, and clearly you're having fun with Devlin."

"But is that enough for a relationship?"

"It's a good start. If you don't mind my saying so, you're a stickler for what you think a marriage *should* look like. How's that working out for you so far?"

Dora stared at the water.

"Let me ask you this. Is it Cal you want to stay with? Or the marriage?"

Dora didn't reply. She sat twisting her wedding ring on her finger.

Harper asked gently, "Are you *in love* with him?"

Dora raised up her left hand. The luster of the gold shone in the moonlight.

"When you talked about feeling shackled by your fortune, all I could think was how I feel shackled to my marriage. Right now"—Dora lifted her left hand—"this ring feels like a manacle, every bit as heavy and binding to an institution I don't want to be part of anymore."

Dora lowered her hand to her lap. "I loved Cal when I married him." Her gaze met Harper's. "But, no. I'm not in love with him. I can't go back." Looking at the ring, she cried, "I want to be free."

Dora began tugging the ring from her finger, but it was snug and unyielding.

"What are you doing?" asked Harper.

"This ring has been on my finger for fourteen years," Dora said with an edge of panic to her voice. "It won't come off."

"Well, stop pulling at it," Harper told her. "You're just making your finger swell more. Try dipping your hand in the cool water."

Dora leaned far over the edge of the dock and stuck her hand into the water.

"Why are you doing this now?" Harper asked, surprised by her usually cautious sister's impetuousness.

"It's your fault," Dora told her, letting her hand wade back and forth in the water. "When you said that about the shackle, I couldn't get that image out of my mind. I've got to get it off." Dora pulled her hand from the water and moved to sit on the dock. She grabbed the ring once more.

"Wait, wait," Harper said, putting an arresting hand on Dora's arm. "Granny James once had a ring stuck on her finger. The jeweler came to cut it off." She laughed. "The ring, not the finger. But first he had her soak it in cool water and then he eased it off her finger, real slow, so the skin didn't bunch up at the knuckle. He used hand lotion. Or we could use some soap. I'll go inside . . ."

"Let me try first." Dora puffed out some air, then very slowly eased and twisted the ring. "I think it's coming." She kept at it, rolling the ring over her knuckle while her face grimaced in pain. Slowly, it slid down her finger.

"It's off!" she exclaimed, holding the gold band in the air between two fingers.

Harper hooted aloud, bringing Dora's hand closer for perusal. Dora's hand was pink and pickled from the cold water, and there was a bruised spot below the knuckle of her fourth finger.

"I'm free!" Dora shouted, pumping the air with her fist.

"Not legally," Harper said, giving Dora her hand back. "At least not yet," she amended.

"Maybe not. But from now on, Cal can take care of himself!"

"Dora," Harper said. "I think we were meant to find those manacles this summer." She leaned forward, eyes gleaming. "Let's make a pact. You and I will no longer be bound by the expectations of others. No more shackles."

Dora grasped Harper's hand. She'd always been a bit jealous that Harper and Carson had their own rallying call: Death to the ladies! Now she and Harper had their own call, as well. In a burst of joy, Dora reared back and threw the ring into the Cove.

Together they shouted, "No more shackles!" Their whoops of glee echoed over the quiet waters.

Chapter Seventeen

~~~

Florida

Nate's fingers tapped his lips as he and Carson followed Lynne Byrd through the long halls of the Mote Marine cetacean hospital. Lynne was kind enough to take Nate on a tour of the lab and the sea turtle hospital, describing all the patients. His head turned from left to right, seemingly taking in the colorful murals of sea life that adorned the walls. Carson knew, however, that the little guy was searching anxiously for Delphine.

At last Lynne pushed open the doors to the outdoor arena. The sunlight was so bright that Carson had to squint until her eyes adjusted. The enormous pool in the center of the arena now had netting arcing over it.

"Good news," Lynne said to Carson. "Delphine has been doing so well, we've moved her into the large pool, where there's room for her to exercise. She's still on antibiotics, but she's a remarkable healer with a strong will to live."

Lynne led them toward the pool. "She was weighed this

morning and is continuing to gain, which is a very good sign. It's been touch and go with the condition of her mouth. At the beginning we only fed her live mullet and snapper, but now she's accepting the dead fish—a mix of herring and capelin, too. She's also interacting more with her environmental enrichment devices." She turned to smile at Nate. "Toys."

"Where's Delphine?" he asked pointedly.

"You'll see her, don't worry," Carson assured him. Like Nate, she wanted to break free and run to the pool to see Delphine.

At last they reached the edge of the pool. Nate wanted to go closer but was cut off by Lynne's outstretched arms.

"Here's how we're going to do this," Lynne said in a tone that brooked no argument. "Carson, you know the drill. You can help me give Delphine her antibiotics. While I get the meds, you can go in the water and let Delphine know you're here." She turned to Nate. "Sorry, Nate, but you can't go in the water."

Nate looked stricken. "But I went in the water with the other dolphins."

"I know. But this is a hospital. It's not allowed. But . . ." Lynne smiled at Nate, who reluctantly met her eyes. "How about I let you play with Delphine using some of her favorite toys? Her very best favorite is that pink ball in the bin over there." She gestured toward a basket by the wall. "See it?"

Nate scanned the room and, spotting it, nodded.

"Okay, go stand by the wall and wait until I say you can throw it to her, okay? Carson and I have to give Delphine her medicine first. Stay by the wall," she said.

"That's the rule," Carson added for clarity, knowing he'd take it very seriously when put in that context.

"Carson, if Delphine will let you, you can give her a rub-down. She loves those."

Carson was surprised she'd still be allowed to touch Del-phine, now that the dolphin was so much improved. She knew Lynne didn't want human interaction with the wild dolphins if possible, especially not touch. It made her wonder if decisions had been made as to where Delphine would be transferred once she was deemed healthy.

"Is Delphine already slated to go to the Dolphin Research Center?"

Lynne shook her head. "No. We haven't given up on trying to release her into the wild."

"But the rubdown . . ."

"It's helping her heal, which is our top priority. This particu-lar dolphin gets depressed in isolation. We had to make a call based on her needs. As for her release—when and where—the jury's still out on that."

The pool was enormous and deep and the vast screening over it provided lovely dappled light that made patterns on the water. Carson stood at the edge and squinted into the shifting shadows, searching for the dolphin. Not seeing her, she low-ered herself to sit on the edge and slipped her legs into the water. It was cool but not cold, refreshing against the searing temperature of the air. She searched the water for some sign of Delphine. Carson kicked her legs in the water, hoping the vibration would alert the dolphin and bring her close, if only out of curiosity.

Nothing.

Carson added a whistle. Sharp and clear, it pierced the quiet. It was the same whistle she'd always used at the Cove when she called Delphine. She glanced over her shoulder at Nate. He stood keen eyed and alert, watching.

Suddenly she saw a gray shadow streaking through the water toward her. Her heart skipped a beat as the shadow swam close, then veered, doing a glide-by. She knew Delphine was checking out the stranger in the pool. Carson gasped with a laugh when a glistening head suddenly emerged from the water right before her. Two shiny bright eyes studied her for a moment. Then Delphine shot high in a vertical jump and released a whistle that sounded to Carson's ears like a yelp of joy.

"Delphine!" she cried, her heart near bursting. From behind her, she heard Nate shout out Delphine's name and run toward the pool.

"It's her! It's her!" he exclaimed, arching on his toes excitedly and pointing.

Swimming past them again, Delphine tilted to her side, looking up. Passing Nate, she stopped and rose up, whistling.

"She sees me!" Nate exclaimed, rushing to the pool's edge.

Carson watched as Nate looked into the dolphin's eyes, overwhelmed with gratitude that Delphine had recognized Nate. There was an attentiveness between them—a connection—that went beyond words.

Two female volunteers came closer from the other tanks, intrigued by what was happening in the pool.

When Nate crouched at the pool's edge, Carson put her hand out to stop him from getting too close. "Honey, I'm sorry, but you have to go back against the wall until Lynne tells you it's okay to come close."

"No!"

"Remember what Lynne said." Nate was jumping up and

down, getting overexcited. She feared a meltdown and spoke calmly but firmly. "Go stand by the wall. That's the rule. If you do what Lynne says, you can play with Delphine. You'll have your turn."

Reluctantly Nate went to stand by the wall, but he rose up on his toes and kept his eyes glued to Delphine.

Delphine kept rising up in the water to peek out over the edge of the pool, obviously looking for Nate.

"She knows you're here," Lynne called out to Nate. "She's happy to see you. I told you she would be!"

"What are all those marks on her body?" Nate asked, looking stricken.

Carson looked at Lynne, who nodded at Carson, giving her the silent go-ahead to explain.

"Those are her scars. But don't worry, they will get better. Look how healthy she is. That's what's important."

Delphine began chattering excitedly, then took a rapid run around the pool before returning to where Carson stood. She tilted her head to study Carson with her shiny black eyes.

Carson lowered her head closer to the dolphin's. "Yes, it's me. I'm back." She braced herself with her arms and slipped into the pool. Delphine swam very close, her eyes big and eager looking. The dolphin stopped in front of her and waited, as though inviting Carson's touch. Carson tentatively reached out a hand in the water and held it inches from the dolphin, giving her time. Delphine moved to gently nudge the tip of her rostrum against Carson's hand, then nudged her head against Carson's fingertips. Carson felt the old connection and relaxed, letting her hands slide gently over the rubbery skin.

"Hey, Delphine," she murmured.

Over and over Delphine swam past Carson, each time allowing Carson's hands to rub her sides in a circular massage. After several minutes, Delphine faced Carson again, this time remaining under the water. Carson heard a quick staccato sound and felt a tingling on her abdomen, like tickling. Laughing, she tried to shoo Delphine away but Delphine was persistent, returning over and over to send the sonar to her belly.

Lynne walked up carrying medical equipment in her arms. "What's she doing?"

"She's echolocating. She won't stop. She keeps coming back and doing it over and over. Look at her—here she comes again." Delphine was gently poking her rostrum near Carson's abdomen. Still laughing, Carson turned around, showing Delphine her back. "Is this a new game for her?"

"Not that I'm aware of," Lynne replied, slipping into the pool beside Carson. She handed Carson a long plastic feeding tube. "Sometimes she echolocates on the metal pole when we sweep the pool. I can feel the tingling on my palms. It's kind of a weird feeling."

"Exactly."

Lynne gave Carson a curious look. "You're not pregnant, are you?"

Carson barked out a laugh. "God, no. Why do you ask?"

"A few years back I was in here with a dolphin and the same thing happened to me. The dolphin kept coming by and echolocating my belly. Over and over." She laughed. "A week later I found out I was pregnant."

Carson felt her body go cold in the water. "You mean, the dolphin . . ." She couldn't say the words.

". . . saw my fetus before I even did," Lynne finished for her. "Amazing, huh? It could see something was different inside me and was curious. That little fetus is three years old now. Makes for a good story, doesn't it?"

Carson couldn't reply. Of course she wasn't pregnant, her mind screamed. Blake always used protection. Still, just the possibility freaked her out. She turned her head to look at Delphine, who was floating nearby, her mouth open and relaxed, watching her with an angelic smile.

What do you know? Carson thought irritably.

Carson had to focus as she assisted Lynne with administering the medication to a compliant Delphine. Then, at last, it was Nate's turn to play. Carson climbed from the water to sit alongside the pool with her feet dangling in the water and watched Nate toss the ball over and over to Delphine. The dolphin was like a dog, never tiring of going after the ball and tossing it back. The two of them were in heaven. Nate didn't need to get into the water. He was seeing for himself that Delphine was okay, that she didn't blame him.

Delphine isn't the only one on the mend, she thought with a bittersweet smile. She remembered Taylor's words: *Not all wounds are visible.*

An hour after Carson and Nate had said their emotional goodbyes to Delphine, with a promise from Lynne to keep Carson apprised of the dolphin's progress, Carson stood with her hands on her hips, staring uncompromisingly at the little white stick lying on the bathroom counter. It was an exercise in frustration, like waiting for a pot of water to boil. She lowered her head and closed her eyes. She'd never realized how long three minutes could be. Nor that a heart could pound so fast or her hands feel so cold. Lifting her head, she checked the wall clock. Three minutes . . .

She licked her lips, took a breath. Her hands were shaking as she held up the tip of the little stick to the color chart on the box.

Carson stared at the stick and felt the blood draining from her face. She slipped slowly to the floor, feeling faint. Over and over her dazed mind kept screaming, *There must be some mistake*. She lurched for the box and read the directions again. Then she looked at the stick again. The two little lines were a bright, unyielding, mocking pink.

Carson leaned back against the wall and stared at one long, narrow crack in the bathtub's porcelain. It forked in the middle of the tub and became two cracks. She kept tracing the crack back and forth, her brain unable to think beyond the glaring truth of those two lines.

She was pregnant.

Chapter Eighteen

~~~~~~~

Mamaw pulled the Camry into a space in front of the Medical University and craned her neck, searching for Lucille. Usually Lucille drove while Mamaw preferred to be the passenger. The Camry belonged to Lucille, and Mamaw didn't feel comfortable with the strange car, but since she'd given the Blue Bomber to Carson she no longer had "wheels," as Carson said. Today she'd driven Lucille to another of several recent doctor appointments. Mamaw did not like how weak Lucille was looking and insisted on driving her to the city. In turn, Lucille had insisted that Mamaw not wait in the hospital for her. Instead, Mamaw could do a little shopping in town, a rarity these days. She had tried to get into her old groove on King Street, but found that most of her favorite boutiques had closed, replaced by hip little cafés and trendy shops.

There was a time she could walk into a boutique and expect the clerk to have a card on file with her sizes. Today no one knew her name. She'd spent her entire life in this city, was a sixth-generation Charlestonian. Generations of her family were buried in this city—her husband, her son—as someday she would be.

And yet, sitting between these massive hospital buildings, watching the traffic go by and throngs of people crowding the sidewalks, she didn't feel that it was home any longer.

What was keeping her? she wondered. Not more than a minute later she spotted a slightly stooped woman in a navy-and-white shirtdress pushing through the hospital revolving door. She stopped on the sidewalk and stood clutching her bag, looking from left to right, the wind picking up the hem of her dress.

"Lucille!" Mamaw called out the window.

Lucille lifted her hand to acknowledge she'd seen her.

When did Lucille get so old? Mamaw wondered as she eased the car into drive. *And so frail?* It seemed to have happened overnight. Worry creased her brow. A body didn't get so frail so quickly with the flu. A shiver of fear swept over her as she pulled up to the curb.

Lucille climbed into the passenger seat with a soft grunt. She fumbled with the seat belt buckle. Once Mamaw heard the click, she flicked on her blinkers and carefully steered the car back into traffic.

"I'm sorry if I kept you waiting," Lucille said. Her voice sounded tired and she leaned her head back against the seat and closed her eyes.

Mamaw glanced at the woman beside her. Lucille looked drawn, her usually plump cheeks sunken. In her hand she carried a large paper bag from the hospital. Medicine, Mamaw guessed. She drove carefully through the tight traffic on narrow city streets, turned onto East Bay, then headed for the bridge.

She breathed easier once she was on the expansive Ravenel Bridge that towered over the Cooper River. She glanced again at Lucille. Her head was turned as she sat quietly looking out at the expansive view of the Cooper River.

"You have indeed kept me waiting," Mamaw said.

Lucille turned her head to look at her. "What's that?"

"I'm wondering," Mamaw said, her eyes on the road ahead, "just how much longer you're going to keep me waiting."

"What do you mean?"

"When are you going to tell me the truth?" She quickly glanced at Lucille. "What's going on?"

Lucille turned her head and looked straight ahead through the windshield.

"I thought we were friends," Mamaw said.

Lucille said nothing.

Mamaw glanced again from the road. Lucille clutched the bag tighter but her face gave nothing away.

"That we didn't keep secrets from each other," Mamaw continued.

"You told me you didn't want no more bad news," Lucille said.

"What? When did I say that?"

"A while back. In this very car."

Mamaw was flustered. "I don't remember saying that, and even if I did, I certainly didn't mean to be taken literally. Lucille, for pity's sake, I know you don't have the flu. Please tell me what's going on."

Lucille turned to look at her. Then she said in a flat voice, "I got the cancer."

Mamaw felt her heart skip a beat, even as her stomach dropped. "Oh, no." She swallowed hard, then asked, "What kind? What do the doctors say?"

"Slow down," Lucille said, tapping the dashboard. "You're gonna kill us both."

Mamaw hadn't realized she'd been accelerating her speed. She applied the brake and slowed to the speed limit. She took the Sullivan's Island exit from the bridge and drove up Coleman Boulevard to the first parking lot she spied. She pulled in and stopped the car. Turning, she faced Lucille.

"Tell me everything."

Lucille looked at her with compassion in her eyes. "I know what you're thinking. You're already making a list of what doctors to call, what treatments to try. Now, Miz Marietta, you're just gonna have to listen to what I'm going to tell you without interrupting me. Okay?"

Mamaw nodded and said uncertainly, "All right."

Lucille shifted her weight in the seat. "A while back I got these pains. I tried to manage them, but when they wouldn't go away I went to see my doctor. He sent me to another doctor here at the hospital and they gave me a mess of tests."

Mamaw feared the worst. "What kind of—"

Lucille put up her hand to stop Mamaw's question and Mamaw snapped her mouth shut.

"They told me I had cancer. Pancreatic cancer."

Mamaw sucked in her breath, then exhaled. "Oh, Lord."

"Today they told me it spread to my other organs. That's why my stomach pains are so bad."

Mamaw had to ask. "What stage is the cancer?"

"They call it stage four."

Mamaw clenched her hands together. Pancreatic cancer was always bad, but stage four was a death sentence and they both knew it.

Lucille looked down at her lap. "There's nothing to do now but wait," Lucille said. She smiled ruefully. "Today the doctor told me I'm not gonna have to wait too long."

"No!" Mamaw blurted out. She'd agreed to keep silent, but now the story was told and she couldn't hold back any longer. Lucille appeared so defeated, so willing to accept the diagnosis. Mamaw couldn't—she wouldn't—lose Lucille without putting up a fight.

"I won't accept that. There are several procedures you can try. My friend had pancreatic cancer and she had some surgery, something to do with a Whipple. I'll find out her doctor's name. We have to try something. I'm sure there's some procedure."

Lucille put her hand up in a gesture to silence Mamaw. "First off, I ain't got insurance."

"I don't care. I'll pay for it."

"Now, Miz Marietta, we both know you can't afford to take that on right now. And I wouldn't let you. Besides, it's too late. There ain't no cure for what I got."

"Maybe not a cure, but we can buy more time. There's chemotherapy and radiation."

"No." Lucille shook her head, her voice resolute. "I'm not doing no chemo or radiation. I'm not puttin' that poison in my body."

"You don't expect me to just sit here and let you die!"

Lucille smiled sadly. "That's exactly what I expect you to do."

Mamaw choked back a cry as her hand covered her mouth. "That's absurd! I can't do that."

Lucille's face softened. "You must. Miz Marietta, the plain truth is, it's too late for any of that. The cancer's too far gone. I talked to the doctors and I've made up my mind."

Mamaw brought a hand to her face and turned her head away as she wept, shaking her head in denial.

Lucille dug into her purse and pulled out a tissue. Handing it to Mamaw, she said, "Here, now. Take this. Your eyes always puff up like a sea urchin when you cry."

Mamaw let out a laugh and grabbed the tissue. Only Lucille could get away with saying such things to her at a time like this.

"This is such a shock. I didn't see it coming. I'm older than you are. I'm supposed to go before you."

"Seems God has different plans."

Mamaw blew her nose and composed herself. "I can't accept this."

"Now, Miz Marietta, listen to me." Lucille waited for Mamaw to face her again, then spoke in a slow, stern voice. "I've seen you be strong when Parker passed, then Mr. Edward. I'm asking you to be strong for me."

A rush of memories flooded Mamaw's mind—the nursing, the companionship, the steady encouragement, the exhausting hours, and, finally, the unutterable grief. She knew what was coming. She comprehended fully what Lucille was asking of her.

Mamaw nodded almost imperceptibly. "I will. You know I will."

"And be strong for the girls."

"The girls," Mamaw said, suddenly remembering them. "When are you going to tell them? They'll be devastated. They love you so much."

"I was hoping I wouldn't have to tell them. I didn't want to ruin their summer with this sorry business. I figured they'll all be leaving at summer's end, flying off like the shorebirds to wherever their lives take them. I hoped I'd just be like one of them. Flying off. No fuss."

"Flying off and leaving me alone!"

"I know that. But it don't change things, does it? You've got your plans, and now I've got mine."

Mamaw brought her trembling hand to her eyes. "Lucille . . ."

"I'm not afraid to go," Lucille said in a peaceful tone. "Seeing those manacles made it right clear in my mind. We're all shackled to this life for the duration. We carry our load. Looking back, I've lived a good life. I've no regrets. Way I see it, it's my time to cross the water. I like to think I'll face the crossing with the same courage of my ancestors." She looked up and smiled. "I'm gonna be set free."

Mamaw tightened her lips.

"I'm only afraid of one thing," Lucille said in a soft voice, looking at the bag of medicine in her lap.

"What's that?"

Lucille lifted the bag. "The pain. They give me all these pills. But they're not working so good no more. The cancer's taken a turn. The time for all this hospital rigmarole is done." She shook her head resolutely. "I don't want no treatments. I know that. But . . . I don't want to face this alone."

Mamaw looked into Lucille's dark, watery eyes. They bulged slightly, unblinking against a chalky face. Mamaw saw a ghostly image of what was coming. She grasped Lucille's hand and held it tight. "I'll be right here, sitting by your side all the way. You won't be alone."

Lucille's lips quivered and she held tight to Mamaw's hand. "That's all I needed to know."

Chapter Nineteen

≈ ≈ ≈

Carson crossed the Ben Sawyer Bridge over the Intracoastal Waterway as dusk settled over the lowcountry. The water shimmered in dusky twilight pinks, and bordering the banks, thick rows of palms formed dark shadows.

She turned off the air-conditioning, rolled down the windows, and let the sultry air flow into the stale car. She breathed deep the scents of mud and salt, raking her hand through her hair, loosening the elastic, and letting her hair catch the wind. She was nearing home.

When she'd arrived at Sea Breeze the previous May without a job or a place to live, she'd thought that she'd hit rock bottom. She'd been penniless and adrift. In retrospect, compared to how she felt now, that seemed like a cakewalk.

During the long trip home from the Keys, Nate had mostly slept, exhausted from his busy week, and she had plenty of time to think about the new life growing inside of her. She vacillated between benign curiosity, idly tapping her belly like a cat playing with a bug, and abject terror of an alien life growing inside of her. She had to first decide whether to tell Blake. Part of her wanted to make her decisions without involving him. It wasn't his body, after all.

Despite her independence, however, it felt selfish, even wrong, not to tell him. Blake wasn't a one-night stand. He was someone she had a relationship with, someone she cared deeply for. Someone she might even love. The father of this unborn child. Didn't he have the right to know?

She'd always been self-reliant. She'd spent most of her youth taking care of her father; she'd been more a maid than a daughter. When she turned eighteen she'd left to live alone, existing hand to mouth most of the time. She was not accustomed even to accepting help, let alone asking for it.

Carson ran her hand through her hair, weary and bleary-eyed. She'd been going over and over this issue in her head for twelve hours and was no closer to a decision. All she knew for certain was that she was exhausted and thirsty, and needed to pee. And that this fetus inside of her felt like an uninvited guest.

She glanced in the rearview mirror at the young boy sleeping in the backseat, strapped in by his seat belt. His head hung loosely to the side and his mouth was open; he was snoring gently. Her heart pinged with affection as tears filled her eyes. She loved that little boy and knew he loved her, in his own way. In retrospect, she had truly enjoyed being with Nate, taking care of him, watching him mature. Would she have these feelings for her own child? Could she be a good mother?

Glancing at the road, Carson saw she was nearing the turnoff for Sea Breeze. Her hands clenched the wheel and her heart rate shot up as her base instincts reared. All she wanted to do was to drop off Nate, then put the pedal to the metal and roar out of the driveway. To keep on driving. To run far, far away.

⟋⟋⟋

The following evening, Carson was sitting at the wood table in Blake's apartment staring at a plate of shrimp and grits. It was a hot and humid night heralding the oncoming storm, but he'd slaved over the stove to prepare the meal for her homecoming. Thunder rumbled and the ceiling fan over the table was causing the tapered candles to drip wax onto the tablecloth.

Across the table from her, Blake was looking anxiously at her face. Shrimp and grits was her favorite dish but she couldn't eat. She'd managed a few bites of the grits but the rich, buttery sauce was too much for her. Just the smell of seafood made her feel sick. More than the smells, however, the news she had to share had her stomach tied in knots.

Hobbs lay patiently under the table, watching for the piece of shrimp she slid under the table into his waiting mouth.

"More water?" Blake asked, already lifting the pitcher.

"Yes, thank you." Her mouth felt filled with unspoken words.

Carson quietly watched him pour, heard the ice clink as it fell into her glass. She knew she was being sullen and withdrawn. To make up for it, he was being exceedingly solicitous, tiptoeing around her.

He set down the pitcher and looked at her full plate. "Aren't you hungry? You've hardly taken a bite."

"No," she said, slowly shaking her head. She felt bad for all his effort for naught. "I'm not feeling well."

"Oh, baby, I'm sorry. You should've told me. You do look a little off."

She snorted a short laugh. "Do I?"

"You still look great," he hurried to add. "Beautiful. As always."

Carson's face was glistening with sweat, and she knew she was being testy. It wasn't Blake's fault she was pregnant . . . at least not entirely. She set her napkin on the table and pushed back a bit in her chair. Hobbs moved back with a dissatisfied grunt.

"Blake, I have something to tell you."

Blake looked at her warily. "Okay."

"I'm pregnant."

Blake sat motionless, his eyes wide. After a moment he blinked, and she could see he was gathering his wits. "Are you sure?"

She wanted to scream, *No, I'm making it up!* "Yes, of course I'm sure. I was late and took a pregnancy test in Florida. It's positive. I took the test three times to be sure."

He leaned back against his chair and averted his gaze. Then, meeting her eyes, he smiled with a kind of wonderment. "You're pregnant," he said. "That's, well, wow . . . that's great."

Carson blinked, not sure she'd heard right. "Great? What do you mean, that's great? It's *not* great."

"It's better than what I thought you might say. Look," he said, laying his palms on the table. "I know we didn't plan it, but it happened." He leaned back on the hind legs of his chair and scratched his head. "How *did* it happen?"

Carson snorted again and looked at him askance.

He brought the chair back aright and grinned wickedly. "I know *how* . . ." His smile fell and he grew serious. "But how did you get pregnant? We were careful."

"That's what I want to know," she replied, narrowing her eyes with accusation.

Anger flashed in Blake's eyes. "What? No way. What do you take me for? If I wanted to knock you up, I'd be up-front and honest about it."

"Well, you *did* knock me up!" she shouted.

"Well, I'm sorry!" he shouted back.

Hobbs jumped up and ran to the door, barking.

"Hobbs, hush," Blake fired off.

The dog immediately stopped barking and returned to sit on the floor by Blake's feet with a grunt.

Blake and Carson stared each other down for a moment, the silence thick around them.

Finally Blake wiped his brow, his face pinched in concentration. "Look," Blake said in a calmer voice. "Obviously something just failed. It's rare but here we are. And you weren't on the pill . . ."

"You knew that," she said defensively, and looked away, embarrassed for her lapse in good judgment. She'd gone off the pill before she'd left Los Angeles. She wanted to give her body a break from the hormones and she wasn't planning on starting up any relationships. She had meant to go back on the pill when she returned from Florida. She'd thought they were being careful. Stupid, stupid, stupid.

"I'm just saying . . ." Blake said in a conciliatory tone. "We're in this together, okay?" He reached out to tap her hand lying flat on the table. When she looked up he held her gaze. "*Okay?*"

Carson reluctantly nodded.

"When did you find out?"

"Day before yesterday. It was so bizarre. I was in the water with Delphine and she started echolocating on my abdomen. Turns out she knew I was pregnant before I did."

"No kidding?" he said, incredulous.

"It freaked me out, let me tell you. As soon as we left the Mote I went to the pharmacy to buy one of those home pregnancy tests. I took all three in the box and all three of them said I was pregnant." She wiped a wayward lock of hair from her face. "When I found out, it turned on some goddamned switch in my body. Suddenly I'm as sick as a dog. I'd think it was psychosomatic except I couldn't fake being this sick."

"Okay," he said, pushing away his unfinished plate. "It's going to be okay. I have money in savings and I've got good insurance."

"Wha— Wait!" Carson blurted, sitting straight with alarm. "I'm not sure I'm even having it!"

Blake's face tightened. "Not sure you're having it?"

"It's a big decision. I need to take a step back and think about it."

"I love you. You love me. What do you need to think about?"

Carson tossed her napkin on the table and stood. She felt the walls of the room closing in on her. "I need to go."

Blake pushed back his chair and went to her side to take hold of her arm.

"I know you're freaked out. You're afraid. But don't be. I'm here."

He was saying all the right things and she wished they made her feel better, but they didn't.

"Carson, you know I love you, right?"

She sniffed, unable to look him in the eye. "Yes."

"There's a simple answer. We can get married."

"No . . ." she said, shaking her head. "Not like this."

"Honey, I want to marry you. I've wanted to marry you from the first moment I saw you at Dunleavy's."

"You wouldn't be asking me if I wasn't pregnant."

"Maybe not tonight. But whether it's now or next year, it doesn't matter as long as we're together." He lowered his lips to kiss the top of her head, then slipped his arms around her, holding her close to his chest.

"We can get married right away, it doesn't have to be fancy. Then you can move in here. We'll make my office the nursery. At least until we find a bigger place."

Blake had it all planned out, apparently. Except Carson didn't come here tonight for him to have all the answers or to plan her life. She just wanted him to listen to her, to be there for her and let her spill out all her fears and worries, to be her sounding board so she could gain some perspective on what decision to make. Instead, he was pushing her to do what he wanted her to do. Planning her life so she would just say yes. Getting married, having a baby . . . these things were on his agenda, not hers.

Carson felt her breath come quick in a panic. His arms around her felt like a trap. She tensed and broke free of his arms.

"Blake," she said in a shaky voice, putting her fingers to her temples. "Right now my head feels like it's going to burst into flames. I can't talk about getting married and moving in. I'm not sure I want to have a baby at all, much less get married! This is all going way too fast. We've only known each other a few months!"

He stared back at her, arms hanging at his sides.

"I didn't ask you to marry me. I don't want you to tell me what to do. That's not why I'm here tonight." She began pacing the room, eyeing the door. "I'm just trying to do the right thing, to tell you that I'm pregnant. That's all. That in itself is a stretch for me. I'm not ready to be a mother. I don't even have a job! How am I going to take care of a baby?"

"I'll support you and the baby."

"I don't want you to! I don't want to depend on you. Don't you get that yet?"

He went still, his expression bruised. "I'm beginning to."

She hadn't meant to hurt him. That's not why she came here. Now everything was worse. "I'm sorry," she said. "It's just that I'm afraid of this . . ." She trailed off, indicating her belly with a swipe of her hand. "This thing."

"Why?"

"Everything will change."

"Nothing will change. Not between us."

"Of course it will. Because I'll change."

"How will you change?"

"I don't know!" she cried, knowing she was sounding irrational, but that she was right. "I just will."

"Carson . . ."

"No! I'm not ready to talk about this. About us. I thought I was strong enough to handle it, but I can't do it."

Blake's eyes dimmed and he lowered his head.

"I have to go."

Blake's arm shot out to grab her hand, stopping her.

"Carson. Don't have an abortion."

"Blake . . ."

"I mean it." His dark eyes deepened.

Carson felt an instinctive rush of rage, rearing back and swiping away his firm grip. "It's my body. I'll decide what I'm going to do."

"I love you, Carson. But if you do that, it's a deal-breaker for me."

Her breath caught in her throat. This was precisely why she hadn't wanted to tell him. She came here hoping he'd be sensitive and understanding, the man who listened to her, helped her make decisions without judgment. But why did she think that? Blake was one of the most opinionated men she'd ever met.

Carson grabbed her purse from the chair as she made her way to the door. She opened it, but before leaving she turned and said, "Please, don't call me for a while, okay?"

"Are you breaking up with me?"

"No. Yes . . ." She gave a huge sigh. "I don't know," she said, and fled, closing the door behind her.

That evening, Dora lay on Devlin's big sleigh bed, her head on his shoulder, drowsy in a post-sex daze. It had been the first time they'd made love on his king-size bed—on land, for that matter. The space seemed luxurious compared to the cramped boat.

It would feel luxurious under any circumstances, Dora thought as her gaze swept the room. His was a large house on the Breach Inlet side of Sullivan's Island, new construction in the Southern style, with lots of porches with rockers facing the ocean. The bedroom porch doors were open wide, allowing the ocean breezes to flow in. Those who grew up on the island preferred the sultry air to air-conditioning. It was indeed an impressive house, she thought again, but she wasn't sure she didn't prefer the quaint cottage on the marsh.

They'd kicked off the sheets and lay exposed to the cooling breeze. Her hand caressed his bare chest, her fingers mingling with the soft curls. Devlin's hand stroked her shoulder in a lazy swirling pattern, as he hummed to the song that was playing on his CD.

"I like this song," Devlin said in a low voice. "Makes me think of us." He began to join in the chorus, singing in an off-key baritone.

"*I saw you last night and got that old feeling.*"

"You know the words," Dora said teasingly. "I'm impressed."

"I live to impress you."

Dora burrowed her head comfortably into his shoulder. Cal was not a cuddler, and of course, neither was her son. With Devlin she found she craved this gentle intimacy, almost more than the sex. The sex was wonderful, but this . . . Dora sighed. She needed to be held, to feel treasured.

Devlin began to sing again in his wobbly voice, "*The spark of love is still burning.*"

"Nice . . ." she murmured absently.

"Woman, didn't you listen to the lyrics? I'm trying to say something here."

Dora went very still, suddenly appreciating that Devlin wasn't joking around.

"That's how I feel about you, Dora. About us. That old feeling is back. It's like we're getting a second chance."

"Honey, we've only just started dating. Let's not get ahead of ourselves."

"How long don't matter. It's like the song says. I saw you and got that old feeling."

"Dev, wait," Dora stammered, sitting up and pulling the sheet around herself.

"What's the matter, honey?" Devlin asked, his smile falling. He moved to sit up, exposing his nakedness. Dora had to look away, still embarrassed at the sight. She'd never felt comfortable naked, not even as a young woman and never before Cal, who was, she could see in retrospect, a prude.

Devlin took the hand that clutched the sheet tight and pulled it away. As it slipped off she lurched to clutch it back, but he reached out to hold both of her hands in his. She blushed, flustered.

"You're not wearing your wedding ring," he said, looking down at the pale skin on her ring finger.

"No."

He didn't say anything; he just nodded and let his finger rub the empty space on her ring finger for a moment.

"I thought you'd be glad to know how I feel about you. How I've always felt about you."

She dragged her gaze to his and was caught by the sincerity in the brilliant blue.

"You were the one for me back when we were teenagers, and you're still the one for me now. All these years we've been apart, I think I've been lost. I know now that I never got over you. I never should have let you go."

Dora felt the impact of those words deep in her heart. She couldn't respond. Couldn't move.

"Did you hear what I said?" he asked.

"Yes."

"I know you feel it, too," he said. "I know it."

"I do," she replied. "When I saw you after all these years, you made me feel like I was sixteen again."

"That's how you always will be to me."

"But I'm not sixteen. I'm thirty-six. With a child."

"Hell, I know all that. What matters is that we feel the same about each other. Right here, right now."

"Right now," she said, "I don't feel sixteen. Nor do I think of you as that teenager anymore." She laughed at his puzzled expression. "Thank God! I've lived those years, gone through so many experiences, learned so much . . . I don't want to be that young, foolish girl any longer. Malleable, obedient, gullible even. I like being the woman I am today. Devlin, you've made me feel beautiful again. Womanly. Sexy. Right now."

She looked at Devlin and leaned forward to stroke his face. "And I like who *you* are today. The man you've become. I don't want to go back to being those kids again."

Devlin reached out to take hold of her shoulders. "I feel the same. That's what I've been trying to say in my own clumsy way. "Dora . . ." he said, his voice tight with emotion. "I . . . I love you. I always have and I always will."

Dora drew back, and her heart began to flutter. "Dev . . . this is all moving so fast."

Devlin's smile slipped and he released her shoulders.

"Because you don't have feelings for me? You don't love me."

Dora let out a guttural groan. "Of course I have feelings for you. Deep and very real. But love? I'm not going to rush into using that word again. I'm not ready. I'm not even divorced yet!"

"Well, I am," he shot back. "And I'll tell you what. A piece of paper don't make a damn bit of difference. It's what's in here that counts." He made a fist and pounded his heart. He went very still. His tone turned indignant. "Eudora Tupper, do you still love your husband?"

"Devlin, how can you ask me that?"

"I can because you broke my heart once over that man. I don't aim to have it broken again."

"When did I break your heart?"

He looked stunned that she could ask. "When you broke up with me!"

"Oh, for . . . Dev, I was eighteen years old!"

"Nineteen. We dated all freshman year you were at Converse and I was at USC. All that summer and part of the next year."

Dora stared back at him, stunned that he knew this, and by the raw hurt and pain so evident in his voice.

"Then you met your high-and-mighty Calhoun Tupper and you traded me in for a fancier model."

"I did not!" she said, annoyed that he would say such a thing. "That's not why we broke up."

"Then why?" he asked, eyes glaring. "You never told me. Not really."

Dora shifted. "I . . . I don't know. We grew up. We changed. I fell in love with Cal," she stammered.

"Or your mama did." His tone was bitter.

"Don't be ridiculous."

"Am I? You know your mama never liked me. She never thought I'd amount to much."

Dora crossed her arms. "What does she have to do with this?"

"Everything! You were a mama's girl. She said jump, you said how high. It was always like that with her. She never liked me, but I can just imagine her putting Cal's picture in front of you whenever I called. I'm damn sure she never gave you half of my messages once you hooked up with Tupper."

Dora averted her gaze.

"You married him because your mama told you to."

"Stop, Dev," Dora said, looking into his eyes. "That's not fair. I married Cal because I loved him."

"Shit," he said in a long drawl, shaking his head. Pointing his finger at her, he declared, "I don't believe you."

Dora straightened, mouth agape.

Devlin angrily flipped back the covers and rose from the bed. He crossed the room in long strides, slamming the bathroom door behind him.

Dora wrapped her arms around herself and sat alone in the king-size bed. The moon rose higher in the sky, like a resplendent queen. A few minutes ago, she'd felt as golden and full of light as that moon. Now she felt eclipsed and cold. She dragged the thick coverlet from the bottom of the bed over her shoulders. Staring out at the night, she ran her fingers along the cable pattern of the wool.

Patterns, she thought—there was that word again. Dora was beginning to comprehend the power that patterns had to influence behavior. What Devlin had said was true. Winnie had made no secret of her disapproval of Devlin. Was she being a good girl and following the pattern set by her mother, and her mother before her, when she'd married Cal? She thought back to how Winnie had pointed out to Dora that Cal wasn't the heavy drinker her father was, or Devlin was. Winnie had always railed against the evils of alcohol, using her father as the prime example of how a life could be corrupted by it. She'd also reminded Dora how Cal was from a family with deep Charleston roots and strong connections. He would provide for her the comfortable lifestyle she was accustomed to.

Dora had loved Cal in her girlish fashion. She had felt from the first that with Cal she was on a trajectory toward marriage. When he dropped to one knee and proposed, she could only answer yes.

They'd married at St. Philip's Episcopal Church in a traditional ceremony on a sunny day in June. She'd worn white lace; the bridesmaids blush-pink taffeta. Dora had chosen an Aynsley China pattern like her mother's and her grandmother's silver pattern.

Was it fair to say that she had judged Devlin by her mother's stringent measures? Dora swallowed hard. She had to admit it was. Lord help her, she thought, feeling the sting of shame.

Dora tossed the throw off her shoulders. The thick, unyielding wool was irritating her tender skin. As she sat scratching her neck and arms, she wondered how long she would continue to blanket herself in the old patterns that had only brought her unhappiness.

The bathroom door opened and Devlin walked out, tying the belt of an expensive-looking waffle-weave robe. His blond hair was disheveled and his feet bare. He had the heavy-footed walk of confidence mixed with anger.

How times had changed, she thought. She couldn't help but wonder what her mama would think of Devlin now. This was no longer the clever but poor island boy she'd grown up with. Dev was a self-made millionaire. He'd brought himself up from almost nothing. He'd become a man, had a successful business, married, divorced, was a father. Yet despite the changes and years, he still loved her.

He stopped at a tray table laden with bottles of liquor and poured himself a drink. He turned to glance her way.

"Want a cognac?"

She could tell from his tone he was upset, but still resigned to being a gentleman. "No, thanks. I'd love a water."

He paused, then turned back to the tray and put the stopper back on the crystal bottle. He then opened two bottles of water and carried them to the bed.

He handed her a bottle, then slid beside her on the mattress. She moved to make room for him against the headboard. He stretched his legs out beside hers and leaned back, taking a long swallow.

Dora leaned against his shoulder, relieved that he'd returned to the bed and not stayed away in a show of pique. Only a man with confidence would do that, she thought. She reached out to take hold of his hand on his lap. Immediately, he squeezed it.

"Dev, we haven't talked yet about *your* marriage," she said, glad that they were both sitting against the headboard, looking out at the ocean, not at each other. It made the honesty somehow easier. "Did you love your wife?"

"I thought I did. I won't deny it."

"I'm glad," Dora said. She wouldn't have liked to think he hadn't been in love with his wife.

"Ashley and I got married a long time after you and I broke up," he clarified.

"Why did you divorce?"

A long sigh rumbled in Devlin's chest. "I screwed up. Screwed around. I was too young to get married and too stupid to appreciate what I had. We hung on for longer than we should've. I don't think either of us wanted to admit we'd made a mistake. Especially after Leigh Anne came along. But when Ashley finally made the call, I didn't fight her. I couldn't. I'm not gonna lie. The divorce was hard to go through. We both still bear the scars. But I can look back and see it was for the best."

"How is she?"

"Ashley's doing okay. Getting married again."

She looked over at him. "Are you okay with that?"

"Sure," he replied quickly. Then, more sincerely, "I'm happy for her. He's a good guy. He'll be a good father for Leigh Anne. But she'll always be *my* little girl. I'd do anything for her. Getting a divorce doesn't change how a father feels about his child."

Dora thought about Cal and believed Devlin was right, unfortunately for Nate.

"Where do they live?"

"Over in Mt. Pleasant. They have a real nice house on the creek. Not far."

"Do you see your daughter often?"

"Every other weekend, and we work out holidays. I haven't missed a school function or a dance recital," he said with a measure of pride.

She smiled, glad to hear that.

He shifted against the headboard to look into her eyes. "Honey, I know we talk about the past a lot and what we remember from back when we were sixteen. I like that you make me feel like that again. And that I make you remember." He paused, playing with her fingers.

"But I know we aren't kids any longer. I got the aches and pains to remind me." His laugh rumbled low. "I'm not that reckless surfer that you used to know. I'm a man now. But just because I've grown up doesn't mean I have to be old, now does it?"

She shook her head and moved a hand to place it over his. "No, not at all. I love that you're still spontaneous and fun. You make me happy."

He cocked his head. "I hear a 'but' coming . . ."

She smiled ruefully. "But . . . like you said, I enjoy a quiet life, my home and my garden. My son. I like staying home at night. While you . . ." She looked into his eyes. "You go out all the time. You walk into the bar and Bill knows your drink. You called Dunleavy's your office."

"It's the nature of my business. I go out with clients when they can go, which is often on weekends and in the evenings. I take them to restaurants to talk about deals and to add some local color."

"It's all business?"

"No, of course not." He paused. "What are you asking? Do you think I can't settle down?"

"I only know what I see."

He looked at her hands again. "Did it occur to you that I might be lonely?"

She abruptly looked up at his face. The blue of his eyes burned like torches against the ruddy tan and burned a hole right through her arguments. She couldn't quite grasp the concept: Devlin Cassell, lonely?

Dora had not considered that possibility. She shook her head, then lowered it onto his broad, strong, capable shoulder. He wrapped his arm tighter around her.

"Dev," she said, pushing herself to be honest. "It means so much to me that you love me. Be patient with me. I can't say the words. Not yet. It might just be paper, but I need to get my divorce signed, sealed, and delivered before I can move forward. I'm not ready for anything more."

He sighed, but his hand gently patted her shoulder. "Okay, honey. I won't rush you."

"Thank you."

"As long as you're not pushing me away again."

"I'm not. I promise." Dora patted his chest with her hand. "I'm right here."

He bent and kissed the top of her head. "That's where I want you to stay."

Dora awoke the following morning filled with light. As soon as she reached the beach she began to run. She didn't stretch. She simply took off, with her fists pumping at her sides. Her feet pounded the hard-packed sand, one foot after the other. To her right, the ocean was a roiling mass of choppy, white-tipped waves.

You're strong. You can do it. You can make your goal.

She said the words over and over, like a metronome keeping the pace. She had to believe the words, too.

Sweat poured down her brow, but she pushed on, past the lighthouse on her way to Breach Inlet. She remembered the first time she'd reached this point, the first day of her walking program. She was tired, thirsty, barely able to put one foot in front of the other. That was the morning Devlin had found her. She'd looked her absolute worst and he'd thought she was beautiful. Dora laughed out loud, hearing the joyful sound like a clarion call in the early morning wind.

She reached the inlet and turned back, keeping up the pace. Her heart felt ready to burst, but Dora kept on running the final lap. Her muscles were screaming, but she'd come too far to quit before she reached her goal. No more excuses. Today she was going to make it.

She ran, her strong heart pounding, until she reached as far north as she could run on the tip of Sullivan's Island. At last Dora came to a stop, panting hard, her hands on her hips, sweat pouring down her face. She was exhausted but triumphant. A grin stretched wide across her face. She'd made it!

She stood on the sand, letting the brisk wind cool her body, as her gaze swept across the stretch of beach of this small island she loved. Beyond, the vast Atlantic Ocean was stirring like a great beast, growling and spitting, awakened by the storm.

She laughed out loud, her voice minging with the roar of the waves. She had come a long way to reach this morning. Her namesake, Eudora Welty, had been right, she thought. A love of place could heal the soul.

Dora turned her head to look toward the back of the island, to where the Cove raced with the tides, where the cordgrass rustled in the wind, where the egrets feasted. Above the treeline she could barely make out the widow's walk of Sea Breeze. She smiled as Mamaw's words sang out in her mind.

Find yourself, and you will find your way home.

Chapter Twenty

≈≈ ≈ ≈

*D*ora showered and dressed in a light summer shift, then carried her coffee and bowl of whole grain cereal out to the back porch. The sun was a ghostly eye in the sky, obscured by an armada of gray clouds. She sidestepped several vegetable and herb flats as she crossed the porch to join Mamaw and Lucille playing cards in their usual spot under the awning. The awning was rattling in the gusts of wind.

She took a seat at the table beside Carson, who was reading the *Island Eye*.

"Good morning," she called out as she approached. "Storm's coming."

The women looked up and greeted her warmly.

"You were up and out early," Mamaw said.

"I hope I didn't wake you."

"Lord, no," Mamaw said. "At my age one never sleeps well. Harper woke up just minutes after you left." Mamaw looked out to the garden. "Dear girl made coffee, fueled up, and went straight to work on planting those flower beds." She sipped her tea, watching, then as she lowered her cup said, "I swanny, look at that girl lift those bags of soil. They must weigh as much as she does."

Looking out to the backyard, Dora saw Harper lifting enormous bags of compost and dumping the contents into two new raised garden beds.

Lucille chuckled. "She's little but she's feisty."

"Dora, why aren't you out in the garden with her?" Mamaw asked. "Isn't it your project, too?"

"Hell, no," Dora said, chewing her cereal. "Harper took over that garden. I just get in her way."

Carson lowered her newspaper and laughed. "That's a switch."

"Not really," Dora said with a bemused expression. "She's not the meek little mouse I used to think she was. I'm kind of afraid of her."

Mamaw laughed as she picked up a playing card and held it in the air, deciding whether to keep or discard it. "She must've ordered every garden book ever written. Her room is littered with them. I'll wager she'll read each one, too."

"What are all of those?" Carson asked, pointing to the flats.

"Vegetable starter plants," Dora replied.

"Just what we need," Lucille muttered, picking up a card. "More vegetables. Wish she took a hankering to raising me a nice pig. Or a couple of chickens."

"Don't mention it to her!" Mamaw exclaimed. "Or we'll have chickens arriving tomorrow." She threw down a card.

"Don't worry. Sullivan's isn't zoned for livestock," Dora said.

"That won't stop Miss Harper if she puts her mind to it," Lucille said, picking up Mamaw's card.

"Bless her heart," Mamaw muttered. "Hush now, here she comes."

The women stopped talking as they watched Harper walking across the yard, slapping dirt from her clothes. It was a futile gesture. She was streaked from head to toe with soil that was fast becoming mud in her sweat.

"She doesn't even look winded," Dora said with awe.

"Hi, y'all," Harper said as she approached.

The three women stared at her wide-eyed with shock that their New Yorker greeted them in the Southern style.

"If that don't beat all," Lucille said under her breath.

"I'm just playing with you," Harper said with a light laugh. "Though I must say that expression is catchy." She turned to Dora as she poured herself a glass of water from a thermos. "Dora, glad you're back. I could use your help. I've got to get all these plants in before the rain comes."

"Sorry, Mrs. Green Jeans," Dora said, but she didn't look the least bit sorry.

Harper harrumphed and turned an imploring gaze on Carson.

"Carson . . ."

"Don't look at me," Carson said. "I hate gardening."

"Aw, come on," Harper moaned. "I need to get all those plants in before the rain." Her eyes sparkled with enthusiasm as she launched into a monologue of her progress. "I've come too far to mess it all up now. There's three different kinds of lettuce, patio tomatoes, and oh, the herbs! They smell heavenly. Parsley, thyme, rosemary, sage, oregano, dill, and lots of basil.

Aren't they sweet? So tiny and all. I call them my babies." She turned to Lucille. "Lucille, this will be your very own kitchen garden," she said proudly. "In a few weeks, you can just saunter out and pick whatever you like."

Lucille smiled sweetly. "That's nice. Thank you, baby." She glanced at Mamaw.

"I really would help you, Harper," Dora said. "But I'm going out to play with Nate. We have a kayaking lesson this morning. Although . . ." She looked up at the gathering clouds. "I hope it isn't canceled because of this storm."

They all looked up at the clouds heralding the tropical storm that was barreling in from the south.

"It's really moving in," Mamaw said. "You shouldn't go out on the water today no matter what."

"Those clouds now have an official name," Carson informed them. She looked to Lucille. "Guess what it is." When Lucille shrugged, Carson said, "They named it Tropical Storm Lucy! Isn't that a hoot? I think it's only fitting they named a storm after you, you ol' windbag."

The girls laughed at the joke as Carson moved to kiss Lucille's cheek.

Lucille grunted. "I ain't never been called Lucy in my life and never will. I've always been Lucille."

Mamaw didn't laugh. "These midsummer storms can be surprisingly strong. They can pack a punch. I've lived through too many of them not to take each one seriously. Last summer Tropical Storm Debby wiped out our dunes. Cut them clean away." She clapped her hands together, rousing the group to action. "Girls, plans or no plans, today we have to prepare for this storm. We must take all the cushions inside, put anything light or loose that can be picked up by the wind into the garage. Harper, all your garden tools have to be put away. We don't want anything to become a missile in the wind and break a window. We can't be too careful."

"Mamaw, you always panic with every storm," Dora said. "This house has weathered storms for over a century."

"That's because I prepare! And I'll have you know, young lady, that this house might still be standing, but I've done many repairs over those years. Hugo almost took the whole house away. Once you live through that, you never turn your back on the ocean."

"Amen," Lucille muttered.

"Lucy's gonna be a real storm," Carson said, looking up at the sky. "I can always feel it in my bones. It's the shift in the barometric pressure."

Dora looked at the sky again, feeling the foreboding every person in the lowcountry experiences at the approach of a named summer storm. "At least it's not a hurricane."

"But the forecast calls for high winds," Harper said, looking warily at the sky. "I'm worried about my plants." She took a deep breath. "I'm off. Got to get them in before the storm hits." Harper marched off to retrieve a flat of herbs and hoisted them in her thin arms with the ease of a common laborer.

"Who is that girl?" Carson asked, resting her chin in her palm. "And where does she get all that energy?"

"It's the enthusiasm of a convert, my dear," Mamaw replied. "It's irrepressible."

"Speaking of energy," Dora said to Carson, "I noticed you slept in again this morning. You haven't been out surfing or kiting since you got back. With those waves building in the storm,

I thought for sure you'd be with those other crazy risk takers out there."

"I'm still just tired from the trip. Not feeling that good, that's all." She looked to Lucille. "I think I've got what you've got."

Lucille snorted. "Honey, you ain't got what I got."

Carson leaned against Lucille's shoulder and declared with humor, "Well, you sure ain't got what I got."

The way Carson said it had Mamaw looking up quickly to catch Dora's eye, then Lucille's. In that moment the three women shared a knowing look. In a synchronized movement, all heads turned toward Carson with narrowed eyes.

Dora bent closer to her sister. "Carson, are you pregnant?"

〰〰

"The air's so wet I could drink it," Mamaw said. Pearls of sweat formed on her brow, and her hair was frizzing.

Tropical Storm Lucy was gathering strength as it moved north along the coast. The sea was roaring in anticipation, echoing throughout the island. A heavy humidity hovered over the lowcountry like a pall. They'd all pitched in to prepare for the storm's predicted arrival that evening.

Mamaw took a final look-see around the property to make certain all the flowerpots, garden supplies, cushions, and knickknacks were safely stored indoors.

"We're done here. And we're hot and sweaty," Carson said, her arms above her head to redo her ponytail. "We're going to the beach."

Mamaw was glad to see a little more color in her face this morning. She was wearing a bikini top and yoga pants that hung low off her hips. Looking at her flat belly, Mamaw found it hard to believe a new life was growing in there. Carson refused to discuss her pregnancy, not even with her. After she'd admitted to the truth, she'd stormed off to her room and shut the door. Mamaw had thought she might hear a rap on her bedroom door and that Carson would slip in, like she usually did for a chat. Carson was resolutely silent.

Harper approached in a black Speedo suit and sarong, and on her head she wore a large floppy hat. She carried beach towels under her arm.

"Want to come?" she asked Mamaw.

"Oh, I don't think so, dear. Not today."

Behind her, Dora carried a large canvas bag. Nate's face bore streaks of white suntan lotion.

"Why don't you come, Mamaw?" Dora asked. "You haven't been to the beach much this summer. It'll be like old times."

"I don't want to leave Lucille alone," Mamaw replied. "Besides, I have a few things I want to get done before the storm. You children go on and have a good time. But Carson"— she pinned her granddaughter with a no-nonsense look—"no going in that ocean, hear? Listen to it roar. That undercurrent is deadly."

Carson only smirked and did not reply. Mamaw knew that good waves in Charleston waters were powerful bait for local surfers. She also knew that as with everything else, Carson would do what Carson wanted to do.

"You, too, Nate," she said, turning to Dora. "Don't you let him in the water."

"Don't worry, Mamaw. We won't."

Mamaw watched the group saunter off, her fingers tapping her thigh. As soon as they disappeared around the hedge,

Mamaw checked her watch and hurried back up the stairs into the house. She went directly to the kitchen phone and dialed a number she'd written on a Post-it note. After two rings, a man answered the phone.

"Devlin Cassell."

"Devlin, it's Marietta Muir."

"Mamaw!" The reply rang with warmth.

Mamaw couldn't respond for a moment, taken aback at the shock of Devlin calling her Mamaw.

"Forgive me for being so familiar, Mrs. Muir. Old habits die hard."

"That's quite all right. But perhaps *Mrs. Muir* is better, given the nature of our business."

"Yes, ma'am, Mrs. Muir."

"The girls have gone to the beach. Do you have time now?"

"For you? Of course I do. I'll be right over." He chuckled low in that easy manner she remembered from long ago. "I know the way."

Mamaw opened the door to a broad-shouldered, well-dressed man wearing dark sunglasses. He removed the sunglasses and smiled, and she recognized the astonishing blue eyes.

"Devlin Cassell. I hardly recognized you!"

He was taller and broader than she remembered. His blond hair was trimmed neatly around his head, but still uncontrolled. It gave him a youthful look, even in his sophisticated creased khaki pants and bright blue, expensive polo shirt.

"Mrs. Muir, you haven't changed a bit," he said with a wide grin.

"Please come in." She ushered him inside. "You'll have to excuse the look of the place at the moment. The girls and I have spent the day turning the house upside down, readying it for the storm!"

Devlin's head moved from left to right as he entered, allowing his gaze to sweep the rooms. She wished the sun were shining. Sea Breeze showed so well with sunlight pouring in through the windows, but with the storm coming, the rooms appeared gloomy. Mamaw had turned the lights on in each room. As they walked through the house, the golden light gave the pine floors an added luster. Devlin paid close attention to the historic details they both knew added value to the house. From time to time he'd stop to jot something in his notebook or make a comment. *You don't see moldings like that every day.* When they stepped out onto the back porch, Devlin paused, put his hands on his hips, and stared out at the vast expanse of the Cove. It was high tide and a silvery mist from the incoming storm hung low over the wetlands, making the scene appear otherworldly.

"This is what they'll come for. The million-dollar view," he said after a while. "Or in this case, multimillion." He released a soft whistle. "I'd forgotten how well situated the house is."

"Yes, well, I believe you had your eyes on Dora at the time."

He caught her eye and chuckled. "I surely did. Still do." He paused, then asked, "Do you mind?"

She was touched that he cared enough about her opinion to ask. "It depends on your sincerity." She tilted her head and clasped her hands, choosing her words carefully. "She's a traditional woman with traditional values. This divorce is hard on her."

"I know that."

Mamaw wrapped her arms around herself, surprised by the drop in temperature.

"I've always found that if a person truly wants to be a part of your life, he will make an effort to do so." She turned toward Devlin, her gaze direct. "We haven't seen hide nor hair of Calhoun Tupper since Dora returned from the hospital. But I believe she's seen quite a bit of you in the past few weeks."

He nodded.

"Have you met Nate?"

"Not yet. I'd like to. But Dora wants to wait."

"She's very protective of that boy. Too protective, perhaps, but she has good reason."

Devlin turned back to face her, his gaze sincere. "I'm trying not to rush her. She told me not to. But," he said in earnest, "I want you to know that my feelings for Dora are true. And they run deep. I won't hurt her. Or Nate. In fact, the one who's likely to get hurt in this deal is me."

Mamaw's smile lit up her face. What a nice, genuine man Devlin had grown up to be.

"Then I think neither of us has anything to be worried about. Let's go inside, shall we? It must've dropped ten degrees just since you arrived and the rain can't be far behind."

They returned to the front of the house. Devlin's gaze fell on the cottage and he stopped in front of it, studying the quaint house. "May we go in and take a look?"

"Not today. Lucille isn't well and she's resting. I don't want to disturb her. And with the change in the weather, I fear the girls will return momentarily. It's as tidy and tight as a ship."

"And the garage?"

"Dusty and filled with cobwebs and junk, but solid."

"Good. Well, then. I'll go to the office and work up some comps so we can begin talking about the price." His eyes gleamed. "But I can tell you right now, there's nothing else like it on the market right now. With both the historic factor and the killer views . . ."

"So you think it might sell quickly?"

He smiled. "I've got folks on my Rolodex I can call right now who are just waiting for a house like yours to come on the market. Yes, Mrs. Muir. I think it could sell very quickly."

Mamaw was filled with relief and sudden gratitude toward him. She looked over to the cottage, imagined Lucille lying in there. Mamaw planned to call a few doctors and see whether there were some procedures that could be done. With money in hand, she could fight the cancer.

"I'm so pleased."

"When would you like to put it on the market?"

"As soon as possible."

Devlin's brows shot up. "Really? I thought Dora said you were going to wait until the fall."

"That was my original thinking. But some recent developments have changed my mind. Though I do not want to leave Sea Breeze until the summer's end."

"Yes, ma'am. I reckon I have my marching orders. I'll get back to you as soon as possible." He turned and walked to his car. It was a large German automobile, black, polished, and expensive-looking. He bent to open his car door, then stopped and looked toward the street.

Mamaw heard the voices as well and felt her stomach drop. She'd hoped they'd finish their business before the girls returned home. Thunder rumbled and a gust of wind sent dry sand swirling in the air. Dora and Nate appeared, walking between the tall hedges that bordered the property. Dora was talking to Nate but stopped short when she saw Devlin. Harper soon followed, then Carson, who smiled and waved when she saw Devlin.

"Well, hey, Dev!" Carson called out, coming to Devlin's side. "I was wondering when you'd show up. How are you?"

"Good. Real good," he replied genially, and glanced worriedly at Dora.

Dora said nothing. She stood silently beside Nate.

"My, don't you look handsome, all dressed up," Carson teased. "Are you here to whisk our girl out to dinner?" She looked over her shoulder at Dora and gave her a questioning look.

"I, uh . . ." Devlin hesitated and glanced at Mamaw for guidance.

Mamaw stepped forward. "I asked Devlin to come. He's here to give me an estimate on the house's value."

Carson looked stricken. "You're putting the house on the market *now*?"

"I'm just getting some information, so let's not fuss. Let the poor man get home before the storm hits."

"Devlin, wait," Dora said, coming closer to him. "Since you're here, I'd like you to meet my son." She waved Nate closer. "Nate, come meet my good friend Mr. Cassell."

Devlin's eyes widened along with his smile. "Hey there, Nate. I'm glad to meet you at last. Your mama told me all about you. In fact, she can't stop talking about you." He held out his hand.

Dora cringed inwardly, knowing Nate would not shake it.

"Hi," said Nate, looking away at the house.

To Devlin's credit, he let his hand move to his hips without offense. "I hope you'll come out on my boat sometime. I know spots where there are lots of dolphins and where they do that strand feeding. Do you know what that is?"

Nate shook his head.

"Then I'll show you. Your mama tells me you like dolphins."

Nate glanced at the man, nodded abruptly, then turned to Dora. "Can I go inside now? I'm cold."

"I'll take him in," Harper said. "Hi, Devlin," she added in passing.

"See you, Dev," said Carson with a short wave, following Harper. "You'd better hurry. The sky looks ready to rip."

Mamaw offered her hand. "I'll be looking forward to your report," she said, and without further word turned and hurried up the stairs.

Dora waited until the others went indoors. Lightning flashed across the sky and by the time the front door was closed, a ripping crack of thunder rent the air. Dora stepped closer to Devlin and he wrapped his arms around her, tugging her against him. Looking up with a coy smile, she surprised him with a long, slow kiss.

"What did I do to deserve that?" he asked lazily, not ready to stop.

"You were kind to my son. And I missed you."

"I'm *here*," Devlin said. Then, locking her gaze in his, he said, "Every day and every night. And I'm not going anywhere."

Chapter Twenty-One

~~~~~~

That evening, as predicted by the forecasters, Tropical Storm Lucy whistled and rattled the windows. Rain pounded the roof. But inside Sea Breeze, the lamps were glowing cheerfully. The women decided to mock the storm by having an indoor picnic. They moved the living room furniture, laid out blankets on the floor, and pulled out food from the refrigerator.

Mamaw sat back in her chair and listened to her granddaughters chatting like magpies as they stretched out on the blankets. When they got together, it was almost as if she were invisible. It was a revelation to hear their stories of their worst dates, fad diets they'd tried, fashions they adored, and favorite memories of their days as children at Sea Breeze. As the evening drew on, the stories became more serious. Occasionally she'd spy Harper jotting down notes on her ever-present computer.

While they talked they feasted on cold chicken and shrimp, savory crackers and assorted cheeses, pickles and olives, ripe avocados, and as much ice cream as they could eat. Mamaw feared the electricity would go out and it would all melt.

At nine o'clock the storm ratcheted up a notch. The wind started screaming like a banshee and rain hit the windows horizontally. Suddenly the lights flickered, then everything went black. Mamaw clutched Lucille's hand beside her, heard the girls suck in a collective breath and Nate's shriek.

Carson reached for the flashlight she had at her side. With a flick, the long beam of light immediately restored calm to the room. "No need to worry," she called out. "There are candles and matches on the table."

Soon the room was alive with dancing light on the walls and ceiling.

"It's like camping." Dora turned to Nate. He was sitting rigid, knees close to his cheeks and eyes wide. She smiled encouragingly. "Isn't it?"

He didn't reply but scooted closer to her.

"The storm's getting pretty strong," Harper said. She looked at the windows with a worried frown. "Are you sure it's not a hurricane?"

"No, child, that ain't no hurricane," Lucille said with a light, cackling laugh. "If it were, you'd know it. This whole house would be rattling, not just the windows. And we wouldn't be sitting here. We'd be off this island waitin' it out somewhere north. After Hugo, I won't stay on the island for no hurricane. Uh-uh," she said with a shake of her head. "So don't you worry none. This be just a good summer storm."

Suddenly the lights were back on.

There was a gasp of surprised delight.

"See?" Lucille said with a smug smile. "What'd I tell you? Just the summer wind."

Mamaw had an idea that she hoped might distract everyone from the worsening weather. She went to the stereo and searched her CD collection. Her fingers ran along the cases until she found Frank Sinatra. Pulling the CD out, she put it in the stereo and pushed play. There was a click and whirr, then the velvet voice of Frank Sinatra sang out.

The summer wind came blowin' in from across the sea.

"Edward and I used to dance to this during storms," Mamaw said, remembering with wistfulness to her tone.

"I remember," Carson said, rising to her feet. "At the big house on East Bay. Once, I hid on the stairs and watched you." She held out her arms. "Mamaw, dance with me."

Mamaw took Carson's outstretched hand. "I'd love to," she said, then laughed lightly as Carson led her in the dance. They were both tall and glided gracefully across the floor.

Dora stood and held out her hands to Nate. "Come on, Nate. You're the man of the house. You have to dance with the ladies."

To everyone's surprise, Nate stood up. They all cheered him on as he took his mother's hands and began to dance a clumsy two-step.

"I don't think she'll ever forget this dance," Carson whispered to Mamaw.

"Nor shall I."

"I love you, Mamaw."

"I know you do. I love you, too. My love is unconditional. You know that, don't you?"

Tears sprang to Carson's eyes and she nodded, tightening her lips.

Harper sprang to her feet. "Come on, Lucille. We can't be left out!"

Harper helped Lucille to her feet and as she took her hands, they began to dance, slow and easy.

Mamaw felt aglow as she looked around the candlelit room to see everyone dancing. No one was running out the door, catching a plane, or sulking in her room. Here they all were, her summer girls, together as she'd always hoped they would be. She said a prayer of thanks for this midsummer storm that had brought them all together for this special night.

They played the song again and switched partners, dancing once more to the heavy beat. Nate wouldn't dance with anyone except Dora, so this time Carson danced with Harper. Mamaw took Lucille's hand and led her in a gentle weaving back and forth, humming the tune.

Suddenly Lucille gasped and bent over in pain.

Everyone froze.

Mamaw clutched Lucille's arms and held on tight as she fired off orders. "Carson! Help me get her to the sofa. Dora, her pills are in my bathroom. Run and get them. Harper, fetch a glass of water."

The girls sprang to action. Within minutes, Lucille was resting on the sofa with Mamaw's arm still around her shoulder. Carson, Dora, and Harper clustered around them, unsure and anxious. Nate sat quietly on the blanket.

"This isn't the flu." Carson looked to Mamaw for confirmation.

Mamaw shook her head. "It's not for me to say." She looked to Lucille.

There was a silence in the room, save for the howling wind outside the windows. Lucille slowly brought her eyes up to look at Carson. Then she turned to look at Harper and Dora. The pain had subsided some, and though she still gripped her abdomen, her face appeared serene.

"Now don't look so worried," Lucille said, her voice weak. "What's happening is as natural as the wind blowing outside those windows. I'm sick, is all."

"What kind of sick?" Dora asked.

Lucille sighed with resignation. "Cancer."

There was a shocked silence, then Carson went to her knees and laid her head on Lucille's lap. "Oh, Lucille."

"What kind of cancer?" Harper wanted to know.

The girls all jumped in after that, with an outpouring of follow-up questions, suggestions, and recommendations of the top medical centers Lucille could go to for treatment.

"Stop all this jabbering," Lucille said, putting her hands up. "I've gone through all this with your grandmother and I don't have the energy to go through it again. I made up my mind, hear?" she said firmly, silencing them all. "I lived my life with dignity. I intend to die with dignity."

"I know how hard it is to accept," Mamaw told the girls. "But Lucille's made her decision. It's up to us now to make sure she's as comfortable as possible."

"Now I hate to break up the party," Lucille said, "but I'm tired and need to go to bed. Gimme your hand, girl," she said to Carson. "Help an old woman up."

Mamaw and Carson each took an arm and helped Lucille slowly to her feet. She grunted softly and grimaced, the pain obvious. Dora and Harper grasped each other's hand for support.

"Take her to my room," Mamaw said.

"What? No, no. I want to lie in my own bed," Lucille said.

"Later, when the storm subsides. For now, just rest awhile in my bed."

Despite Lucille's complaints, she settled in Mamaw's big four-poster bed. Dora and Harper fluffed up pillows behind her.

"Go on back to your party." Lucille waved her hand dismissively. "This ain't no death watch. I'm just tired. Go on with you." She added, "My precious girls."

Carson, Harper, and Dora took turns kissing Lucille good night, reluctantly leaving the room. Mamaw ushered them out the door. "She'll be all right. She needs her rest. I'm going to bed, too. We'll see you in the morning. Mind you blow out the candles before you retire."

She closed the bedroom door with a sigh of relief. What a night it had been. She felt exhausted by the whole of it. She quickly changed into her nightgown and brushed her teeth, listening to the storm still pounding the rooftop like a drum. Turning off the light, she entered her bedroom, lit only by the eerie blue light of her night-light.

"I can go to my own bed now," Lucille said, flipping off the blanket.

"Oh, no, you don't," Mamaw said, hurrying to Lucille's side and smoothing the blanket back over her chest. "It's gale winds out there, as bad as we've had in a long spell. I don't want you alone out there in that cottage. You just settle in, my friend, because you're sleeping in this house till it's over."

"But there's no extra bed!"

"That's why you're going to sleep here."

"Where will you sleep?"

"Right next to you."

"I can't . . ."

"Don't fuss at me. I'm too tired to argue. I doubt either of us will get much sleep anyway, with that wind howling like that and the rain beating against the roof."

Lucille looked to the window. "It's raining like the Lord's flood."

"I hope Harper's poor little plants survive. She worked so hard . . ." Mamaw sighed as she climbed into the bed beside Lucille. She tried to move slowly so as not to jiggle the mattress. Lucille had told her the pain was worsening and it weighed heavily on Mamaw's mind. Mamaw knew it was only a short while before she'd have to call hospice.

Mamaw lay on her back and brought the blanket up to her chin. Glancing over, she saw Lucille beside her, propped up by pillows, lying absolutely still as though afraid to move.

"This is a first," Mamaw said with a giggle.

Lucille chuckled softly. "One for the books."

Mamaw giggled. She certainly couldn't imagine lying in the same bed with her maid fifty years ago. "We've lived a lot of years, my friend. Gone through many changes."

"Maybe not as many as just this summer."

Mamaw laughed a tired laugh.

Lucille smacked her lips.

"Want a glass of water?" Mamaw asked.

"No. This medicine makes my mouth dry, is all."

"Some ice, then? You could chew it."

"I'm fine."

They lay in silence, listening to the storm.

"I'm glad you told them. They needed to know. To prepare."

"I expect so."

"They love you very much."

"I know that." Lucille turned her head toward her. "It's a comfort."

"I'm going to miss you," Mamaw said in a broken voice.

"I know that, too," Lucille said. "But I'll be watching over you, same as always."

"It won't be the same. Who will give me what-for after you're gone? You're the only one who keeps me in line."

Lucille laughed lightly in the dark. "Oh, I 'spect them girls will carry on."

Mamaw sighed. "I expect you're right."

Mamaw and Lucille could hear the sounds of the three women talking in the living room.

"I worry about them," Mamaw said softly.

"Mmm-hmm."

"Harper seems so alone. She carries such a burden of expectations from her family. Her mother . . . How will she ever find what *she* wants to do? Or find a husband who can measure up to the James standards?"

"You worry about *Harper*?" Lucille huffed. "Why, she's the one I'm *least* worried about."

"Why do you say that?"

"First off, she's the youngest. Only twenty-eight. What cause have you to worry if she finds herself a fella or not? She's got plenty of time."

"In my time, most young women were married by twenty-eight," Mamaw said primly.

"Well, that time is long, long gone. Second, she's rich as

Croesus. Or her mama is. That child don't need to find no husband or no job to live. And live proud." She jerked her chin, emphasizing that point. "I never got married on account I never wanted no man to tell me what to do. I like living on my own. Who's to say Harper don't feel the same way?" A grin eased across Lucille's face. "If I had money like Harper. Lord . . ." She rolled her eyes and grinned.

"What would you do?" Mamaw said, curious.

"What wouldn't I do?"

The women laughed together in the manner of old friends, comfortable in the bond of their decades-long friendship.

"You don't need to worry about our Dora, neither," Lucille added.

"Don't I? She still has so many decisions to make. The divorce isn't final . . . if there's even going to be a divorce."

"Oh, there'll be a divorce."

"What do you know?" Mamaw asked.

"Can't say. Just that it ain't Calhoun Tupper she's dreaming of no more."

Mamaw half smiled, having come to the same conclusion.

"It's that other one I lose sleep over." Lucille wagged her head.

"Carson . . ."

"What we gonna do with that girl?"

"I don't know," Mamaw confessed. She was very afraid for Carson.

"I thought we got her on the road to mend. Now this baby. What's become of her young man? I ain't seen him come by in a while."

"Blake? I heard she's broken it off."

"Lord have mercy. She runnin' from another one?"

Mamaw sighed. "She needs us now more than ever."

"She needs you," Lucille amended. "I'm not going to be here."

"Don't say that! Of course you will."

Lucille didn't reply.

"Thank heavens she stopped drinking," Mamaw mused. "To think if she'd been drinking when she conceived that baby. It's a small miracle. Poor girl has her father's curse and I'm proud of how hard she's trying. But she can't drink a drop while she's carrying."

"Is she even gonna have the baby?" Lucille asked.

"Of course she'll have it."

"Best to just wait and see what happens." She gave Mamaw a long look. "No meddlin'."

"I have a right to worry."

"Worry, yes. Meddle, no."

"Stop giving me the eye, you old banty hen."

Lucille just cackled a laugh in response.

"We raise our girls to grow up to be strong and independent women," Mamaw said in a more serious tone. "And they are. But Lord, I'm embarrassed to admit I still think of them as my little girls. I want to see them all settled. Married. Am I too old-fashioned? The girls think I am . . ."

"You and me, we're from another era. Things are different now. These girls want more, expect more, even demand more. Who's to say being married is the answer? Look at Dora! She done everything right. Got married at a tender age to a respectable man in that fancy wedding you and Mr. Edward paid for. She moved into a big house, had a child. Marched to the tune y'all been singing since she was born. And now what?"

Mamaw was silent.

"I'll tell you what," Lucille said. "Our girl Dora's pickin' herself off the floor, straightenin' her shoulders, and startin' anew. She's settin' a good example for her younger sisters. I'm so proud of her my buttons are poppin' off my chest."

Mamaw reached out and grasped Lucille's hand. "Thank you, Lucille. I needed to hear that. See? That's what I mean," she said with a sniff. "You're my best friend. What am I going to do without you?"

"You gonna get older and wiser. That's the way of things." She paused. "We had fun tonight, didn't we?"

"We did," Mamaw said with a whisper of a smile.

"That summer wind was blowin' but we danced. You needs to remember tonight, Marietta. When the hard times come, just dance."

Chapter Twenty-Two

~~~~~ ~~~~~

Dora sat cross-legged beside Harper on the four-poster brass bed. The storm and the late hour had brought a chill and dampness, and they were wrapped in blankets. She let her gaze wander over the changes in her bedroom—the petal-pink-and-white wallpaper, the brass-and-mirrored vanity, the Aubusson rug. The physical changes of the room reflected Dora's taste and were an outward sign of the changes that had taken place within herself this summer.

And for her sisters, as well. Harper's room was more serene and classic. Carson's was lowcountry, more shabby chic. In giving them rooms of their own, Mamaw had offered each granddaughter a safe haven at Sea Breeze from the storms they each faced.

Dora looked up to see Carson standing at the window, her arms crossed like a shield in front of her, looking out at the fronds of the palm trees shaking in the wind. The relentless roar of the surf echoed, and Dora wondered at the changes she'd see on the beach in the morning.

"Carson, come join us," Dora called.

Carson came to join her sisters on the bed. Harper scooted closer and tugged at the blanket around her shoulders to place part of it over Carson.

"This is nice, all of us huddled together, talking," Dora said.

"Like old times," Harper agreed.

"But it won't always be like this, will it?" Carson asked, her tone depressed. "The thought of losing Sea Breeze is hard enough. But now Lucille?" She shook her head. "Unbearable."

"But that doesn't mean we can't still be together," Dora said. "Somewhere."

"Doesn't it?" Carson asked.

"That depends on us," Harper answered. "All those years Sea Breeze sat here and none of us came. We have to decide to make the effort."

"Yeah, well, let's remember it was Mamaw who brought us back," Carson said. "What happens when she is gone? When Sea Breeze is gone?"

"Don't be morbid," Dora said.

"I'm not. I'm just facing reality. I can't help but worry now about what's going to happen to her. She's eighty. What's she going to do without Lucille?" Carson asked. "Especially when we all leave?"

Carson looked at the streaks against the window and thought it looked as though even the house was crying.

"That's *why* Mamaw brought us back," Dora said. "She knew this day was coming and she wanted us to be close again, as sisters should."

"Even if her methods were a little Machiavellian." Harper smiled wryly.

"I feel," Carson said, her voice low and trembling, "like everything I love is slipping through my fingers."

"This place has always been the touchstone for all of us," Dora said, aware of her role as the older sister. "We're all feeling shaken. I admit, even though Mamaw talked about selling Sea Breeze, it just never felt real. Until today when I saw Devlin come by for an appraisal. I don't know about y'all, but that brought it home for me. Mamaw's not fooling around. She's going to sell this house and we won't have Sea Breeze to come back to any longer." She looked at Harper and Carson. "So what are we going to do after Sea Breeze is sold? Are we going to stay in touch?"

"Yes," Harper readily agreed. "Though, I don't know where I'll be or what I'll be doing. I've got a month to figure out where I'll be going from here."

"Aren't you going back to New York?" asked Dora.

"Maybe. But definitely not to live with my mother." She shook her head, then tucked a copper-colored shank of hair away from her face. "I couldn't go back to that. I've thought about going to England," Harper added. "Even if for a visit. Just to sniff around a bit, see how I feel. I'd like to visit Granny James for a while. I thought I'd be nervous and scrambling around, handing in my resume to a zillion companies. But I'm not. I'm not in a hurry." Harper tucked the blanket closer. "I know this sounds a bit out there, but I feel like something's going to happen to make everything clear."

"Like what?" Dora asked, intrigued.

"I don't know," Harper said with a small smile. "I'm not just sitting around," she hastened to add. "I'm looking at my options. Lining up a few things. But, I'm also kind of . . . waiting."

"Waiting?" Dora asked dubiously. "That sounds so not like you."

Harper shrugged and looked a bit embarrassed. "I'll know when it happens. But wherever I end up, I promise I'll stay in touch."

"That's the big question for all of us, isn't it? It's like we're on some ship waiting to dock. I'm not sure where I'll end up either," Dora said. She made a face. "By the end of summer I'll be in the midst of a divorce. *And* selling my house." She put her hands together in supplication. "Please, God, let someone buy it." She lowered her hands and began counting off her fingers. "*And* I have to find a new place to live. A job. A new school for Nate." Dora blew out a plume of air with a soft whistle. "I've got more on my plate than I can eat, that's for sure."

"You've got Devlin in the wings," Harper reminded her.

"Dev . . . He's a good ol' boy with one eye always on the tides. It's what I like most about him. He's laid-back where I'm uptight. But he's also smart, successful. He keeps me grounded. And Lord, he knows how to push my buttons in a good way." She smiled with a little embarrassment. Dora looked at the empty space on her ring finger. The bruising was gone but the skin remained pale where the ring once lay.

"I've made a decision. A big one." She looked up to see Carson and Harper staring at her. "I'm going forward with my divorce. I can't go back to Cal. I feel sad," she admitted. "It's hard to break up a family. Except, we weren't much of a family, and I know I can't live like that anymore. I know we'll both be happier apart than we were together."

"I'm glad you made the decision." Harper reached out to place a hand on her shoulder. "I know it wasn't easy."

Carson looked sideways at Dora. "Is it because of Devlin?"

Dora's cheeks colored. "For sure, my feelings for Dev helped me make the decision. But he wasn't the deciding factor. Cal had already left the marriage, don't forget. We were on the way to a nasty divorce when I had that attack. Sister mine, if I learned one thing this summer, it's that I'm not going back to a loveless marriage. It's not enough for me."

Carson tilted her head and studied Dora as a smile eased across her face. "Good for you."

"But I'm not looking to hitch my star on any man right now, either," Dora continued. "I think I want to be an unmarried woman for a while." She glanced up. "This summer is *my* time. I used to think that was selfish, just focusing on my needs and what I wanted. I've spent my entire life thinking about other people's needs—trying to make them happy, seeking approval. I'm heading on forty. It's high time I start thinking about how I want to spend the next forty years of my life." She sat straighter and the blanket slid from her shoulder. "You know, I've never lived on my own before."

Harper shook her head in disbelief. "Never?"

"Nope," Dora replied, yanking the blanket back over her shoulder. "I went straight from my mother's house to Cal's house." She waved her hand. "Not counting college, of course. But I lived on campus with a slew of roommates. That doesn't count." She sighed. "I've always lived where I was told to. I never rented my own apartment. I'm kind of looking forward to it."

"Where?" asked Carson.

Dora considered this. "I won't go as far as New York or England, that's for sure," she added with a quick smile toward Harper.

Devlin's face flashed in her mind, their times out on the boat together, cooking crabs, drinking beer, watching sunsets. She thought of the exhilaration she felt running on the beach, watching the changing tides, collecting shells with Nate.

"I'll stay in South Carolina, definitely. I want a small house, with a tiny bit of land I can garden that needs little to no maintenance. I see now how I isolated myself. And ate to compensate for the void I was feeling. This time, I'm going to reconnect with old friends, make some new ones, rejoin my community. I think I'll stay right here in the lowcountry. I love it here," she admitted with heart. "Nate does, too." Her son's smiling face came to mind. "He's better when he's near the sea." She took a breath and looked at Carson and Harper.

"Wherever I end up, I'll keep in touch. I promise. I'm going to need my sisters to get through this."

Dora and Harper turned to look at Carson.

"What about you, Carson?" Harper prodded.

Carson only looked down and offered a noncommittal shrug.

"Are you okay?" asked Dora.

"No. I'm not okay," she fired back, almost as a challenge. "I'm pretty far from okay." She looked at her sisters, her eyes flashing. "You both have support systems in place, imperfect as they might be. You have families who've got your back. For me, it's only Lucille and Mamaw. This house. And now that's all being blown away like the sand out there in the wind. Predicting what I'll be doing in the fall feels damn impossible. Forgive me if I can't get past next week."

Dora reached over to put her hand on Carson's shoulder. "You have us, too. Me and Harper are right here. Oh, honey, we know this is a tough time for you. But we'll be here for you all the way.

Hey, you can come live with me," she said with a nudge of encouragement. "It won't be fancy, but I'll help you take care of that baby."

Carson recoiled from Dora's hand. "Baby? I'm not having a baby."

Dora looked confused. "But I thought . . ."

Carson went rigid and her voice turned cold. "You thought wrong."

Understanding flooded Dora's features. "You're considering an abortion?"

"Of course I am," Carson said, clenching her fists under the blanket. "I'm unmarried, without a job, without a place to live . . ."

"Carson," Dora said, leaning forward and slipping off her blanket. "What about Blake?"

Carson's voice trembled with raw emotion. "Don't go there."

"Carson, I—"

"Dora," Harper said in a warning tone. "Can't you see she's struggling? This isn't your decision. Let it go."

Dora stared at Harper, letting her words penetrate. *Let it go.* Letting things go without a fight was what she'd been trying to do all summer. But this was so important. She had things she should say to stop Carson from making a decision she might live to regret. Like how hard it was for her to conceive Nate. How she'd suffered one miscarriage after another, staying in bed for months at a time and gaining fifty pounds in the process. How Carson should keep the baby.

Dora looked at Carson, sitting straight, bowed up for a fight, tears flashing in those blue Muir eyes. Then it hit her. She thought of her mother and how she always had a *should* at the ready at moments like this to keep her daughter in line. Dora didn't want to tell Carson what she *should* do. That hadn't worked out well between them in the past.

Dora wanted a relationship with her sister, one based on love and trust. She thought again of all the phone calls they'd shared while Carson was in Florida and how they'd talked about everything and nothing. Dora wanted her sister to pick up the phone and call her after they left Sea Breeze.

Dora pressed her fingers to her eyelids. Harper was right. Her opinions were not what her sister needed to hear now. Dora's life might be a shit storm at the moment, but she was beginning to see the light breaking through the clouds. That's what Carson needed now. Just a sliver of luminosity to give her hope.

Dora looked at Carson and spoke in a calm voice without contention. "A few months ago, I might have told you what I thought you should do." She laughed in a self-deprecating manner. "I wouldn't have been shy to tell you my opinions, either."

"I think I can guess what you'd say," Carson said flatly.

"Probably. Those are *my* opinions," Dora said honestly. "We're so different. We share the same father, but we haven't had the same upbringing, the same religious beliefs, culture, lifestyle. The list goes on and on."

"Even if we grew up in the same house," said Harper, "we'd all be different."

"Well, yeah," Dora conceded. "Honey, I'm stuck in my own mud pile right now. I don't need to be flinging any of it around. I'm the last person who should give you advice."

She stopped when she saw the stunned expressions on Carson's and Harper's faces. It was slightly irritating, but gratifying at the same time—their shock confirmed for Dora that she had done the right thing.

"What I'm trying to say," Dora pressed on, needing to get the words out, "is I don't really know what you're going through. When I got pregnant I didn't have to make a choice. I was married. I wanted a baby. And yet I still had problems."

Carson's face lost its belligerence, and Dora saw that she was listening.

"I had miscarriage after miscarriage. Each one broke my heart. I wanted a baby so badly and I just couldn't carry one. I felt I'd failed. And then I had Nate. My sweet, darling boy."

Tears came to her eyes, and Dora wiped them away. She didn't want to be emotional now, just honest.

"Being a mother is hard." She took a long breath and exhaled. "Okay, I'm just going to say this. I've never said it before, at least not aloud." She clenched the blanket tighter around her shoulders. "I was brokenhearted when I got Nate's diagnosis of autism. At the beginning I didn't know how bad it was going to be, if he'd learn to speak, to communicate at all, even go to the bathroom. I was told I was being selfish, that I had to think about my child and not myself. I tried. I really did." Dora swallowed hard, feeling the old emotions well up.

"But deep inside I grieved over the loss of the child I'd planned on having. The perfect child . . ." She shook her head. "I know that sounds awful. That's why I could never talk to anyone about those feelings. Not even Cal." She snorted. "Especially not Cal."

Dora looked up to gauge her sisters' reactions, sensitive to criticism or judgment in their eyes. Not finding any, she continued. "I've been on a long journey since then. I know now there is no such thing as a perfect child. I love Nate for who he is, just the way he is. I may have to teach him about emotional cues, but he's had to teach me, too. Sure, I know it will always hurt when I visit my son at school and find him eating alone, or when he's not invited to a birthday party. Or when I can't take away his anguish when he's trapped in the throes of a tantrum. But any mother feels this when she can't make life perfect for her child." She smiled tremulously and shrugged. "It's not easy being a mother. But this is the part I want you to know. I'll be thankful every day because I thought I'd never be able to have a child and now I have this amazing gift."

Dora searched Carson's face and saw the vulnerability in her eyes. She knew there was so much more she could say. She felt the words aching in her chest. But Carson was too fragile. Dora needed to tread softly.

"It's not going to be easy, no matter what you decide. In either case, your life will never be the same." She reached out and put her hand on Carson's shoulder. "You're my sister and I love you. Whatever you decide, I'll be here for you."

Carson leaned forward and slipped her arms around Dora.

"Thank you," Carson said, with a tremulous whisper.

"I'm here, too," Harper said, wrapping her slender arms around both her sisters.

⁓

Carson lay on her side, her hands tucked under her head and her eyes wide open. She'd been lying in bed, listening to the storm slowly dissipate as it moved off island. Outside the house, as well as inside, a temporary peace had been restored. She saw the first faint gray light of dawn through the slats of the shutters. She heard the dawn song of the birds in the surrounding trees, vigorously heralding the new day.

The dawn had always called to Carson. She rose from her

bed and slipped a silk kimono over her underwear. Tying it at the waist, she walked out into the hallway, careful not to awaken her two sisters sleeping side by side on Dora's bed. She'd heard them talking into the wee hours of the morning.

She opened the front door, cringing when it creaked loudly in the silence. Stepping outdoors, she was met immediately with the moist sweetness in the air that always followed summer storms. Raindrops lay heavy on the leaves of the oak tree, along the bark, and in puddles on the ground. A pearly mist hung over the island, and as she walked down the stairs she felt as though she were entering another world.

A noise caught her attention and she followed the sound, turning her head toward the cottage. She saw Lucille in her robe and slippers slowly climbing the stairs up to her front porch. Carson hurried across the cold gravel to Lucille's side.

"Let me help you up the stairs," she said, taking hold of Lucille's arm. The old woman's bones felt as light and hollow as a bird's. They reached the porch and paused while Lucille caught her breath. Carson couldn't remember ever seeing Lucille so winded and it scared her.

"I want to lie in my own bed," Lucille told her.

"Of course. I'll open the door for you and turn on a light. We don't want you falling in the dark."

"I could walk through my house with my eyes closed," Lucille muttered, but she waited while Carson turned on the lights, then held open the door for her.

Carson followed Lucille into the cottage. All was as neat as a pin. The walls were painted stark white but the artwork covering the walls was alive with the vivid colors of popular African-

American artists of Charleston. Everywhere she looked she saw signs of Lucille's personality and handiwork—the sweetgrass baskets, the embroidered pillows, the knitted throw. It was easy to see that Lucille loved her cottage and was happy here.

Stepping into Lucille's bedroom, however, Carson caught the stale scent of illness and medicine. She helped Lucille out of her robe and into the black iron bed. Lucille had shrunk in size, and her robustness had disappeared along with the pounds. She looked like a child with her dark eyes wide in her face, her gray hair frizzled around her head like a halo, engulfed in the brightly colored crazy quilt. Carson let her gaze flutter around the room, capturing Lucille's robe lying across the small lady's parlor chair, the large bouquet of summer flowers, and the bedside table filled with medicine bottles.

"There, that's better," Lucille muttered. "I like lying in my own bed. Under my own roof." She blinked heavily several times, seemingly exhausted. Then her gaze sought out Carson, and finding her, Lucille smiled weakly and patted the mattress. "Come closer, child."

Carson came to sit on the edge of the mattress, careful not to jostle Lucille. It was heart-wrenching to see Lucille so weak and frail. For her, Lucille had always been the strong, opinionated, unwavering pillar of support. This woman had raised her. She'd been a mother to her every bit as much as her grandmother had. Carson held her breath, trying in vain to stop the tears.

"Why you crying?" Lucille asked.

Carson sniffed and shook her head. "I don't know," she blurted.

"Must be something, 'cause you hardly never cry. Tell me."

Carson didn't want to tell her she was crying because she couldn't bear to see her so weak, so sick. How she couldn't imagine life without her. So instead she told her of the other source of her tears, knowing Lucille was probably the one person who would listen and not judge her.

"I feel so lost. And scared."

"About that life you got growing inside of you?"

Carson took a deep breath and nodded. "I don't know what to do."

"You don't have to do anything."

Carson couldn't look at her. "I think I do."

"I see." Lucille went quiet.

"You don't think I'm a terrible person?"

Lucille snorted and shook her head. "You're in trouble. And you're scared. I can see that."

"I'm thinking of going away."

"'Course you are."

Carson frowned and looked up. "Why do you say that?"

"'Cause whenever trouble comes, you run away."

"No, I don't!"

Lucille patted her hand, her thick knuckles and stubby nails beautiful to Carson. "Yes, child, you do. Always have. I've known you since you were born. When someone gets too close, you cut loose. Carson, you can't ever outrun the kind of fear you got bottled up inside. You think if you don't let anything or anyone get too close you won't get hurt again, like you were when your mama died, or when your daddy took you away from us to go to California. I never thought your mamaw should've let that happen. You cried then like you're crying now." She sighed heavily. "And now, you're upset I'm gonna leave you, too. Now, don't deny it," she said, waving her hand against Carson's open mouth. "The plain truth is, I *am* going to die and there's nothing you can do and it scares you. I see it in your eyes. And you're afraid your mamaw's gonna die, too. Well, child, one day she is!"

"No," Carson cried, her shoulders shaking as the tears gushed. She lowered her head to Lucille's shoulder as she did when she was a little girl. "Don't leave me. I don't want you to go."

Lucille patted her hand as Carson released the pent-up tears that she'd held at bay for too long. Tears of sorrow for Lucille's illness, for the pregnancy, for her breakup with Blake, for her guilt over Delphine, for all the sorrows she knew were as yet coming.

When she finished Carson pulled herself back up and reached for a tissue.

"Feel better?"

Carson shrugged. "I feel drained."

"A good cry is like letting loose the steam from a pipe. Gotta do it before it bursts."

Carson blew her nose. "I'm crying a lot lately."

"Hormones."

"Oh, God . . ." Carson said with a long sigh.

"You and I, we're both participating in the cycle of life. The beginning and the end. I find that kind of reassuring, don't you?"

Carson looked out the window.

"We all enter and leave this world alone." Lucille tapped Carson's hand, drawing back her attention. "But it's sharing our lives with others what makes life worth living. And makes the leaving easier. When your time comes, you know you're leaving a part of yourself behind, with them."

Lucille moved to sit higher up against the pillows. Her face scrunched up in pain with the effort while Carson fluffed up the pillows. Once she settled back, Lucille looked again at Carson, her dark eyes piercing.

"What's really ailing you, child?"

Carson lowered her head. Her confusion and despair were like a black hole, sucking the light from her life. She squeezed her wildly swinging emotions into three tiny words: "I am afraid." She hastily wiped her eyes. "You're right. I don't like being afraid. I feel frozen, like I did back when I was floating in the ocean staring into the deadly eyes of the shark. I couldn't move. That's how I feel now. My mind can't make a decision."

Lucille made a face and scoffed at the notion. "But you got away! You made it to shore. See? That's what I'm talkin' about. Girl, you got good instincts. I used to watch when you went out in that ocean riding them waves and wonder what that must feel like."

"I didn't know you watched me surf."

"Well, I did. Your mamaw and I both did. You know how to move your feet and your legs, when to move a bit to the left or right, how to ride that wave back to shore." She released a gentle laugh. "You might look like a natural out there, but I know how you got up early and went out there day after day, no matter what the weather. After all them years, your body just knows what to do. And *now* you're doubting yourself? Girl, get out of your head! We might all be cheering you on from the beach, but it's like I was saying. You're alone out there on the water. You got to trust your instincts to take you where you're supposed to go."

"This isn't the ocean. This is life. It's different."

"No it ain't." Lucille gave her a no-nonsense look, her

beautiful, intelligent eyes radiating faith and encouragement. "Carson, honey, life is like that ocean out there. It's deep and bountiful, and the waves just keep on comin'. Sometimes the waves get choppy, sometimes they smooth. You just got to ride them, Carson, same as you always done."

Lucille's smile fell as her voice weakened. "Whatever you decide, don't be afraid. I don't never want to hear you say those words again. You hear?"

Carson nodded.

"You've got good instincts. Listen to them. You'll know what to do." Her eyelids lowered and she patted Carson's hand a final time. "Now I'm tired. Didn't sleep a wink in your mamaw's bed. Go on and let me rest, eh? Just a little while."

Carson bent to kiss Lucille's cheek. She smelled of vanilla.

"Sweet dreams, Lucille," she whispered.

Carson stepped outside the cottage and closed the door quietly behind her. She stood on the edge of the porch and raised her face to the warmth of the morning sun. The fog had lifted, though a soft rain still fell. The shrubs, flowers, and grasses were no longer bent over by the pounding rain and struggled to stand taller, shaking off the drops. Bits of leaves and debris lay scattered across the gravel, remnants of the storm. Looking up, she saw the ball of sun pushing rays of golden color through the dispersing clouds. Behind them, soft hues of rose and blue already were stretching across the morning sky.

Overhead, the calls of the birds grew increasingly strident, and beyond, she heard the roar of the ocean. As always, she followed its call. Carson walked across the gravel toward the beach, eyes on the sky.

Chapter Twenty-Three

~~~

Mamaw awoke slowly. She pried open an eye, yawned, then gathered her wits after the long, trembling night. Suddenly remembering, Mamaw turned to look at the pillow beside her.

Lucille was gone.

Of course she was, she thought with a weary sigh. Lucille no doubt sneaked out at the first sign of the storm's abatement. She did love her own bed.

The sliding door to her former sitting room, Harper's room now, was open. Supporting herself on one elbow, Mamaw craned her neck and peeked in. She saw that the bed had not been slept in. She'd heard the girls chatting like magpies in the other room until she'd fallen asleep. She wondered how late they'd stayed up. She hoped it had been one of those all-night bonding experiences that would stay with them long after the summer had passed, keeping them close despite the distance between them.

The house was silent. Mamaw slipped into her pink silk robe and slippers, then went into her bathroom and took her time with her toiletries, washing her face and brushing her teeth, adding moisturizer and running a comb through her hair. She opened the window and felt the breeze, carrying with it the scent of pluff mud and an earthy sweetness from the storm.

She slipped into underwear, a pair of soft pants, and a tunic, then went out into the living room, relishing the sight of sunlight pouring in through the windows. Peering out, she surveyed the storm's damage. She was especially anxious about the ancient live oak tree that dominated the front yard. Those giant limbs hanging over the house were always a worry. She smiled with relief, seeing that once again the old tree had weathered the strong winds. *Good ol' tree*, she thought with affection.

It would be a good day, she thought with a light step as she made her way into the kitchen. The clock chimed eight times. So late? Strange that the house was still so quiet. She busied herself measuring coffee grinds into the machine and water into the teakettle. Then she put two pieces of whole grain bread into the toaster. Humming a nameless tune, Mamaw pulled out the floral tray that was Lucille's favorite and set out a Limoges floral china bowl, matching teacup and saucer, and silver. She put the kettle on the stove and hurried out the front door to collect the newspaper. The pavers were soaked through and the scattered leaves of trees and shrubs littered the ground like dead soldiers after a war. There was cleanup to be done later in the day, she thought. As she glanced at the cottage, all was quiet. She was glad Lucille was still asleep.

The kettle was whistling when she returned to the kitchen and the rich aroma of fresh coffee filled the air. She poured herself a cup, then set about preparing Lucille's breakfast. She ate so little these days, Mamaw had to tempt her with her favorite foods and a nice presentation. If she served her several small meals a day, Lucille ate more. Mamaw didn't want her to lose any more weight. She plucked the hot toast from the toaster and, skipping the butter that bothered Lucille's stomach, slathered a thick coating of her favorite blackberry jam over the bread. Next she filled a bowl with blueberries, poured the tea, then arranged it all prettily on the tray. Lucille, for all her no-nonsense brashness, liked pretty things.

Humming again, she lifted the tray, steadying herself, feeling its weight. She might feel like a girl, but she had the strength of an old woman, she chided herself. Nonetheless, she moved on through the house, navigating doors, steps, pavers, and gravel to cross the driveway to Lucille's cottage. She set the tray on the porch table, knocked as a courtesy, then opened the door.

"Lucille! It's me!"

Picking up the tray, she walked into the cottage, humming the cheery tune. "Breakfast," she called out as she made her way down the hall to Lucille's bedroom. The drapes were drawn and the room held a strange crepuscular light.

She pushed open the bedroom door with her shoulder. "The storm is over and the sun . . ."

Mamaw stopped talking when she saw that Lucille was still asleep in her bed. Poor thing, she thought. She must be tuckered out after all the excitement of the night. Mamaw set the tray down on the bureau, relieved of the weight, and turned to approach the bed.

She stopped short. Suddenly, all her joy drained from her, replaced by a sudden sense of dread. In the shadowy light,

Lucille lay on her back, her arms at her sides, her head tilted toward the windows. Mamaw felt her blood go cold. Lucille was not asleep. She appeared to be looking out at the morning sun. Only Mamaw knew her eyes no longer saw.

Mamaw's heart beat like a trapped bird's as she stepped closer to the bed. She hesitatingly stretched out her arm and laid a hand on Lucille's chest. There was no heartbeat. She lay still, her gaze vacant and empty. Mamaw moved to grasp Lucille's hand. Her body was not yet cold. Despair immediately filled Mamaw.

Have I just missed her passing? If only I hadn't dallied. If I'd hurried, if I'd woken just a little earlier . . . She was alone when she passed. With a choked cry, Mamaw brought Lucille's hand to her mouth and kissed it, then held it close to her breast. *I didn't get to say good-bye.*

After she had sat by Lucille's bedside for some time, alternating between crying heaving tears and staring blankly at the shell that had housed her dearest friend, Mamaw went out of the cottage. She paused at the threshold of the porch, leaning against the white pillar. She stared out at a world that, though in many ways was the same world she'd stared out at earlier that same morning, was now somehow all changed.

Lucille gone. She couldn't grasp it. She knew Lucille was dying, realized the end would come—but not so soon. Not today. They'd spent the night talking. It still didn't seem possible that they'd never talk again.

She brought her hand to her throat as her practical nature took stock. There were things to do, phone calls to make. She was, sadly, experienced in matters of death. She should go to the house and begin, she thought. But she couldn't so much as move a muscle. All the energy she'd felt only a short while ago when she was rustling through the kitchen had fled, leaving her feeling so very old. Numb.

The weight of her deadened heart made her weary. She walked slowly to the rocking chair. Water had pooled in the seat. She was beyond caring. She eased into the seat, feeling the cold dampness through her silk gown.

Mamaw was no stranger to grief. There could be no grief worse than the death of one's only child. Yet she'd survived. When Edward had passed a year after Parker, she thought she'd go mad. She didn't believe she could continue. Or want to. It was Lucille who had nursed her back, who would not allow her to wallow. And again, she'd persevered.

But now? Lucille wasn't here. Her loved ones were gone. What was the point of continuing the fight?

A gust of wind sprayed droplets of rain from the tree's leaves across her face. Mamaw sucked in her breath at the chill of it. Turning her head from the rain, she saw Lucille's chair beside her rocking back and forth. Mamaw's breath caught in her throat. She sensed Lucille's presence, very real and very close. So close that she called her name.

"Lucille?"

There was no reply. Only the calls of birds and the rustle of leaves. "You old fool," she muttered to herself. It was just the summer wind. Yet, closing her eyes, she still felt Lucille's presence.

Thunder rumbled softly in the distance. Mamaw opened her eyes and saw that the sun had emerged from behind the clouds. She gripped the arms of her rocker and rose to her feet to stand again at the edge of the porch. Stepping into the mist, she felt the cool moisture against her skin. Looking at the dewy, fresh surroundings, Mamaw remembered Lucille's words. *When the hard times come, just dance.*

She stretched out her arms and lifted her face to welcome the sun and the rain. Going up on tiptoe, she swirled around. She was alive! The night had been filled with terror, but the morning sun rose on another day. Lucille would want her to be grateful, even joyful, in this moment, despite the grief and the pain.

Mamaw lowered her arms and walked back toward Sea Breeze, taking the time to let her gaze sweep over her house and the landscape she loved. The old house with its mullioned windows, graceful, sweeping stairs, and gables had survived the storm, too. She didn't want to go inside quite yet. Inside the house, the girls were still sleeping. Mamaw wanted a few more moments alone with her memories.

She took the pebbled path around the side of the house. She passed the outdoor shower and near the porch spotted Harper's raised garden beds. The small stalks of starter plants were bent over from the storm's driving rain and wind. Some of the tiny leaves were plastered with the mud. But a few hearty ones had already straightened, and in time, most of them would perk up in the sunshine.

She stepped out of the dappled shade into the light. The sun felt warm on her damp skin. The wet grass soaked her slippers but she ignored it, walking on toward the Cove. The air was heavy with the pungent scents of pluff mud and that powerful post-rain sweetness she called the perfume of the lowcountry. She breathed deep, feeling cleansed, looking at the refreshed green of the sea grass. She walked with arms swinging across the rain-drenched ground to Harper's garden.

Who knew her Harper had a green thumb? Sweet city girl was growing roots in the lowcountry, she thought as she took in the newly planted flowers. Drops of dew hung fat and heavy on the roses that she knew had been planted especially for her. Bending, she plucked the best one and cradled it in her palms. It was a bright pink, just opening its petals to the sun. She brought it to her nose. The bud didn't have much scent, but she gloried in the fact that it was the first rose she'd gathered from this garden in years.

She heard the piercing cries of an osprey from the Cove. She looked up, searching for the great fish hawk. She'd always loved that plucky bird. Putting her hand like a visor over her eyes, she spotted it, circling gracefully over the water, on the hunt. This time of year there would be babies on the nest, squawking for breakfast.

"There she is!" came a call from the porch.

Turning her head toward the house, she saw her grand-daughters walking toward her in the light. Her summer girls. Dora in a flowing floral robe, Harper in a sleek silk sheath, Carson already in her swimsuit and shorts. So different, yet united by blood. Together . . . Mamaw felt her chest swell, knowing that she and Lucille had done the right thing in bringing the three women back home to Sea Breeze for this final summer. This was their shared triumph. These young women were their legacy.

Mamaw felt her heart warm in her breast and pump with love. Despite all the as-yet-unsettled questions, regardless of the many decisions yet to be made, on this troubled morning, looking at her granddaughters, she rediscovered her purpose for living.

Yes, they needed her, perhaps now more than ever. Yet not, she knew, as much as she needed them.

She raised her arm over her head in a wide-arc wave.

They were coming toward her.

Mamaw opened her arms.

"I'm here!"

Acknowledgments

≈ ≈ ≈

I owe a great debt of thanks to Dr. Pat Fair at NOAA for her mentorship and friendship; to Stephen McCulloch at Florida Atlantic University; and to Lynne Byrd at the Mote Marine cetacean hospital. A heartfelt thanks to the dedicated team at the Dolphin Research Center, especially Joan Mehew, Mandy Rodriguez, Linda Erb, Rita Irwin, Mary Stella, Becky Rhodes, and Sheri Peiloch. A shout of congratulations to Joan Mehew for winning the Wounded Warrior Project's 2013 Carry Forward Award! Some readers may recognize the Dolphin Research Center and the Mote Marine cetacean hospital described in the book, but the depicted sessions, characterizations, and dialogue are strictly from my imagination and presented with their approval.

As always, I send my sincere thanks and love to Marguerite Martino, Angela May, Kathie Bennett, Buzzy Porter, Ruth Cryns, and Lisa Minnick for all their invaluable support.

Heartfelt thanks to the fabulous team at Gallery Books: Lauren McKenna, Louise Burke, Jennifer Bergstrom, Elana Cohen, Jean Anne Rose, Ellen Chan, Natalie Ebel, Liz Psaltis, and everyone there who has continually supported my books. Love and thanks to my agents at Trident Media Group: Robert Gottlieb and Kimberly Whalen, Sylvie Rosokoff, Adrienne Lombardo, and Tara Carberry. Many thanks also to Joseph Veltre at Gersh.

I especially want to acknowledge the children's picture book *Shackles*, written by Marjory Wentworth (Legacy Publications). Her beautiful story of the discovery of slave manacles in her backyard on Sullivan's Island inspired me.

Finally, my love and thanks to my husband, Markus, for all the cups of coffee, glasses of wine, handfuls of almonds, and words of encouragement during all hours of the day and night.

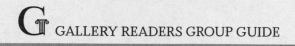
The Summer Wind

Mary Alice Monroe

Introduction

The second book in Mary Alice Monroe's Lowcountry Summer trilogy, *The Summer Wind* continues the story of three half-sisters and their grandmother experiencing the highs and lows of a poignant summer on Sullivan's Island.

For Dora, the winds of change force her to cope with the aftermath of a messy divorce. Dora must let go of her facade of the perfect wife and mother and discover a renewed purpose before she can move on with her future. For Carson, the summer brings a road trip with her nephew that will change and heal them both. For Harper, a summer of self-reflection leads her to reveal the weight of the expectations placed on her as the heir to her family's fortune.

As a rough island storm brews and a health crisis threatens a beloved member of the family, the summer girls' bond strengthens—just as Mamaw had planned.

Discussion Questions

1. Mamaw sometimes reflects on her sneaky methods—
   "blackmail," Harper calls it—for keeping the girls together
   at Sea Breeze for the summer. Do you think she was right to
   use manipulation to get the girls to stay? In other words, do
   you think that a mother's or grandmother's good intentions
   can justify her actions?

2. How do the girls' relationships with one another change
   over the course of the novel? Take time to consider each of
   their one-on-one relationships, as well as the dynamic of the
   three of them together.

3. As Dora stands in her and Cal's old house, she compares
   it both to herself—"She felt rather like this old house. . . .
   Beneath her ever-present smile, she was crumbling"—and
   to her and Cal's marriage—"Everywhere she looked, Dora
   saw . . . that no amount of effort on her part could save it." In
   what ways does Dora feel trapped in the house, and how is
   she able to free herself of it? On a separate but similar note,
   if the old house represents Dora's marriage and unhappiness,
   what does Sea Breeze represent?

4. Which moment do you think was the bigger turning point
   for Dora—her "broken heart syndrome" stress cardiomyopathy attack, or her realization in the store dressing room
   after Harper's outburst? What other major turning points
   does Dora encounter, and how do they affect her life and her
   relationships?

5. Dora's role as Nate's mother is not easy, but her sisters suspect she puts more pressure and strain on herself than she

needs to. What does Dora discover about her relationship with Nate through allowing him to travel to Florida with Carson?

6. Though he is continually withdrawn due to his Asperger's, Nate's transformation from the sad, outburst-prone boy at the start of the novel to the more accepting, slightly more outgoing boy at the end is clear. What factors and events most contributed to this transformation? Do you think the change is temporary or permanent, and why?

7. What do you consider to be the main priorities of each summer girl—Carson, Dora, Harper? How, if at all, do you think their priorities change over the course of the novel?

8. Monroe's theme of humans and animals sharing a connection is evident in *The Summer Wind*. Consider Carson and Nate's connection with Delphine, Cara's connection with the sea-turtle hatchlings, and Taylor's connections with Jax and Thor. How do these bonds affect their lives and the lives of those they love? Discuss ways in which you can develop your connection with animals and with nature.

9. Harper talks of the expectations placed on her as the heir to the Jameses' fortune. How do you think those expectations have shaped the woman she has become?

10. What are the major differences between Dora's relationship with Cal and her relationship with Devlin Cassell? What positives and negatives do you see for her in each relationship, and which would you encourage her to pursue? Why?

11. Consider the role that guilt plays in the novel. Which characters suffer from it, and why? Are all of the characters able to

overcome their guilt? Or are there any characters left with guilty feelings at the end of this book?

12. The unearthing of the slave manacles is a poignant moment for the girls—and especially for Lucille. What do you think the manacles represent to her? What emotions do you imagine are stirred in her when she sees and holds them?

13. "We should never underestimate how important our loved ones are to us. Or how powerful one's grief can be." Mamaw's words foreshadow the loss that is to come in the novel's final pages. Lucille's passing signifies the end of a long era at Sea Breeze; truly she had become a member of the family. Discuss Mamaw and Lucille's long friendship, and the impact each woman had on the other's life.

14. At the end of the novel, Carson is faced with a life-changing decision. Do you think she will decide to have her baby? Do you think she'll repair her relationship with Blake? What are your predictions for her in the final novel of the Lowcountry Summer trilogy?

15. The theme of healing is dominant in this book, as Dora heals from "broken heart syndrome" and the dolphin Delphine heals from her injuries. Discuss the parallels of their healing: What do both Delphine and Dora have to let go of from their past? What must they find? What are the possibilities for their future? Are other characters undergoing healing in this book?

Reading Group Enhancers

1. On the very first page of the novel, we learn that "being out on Sullivan's Island, sitting in the shade of a live oak tree, sipping iced tea, and waiting for the occasional offshore breeze" is Mamaw's "very definition of summer." What's yours? Ask each member of your reading group to write down how they define summer on an index card, then take turns sharing the definitions out loud.

2. Carson's best friends when she was a child were her books— "*A Wrinkle in Time, The Lion, the Witch, and the Wardrobe,* and anything by Judy Blume." Have the members of your group bring their favorite childhood books along to share, and discuss the role reading played in your lives when you were younger.

3. The three summer girls were named after their father's favorite Southern authors—Harper after Harper Lee, Carson after Carson McCullers, and Dora after Eudora Welty. Split your reading group into three teams, and give each of the teams one of these authors to research, asking them to consider what each author may have in common with her namesake.

4. In gardening, Dora and Harper find an activity that brings them closer together. Bring a bit of nature into your reading group: Purchase packets of seeds, small pots, and a bag of soil ahead of your reading group date, then let each member of your group plant their own mini-garden to take home with them.

5. If playing cards is more your speed, skip the gardening and go straight for discussing the novel over a game of gin rummy—

in Mamaw's honor and Lucille's memory. Don't know the rules, or need a quick refresher course? Check out http://www.bicyclecards.com/card-games/rule/gin-rummy.

6. Taylor, the former Marine Carson meets while in Florida, is a participant in the Wounded Warrior Project—a program for which the real-life Joan Mehew won the Carry Forward Award in 2013. To learn more about the vision and purpose of the Wounded Warrior Project, visit http://sandbox.woundedwarriorproject.org.

7. To discover more about Mary Alice Monroe and her books, read her blog, view a list of her upcoming author appearances, and more, visit http://www.maryalicemonroe.com.